GOOD NIGHT,
MR. JAMES

GOOD NIGHT, MR. JAMES

AND OTHER STORIES

The Complete Short Fiction
of Clifford D. Simak,
Volume Eight

Introduction by David W. Wixon

INTEGRATED MEDIA
NEW YORK

All rights reserved, including without limitation the right to reproduce this book or any portion thereof in any form or by any means, whether electronic or mechanical, now known or hereinafter invented, without the express written permission of the publisher.

These are works of fiction. Names, characters, places, events, and incidents either are the product of the author's imagination or are used fictitiously. Any resemblance to actual persons, living or dead, businesses, companies, events, or locales is entirely coincidental.

Copyright © 2016 the Estate of Clifford D. Simak

All stories reprinted by permission of the Estate of Clifford D. Simak.

"Good Night, Mr. James" © 1951 by World Editions, Inc. © 1979 by Clifford D. Simak. Originally published in Galaxy Science Fiction, v. 1, no. 6, March, 1951.

"Brother" © 1977 by Mercury Press, Inc. © 2005 by the Estate of Clifford D. Simak. Originally published in The Magazine of Fantasy & Science Fiction, v. 53, no. 4, Oct., 1977.

"Senior Citizen" © 1975 by Mercury Press, Inc. © 2003 by the Estate of Clifford D. Simak. Originally published in The Magazine of Fantasy & Science Fiction, v. 49, no. 4, October, 1975.

"The Gunsmoke Drummer Sells A War" © 1945 by Fictioneers, Inc. © 1973 by Clifford D. Simak. Originally published in Ace-High Western Stories, v. 10, no. 4, Jan., 1946.

"Kindergarten" © 1953 by Galaxy Publishing Corp. © 1981 by Clifford D. Simak. Originally published in Galaxy Science Fiction, v. 6, no. 4, July, 1953.

"Reunion on Ganymede" © 1938 by Street & Smith Publications, Inc. © 1966 by Clifford D. Simak. First published in Astounding Science Fiction, v. 22, no. 3, Nov, 1938.

"Galactic Chest" © 1956 by Columbia Publications, Inc. © 1984 by Clifford D. Simak. Originally published in (The Original) Science Fiction Stories, v. 7, no. 2, September, 1956.

"Death Scene" © 1957 by Royal Publications, Inc. © 1985 by Clifford D. Simak. Originally published in Infinity Science Fiction, v. 2, no. 6, Oct., 1957.

"Census" © 1944 by Street & Smith Publications, Inc. © 1972 by Clifford D. Simak. Originally published in Astounding Science Fiction, v. 34, no. 1, Sept., 1944.

"Auk House" © 1977 by Random House, Inc. © 2005 by the Estate of Clifford D. Simak. Originally published in Stellar 3, ed. Judy-Lynn del Rey.

Introduction © 2016 by David W. Wixon

Cover design by Jason Gabbert

978-1-5040-6031-8

Published in 2020 by Open Road Integrated Media, Inc.
180 Maiden Lane
New York, NY 10038
www.openroadmedia.com

CONTENTS

Introduction: The Non-Fiction of Clifford D. Simak	vii
Good Night, Mr. James	1
Brother	25
Senior Citizen	49
The Gunsmoke Drummer Sells a War	55
Kindergarten	103
Reunion on Ganymede	159
Galactic Chest	187
Death Scene	217
Census	225
Auk House	259

INTRODUCTION: THE NON-FICTION OF CLIFFORD D. SIMAK

"I sometimes wonder if there is any reality at all—if there is anything but thought. Whether it may not be that some gigantic intelligence has dreamed all these things we see and believe in and accept as real . . . if the giant intelligence may not have set mighty dream stages and peopled them with actors of his imagination. I wonder at times if all the universes may be nothing more than a shadow show."
—*Clifford D. Simak, in* Cosmic Engineers

I'm certain no one has ever included Clifford D. Simak in any list of the writers of so-called "hard science fiction"— science fiction arising out of, or based on extrapolations from, the purported "hard sciences" (sciences heavily weighted with technology)—but Cliff was no science lightweight, by any means.

Anyone with even a superficial knowledge of the life of Clifford D. Simak knows that, for most of the fifty-five-year period during which he was a published writer of science fiction, he was also a working journalist—a newspaperman at a time when that career carried a much higher freight of meaning and importance than it does now. And so, of course, he wrote many news stories of various sorts, but those are seldom, if ever, included in the bibliographies of his fiction (even if they can be identified).

But newspapers frequently publish material that is different, in one way or another, from what we think of as "the news," and for Cliff Simak, this began during his very first newspaper job, when, only a few years after coming to the *Iron River Reporter* (Michigan), he became the paper's editor and, among other duties, wrote a regular column entitled "Driftwood."

It is now impossible to ascertain all of the sorts of things Cliff might have written during his subsequent years working on a variety of newspapers across the Upper Midwest. In those days, most of a reporter's work went uncredited when the issue was published, making a byline a sought-after reward for good work. But at some point after 1959, during Cliff's time with the *Minneapolis Star* and later with the *Tribune*—with which the *Star* eventually merged after a period during which they both continued to publish, the *Tribune* as the morning paper and the *Star* as the evening paper—Cliff became the go-to guy for the paper's science-oriented stories, writing stories that ranged from meteorology and climate studies to space exploration (he interviewed Willy Ley), astronomy (he interviewed Harlow Shapley), anthropology, computers, geology, nuclear physics (he interviewed Edward Teller), and energy-oriented issues to hypnosis, unidentified flying objects, and matters concerning how both society and individuals dealt with death. By 1966, Cliff was identified in the paper as the *Star*'s "science writer" and as the "coordinator for the Science Reading Program" for the *Tribune*.

Aimed at encouraging an interest in science among young people, the Science Reading Program—perhaps reflecting new national priorities arising following the shock to American complacencies caused by the USSR's launching of the first artificial satellite—worked with schools to provide students with insights into a variety of the fields of science. It did so well, apparently, that the series was translated for use in schools in India and South America.

Although Cliff was clearly interested in science and the development of technology for most of his life—he used to speak, with a chuckle, of the days of his youth when, on the rare occasions an automobile drove down the roads of his rural area, each resident that saw it would use the telephone to call up the neighbors to let them know it was coming so that they could step outside and see it themselves—most of his education and early career involved no technology or science beyond the typewriter, the printing press, and the telephone. The earliest of Cliff's surviving journals contains what appears to be a list of out-of-town radio stations that he had listened to, and I wonder if that might reflect enthusiasm following his first ownership of a radio. Those entries are undated, but the first page following them, which lists a series of purchases of firewood, was headed "1932–33."

And yet, by the early 1960s, he became a writer of books about science—and, specifically, of books that could be called popularizations of a variety of scientific fields for the edification of younger readers. It is unfortunate that any journals he might have akept during those years have not survived to give us an insight into his thinking on such matters, but then, considering that he was still working full time at his newspaper and writing science fiction (this was the period during which he wrote the celebrated *Way Station*, among other things), as well as writing a series of non-fiction books, perhaps he had no time to bother with a journal.

In 1962, St. Martin's Press published *The Solar System: Our New Front Yard*. Its subject was astronomy. *From Atoms to Infinity: Readings in Modern Science* was published by Harper & Row in 1965. A sort of anthology of essays, edited by Cliff, that had appeared in the *Tribune*'s Science Reading series in 1963 and 1964, it also included an article by Cliff, entitled "Our Place in the Galaxy," that was in the section on astronomy, to which the great astronomer Harlow Shapley contributed three articles. Other sections touched on fields such as mathematics (four short articles by Isaac Asimov), meteorology, archaeology, Earth, rocketry (four short articles by Willy Ley), plasma physics, the atom, and cancer. St. Martin's Press then published *Trilobite, Dinosaur, and Man: The Earth's Story*, a book on historical geology, in 1966, followed by *Wonder and Glory: The Story of the Universe* in 1969. In 1969, Harper & Row published *The March of Science*, which was an anthology of scientific articles by ten writers on such subjects as relativity, archaeology, virology, and the stars. And finally, in 1971, St. Martin's Press published *Prehistoric Man*.

It would be easy to dismiss these books as lightweight; the description "popularization" carries unappealing connotations to most educated readers, and the fact that the volumes are all now over forty-five years old strongly implies that they are certainly outdated—and, in some senses, that is true. Moreover, these books were clearly aimed at young readers.

Nonetheless, value can be found in at least some of these books. I decided to read *Wonder and Glory*, for instance, simply because of the title. Having read every piece of Cliff's fiction that I could reach multiple times, I noticed that he used the phrase "wonder and glory" on a number of occasions, generally in some context relating to outer space, and I came to the conclusion that the phrase had some particular, perhaps strongly psychological, meaning to him.

Now over forty-seven years old, *Wonder and Glory* lacks the tremendous knowledge and insights that have been given the field of astronomy in those superseding years, of course, and yet the book has more value than I expected, providing a smooth, easily understood primer on the basics of that field—much of which I had once known, but had forgotten. Clearly, Cliff had a touch for explaining things; and the only things missing from the book are the things that would later be built on the matters he explained. (The contemporary reviews of the book seem to have focused on the fact that it did not bother with footnotes and citations, a short-sighted criticism given that the idea was not to drive away young readers.)

Similarly, I decided to read *Prehistoric Man* largely because I had noticed that Cliff made a number of references in his fiction to, well, the images we have of prehistoric mankind (see such stories as "The Loot of Time" and "Final Gentleman," for example). And I was charmed by the book, short though it is. Using the device of portraying the life of two prehistoric societies through the eyes of two old men—one, a member of a hunter society, at the beginning of the book, the other, a member of an early farming community, at the end—it challenges the reader to treat early men as already human rather than as vicious or animalistic. And in the midst of presenting the basic facts known by the experts (in 1970, I suppose) regarding our prehistoric ancestors (again, in smooth, easily flowing prose that eschews footnotes and citations), Cliff did not hesitate to provide some interesting opinions, such as:

> "So finally . . . creatures like us came to exist, evolving into a life form so competent and efficient, so brutal and so selfish and so ruthless, that it took over the entire earth."

And:

> "We should not fall into the error of thinking of prehistoric Man as something less than human. . . . We cannot divorce ourselves from any single one of them."

And:

> "The question . . . is whether man domesticated the dog or the dog domesticated man. Dogs are affable and intelligent animals and forever on the make."

As he did with *Wonder and Glory*, Cliff made his summary of the basics of anthropological knowledge easy and attractive to read; but in this case, he did not hesitate to fill in blank spots in the available knowledge with his own speculations and suggestions—whenever he did so, however, he clearly labeled his imaginings as exactly that: speculations that, although at that point unproven, were still possible—and that still had the value of being both educational and able to stretch the imaginations of the readers.

Cliff's daughter remembers nights when, as a child, she and her father delved into the books that reproduced cave paintings preserved from prehistory; it is significant that his interest in prehistoric people, already in existence well before his children were born, may have had some effect on his daughter's eventual career as a museum curator.

David W. Wixon

GOOD NIGHT, MR. JAMES

"Good Night, Mr. James" was originally published in the March 1951 issue of Galaxy Science Fiction, *then a very new magazine just beginning its run to a prominence—a run that would nearly eclipse that of the legendary Astounding Science Fiction. That publication date suggests that the story was written in late 1949 or early 1950, a period not represented in Cliff Simak's surviving journals. And I regret that fact, because I would like to be able to see whether Cliff had anything to say about how he came to write this story.*

For although Cliff frequently commented that there was "little violence in [his] work," he would later describe "Good Night, Mr. James" as "vicious." In fact, it was so vicious, he said, that "it is the only one of [his] stories adapted to television. It is so unlike anything [he had] ever written that at times [he found himself] wondering how [he] came to do it."

Me, too.

—*dww*

I

He came alive from nothing. He became aware from unawareness.

He smelled the air of the night and heard the trees whispering on the embankment above him and the breeze that had set the trees to whispering came down to him and felt him over with soft and tender fingers, for all the world as if it were examining him for broken bones or contusions and abrasions.

He sat up and put both his palms down upon the ground beside him to help him sit erect and stared into the darkness. Memory came slowly and when it came it was incomplete and answered nothing.

His name was Henderson James and he was a human being and he was sitting somewhere on a planet that was called the Earth. He was thirty-six years old and he was, in his own way, famous, and comfortably well-off. He lived in an old ancestral home on Summit Avenue, which was a respectable address even if it had lost some of its smartness in the last twenty years or so.

On the road above the slope of the embankment a car went past with its tires whining on the pavement and for a moment its headlights made the treetops glow. Far away, muted by the distance, a whistle cried out. And somewhere else a dog was barking with a flat viciousness.

His name was Henderson James and if that were true, why was he here? Why should Henderson James be sitting on the slope of an embankment, listening to the wind in the trees and to a wailing whistle and a barking dog? Something had gone wrong, some incident that, if he could but remember it, might answer all his questions.

There was a job to do.

He sat and stared into the night and found that he was shivering, although there was no reason why he should, for the night was not that cold. Beyond the embankment he heard the sounds of a city late at night, the distant whine of the speeding car and the far-off wind-broken screaming of a siren. Once a man walked along a street close by and James sat listening to his footsteps until they faded out of hearing.

Something had happened and there was a job to do, a job that he had been doing, a job that somehow had been strangely interrupted by the inexplicable incident which had left him lying here on this embankment.

He checked himself. Clothing . . . shorts and shirt, strong shoes, his wristwatch and the gun in the holster at his side.

A gun?

The job involved a gun.

He had been hunting in the city, hunting something that required a gun. Something that was prowling in the night and a thing that must be killed.

Then he knew the answer, but even as he knew it he sat for a moment wondering at the strange, methodical, step-by-step progression of reasoning that had brought him to the memory. First his name and the basic facts pertaining to himself, then the realization of where he was and the problem of why he happened to be there and finally the realization that he had a gun and that it was meant to be used. It was a logical way to think, a primer schoolbook way to work it out:

I am a man named Henderson James.
I live in a house on Summit Avenue.
Am I in the house on Summit Avenue?
No, I am not in the house on Summit Avenue.
I am on an embankment somewhere.

Why am I on the embankment?
But it wasn't the way a man thought, at least not the normal way a normal man would think. Man thought in shortcuts. He cut across the block and did not go all the way around.

It was a frightening thing, he told himself, this clear-around-the-block thinking. It wasn't normal and it wasn't right and it made no sense at all . . . no more sense than did the fact that he should find himself in a place with no memory of getting there.

He rose to his feet and ran his hands up and down his body. His clothes were neat, not rumpled. He hadn't been beaten up and he hadn't been thrown from a speeding car. There were no sore places on his body and his face was unbloody and whole and he felt all right.

He hooked his fingers in the holster belt and shucked it up so that it rode tightly on his hips. He pulled out the gun and checked it with expert and familiar fingers and the gun was ready.

He walked up the embankment and reached the road, went across it with a swinging stride to reach the sidewalk that fronted the row of new bungalows. He heard a car coming and stepped off the sidewalk to crouch in a clump of evergreens that landscaped one corner of a lawn. The move was instinctive and he crouched there, feeling just a little foolish at the thing he'd done.

The car went past and no one saw him. They would not, he now realized, have noticed him even if he had remained out on the sidewalk.

He was unsure of himself; that must be the reason for his fear. There was a blank spot in his life, some mysterious incident that he did not know and the unknowing of it had undermined the sure and solid foundation of his own existence, had wrecked the basis of his motive and had turned him, momentarily, into a furtive animal that darted and hid at the approach of his fellow men.

That and something that had happened to him that made him think clear around the block.

He remained crouching in the evergreens, watching the street and the stretch of sidewalk, conscious of the white-painted, ghostly bungalows squatting back in their landscaped lots.

A word came into his mind. *Puudly*. An odd word, unearthly, yet it held terror.

The *puudly* had escaped and that was why he was here, hiding on the front lawn of some unsuspecting and sleeping citizen, equipped with a gun and a determination to use it, ready to match his wits and the quickness of brain and muscle against the most bloodthirsty, hate-filled thing yet found in the Galaxy.

The *puudly* was dangerous. It was not a thing to harbor. In fact, there was a law against harboring not only a *puudly*, but certain other alien beasties even less lethal than a *puudly*. There was good reason for such a law, reason which no one, much less himself, would ever think to question.

And now the *puudly* was loose and somewhere in the city.

James grew cold at the thought of it, his brain forming images of the things that might come to pass if he did not hunt down the alien beast and put an end to it.

Although beast was not quite the word to use. The *puudly* was more than a beast . . . just how much more than a beast he once had hoped to learn. He had not learned a lot, he now admitted to himself, not nearly all there was to learn, but he had learned enough. More than enough to frighten him.

For one thing, he had learned what hate could be and how shallow an emotion human hate turned out to be when measured against the depth and intensity and the ravening horror of the *puudly's* hate. Not unreasoning hate, for unreasoning hate defeats itself, but a rational, calculating, driving hate that motivated a clever and deadly killing machine which directed its rapacity and its cunning against every living thing that was not a *puudly*.

For the beast had a mind and a personality that operated upon the basic law of self-preservation against all comers, whoever they might be, extending that law to the interpretation that safety lay in one direction only . . . the death of every other living being. No other reason was needed for a *puudly's* killing. The fact that anything else lived and moved and was thus posing a threat, no matter how remote, against a *puudly*, was sufficient reason in itself.

It was psychotic, of course, some murderous instinct planted far back in time and deep in the creature's racial consciousness, but no more psychotic, perhaps, than many human instincts.

The *puudly* had been, and still was for that matter, a unique opportunity for a study in alien behaviorism. Given a permit, one could have studied them on their native planet. Refused a permit, one sometimes did a foolish thing, as James had.

And foolish acts backfire, as this one did.

James put down a hand and patted the gun at his side, as if by doing so he might derive some assurance that he was equal to the task.

There was no question in his mind as to the thing that must be done.

He must find the *puudly* and kill it and he must do that before the break of dawn. Anything less than that would be abject and horrifying failure.

For the *puudly* would bud. It was long past its time for the reproductive act and there were bare hours left to find it before it had loosed upon the Earth dozens of baby *puudlies*. They would not remain babies for long. A few hours after budding they would strike out on their own. To find one *puudly*, lost in the vastness of a sleeping city, seemed bad enough; to track down some dozens of them would be impossible.

So it was tonight or never.

Tonight there would be no killing on the *puudly's* part, Tonight the beast would be intent on one thing only, to find a place where it could rest in quiet, where it could give itself over, wholeheartedly and with no interference, to the business of bringing other *puudlies* into being.

It was clever. It would have known where it was going before it had escaped. There would be, on its part, no time wasted in seeking or in doubling back. It would have known where it was going and already it was there, already the buds would be rising on its body, bursting forth and growing.

There was one place, and one place only, in the entire city where an alien beast would be safe from prying eyes. A man could figure that one out and so could a *puudly*. The question was: Would the *puudly* know that a man could figure it out? Would the *puudly* underestimate a man? Or, knowing that the man would know it, too, would it find another place of hiding?

James rose from the evergreens and went down the sidewalk. The street marker at the corner, standing underneath a swinging street light, told him where he was and it was closer to the place where he was going than he might have hoped.

II

The zoo was quiet for a while, and then something sent up a howl that raised James' hackles and made his blood stop in his veins.

James, having scaled the fence, stood tensely at its foot, trying to identify the howling animal. He was unable to place it. More than likely, he told himself, it was a new one. A person simply couldn't keep track of all the zoo's occupants. New ones were coming in all the time, strange, unheard of creatures from the distant stars.

Straight ahead lay the unoccupied moat cage that up until a day or two before had held an unbelievable monstrosity from the jungles of one of the Arctian worlds. James grimaced in the dark, remembering the thing. They had finally had to kill it.

And now the *puudly* was there . . . well, maybe not there, but one place that it could be, the one place in the entire city where it might be seen and arouse no comment, for the zoo was filled with animals that were seldom seen and another strange one would arouse only momentary wonder. One animal more would go unnoticed unless some zoo attendant should think to check the records.

There, in that unoccupied cage area, the *puudly* would be undisturbed, could quietly go about its business of budding out more *puudlies*. No one would bother it, for things like *puudlies* were the normal occupants of this place set aside for the strangers brought to Earth to be stared at and studied by that ferocious race, the humans.

James stood quietly beside the fence.

Henderson James. Thirty-six. Unmarried. Alien psychologist. An official of this zoo. And an offender against the law for having secured and harbored an alien being that was barred from Earth.

Why, he asked himself, did he think of himself in this way? Why, standing here, did he catalogue himself? It was instinctive to know one's self . . . there was no need, no sense of setting up a mental outline of one's self.

It had been foolish to go ahead with this *puudly* business. He recalled how he had spent days fighting it out with himself, reviewing all the disastrous possibilities which might arise from it. If the old renegade spaceman had not come to him and had not said, over a bottle of most delicious Lupan wine, that he could deliver, for a certain, rather staggering sum, one live *puudly*, in good condition, it never would have happened.

James was sure that of himself he never would have thought of it. But the old space captain was a man he knew and admired from former dealings. He was a man who was not averse to turning either an honest or a dishonest dollar, and yet he was a man, for all of that, that you could depend upon. He would do what you paid him for and keep his lip buttoned tight once the deed was done.

James had wanted a *puudly*, for it was a most engaging beast with certain little tricks that, once understood, might open up new avenues of speculation and approach, might write new chapters in the tortuous study of alien minds and manners.

But for all of that, it had been a terrifying thing to do and now that the beast was loose, the terror was compounded. For it was not wholly beyond speculation that the descendants of this one brood that the escaped *puudly* would spawn might wipe out the population of the Earth, or at the best, make the Earth untenable for its rightful dwellers.

A place like the Earth, with its teeming millions, would provide a field day for the fangs of the *puudlies*, and the minds that drove the fangs. They would not hunt for hunger, nor for the sheer madness of the kill, but because of the compelling conviction that no *puudly* would be safe until Earth was wiped clean of life. They would be killing for survival, as a cornered rat would kill . . . except that they would be cornered nowhere but in the murderous insecurity of their minds.

If the posses scoured the Earth to hunt them down, they would be found in all directions, for they would be shrewd enough to scatter. They would know the ways of guns and traps and poisons and there would be more and more of them as time went on. Each of them would accelerate their budding to replace with a dozen or a hundred the ones that might be killed.

James moved quietly forward to the edge of the moat and let himself down into the mud that covered the bottom. When the monstrosity had been killed, the moat had been drained and should long since have been cleaned, but the press of work, James thought, must have prevented its getting done.

Slowly he waded out into the mud, feeling his way, his feet making sucking noises as he pulled them through the slime. Finally he reached the rocky incline that led out of the moat to the island cage.

He stood for a moment, his hands on the great, wet boulders, listening, trying to hold his breath so the sound of it would not interfere with hearing. The thing that howled had quieted and the night was deathly quiet. Or seemed, at first, to be. Then he heard the little insect noises that ran through the grass and bushes and the whisper of the leaves in the trees across the moat and the far-off sound that was the hoarse breathing of a sleeping city.

Now, for the first time, he felt fear. Felt it in the silence that was not a silence, in the mud beneath his feet, in the upthrust boulders that rose out of the moat.

The *puudly* was a dangerous thing, not only because it was strong and quick, but because it was intelligent. Just how intelligent, he did not know. It reasoned and it planned and schemed. It could talk, though not as a human talks . . . probably better than a human ever could. For it not only could talk words, but it could talk emotions. It lured its victims to it by the thoughts it put into their minds; it held them entranced with dreams and illusion until it slit their throats. It could purr a man to sleep, could lull him to suicidal inaction. It could drive him crazy with a single flicking thought, hurling a perception so foul and alien that the mind recoiled deep inside itself and stayed there, coiled tight, like a watch that has been overwound and will not run.

It should have budded long ago, but it had fought off its budding, holding back against the day when it might escape, planning, he realized now, its fight to stay on Earth, which meant its conquest of Earth. It had planned, and planned well, against this very moment, and it would feel or show no mercy to anyone who interfered with it.

His hand went down and touched the gun and he felt the muscles in his jaw involuntarily tightening and suddenly there was at once a lightness and a hardness in him that had not been there before. He pulled himself up the boulder face, seeking cautious hand- and toeholds, breathing shallowly, body pressed against the rock. Quickly, and surely, and no noise, for he must reach the top and be there before the *puudly* knew there was anyone around.

The *puudly* would be relaxed and intent upon its business, engrossed in the budding forth of that numerous family that in days to come would begin the grim and relentless crusade to make an alien planet safe for *puudlies* . . . and for *puudlies* alone.

That is, if the *puudly* were here and not somewhere else. James was only a human trying to think like a *puudly* and that was not an easy or a pleasant job and he had no way of knowing if he succeeded. He could only hope that his reasoning was vicious and crafty enough.

His clawing hand found grass and earth and he sank his fingers deep into the soil, hauling his body up the last few feet of the rock face above the pit.

He lay flat upon the gently sloping ground, listening, tensed for any danger. He studied the ground in front of him, probing every foot. Distant street lamps lighting the zoo walks threw back the total blackness that had engulfed him as he climbed out of the moat, but there still were areas of shadow that he had to study closely.

Inch by inch, he squirmed his way along, making sure of the terrain immediately ahead before he moved a muscle. He held the gun in a rock-hard fist, ready for instant action, watching for the faintest hint of motion, alert for any hump or irregularity that was not rock or bush or grass.

Minutes magnified themselves into hours, his eyes ached with staring and the lightness that had been in him drained away, leaving only the hardness, which was as tense as a drawn bowstring. A sense of failure began to seep into his mind and with it came the full-fledged, until now unadmitted, realization of what failure meant, not only for the world, but for the dignity and the pride that was Henderson James.

Now, faced with the possibility, he admitted to himself the action he must take if the *puudly* were not here, if he did not find it here and kill it. He would have to notify the authorities, would have to attempt to alert the police, must plead with newspapers and radio to warn the citizenry, must reveal himself as a man who, through pride and self-conceit, had exposed the people of the Earth to this threat against their hold upon their native planet.

They would not believe him. They would laugh at him until the laughter died in their torn throats, choked off with their blood. He sweated, thinking of it, thinking of the price this city, and the world, would pay before it learned the truth.

There was a whisper of sound, a movement of black against deeper black.

The *puudly* rose in front of him, not more than six feet away, from its bed beside a bush. He jerked the pistol up and his finger tightened on the trigger.

"Don't," the *puudly* said inside his mind. "I'll go along with you."

His finger strained with the careful slowness of the squeeze and the gun leaped in his hand, but even as it did he felt the whiplash of terror slash at his brain, caught for just a second the terrible import, the mind-shattering obscenity that glanced off his mind and ricocheted away.

"Too late," he told the *puudly*, with his voice and his mind and his body shaking. "You should have tried that first. You wasted precious seconds. You would have got me if you had done it first."

It had been easy, he assured himself, much easier than he had thought. The *puudly* was dead or dying and the Earth and its millions of unsuspecting citizens were safe and, best of all, Henderson James was safe . . . safe from indignity, safe from being stripped naked of the little defenses he had built up through the years to shield him against the public stare. He felt relief flood over him and it left him pulseless and breathless and feeling clean, but weak.

"You fool," the dying *puudly* said, death clouding its words as they built up in his mind. "You fool, you half-thing, you duplicate . . ."

It died then and he felt it die, felt the life go out of it and leave it empty.

He rose softly to his feet and he seemed stunned and at first he thought it was from knowing death, from having touched hands with death within the *puudly's* mind.

The *puudly* had tried to fool him. Faced with the pistol, it had tried to throw him off his balance to give it the second that it needed to hurl the mind-blasting thought that had caught at the edge of his brain. If he had hesitated for a moment, he knew, it would have been all over with him. If his finger had slackened for a moment, it would have been too late.

The *puudly* must have known that he would think of the zoo as the first logical place to look and, even knowing that, it had held him in enough contempt to come here, had not even bothered to try to watch for him, had not tried to stalk him, had waited until he was almost on top of it before it moved.

And that was queer, for the *puudly* must have known, with its uncanny mental powers, every move that he had made. It must have maintained a casual contact with his mind every second of the time since it had escaped. He had known that and . . . wait a minute, he hadn't known it until this very moment, although, knowing it now, it seemed as if he had always known it.

What is the matter with me, he thought. There's something wrong with me. I should have known I could not surprise the *puudly*, and yet I didn't know it. I must have surprised it, for otherwise it would have finished me off quite leisurely at any moment after I climbed out of the moat.

You fool, the *puudly* had said. You fool, you half-thing, you duplicate . . .

You duplicate!

He felt the strength and the personality and the hard, unquestioned identity of himself as Henderson James, human being, drain out of him, as if someone had cut the puppet string and he, the puppet, had slumped supine upon the stage.

So that was why he had been able to surprise the *puudly!*

There were two Henderson Jameses. The *puudly* had been in contact with one of them, the original, the real Henderson James, had known every move he made, had known that it was safe so far as that Henderson James might be concerned. It had not known of the second Henderson James that had stalked it through the night.

Henderson James, duplicate.

Henderson James, temporary.

Henderson James, here tonight, gone tomorrow.

For they would not let him live. The original Henderson James would not allow him to continue living, and even if he did, the world would not allow it. Duplicates were made only for very temporary and very special reasons and it was always understood that once their purpose was accomplished they would be done away with.

Done away with . . . those were the words exactly. Gotten out of the way. Swept out of sight and mind. Killed as unconcernedly and emotionlessly as one chops off a chicken's head.

He walked forward and dropped on one knee beside the *puudly*, running his hand over its body in the darkness. Lumps stood out all over it, the swelling buds that now would never break to spew forth in a loathsome birth a brood of *puudly* pups.

He rose to his feet.

The job was done, The *puudly* had been killed—killed before it had given birth to a horde of horrors.

The job was done and he could go home.

Home?

Of course, that was the thing that had been planted in his mind, the thing they wanted him to do. To go home, to go back to the house on Summit Avenue, where his executioners would wait, to walk back deliberately and unsuspectingly to the death that waited.

The job was done and his usefulness was over. He had been created to perform a certain task and the task was now performed and while an hour ago he had been a factor in the plans of men, he was no longer wanted. He was an embarrassment and superfluous.

Now wait a minute, he told himself. You may not be a duplicate. You do not feel like one.

That was true. He felt like Henderson James. He was Henderson James. He lived on Summit Avenue and had illegally brought to Earth a beast known as a *puudly* in order that he might study it and talk to it and test its alien reactions, attempt to measure its intelligence and guess at the strength and depth and the direction of its non-humanity. He had been a fool, of course, to do it, and yet at the time it had seemed important to understand the deadly, alien mentality.

I am human, he said, and that was right, but even so the fact meant nothing. Of course he was human. Henderson James was human and his duplicate would be exactly as human as the original. For the duplicate, processed from the pattern that held every trait and characteristic of the man he was to become a copy of, would differ in not a single basic factor.

In not a single basic factor, perhaps, but in certain other things. For no matter how much the duplicate might be like his pattern, no matter how full-limbed he might spring from his creation, he still would be a new man. He would have the capacity for knowledge and for thought and in a little time he would have and know and be all the things that his original was . . .

But it would take some time, some short while to come to a full realization of all he knew and was, some time to coordinate and recognize all the knowledge and experience that lay within his mind. At first he'd grope and search until he came upon the things that he must know. Until he became acquainted with himself, with the sort of man he was, he could not reach out blindly in the dark and put his hand exactly and unerringly upon the thing he wished.

That had been exactly what he'd done. He had groped and searched. He had been compelled to think, at first, in simple basic truths and facts.

I am a man.

I am on a planet called Earth.

I am Henderson James.

I live on Summit Avenue.

There is a job to do.

It had been quite a while, he remembered now, before he had been able to dig out of his mind the nature of the job.

There is a *puudly* to hunt down and destroy.

Even now he could not find in the hidden, still-veiled recesses of his mind the many valid reasons why a man should run so grave a risk to study a thing so vicious as a *puudly*. There were reasons, he knew there were, and in a little time he would know them quite specifically.

The point was that if he were Henderson James, original, he would know them now, know them as a part of himself and his life, without laboriously searching for them.

The *puudly* had known, of course. It had known, beyond any chance of error, that there were two Henderson Jameses. It had been keeping tab on one when another one showed up. A mentality far less astute than the *puudly's* would have had no trouble in figuring that one out.

If the *puudly* had not talked, he told himself, I never would have known. If it had died at once and not had a chance to taunt me, I would not have known. I would even now be walking to the house on Summit Avenue.

He stood lonely and naked of soul in the wind that swept across the moated island. There was a sour bitterness in his mouth.

He moved a foot and touched the dead *puudly*.

"I'm sorry," he told the stiffening body. "I'm sorry now I did it. If I had known, I never would have killed you."

Stiffly erect, he moved away.

III

He stopped at the street corner, keeping well in the shadow. Halfway down the block, and on the other side, was the house. A light burned in one of the rooms upstairs and another on the post beside the gate that opened into the yard, lighting the walk up to the door.

Just as if, he told himself, the house were waiting for the master to come home. And that, of course, was exactly what it was doing. An old lady of a house, waiting, hands folded in its lap, rocking very gently in a squeaky chair . . . and with a gun beneath the folded shawl.

His lip lifted in half a snarl as he stood there, looking at the house. What do they take me for, he thought, putting out a trap in plain sight and one that's not even baited? Then he remembered. They would not know, of course, that he knew he was a duplicate. They would think that he would think that he was Henderson James, the one and only. They would expect him to come walking home, quite naturally, believing he belonged there. So far as they would know, there would be no possibility of his finding out the truth.

And now that he had? Now that he was here, across the street from the waiting house?

He had been brought into being, had been given life, to do a job that his original had not dared to do, or had not wanted to do. He had carried out a killing his original didn't want to dirty his hands with, or risk his neck in doing.

Or had it not been that at all, but the necessity of two men working on the job, the original serving as a focus for the *puudly's* watchful mind while the other man sneaked up to kill it while it watched?

No matter what, he had been created, at a good stiff price, from the pattern of the man that was Henderson James. The wizardry of man's knowledge, the magic of machines, a deep understanding of organic chemistry, of human physiology, of the mystery of life, had made a second Henderson James. It was legal, of course, under certain circumstances . . . for example, in the case of public policy, and his own creation, he knew, might have been validated under such a heading. But there were conditions and one of these was that a duplicate not be allowed to continue living once it had served the specific purpose for which it had been created.

Usually such a condition was a simple one to carry out, for the duplicate was not meant to know he was a duplicate. So far as he was concerned, he was the original. There was no suspicion in him, no foreknowledge of the doom that was invariably ordered for him, no reason for him to be on guard against the death that waited.

The duplicate knitted his brow, trying to puzzle it out.

There was a strange set of ethics here.

He was alive and he wanted to stay alive. Life, once it had been tasted, was too sweet, too good, to go back to the nothingness from which he had come . . . or would it be nothingness? Now that he had known life, now that he was alive, might he not hope for a life after death, the same as any other human being? Might not he, too, have the same human right as any other human to grasp at the shadowy and glorious promises and assurances held out by religion and by faith?

He tried to marshal what he knew about those promises and assurances, but his knowledge was illusive. A little later he would remember more about it. A little later, when the neural bookkeeper in his mind had been able to coordinate and activate the knowledge that he had inherited from the pattern, he would know.

He felt a trace of anger stir deep inside of him, anger at the unfairness of allowing him only a few short hours of life, of allowing him to learn how wonderful a thing life was, only to snatch it from him. It was a cruelty that went beyond mere human cruelty. It was something that had been fashioned out of the distorted perspective of a machine society that measured existence only in terms of mechanical and physical worth, that discarded with a ruthless hand whatever part of that society had no specific purpose.

The cruelty, he told himself, was in ever giving life, not in taking it away.

His original, of course, was the one to blame. He was the one who had obtained the *puudly* and allowed it to escape. It was his fumbling and his inability to correct his error without help which had created the necessity of fashioning a duplicate.

And yet, could he blame him?

Perhaps, rather, he owed him gratitude for a few hours of life at least, gratitude for the privilege of knowing what life was like. Although he could not quite decide whether or not it was something which called for gratitude.

He stood there, staring at the house. That light in the upstairs room was in the study off the master bedroom. Up there Henderson James, original, was waiting for the word that the duplicate had come home to death. It was an easy thing to sit there and wait, to sit and wait for the word that was sure to come. An easy thing to sentence to death a man one had never seen, even if that man be the walking image of one's self.

It would be a harder decision to kill him if you stood face to face with him ... harder to kill someone who would be, of necessity, closer than a brother, someone who would be, even literally, flesh of your flesh, blood of your blood, brain of your brain.

There would be a practical side as well, a great advantage to be able to work with a man who thought as you did, who would be almost a second self. It would be almost as if there were two of you.

A thing like that could be arranged. Plastic surgery and a price for secrecy could make your duplicate into an unrecognizable other person. A little red tape, some finagling . . . but it could be done. It was a proposition that Henderson James, duplicate, thought would interest Henderson James, original. Or at least he hoped it would.

The room with the light could be reached with a little luck, with strength and agility and determination. The brick expanse of a chimney, its base cloaked by shrubs, its length masked by a closely growing tree, ran up the wall. A man could climb its rough brick face, could reach out and swing himself through the open window into the lighted room.

And once Henderson James, original, stood face to face with Henderson James, duplicate . . . well, it would be less of a gamble. The duplicate then would no longer be an impersonal factor. He would be a man and one that was very close to his original.

There would be watchers, but they would be watching the front door. If he were quiet, if he could reach and climb the chimney without making any noise, he'd be in the room before anyone would notice.

He drew back deeper in the shadows and considered. It was either get into the room and face his original, hope to be able to strike a compromise with him, or simply to light out . . . to run and hide and wait, watching his chance to get completely away, perhaps to some far planet in some other part of the Galaxy.

Both ways were a gamble, but one was quick, would either succeed or fail within the hour; the other might drag on for months with a man never knowing whether he was safe, never being sure.

Something nagged at him, a persistent little fact that skittered through his brain and eluded his efforts to pin it down. It might be important and then, again, it might be a random thing, simply a floating piece of information that was looking for its pigeonhole.

His mind shrugged it off.

The quick way or the long way?

He stood thinking for a moment and then moved swiftly down the street, seeking a place where he could cross in shadow.

He had chosen the short way.

IV

The room was empty.

He stood beside the window, quietly, only his eyes moving, searching every corner, checking against a situation that couldn't seem quite true . . . that Henderson James was not here, waiting for the word.

Then he strode swiftly to the bedroom door and swung it open. His finger found the switch and the lights went on. The bedroom was empty and so was the bath. He went back into the study.

He stood with his back against the wall, facing the door that led into the hallway, but his eyes went over the room, foot by foot, orienting himself, feeling himself flow into the shape and form of it, feeling familiarity creep in upon him and enfold him in its comfort of belonging.

Here were the books, the fireplace with its mantel loaded with souvenirs, the easy chairs, the liquor cabinet . . . and all were a part of him, a background that was as much a part of Henderson James as his body and his inner thoughts were a part of him.

This, he thought, is what I would have missed, the experience I never would have had if the *puudly* had not taunted me. I would have died an empty and unrelated body that had no actual place in the universe.

The phone purred at him and he stood there startled by it, as if some intruder from the outside had pushed its way into the room, shattering the sense of belonging that had come to him.

The phone rang again and he went across the room and picked it up.

"James speaking," he said.

"That you, Mr. James?"

The voice was that of Anderson, the gardener.

"Why, yes," said the duplicate. "Who did you think it was?"

"We got a fellow here who says he's you."

Henderson James, duplicate, stiffened with fright and his hand, suddenly, was grasping the phone so hard that he found the time to wonder why it did not pulverize to bits beneath his fingers.

"He's dressed like you," the gardener said, "and I knew you went out. Talked to you, remember? Told you that you shouldn't? Not with us waiting for that . . . that thing."

"Yes," said the duplicate, his voice so even that he could not believe it was he who spoke. "Yes, certainly I remember talking with you."

"But, sir, how did you get back?"

"I came in the back way," the even voice said into the phone. "Now what's holding you back?"

"He's dressed like you."

"Naturally. Of course he would be, Anderson."

And that, to be sure, didn't quite follow, but Anderson wasn't too bright to start with and now he was somewhat upset.

"You remember," the duplicate said, "that we talked about it."

"I guess I was excited and forgot," admitted Anderson. "You told me to call you, to make sure you were in your study, though. That's right, isn't it, sir?"

"You've called me," the duplicate said, "and I am here."

"Then the other one out here is him?"

"Of course," said the duplicate. "Who else could it be?"

He put the phone back into the cradle and stood waiting. It came a moment after, the dull, throaty cough of a gun. He walked to a chair and sank into it, spent with the knowledge of how events had so been ordered that now, finally, he was safe, safe beyond all question.

Soon he would have to change into other clothes, hide the gun and the clothes that he was wearing. The staff would ask no questions, most likely, but it was best to let nothing arouse suspicion in their minds.

He felt his nerves quieting and he allowed himself to glance about the room, take in the books and furnishings, the soft and easy . . . and earned . . . comfort of a man solidly and unshakably established in the world.

He smiled softly.

"It will be nice," he said.

It had been easy. Now that it was over, it seemed ridiculously easy. Easy because he had never seen the man who had walked up to the door. It was easy to kill a man you have never seen.

With each passing hour he would slip deeper and deeper into the personality that was his by right of heritage. There would be no one to question, after a time not even himself, that he was Henderson James.

The phone rang again and he got up to answer it. A pleasant voice told him, "This is Allen, over at the duplication lab. We've been waiting for a report from you."

"Well," said James, "I . . ."

"I just called," interrupted Allen, "to tell you not to worry. It slipped my mind before."

"I see," said James, though he didn't.

"We did this one a little differently," Allen explained. "An experiment that we thought we'd try out. Slow poison in his bloodstream. Just another precaution. Probably not necessary, but we like to be positive. In case he fails to show up, you needn't worry any."

"I am sure he will show up."

Allen chuckled. "Twenty-four hours. Like a time bomb. No antidote for it even if he found out somehow."

"It was good of you to let me know," said James.

"Glad to," said Allen. "Good night, Mr. James."

BROTHER

Many people take Clifford Simak's story "Brother" as autobiographical; and to a limited, but enticing, extent, they are correct—particularly with regard to Anderson's description of Edward Lambert as the "pastoral spokesman of the century," based on his nature writing. Of course, this is strikingly parallel to the numerous portraits of Simak as the "pastoralist of science fiction," but what few of Cliff's fans realize is that he did have a certain amount of interest in the field of nature writing. In the early 1930s, when he was just beginning to try to sell short stories and articles to magazines, Cliff submitted several articles to nature magazines such as Field & Stream and Sports Afield. And his personal library contained several volumes by writers such as the great Sigurd F. Olson.

"Brother" was originally published in the October 1977 issue of the Magazine of Fantasy & Science Fiction.

—dww

He was sitting in his rocking chair on the stone-flagged patio when the car pulled off the road and stopped outside his gate. A stranger got out of it, unlatched the gate and came up the walk. The man coming up the walk was old—not as old, judged the man in the rocking chair, as he was, but old. White hair blowing in the wind and a slow, almost imperceptible, shuffle in his gait.

The man stopped before him. "You are Edward Lambert?" he asked. Lambert nodded. "I am Theodore Anderson," said the man. "From Madison. From the university."

Lambert indicated the other rocker on the patio. "Please sit down," he said. "You are far from home."

Anderson chuckled. "Not too far. A hundred miles or so."

"To me, that's far," said Lambert. "In all my life I've never been more than twenty miles away. The spaceport across the river is as far as I've ever been."

"You visit the port quite often?"

"At one time, I did. In my younger days. Not recently. From here, where I sit, I can see the ships come in and leave."

"You sit and watch for them?"

"Once I did. Not now. I still see them now and then. I no longer watch for them."

"You have a brother, I understand, who is out in space."

"Yes, Phil. Phil is the wanderer of the family. There were just the two of us. Identical twins."

"You see him now and then? I mean, he comes back to visit."

"Occasionally. Three or four times, that is all. But not in recent years. The last time he was home was twenty years ago. He was always in a hurry. He could only stay a day or two. He had great tales to tell."

"But you, yourself, stayed home. Twenty miles, you said, the farthest you've ever been away."

"There was a time," said Lambert, "when I wanted to go with him. But I couldn't. We were born late in our parents' life. They were old when we were still young. Someone had to stay here with them. And after they were gone, I found I couldn't leave. These hills, these woods, the streams had become too much a part of me."

Anderson nodded. "I can understand that. It is reflected in your writing. You became the pastoral spokesman of the century. I am quoting others, but certainly you know that."

Lambert grunted. "Nature writing. At one time, it was in the great American tradition. When I first started writing it, fifty years ago, it had gone out of style. No one understood it, no one wanted it. No one saw the need for it. But now it's back again. Every damn fool who can manage to put three words together is writing it again."

"But none as well as you."

"I've been at it longer. I have more practice doing it."

"Now," said Anderson, "there is greater need of it. A reminder of a heritage that we almost lost."

"Perhaps," said Lambert.

"To get back to your brother..."

"A moment, please," said Lambert. "You have been asking me a lot of questions. No preliminaries. No easy build up. None of the usual conversational amenities. You simply came barging in and began asking questions. You tell me your name and that you are from the university, but that is all. For the record, Mr. Anderson, please tell me what you are."

"I am sorry," said Anderson. "I'll admit to little tact, despite the fact that is one of the basics of my profession. I should know its value. I'm with the psychology department and..."

"Psychology?"

"Yes, psychology."

"I would have thought," said Lambert, "that you were in English or, perhaps, ecology or some subject dealing with the environment. How come a psychologist would drop by to talk with a nature writer?"

"Please bear with me," Anderson pleaded. "I went at this all wrong. Let us start again. I came, really, to talk about your brother."

"What about my brother? How could you know about him? Folks hereabouts know, but no one else. In my writings, I have never mentioned him."

"I spent a week last summer at a fishing camp only a few miles from here. I heard about him then."

"And some of those you talked with told you I never had a brother."

"That is it, exactly. You see, I have this study I have been working on for the last five years...."

"I don't know how the story ever got started," said Lambert, "that I never had a brother. I have paid no attention to it, and I don't see why you..."

"Mr. Lambert," said Anderson, "please pardon me. I've checked the birth records at the county seat and the census..."

"I can remember it," said Lambert, "as if it were only yesterday, the day my brother left. We were working in the barn, there across the road. The barn is no longer used now and, as you can see, has fallen in upon itself. But then it was used. My father farmed the meadow over there that runs along the creek. That land grew, still would grow if someone used it, the most beautiful corn that you ever saw. Better corn than the Iowa prairie land. Better than any place on earth. I farmed it for years after my father died, but I no longer farm it. I went out of the farming business a good ten years ago. Sold off all the stock and machinery. Now I keep a little kitchen garden. Not too large. It needn't be too large. There is only..."

"You were saying about your brother?"

"Yes, I guess I was. Phil and I were working in the barn one day. It was a rainy day—no, not really a rainy day, just drizzling. We were repairing harness. Yes, harness. My father was a strange man in many ways. Strange in reasonable sorts of ways. He didn't believe in using machinery any more than necessary. There was never a tractor on the place. He thought horses were better. On a small place like this, they were. I used them myself until I finally had to sell them. It was an emotional wrench to sell them. The horses and I were friends. But, anyhow, the two of us were working at the harness when Phil said to me, out of the thin air, that he was going to the port and try to get a job on one of the ships. We had talked about it, off and on, before, and both of us had a hankering to go, but it was a surprise to me when Phil spoke up and said that he was going. I had no idea that he had made up his mind. There is something about this that you have to understand—the time, the circumstance, the newness and excitement of travel to the stars in that day of more than fifty years ago. There were days, far back in our history, when New England boys ran off to sea. In that time of fifty years ago, they were running off to space. . . ."

Telling it, he remembered it, as he had told Anderson, as if it were only yesterday. It all came clear and real again, even to the musty scent of last year's hay in the loft above them. Pigeons were cooing in the upper reaches of the barn, and, up in the hillside pasture, a lonesome cow was bawling. The horses stamped in their stalls and made small sounds, munching at the hay remaining in their mangers.

"I made up my mind last night," said Phil, "but I didn't tell you because I wanted to be sure. I could wait, of course, but if I wait, there's the chance I'll never go. I don't want to live out my life here wishing I had gone. You'll tell pa, won't you? After I am gone. Sometime this afternoon, giving me a chance to get away."

"He wouldn't follow you," said Edward Lambert. "It would be best for you to tell him. He might reason with you, but he wouldn't stop your going."

"If I tell him, I will never go," said Phil. "I'll see the look upon his face and I'll never go. You'll have to do this much for me, Ed. You'll have to tell him so I won't see the look upon his face."

"How can you get on a ship? They don't want a green farm boy. They want people who are trained."

"There'll be a ship," said Phil, "that is scheduled to lift off, but with a crew member or two not there. They won't wait for them, they won't waste the time to hunt them down. They'll take anyone who's there. In a day or two, I'll find that kind of ship."

Lambert remembered once again how he had stood in the barn door, watching his brother walking down the road, his boots splashing in the puddles, his figure blurred by the mist-like drizzle. For a long time after he could no longer see him, long after the grayness of the drizzle had blotted out his form, he had still imagined he would see him, an ever smaller figure trudging down the road. He recalled the tightness in his chest, the choke within his throat, the terrible, gut-twisting heaviness of grief at his brother's leaving. As if a part of him were gone, as if he had been torn in two, as if only half of him were left.

"We were twins," he told Anderson. "Identical twins. We were closer than most brothers. We lived in one another's pocket. We did everything together. Each of us felt the same about the other. It took a lot of courage for Phil to walk away like that."

"And a lot of courage and affection on your part," said Anderson, "to let him walk away. But he did come back again?"

"Not for a long time. Not until after both our parents were dead. Then he came walking down the road, just the way he'd left. But he didn't stay. Only for a day or two. He was anxious to be off. As if he were being driven."

Although that was not exactly right, he told himself. Nervous. Jumpy. Looking back across his shoulder. As if he were being followed. Looking back to make sure the Follower was not there.

"He came a few more times," he said. "Years apart. He never stayed too long. He was anxious to get back."

"How can you explain this idea that people have that you never had a brother?" asked Anderson. "How do you explain the silence of the records?"

"I have no explanation," Lambert said. "People get some strange ideas. A thoughtless rumor starts—perhaps no more than a question: 'About this brother of his? Does he really have a brother? Was there ever any brother?' And others pick it up and build it up and it goes on from there. Out in these hills there's not much to talk about. They grab at anything there is. It would be an intriguing thing to talk about—that old fool down in the valley who thinks he has a brother that he never had, bragging about this nonexistent brother out among the stars. Although it seems to me that I never really bragged. I never traded on him."

"And the records? Or the absence of the records?"

"I just don't know," said Lambert. "I didn't know about the records. I've never checked. There was never any reason to. You see, I know I have a brother."

"Do you think that you may be getting up to Madison?"

"I know I won't," said Lambert. "I seldom leave this place. I no longer have a car. I catch a ride with a neighbor when I can to go to the store and get the few things that I need. I'm satisfied right here. There's no need to go anywhere."

"You've lived here alone since your parents died?"

"That is right," said Lambert. "And I think this has gone far enough. I'm not sure I like you, Mr. Anderson. Or should that be Dr. Anderson? I suspect it should. I'm not going to the university to answer questions that you want me to or to submit to tests in this study of yours. I'm not sure what your interest is and I'm not even faintly interested. I have other, more important things to do."

Anderson rose from the chair. "I am sorry," he said. "I had not meant . . ."

"Don't apologize," said Lambert.

"I wish we could part on a happier note," said Anderson.

"Don't let it bother you," said Lambert. "Just forget about it. That's what I plan to do."

He continued sitting in the chair long after the visitor had left. A few cars went past, not many, for this was a lightly traveled road, one that really went nowhere, just an access for the few families that lived along the valley and back in the hills.

The gall of the man, he thought, the arrogance of him, to come storming in and asking all those questions. That study of his—perhaps a survey of the fantasies engaged in by an aged population. Although it need not be that; it might be any one of a number of other things.

There was, he cautioned himself, no reason to get upset by it. It was not important; bad manners never were important to anyone but those who practiced them.

He rocked gently back and forth, the rockers complaining on the stones, and gazed across the road and valley to the place along the opposite hill where the creek ran, its waters gurgling over stony shallows and swirling in deep pools. The creek held many memories. There, in long, hot summer days, he and Phil had fished for chubs, using crooked willow branches for rods because there was no money to buy regular fishing gear—not that they would have wanted it even if there had been. In the spring great shoals of suckers had come surging up the creek from the Wisconsin River to reach their spawning areas. He and Phil would go out and seine them, with a seine rigged from a gunny sack, its open end held open by a barrel hoop.

The creek held many memories for him and so did all the land, the towering hills, the little hidden valleys, the heavy hardwood forest that covered all except those few level areas that had been cleared for farming. He knew every path and byway of it. He knew what grew on and lived there and where it grew or lived. He knew of the secrets of the few surrounding square miles of countryside, but not all the secrets; no man was born who could know all the secrets.

He had, he told himself, the best of two worlds. Of two worlds, for he had not told Anderson, he had not told anyone, of that secret link that tied him to Phil. It was a link that never had seemed strange because it was something they had known from the time when they were small. Even apart, they had known what the other might be doing. It was no wondrous thing to them; it was something they had taken very much for granted. Years later, he had read in learned journals the studies that had been made of identical twins, with the academic speculation that in some strange manner they seemed to hold telepathic powers which operated only between the two of them—as if they were, in fact, one person in two different bodies.

That was the way of it, most certainly, with him and Phil, although whether it might be telepathy, he had never even wondered until he stumbled on the journals. It did not seem, he thought, rocking in the chair, much like telepathy, for telepathy, as he understood it, was the deliberate sending and receiving of mental messages; it had simply been a knowing, of where the other was and what he might be doing. It had been that way when they were youngsters and that way ever since. Not a continued knowing, not continued contact, if it was contact. Through the years, however, it happened fairly often. He had known through all the years since Phil had gone walking down the road the many planets that Phil had visited, the ships he'd traveled on—had seen it all with Phil's eyes, had understood it with Phil's brain, had known the names of the places Phil had seen and understood, as Phil had understood, what had happened in each place. It had not been a conversation; they had not talked with one another; there had been no need to talk. And although Phil had never told him, he was certain Phil had known what he was doing and where he was and what he might be seeing. Even on the few occasions that Phil had come to visit, they had not talked about it; it was no subject for discussion since both accepted it.

In the middle of the afternoon, a beat-up car pulled up before the gate, the motor coughing to a stuttering halt. Jake Hopkins, one of his neighbors up the creek, climbed out, carrying a small basket. He came up on the patio and, setting the basket down, sat down in the other chair.

"Katie sent along a loaf of bread and a blackberry pie," he said. "This is about the last of the blackberries. Poor crop this year. The summer was too dry."

"Didn't do much blackberrying myself this year," said Lambert. "Just out a time or two. The best ones are on that ridge over yonder, and I swear that hill gets steeper year by year."

"It gets steeper for all of us," said Hopkins. "You and I, we've been here a long time, Ed."

"Tell Katie thanks," said Lambert. "There ain't no one can make a better pie than she. Pies, I never bother with them, although I purely love them. I do some cooking, of course, but pies take too much time and fuss."

"Hear anything about this new critter in the hills?" asked Hopkins.

Lambert chuckled. "Another one of those wild talks, Jake. Every so often, a couple of times a year, someone starts a story. Remember that one about the swamp beast down at Millville? Papers over in Milwaukee got hold of it, and a sportsman down in Texas read about it and came up with a pack of dogs. He spent three days at Millville, floundering around in the swamps, lost one dog to a rattler, and, so I was told, you never saw a madder white man in your life. He felt that he had been took, and I suppose he was, for there was never any beast. We get bear and panther stories, and there hasn't been a bear or panther in these parts for more than forty years. Once, some years ago some damn fool started a story about a big snake. Big around as a nail keg and thirty feet long. Half the county was out hunting it."

"Yes, I know," said Hopkins. "There's nothing to most of the stories, but Caleb Jones told me one of his boys saw this thing, whatever it may be. Like an ape, or a bear that isn't quite a bear. All over furry, naked. A snowman, Caleb thinks."

"Well, at least," said Lambert, "that is something new. There hasn't been anyone, to my knowledge, claimed to see a snowman here. There have been a lot of reports, however, from the West Coast. It just took a little time to transfer a snowman here."

"One could have wandered east."

"I suppose so. If there are any of them out there, that is. I'm not too sure there are."

"Well, anyhow," said Hopkins, "I thought I'd let you know. You are kind of isolated here. No telephone or nothing. You never even run in electricity."

"I don't need either a telephone or electricity," said Lambert. "The only thing about electricity that would tempt me would be a refrigerator. And I don't need that. I got the springhouse over there. It's as good as any refrigerator. Keeps butter sweet for weeks. And a telephone. I don't need a telephone. I have no one to talk to."

"I'll say this," said Hopkins. "You get along all right. Even without a telephone or the electric. Better than most folks."

"I never wanted much," said Lambert. "That's the secret of it—I never wanted much."

"You working on another book?"

"Jake, I'm always working on another book. Writing down the things I see and hear and the way I feel about them. I'd do it even if no one was interested in them. I'd write it down even if there were no books."

"You read a lot," said Hopkins. "More than most of us."

"Yes, I guess I do," said Lambert. "Reading is a comfort."

And that was true, he thought. Books lined up on a shelf were a group of friends—not books, but men and women who talked with him across the span of continents and centuries of time. His books, he knew, would not live as some of the others had. They would not long outlast him, but at times he liked to think of the possibility that a hundred years from now someone might find one of his books, in a used bookstore, perhaps, and, picking it up, read a few paragraphs of his, maybe liking it well enough to buy it and take it home, where it would rest on the shelves a while, and might, in time, find itself back in a used bookstore again, waiting for someone else to pick it up and read.

It was strange, he thought, that he had written of things close to home, of those things that most passed by without even seeing, when he could have written of the wonders to be found light-years from earth—the strangenesses that could be found on other planets circling other suns. But of these he had not even thought to write, for they were secret, an inner part of him that was of himself alone, a confidence between himself and Phil that he could not have brought himself to violate.

"We need some rain," said Hopkins. "The pastures are going. The pastures on the Jones place are almost bare. You don't see the grass; you see the ground. Caleb has been feeding his cattle hay for the last two weeks, and if we don't get some rain, I'll be doing the same in another week or two. I've got one patch of corn I'll get some nubbins worth the picking, but the rest of it is only good for fodder. It does beat hell. A man can work his tail off some years and come to nothing in the end."

They talked for another hour or so—the comfortable, easy talk of countrymen who were deeply concerned with the little things that loomed so large for them. Then Hopkins said good-by and, kicking his ramshackle car into reluctant life, drove off down the road.

When the sun was just above the western hills, Lambert went inside and put on a pot of coffee to go with a couple of slices of Katie's bread and a big slice of Katie's pie. Sitting at the table in the kitchen—a table on which he'd eaten so long as memory served—he listened to the ticking of the ancient family clock. The clock, he realized as he listened to it, was symbolic of the house. When the clock talked to him, the house talked to him as well—the house using the clock as a means of communicating with him. Perhaps not talking to him, really, but keeping close in touch, reminding him that it still was there, that they were together, that they did not stand alone. It had been so through the years; it was more so than ever now, a closer relationship, perhaps arising from the greater need on both their parts.

Although stoutly built by his maternal great-grandfather the house stood in a state of disrepair. There were boards that creaked and buckled when he stepped on them, shingles that leaked in the rainy season. Water streaks ran along the walls, and in the back part of the house, protected by the hill that rose abruptly behind it, where the sun's rays seldom reached, there was the smell of damp and mold.

But the house would last him out, he thought, and that was all that mattered. Once he was no longer here, there'd be no one for it to shelter. It would outlast both him and Phil, but perhaps there would be no need for it to outlast Phil. Out among the stars, Phil had no need of the house. Although, he told himself, Phil would be coming home soon. For he was old and so, he supposed, was Phil. They had, between the two of them, not too many years to wait.

Strange, he thought, that they, who were so much alike, should have lived such different lives—Phil, the wanderer, and he, the stay-at-home, and each of them, despite the differences in their lives, finding so much satisfaction in them.

His meal finished, he went out on the patio again. Behind him, back of the house, the wind soughed through the row of mighty evergreens, those alien trees planted so many years ago by that old great-grandfather. What a cross-grained conceit, he thought—to plant pines at the base of a hill that was heavy with an ancient growth of oaks and maples, as if to set off the house from the land on which it was erected.

The last of the fireflies were glimmering in the lilac bushes that flanked the gate, and the first of the whippoorwills were crying mournfully up the hollows. Small, wispy clouds partially obscured the skies, but a few stars could be seen. The moon would not rise for another hour or two.

To the north a brilliant star flared out, but watching it, he knew it was not a star. It was a spaceship coming in to land at the port across the river. The flare died out, then flickered on again, and this time did not die out but kept on flaring until the dark line of the horizon cut it off. A moment later, the muted rumble of the landing came to him, and in time it too died out, and he was left alone with the whippoorwills and fireflies.

Someday, on one of those ships, he told himself, Phil would be coming home. He would come striding down the road as he always had before, unannounced but certain of the welcome that would be waiting for him. Coming with the fresh scent of space upon him, crammed with wondrous tales, carrying in his pocket some alien trinket as a gift that, when he was gone, would be placed on the shelf of the old breakfront in the living room, to stand there with the other gifts he had brought on other visits.

There had been a time when he had wished it had been he rather than Phil who had left. God knows, he had ached to go. But once one had gone, there had been no question that the other must stay on. One thing he was proud of—he had never hated Phil for going. They had been too close for hate. There could never be hate between them.

There was something messing around behind him in the pines. For some time now, he had been hearing the rustling but paying no attention to it. It was a coon, most likely, on its way to raid the cornfield that ran along the creek just east of his land. The little animal would find poor pickings there, although there should be enough to satisfy a coon. There seemed to be more rustling than a coon would make. Perhaps it was a family of coons, a mother and her cubs.

Finally, the moon came up, a splendor swimming over the great dark hill behind the house. It was a waning moon that, nevertheless, lightened up the dark. He sat for a while longer and began to feel the chill that every night, even in the summer, came creeping from the creek and flowing up the hollows.

He rubbed an aching knee, then got up slowly and went into the house. He had left a lamp burning on the kitchen table, and now he picked it up, carrying it into the living room and placing it on the table beside an easy chair. He'd read for an hour or so, he told himself, then be off to bed.

As he picked a book off the shelf behind the chair, a knock came at the kitchen door. He hesitated for a moment and the knock came again. Laying down the book, he started for the kitchen, but before he got there, the door opened, and a man came into the kitchen. Lambert stopped and stared at the indistinct blur of the man who'd come into the house. Only a little light came from the lamp in the living room, and he could not be sure.

"Phil?" he asked, uncertain, afraid that he was wrong.

The man stepped forward a pace or two. "Yes, Ed," he said. "You did not recognize me. After all the years, you don't recognize me."

"It was so dark," said Lambert, "that I could not be sure."

He strode forward with his hand held out, and Phil's hand was there to grasp it. But when their hands met in the handshake, there was nothing there. Lambert's hand closed upon itself.

He stood stricken, unable to move, tried to speak and couldn't, the words bubbling and dying and refusing to come out.

"Easy, Ed," said Phil. "Take it easy now. That's the way it's always been. Think back. That has to be the way it's always been. I am a shadow only. A shadow of yourself."

But that could not be right, Lambert told himself. The man who stood there in the kitchen was a solid man, a man of flesh and bone, not a thing of shadow.

"A ghost," he managed to say. "You can't be a ghost."

"Not a ghost," said Phil. "An extension of yourself. Surely you had known."

"No," said Lambert. "I did not know. You are my brother, Phil."

"Let's go into the living room," said Phil. "Let's sit down and talk. Let's be reasonable about this. I rather dreaded coming, for I knew you had this thing about a brother. You know as well as I do you never had a brother. You are an only child."

"But when you were here before . . ."

"Ed, I've not been here before. If you are only honest with yourself, you'll know I've never been. I couldn't come back, you see, for then you would have known. And up until now, maybe not even now, there was no need for you to know. Maybe I made a mistake in coming back at all."

"But you talk," protested Lambert, "in such a manner as to refute what you are telling me. You speak of yourself as an actual person."

"And I am, of course," said Phil. "You made me such a person. You had to make me a separate person or you couldn't have believed in me. I've been to all the places you have known I've been, done all the things that you know I've done. Not in detail, maybe, but you know the broad outlines of it. Not at first, but later on, within a short space of time, I became a separate person. I was, in many ways, quite independent of you. Now let's go in and sit down and be comfortable. Let us have this out. Let me make you understand, although in all honesty, you should understand, yourself."

Lambert turned and stumbled back into the living room and let himself down, fumblingly, into the chair beside the lamp. Phil remained standing, and Lambert, staring at him, saw that Phil was his second self, a man similar to himself, almost identical to himself—the same white hair, the same bushy eyebrows, the same crinkles at the corners of his eyes, the same planes to his face.

He fought for calmness and objectivity. "A cup of coffee, Phil?" he asked. "The pot's still on the stove, still warm."

Phil laughed. "I cannot drink," he said, "or eat. Or a lot of other things. I don't even need to breathe. It's been a trial sometimes, although there have been advantages. They have a name out in the stars for me. A legend. Most people don't believe in me. There are too many legends out there. Some people do believe in me. There are people who'll believe in anything at all."

"Phil," said Lambert, "that day in the barn. When you told me you were leaving, I did stand in the door and watch you walk away."

"Of course you did," said Phil. "You watched me walk away, but you knew then what it was you watched. It was only later that you made me into a brother—a twin brother, was it not?"

"There was a man here from the university," said Lambert. "A professor of psychology. He was curious. He had some sort of study going. He'd hunted up the records. He said I never had a brother. I told him he was wrong."

"You believed what you said," Phil told him. "You knew you had a brother. It was a defensive mechanism. You couldn't live with yourself if you had thought otherwise. You couldn't admit the kind of thing you are."

"Phil, tell me. What kind of thing am I?"

"A breakthrough," said Phil. "An evolutionary breakthrough. I've had a lot of time to think about it, and I am sure I'm right. There was no compulsion on my part to hide and obscure the facts, for I was the end result. I hadn't done a thing; you were the one who did it. I had no guilt about it. And I suppose you must have. Otherwise, why all this smokescreen about dear brother Phil?"

"An evolutionary breakthrough, you say. Something like an amphibian becoming a dinosaur?"

"Not that drastic," said Phil. "Surely you have heard of people who had several personalities, changing back and forth without warning from one personality to another. But always in the same body. You read the literature on identical twins—one personality in two different bodies. There are stories about people who could mentally travel to distant places, able to report, quite accurately, what they had seen."

"But this is different, Phil."

"You still call me Phil."

"Dammit, you are Phil."

"Well, then, if you insist. And I am glad you do insist. I'd like to go on being Phil. Different, you say. Of course, it's different. A natural evolutionary progression beyond the other abilities I mentioned. The ability to split your personality and send it out on its own, to make another person that is a shadow of yourself. Not mind alone, something more than mind. Not quite another person, but almost another person. It is an ability that made you different, that set you off from the rest of the human race. You couldn't face that. No one could. You couldn't admit, not even to yourself, that you were a freak."

"You've thought a lot about this."

"Certainly I have. Someone had to. You couldn't, so it was up to me."

"But I don't remember any of this ability. I still can see you walking off. I have never felt a freak."

"Certainly not. You built yourself a cover so fast and so secure you even fooled yourself. A man's ability for self-deception is beyond belief."

Something was scratching at the kitchen door, as a dog might scratch to be let in.

"That's the Follower," said Phil. "Go and let him in."

"But a Follower . . ."

"That's all right," said Phil. "I'll take care of him. The bastard has been following me for years."

"If it is all right . . ."

"Sure, it is all right. There's something that he wants, but we can't give it to him."

Lambert went across the kitchen and opened the door. The Follower came in. Never looking at Lambert, he brushed past him into the living room and skidded to a halt in front of Phil.

"Finally," shouted the Follower, "I have run you to your den. Now you cannot elude me. The indignities that you have heaped upon me—the learning of your atrocious language so I could converse with you, the always keeping close behind you, but never catching up, the hilarity of my acquaintances who viewed my obsession with you as an utter madness. But always you fled before me, afraid of me when there was no need of fear. Talk with you, that is all I wanted."

"I was not afraid of you," said Phil. "Why should I have been? You couldn't lay a mitt upon me."

"Clinging to the outside of a ship when the way was barred inside to get away from me! Riding in the cold and emptiness of space to get away from me. Surviving the cold and space—what kind of creature are you?"

"I only did that once," said Phil, "and not to get away from you. I wanted to see what it would be like. I wanted to touch interstellar space, to find out what it was. But I never did find out. And I don't mind telling you that once one got over the wonder and the terror of it, there was very little there. Before the ship touched down, I damn near died of boredom."

The Follower was a brute, but something about him said he was more than simple brute. In appearance, he was a cross between a bear and an ape, but there was something manlike in him, too. He was a hairy creature, and the clothing that he wore was harness rather than clothing, and the stink of him was enough to make one gag.

"I followed you for years," he bellowed, "to ask you a simple question, prepared well to pay you if you give me a useful answer. But you always slip my grasp. If nothing else, you pale and disappear. Why did you do that? Why not wait for me: Why not speak to me? You force me to subterfuge, you force me to set up ambush. In very sneaky and expensive manner, which I deplore, I learned position of your planet and location where you home, so I could come and wait for you to trap you in your den, thinking that even such as you surely must come home again. I prowl the deep woodlands while I wait, and I frighten inhabitants of here, without wishing to, except they blunder on me, and I watch your den and I wait for you, seeing this other of you and thinking he was you, but realizing, upon due observation, he was not. So now . . ."

"Now just a minute," said Phil. "Hold up. There is no reason to explain."

"But explain you must, for to apprehend you, I am forced to very scurvy trick in which I hold great shame. No open and above board. No honesty. Although one thing I have deduced from my observations. You are no more, I am convinced, than an extension of this other."

"And now," said Phil, "you want to know how it was done. This is the question that you wish to ask."

"I thank you," said the Follower, "for your keen perception, for not forcing me to ask."

"But first," said Phil, "I have a question for you. If we could tell you how it might be done, if we were able to tell you and if you could turn this information to your use, what kind of use would you make of it?"

"Not myself," said the Follower. "Not for myself alone, but for my people, for my race. You see, I never laughed at you; I did not jest about you as so many others did. I did not term you ghost or spook. I knew more to it than that. I saw ability that if rightly used. . . ."

"Now you're getting around to it," said Phil. "Now tell us the use."

"My race," said the Follower, "is concerned with many different art forms, working with crude tools and varying skills and in stubborn materials that often take unkindly to the shaping. But I tell myself that if each of us could project ourselves and use our second selves as medium for the art, we could shape as we could wish, creating art forms that are highly plastic, that can be worked over and over again until they attain perfection. And, once perfected, would be immune against time and pilferage. . . ."

"With never a thought," said Phil, "as to its use in other ways. In war, in thievery . . ."

The Follower said, sanctimoniously, "You cast unworthy aspersions upon my noble race."

"I am sorry if I do," said Phil. "Perhaps it was uncouth of me. And now, as to your question, we simply cannot tell you. Or I don't think that we can tell you. How about it, Ed?"

Lambert shook his head. "If what both of you say is true, if Phil really is an extension of myself, then I must tell you I do not have the least idea of how it might be done. If I did it, I just did it, that was all. No particular way of doing it. No ritual to perform. No technique I'm aware of."

"Ridiculous that is," cried the Follower. "Surely you can give me hint or clue."

"All right, then," said Phil, "I'll tell you how to do it. Take a species and give them two million years in which they can evolve, and you might come to it. Might, I say. You can't be certain of it. It would have to be the right species, and it must experience the right kind of social and psychological pressure, and it must have the right kind of brain to respond to these kinds of pressures. And if all of this should happen, then one day one member of the species may be able to do what Ed has done. But that one of them is able to do it does not mean that others will. It may be no more than a wild talent, and it may never occur again. So far as we know, it's not happened before. If it has, it's been hidden, as Ed has hidden his ability, even from himself, forced to hide it from himself because of the human conditioning that would make such an ability unacceptable."

"But all these years," said the Follower, "all these years, he has kept you as you are. That seems . . ."

"No," said Phil. "Not that at all. No conscious effort on his part. Once he created me, I was self-sustaining."

"I sense," the Follower said, sadly, "that you tell me true. That you hold nothing back."

"You sense it, hell," said Phil. "You read our minds, that is what you did. Why, instead of chasing me across the galaxy, didn't you read my mind long ago and have done with it?"

"You would not stand still," said the Follower, accusingly. "You would not talk with me. You never bring this matter to the forefront of your mind so I have a chance to read it."

"I'm sorry," said Phil, "that it turned out this way for you. But until now, you must realize, I could not talk with you. You make the game too good. There was too much zest in it."

The Follower said, stiffly, "You look upon me and you think me brute. In your eyes I am. You see no man of honor, no creature of ethics. You know nothing of us and you care even less. Arrogant you are. But, please believe me, in all that's happened, I act with honor according to my light."

"You must be weary and hungry," said Lambert. "Can you eat our food? I could cook up some ham and eggs, and the coffee is still hot. There is a bed for you. It would be an honor to have you as our guest."

"I thank you for your confidence, for your acceptance of me," said the Follower. "It warms—how do you say it—the cockle of the heart. But the mission's done and I must be going now. I have wasted too much time. If you, perhaps, could offer me conveyance to the spaceport."

"That's something I can't do," said Lambert. "You see, I have no car. When I need a ride, I bum one from a neighbor, otherwise I walk."

"If you can walk, so can I," said the Follower. "The spaceport is not far. In a day or two, I'll find a ship that is going out."

"I wish you'd stay the night," said Lambert. "Walking in the dark . . ."

"Dark is best for me," said the Follower. "Less likely to be seen. I gather that few people from other stars wander about this countryside. I have no wish to frighten your good neighbors."

He turned briskly and went into the kitchen, heading for the door, not waiting for Lambert to open it for him.

"Good-by, pal," Phil called after him.

The Follower did not answer. He slammed the door behind him.

When Lambert came back into the living room, Phil was standing in front of the fireplace, his elbow on the mantel.

"You know, of course," he said, "that we have a problem."

"Not that I can see," said Lambert. "You will stay, won't you. You will not leave again. We are both getting old."

"If that is what you want. I could disappear, snuff myself out. As if I'd never been. That might be for the best, more comfortable for you. It could be disturbing to have me about. I do not eat or sleep. I can attain a satisfying solidity but only with an effort and only momentarily. I command enough energy to do certain tasks, but not over the long haul."

"I have had a brother for a long, long time," said Lambert. "That's the way I want it. After all this time, I would not want to lose you."

He glanced at the breakfront and saw that the trinkets Phil had brought on his other trips still stood solidly in place.

Thinking back, he could remember, as if it were only yesterday, watching from the barn door as Phil went trudging down the road through the grey veil of the drizzle.

"Why don't you sit down and tell me," he said, "about the incident out in the Coonskin system. I knew about it at the time, of course, but I never caught quite all of it."

SENIOR CITIZEN

Originally published in the October 1975 issue of the Magazine of Fantasy & Science Fiction, *this story was one of several Simak stories that led some critics to suggest that the author seemed to be obsessed with old age. Even if true, so what? Cliff was in his early seventies when he wrote this story, and retirement from the job he had loved all his life was looming on the horizon.*

I do wonder, at times, why he chose the name Anson Lee for the old man in this story—it was a name he used several times in other stories, but I know of nothing in Cliff's history to explain why it seemed to stick in his mind—but I don't think about it too often, because this story, with its images of the way that dignity can die before the body does, makes me very uncomfortable.

—*dww*

The music wakened him, and a soft, sweet, feminine voice said, "Good morning, Mr. Lee. If you should not, for the moment, remember, you are Anson Lee. You are a lucky senior citizen in your retirement home in space."

He sat up blindly and swung his feet out of bed. He sat on the edge of the bed and scrubbed his eyes with closed fists, ran a hand through his thinning hair. It would be nice if he could fall back on the bed again and get another hour of sleep.

"We have so much to do today, Mr. Lee," said the sweet voice, but it seemed to him that behind the sweetness he could detect the hidden steel of authority. Women, he thought—bitches, all of them.

"There is a nice change of clothes for you," the voice said. "Hurry up and dress. Then we'll have breakfast."

I'll have breakfast, he thought. Not we, but I. You won't have any breakfast, for you aren't even here.

He reached out his hand for the clothes. "I don't like new clothes," he complained. "I like old clothes. I like to break them in and get them comfortable. Why do I have to have new clothes every day? I know what you do with my old clothes. You throw them in the converter every night when I take them off to go to bed."

"But these are nice," said the voice. "They are nice and clean. The pants are blue, the shirt is green. You like blue and green."

"I like old clothes," he said.

"You cannot have old clothes," the voice said. "New clothing is so much better for you. And the clothing fits. It always fits. We have your measurements."

He put on the shirt. He stood up and put on the pants. There was no use in arguing, he knew. They always had their way. He never won. Just once he'd like to win. Just once he'd like to have old clothes. They were comfortable and soft, once you wore them for a while. He remembered his old fishing clothes. He'd had them for years and had treasured them. But now he had no fishing clothes. There was no place to fish.

"Now," said the voice, "we'll have breakfast. Scrambled eggs and toast. You like scrambled eggs."

"I won't eat any breakfast," he said. "I don't want any breakfast. I might be eating Nancy."

"What foolishness is this?" asked the voice, not so sweet, a little sharper now. "You remember Nancy's gone. She went away and left us."

"Nancy died," he said. "You put her in the converter. You put everything into the converter. We have only so much matter, and we must use it over and over again. I know the theory. I was a chemist. I know exactly how it works. Matter to energy, energy to matter. We are a closed ecology and . . ."

"But Nancy. It was so long ago."

"It doesn't matter how long ago it was. There's Nancy in the clothes. There'll be Nancy in the eggs."

"I think we'd better," said the voice, which was no longer sweet.

A hand reached out behind him and grasped him around the waist. "Let's have a look at you, old-timer," said a voice in his ear, this time an authoritative voice, a man's voice.

He felt himself being urged into a cubicle. He was grasped by things other than hands. Tentacles wormed their way inside his clothes, fastened on his flesh. He could not move. A cold liquid sprayed forcefully against his arm. Then everything let loose of him.

"You're fine," said the hard, firm medic voice. "You are in finer shape than you were yesterday."

Yes, fine, he told himself. So fine that when he woke they thought it necessary to tell him who he was. So fine they had to shoot some dope into his arm to keep him from fantasizing.

"Come now," said the voice, grown sweet again. "Come and eat your breakfast."

He hesitated for a moment, trying to force himself to think. It seemed there was some reason he should not be eating breakfast, but he had forgotten. If there had ever been a reason.

"Come along, now," said the voice, wheedling.

He shuffled toward the table and sat down, staring at the cup of coffee, the plate of scrambled eggs.

"Now pick up your fork and eat," said the urgent voice. "It's the breakfast you like best. You have always told me you like scrambled eggs the best. Hurry up and eat. There's a lot to do today."

She was bullying him again, he told himself, patronizing him, treating him in the same manner she would use with a sulking child. But there was nothing he could do about it. He might resent it, but he could not act upon the resentment. He could never reach her. She was not really there. There was no one really there. They tried to make him think there was, but he knew he was alone. Even if he could not act upon the resentment, he tried to cherish it, but it slipped away. It was something, he knew, that was done in the diagnostic cubicle. Maybe it was the stuff they shot into his arm. Stuff to make him feel good, to block off resentment, to wipe the self-nagging from his mind.

Although it didn't really matter. Nothing really mattered. He drank his urine, he ate his feces, and it didn't really matter. And there was something else that he ate as well, but he could not remember. He had known once, but he had forgotten.

He finished the plate of eggs and drank the cup of coffee, and the voice said, "What will we do now? What would you like to do today. I can read to you or we can play some music or we can play cards or chess. Would you like to paint? You used to like to paint. You were very good at it."

"No, God damn it," he said. "I would not like to paint."

"Tell me why you don't want to paint. You must have a reason. When you do so well, you must have a reason."

Bullying him again, he thought, using schoolboy psychology upon him—and, worst of all, lying to him. For he could not paint. He did not do well at it. The daubs he turned out were not painting. But there was no use to go into that, he told himself; she would keep on insisting he did well at painting, operating on the conviction that the self-concept of the old must at all times be supported and improved upon.

"There's nothing to paint," he said.

"There are many things to paint."

"There are no trees, no flowers, no sky or clouds, no people. There once were trees and flowers, but now I'm not sure there are. I can't remember any more what a tree or flower looks like. A man can carry memory only for so long. There once were flowers and trees on Earth."

And there had been, as well, a house upon the Earth. But the house was dim in his memory as well. What did the house look like, he wondered. How does another human being look? What is a river like?

"You do not need to see things to paint them," she said. "You can paint out of your mind."

Perhaps he could, he thought. But how do you paint loneliness? How does one depict dejection and abandonment?

When he made no answer, she asked, "There is nothing you want to do?"

He made no answer to her. Why bother to answer a simulated voice produced by a data core that was crammed with social welfare concepts and with little else? Why, he wondered, did they go to so much trouble to take good care of him? Although, come to think of it, perhaps it was not so much trouble as if might seem. The satellite would be out here, anyhow, gathering and monitoring data, perhaps performing other tasks of which he was not aware. And if such satellites could also serve to get the useless aged off the Earth, the care would cost them nothing.

He remembered how he and Nancy had been persuaded to make the satellite their home by a clever young man with a sincere and authoritative voice, carefully reciting all the benefits of it. Perhaps, even so, they would not have gone if their little house had not been condemned to make way for a transportation project. After that it had not really mattered where they'd gone or where they might be sent, for their home was gone. You'll be out of this world's rat race, the sincere young man had said. You'll have peace and comfort in your final years; everything will be done for you. All your friends are gone, and the changes that you see must be distressful to you; there's no reason you should stay. Your son? Why, he can come and see you as often, perhaps oftener, than you see him now—but, of course, he'd never come.

Up there, you'll have everything you need. You'll never have to cook or clean; it'll be done for you. No more bother going to a doctor; there'll be a diagnostic cubicle just a step away. There'll be music and reading tapes and all your favorite programs, just like here on Earth.

Once a man gets old, he thought, he gets somewhat confused, and he's not sure of his rights and, even if he is, doesn't have the courage to stand up for them, not the courage to face down authority, no matter how much he may despise authority. His strength is gone and the sharpness of his mind, and he is tired of fighting for his heritage.

Now, he thought, there was nothing left but the sweet authority (more hateful, perhaps, because it was so sweet) and the scarcely concealed contempt for the old, although the sweetness tried to hide it.

"Well then," said the social-worker voice, "since you do not care to do anything, I'll leave you sitting here, by the port, where you can look out."

"There is no sense of looking out," he said. "There's nothing one can see."

"But there is," she said. "There are all the pretty stars."

Sitting by the port, he watched the pretty stars.

THE GUNSMOKE DRUMMER SELLS A WAR

If the title of this story does not seem like a Clifford Simak creation, that's probably because the title was created by someone at Ace-High Western Stories, to whom Cliff sent the story, and who published it in their January 1946 issue. And the magazine's editor (whose name does not appear on the masthead) apparently liked it well enough to make it the lead story in the issue, giving it top billing on the cover and the first position among the stories inside.

In keeping with his desire to feature characters other than cowboys and Indians in his Westerns, Cliff created his protagonist as a drummer—that is, a peddler, a person who drove a wagon from town to town, carrying goods to sell and performing the occasional service, such as sharpening scissors. But for there to be a story at all, Johnny Harrison had to ride into a bad situation; and he drove his wagon into an effort to take control of the county.

—dww

Chapter One
A Deadly Message

There was no time to draw a gun.

The horseman with the blue shirt and the blue bandana tied across his face simply rode out of the brush that screened the trail and was there, sitting the sorrel, a six-gun in his hand.

Johnny Harrison pulled the team to a halt and sat motionless on the seat of the peddler rig, staring at the man.

The bushes rustled and another man rode out, a man with a red shirt and a blue handkerchief, mounted on a bay horse with a blaze slashed across its face from nose to ears. And then another rustle and another man, big and beefy in a black coat, with red whiskers sticking out beneath the mask.

"Everybody here?" asked Harrison.

The gun tilted in the first man's hand, belched sudden smoke and thunder. Harrison felt the hat twitch from his head, go rolling in the dust. He fought the startled team to quietness with firm hands on the reins.

"That goes to show you," the gunman told him, "that we aren't fooling. So you better listen close."

"That hat was plumb new, mister," said Harrison. "It will cost you just ten bucks."

"He's got a nice horse tied on behind the wagon," said the man with the black coat and red whiskers. "We might just as well take it along when we up and leave."

The first man snarled behind the mask. "Shut up," he snapped. "And leave the horse alone." Then he said to Harrison: "We've got a little message we'd like you to deliver."

"Speak your piece," Harrison said, curtly, "and fork over that ten bucks."

He was feeling better now, for he knew they wouldn't kill him. Men who want one to deliver a message don't shoot the messenger.

"There's a hombre in jail over at Sundown," said the man, "that ain't got no call to be there. You go and see the marshal and tell him this: Tell him that if he don't turn Jim Westman loose we'll be over and take care of it ourselves."

"But . . ." said Harrison.

"He'll understand," the man assured him. "You won't have to draw no pictures."

"All right, I'll tell him first thing I get to town," Harrison promised. "And now that we got that off our chest, how about some business? Need any pots or pans? Got some . . ."

The horseman in the black coat spurred forward, big and burly on his shaggy mount, face red with sudden anger.

"You go getting gay," he shouted, "and we'll shoot your pans so full of holes you can put them up for sieves."

"Shut up!" yelled the first man, angrily.

"No stinking peddler can go getting gay with . . ."

The man's words broke off and he coughed and swayed jerkily in his saddle. From the barren hilltop that rose like a bald man's head above the brushy hillside came the snarling chuckle of a high power rifle.

The first man spun his horse around with a vicious hand, raised his six-gun in a flashing arc. From the ridge the rifle coughed and a bumbling thing howled above the men grouped on the trail and crashed into the brush.

On his feet, Harrison fought the rearing team with one hand, clawed for one of his six-guns with the other. A .45 crashed beside the wagon and out of the corner of his eye, Harrison saw the bullet raise a trail of dust clouds as it ground-skipped across the ridge-top.

The rifle spat like an angry cat and the horse of the wounded man bolted, the black-coated rider doubled up in his saddle as if a taloned fist were tearing at his vitals. He bounced like a wobbly sack of oats as the horse tore into the brush and wallowed down the hillside.

The man in the blue shirt followed. The man in the red shirt was already gone. When Harrison cleared his gun the trail was empty. Quieting the maddened team, he stood and listened to the crashing of the underbrush on the hillside far below.

Turning to the ridge above him, he saw two riders angling down toward him. One was tall and skinny as a scarecrow and rode without a hat. The other was broad and solid in the saddle and wore a hat that made up in bulk for the one the other didn't wear.

"Ma!" Harrison shouted. "Ma Elden!"

Ma Elden shouted back. "You all right, Johnny?"

"They got my hat," yelled Harrison.

He got down from the rig and waited for them, hunting up his hat, trying to brush off the dirt with an awkward sleeve, staring ruefully at the ragged hole angling through the crown.

"Ten bucks," he told himself. "Ten whole cartwheels."

The horses reached the trail and Ma Elden eased herself out of the saddle, waddled heavily forward, hunting in the pocket of her shirt for makings.

"What did they want?" she asked.

"Wanted me to tell Marshal Haynes to turn somebody loose."

Ma nodded. "Jim Westman. No account rascal. Shot the town up some the other night. Plugged Jack Collins dead center."

"Kill him?"

"Bet your boots," said Ma. "Collins wasn't much good himself and probably wanted killing, but Sundown kind of likes to dish out its own justice. Don't appreciate foreigners coming in and doing it for them."

She poured tobacco into a paper, coaxed it into shape.

Harrison spoke to the skinny man still sitting his horse.

"Howdy, Hatless."

Hatless Joe chuckled softly, tawny mustaches waggling. "Kind of tickled up that pudgy feller some, didn't I?"

"If he lives," said Harrison, "it will be a miracle."

Ma licked the quirly deftly. "Horse thieves," she said. "Horse thieves, sure as I was born. County's plumb infested with them."

Harrison went back to the man in jail. "How come," he asked, "if this Westman killed a man he isn't over in the county jail at Rattlesnake?"

Ma snorted. "Cause they'd turn him loose, that's why. Get the judge all likkered up and load the jury with his friends. That is, if the sheriff didn't sort of forget and let him go before he ever got to trial. Westman worked for Dunham at the Bar X for a while, then drifted over to Rattlesnake and since then's been living without visible means of support, if you don't look too close."

"The way it is," said Hatless, "we figure on giving him a fair trial, then take him out and hang him."

Ma snapped a match across her thumbnail, lit the quirly.

"Westman one of the horse thieves you spoke about?" asked Harrison.

"Could be," Ma told him. "Don't rightly know, of course. He's got all the earmarks, though. Gang's got its hideout somewhere in the badlands up near Rattlesnake. Been cleaning out the county."

"Newest thing in stealing," explained Hatless. "Lifting cows is downright old fashioned now. Horses move faster and bring better prices."

Harrison nodded gravely. "Been hearing some about it. Most everyone has lost some horses, seems. But folks are so stirred up with this county splitting business that you don't hear much of any talk but that."

"It's about time we got shut of that courthouse bunch up at Rattlesnake," Ma said, curtly. "Just a bunch of cutthroats. Me, I been working real hard for setting up a new county, so's we can get some decent government. Trouble is, folks seem to be afraid of

Dunham. Him and the Bar X outfit is plumb set against this two county business. Says we've got along all right so far, so what's the sense of changing."

Hatless guffawed. "Getting along all right the way Dunham wants it. Him with the biggest ranch in the whole dang country and bringing in a batch of men that he don't need around each election time just so they can vote."

Ma moved toward the rear of the wagon. "Got a new horse, I see."

"Picked him up the other day," Harrison told her. "Come sort of high, but once I laid eyes on him . . ."

"Yeah, I know," said Ma. She eyed him closely. "When you going to quit this peddling and get a business of your own?"

"Pretty soon," Harrison told her. "Figured maybe I'd do it right away and then . . ."

"And then you saw this horse."

Harrison grinned. "I call him Satan. Good name for him, don't you think? Black as night. Best horse I ever saw."

"The Smith general store at Sundown is up for sale, I hear," said Ma. "Cheap, too. Jake is figuring on moving farther west. Got an itchy foot."

"Haven't got the money, now. Another year or so."

"Might loan you some," said Ma.

Hatless chuckled. "She'd do most anything . . ."

Ma raged at him. "You keep your trap shut, you old buzzard. Ain't I got trouble enough without you butting into everything I say?"

Harrison put the damaged hat on his head, reached for the reins.

"Thanks for happening along," he said.

"Was hunting some cows when we heard the shot," said Hatless. "Figured we'd better see what was going on."

"You're coming out to the ranch for Sunday dinner, ain't you?" asked Ma.

"Sure," said Harrison. "Always do when I'm around."

"Carolyn will be home," Ma told him. "Coming home tonight."

"All the way from St. Louis," said Hatless. "She's been away to school. Mighty fancy . . ."

"He knows that as well as you do," Ma snapped.

She said to Harrison: "Sing Lee will have some of that chicken fixed the way you like it. That is, if he's sober."

"He's taken to making his own, now," said Hatless. "Beats forty rod all hollow. Got to tie it down before you try to drink it."

Harrison climbed aboard the wagon.

"See you Sunday," he said.

He clucked to the team and the wagon rolled, canvas flapping in the wind, faint rattle of pans coming from the rear, the one dry wheel screaming in protest.

Two miles from Sundown he overtook the man walking along the trail and leading a horse.

Harrison pulled up the rig.

"What's the matter, Doc?"

Doc Falconer grinned lop-sidedly. "You don't know how glad I am to see you."

He climbed to the seat beside Harrison, set his medicine kit on the floor, holding onto the reins of the horse.

"You and the horse have an argument?" asked Harrison.

"Horse went lame," explained Doc. "And I didn't have the heart to ride him. Take it easy, will you. Don't want to make it harder on him than I have to."

"Somebody sick?"

Doc shook his head. "Been out to my gold mine, Johnny."

"You really got a gold mine, Doc?"

Doc Falconer's eyes squeezed together, making tiny wrinkles of dry humor at their corners.

"Nope, but folks think I have. Figure I got a lot more cash than I really have. Figure nobody could make that much cash just doctoring."

He squinted along the dusty trail. "Folks should know how little I have just from the way they pay me," he declared.

The dry clop-clop of the horses' hoofs sounded like faint, dull explosions in the dust. An insect sang stridently in the limp air of late afternoon. Fall flowers nodded beside the trail.

"When are you going to quit this roving life and settle down?" asked Doc.

"Someday," said Harrison casting his eyes down.

"That Carolyn is a darn fine girl," said Doc.

"She's coming home tonight," Harrison told him.

"Knew that," said Doc. "Figured you'd be along."

He hummed beneath his breath.

"Wonder if you'd do something for me, Johnny?"

"Sure would," said Harrison. "That is, if I can."

"Only one around here that could do it," Doc told him. "Only one that knows enough to keep his mouth shut. Wonder," said Doc, "if you'd keep a letter for me and forget you ever saw it."

"Sure," agreed Harrison.

"I may come and ask you for it," said Doc, "and again I might not. If I don't come back in five days or so you mail it."

"Sounds like you figure on something happening to you," said Harrison.

"Something may," Doc told him.

"You usually camp at the spring below town, don't you?" asked Doc.

Harrison nodded.

"I'll get off there and walk in the rest of the way," said Doc. "Thanks for the lift."

"About that letter . . ."

"I'll give it to you in the morning."

At the spring, Harrison stood for a long time beside the wagon, watching Doc and the horse continue their slow way up the trail to town.

Harrison shook his head. "Queer jasper," he told himself.

Folks in Sundown didn't like Doc Falconer . . . mostly because they didn't understand or appreciate the dry humor that made the wrinkles at the corners of his eyes.

And that gold mine yarn. To Doc himself it was just another joke, to many of Sundown's citizens it was actual truth . . . how Doc would go riding off and be gone for several days, then come back and pay up bills that had been accumulating in the stores for weeks.

Harrison shook his head again. It was no business of his . . . Doc's gold mines or Doc's letters.

Hurriedly he made camp, watering the horses and picketing them out, spending an extra moment with Satan, who whickered and nipped playfully at his shoulder.

"Good horse," said Harrison and gave him an extra pat, then hurried up the trail to town.

Marshal Albert Haynes was sprawled in a chair behind his desk, picking with a knife at a sliver in his finger.

"Howdy, Johnny," he said. "Somebody steal some pans?"

"Nope," said Harrison. "Got a message for you."

"Shoot," the marshal invited.

"Some gents stopped me out on the trail with guns. Told me to tell you that if you didn't turn Jim Westman loose they'd come in and tend to it themselves."

The marshal bounced up in his chair, stabbed the knife deep into the desk.

"Oh, they did, did they?"

He glared at Harrison. "You go back and tell them hombres to go plumb to hell. I ain't turning loose no murderer."

"I'm not telling them a thing," said Harrison. "They didn't ask me to. They told me what to tell you and you've said no and that's an end of it."

Haynes hunched forward. "I ain't so sure that's the end of it," he snarled. "Don't look good to me, you coming and telling me all this bosh about being held up and told a message for me. Don't look good . . ."

"Why, you —!" Even as he spoke, Harrison moved forward, one swift step that brought him towering above the desk. One powerful hand shot out and grabbed the marshal by the shoulder, hauled him to his feet. The other hand, doubled into a sledge hammer fist, moved even as the marshal, face twisted with fear and rage, clawed desperately for gun-butts.

The fist smacked with a hollow sound, a thudding sound that almost echoed in the room. Pain shot through Harrison's wrist with the force of the blow and he felt Haynes go limp within his grasp. He opened his hand and the man slid down behind the desk and out of sight.

Harrison turned on his heel and walked out onto the street.

Dusk had come and the first lamps of evening were being lit in the business houses that ran along the single street. Two horses stood slack-hipped at the hitching rail in front of the Silver Dollar. Harrison glanced at them as he went past, his eyes barely sliding along them, then stopping in surprise. A sorrel and a blaze-faced bay!

He halted and stared at the horses. Possible, but not likely. Not likely that two other men would ride a sorrel and blaze-faced bay.

He swung around quickly, but the saloon's porch was empty. From inside came the low buzz of voices and the clink of glasses on the bar.

For a moment, Harrison stood in indecision, then shrugged.

"No business of mine," he told himself. "I'm getting out before that gang starts hemstitching this town with their forty-fives."

Rapidly he strode along the sidewalk. The smell of ham and eggs from a restaurant hurried his gait—he recalled the campfire to be built, the supper to be cooked.

There was a light in Doc Falconer's office over the bank and inside his general store Jake Smith leaned elbows on the counter and talked with a rancher in to buy a month's supplies. Nice business, Harrison thought. And Ma said it could be gotten cheap. Only I bought a horse instead.

And socked the marshal, said his accusing mind. That's a hell of a way to start business in a town.

The horses nickered at him companionably as he came up to the wagon.

"Hello, fellers," he told them. "How's everything?"

They stamped at him, champing grass.

Only there was something wrong, something that it took a long minute for him to place. Then he knew.

There were only two horses, the team.

Satan was gone!

Heart thumping, he strode toward the place where he'd picketed the black.

Maybe he just pulled the pin and wandered off. Maybe . . .

But the pin was there, planted solidly in the ground, with the rope trailing from it. He picked up the rope and hauled it in, ran exploring fingers across the free end.

Cut! Slashed with a knife!

Satan had been stolen!

Chapter Two
A Gun Deal from the Bottom

The sorrel and the blaze-faced bay were gone from the hitching rack in front of the Silver Dollar, but there was some excitement going on up the street in front of the Eagle hotel.

For a moment Harrison hesitated, trying to decide whether to go inside the saloon and ask about the men or to hurry up the street in hopes that he might find some trace of them. Ben, the bartender, he remembered, was a surly hombre and probably wouldn't tell him a thing.

After all, he told himself, standing there in the spatter of light that came from the saloon's dirty window, he had no evidence the two men had taken Satan; no evidence, even, that the men were the ones who had held him up that afternoon. He had only seen the horses . . . and other men might ride horses that looked exactly the same.

Slowly, Harrison turned from the saloon, started up the street.

"Johnny!"

He swung around. Ma Elden had stepped out of the crowd in front of the hotel and was waving at him. And suddenly he remembered . . . remembered a thing that had been shaken from his mind. Carolyn was coming in tonight . . . coming on the stage.

He turned around, walked slowly back toward the crowd in front of the hotel. Ma hurried out to meet him. She was upset, he saw . . . upset and a little angry.

"Johnny, I've been expecting you. And the stage is late. What do you think has happened?"

"Had some trouble, maybe," said Harrison. "Broke a wheel or something."

But even as he said it, he knew the explanation was a weak one. Jack Carter, who drove the stage, prided himself on the time he made. And the road was good.

"I just know . . ."

"Listen," snapped Harrison.

From up the street came the faint sound of pounding hoofs and rattling wheels.

"It's him," someone shouted. "It's Carter and the stage!"

Ma beamed happily. "Maybe there ain't nothing wrong, after all. Maybe it's just . . ."

Her words cut off and one hand went to her mouth. The stage had swung around the corner and was coming down the street, not more than a block away, the horses at a dead run, the stage swaying drunkenly, the long reins dragging in the dust, coiling and looping like snakes behind the frightened horses.

A man was slumped across the high dashboard, where he had lodged when he had fallen from the seat. His head rolled limply in the faint lamplight spearing from the stores and his dangling arms swung like pendulums with the swaying of the coach.

Harrison sprang forward with a shout, hand shooting out to grasp the bridle of one of the leaders. The momentum of the animal swung him off his feet and one driving hoof scraped along his leg.

Someone had dived for the lines and gotten them and the horses were slowing to a stop. Harrison flung himself to one side, heard the rumbling wheels rush past him, then was running alongside as the stage came to a halt.

With a leap, he sprang on the front wheel, scrambled to the seat, reached down and lifted the slumped figure that hung against the dashboard. The man was a dead weight in his arms as he pulled him free and the lolling head flopped back to show the grinning teeth of pain, the eyes staring vacantly at death.

Slowly, Harrison laid him back and straightened up. His hand was wet and the sleeve of his shirt was stained with the sticky blood that had glued the dead man's shirt tight against his back.

Harrison looked down into the white faces that stared up at him.

"It's Carter," he told them. "Shot."

Ma's scream cut above the murmur of the crowd.

"Where is she? Where's Carolyn!"

Harrison vaulted from the seat of the stage and pushed toward the open door. A frightened man in a flowered waistcoat cowered against the coach.

Ma yelled at him, hysteria edging her voice. "Where is she? Where's the girl . . ."

"They took her," the man yelled back. "They must have. They . . ."

"Don't you know?" screamed Ma.

Hatless Joe loomed up beside Ma's squat, angry figure.

"Now, you calm down," he said, "and let the gent get a word in edgewise."

He said to the man: "Take your time and get your wits together and tell us all about it."

The man put up a trembling hand and pulled at his wilted collar.

"They held us up just this side of the river, where the road begins to climb the rise."

"They?" screamed Ma. "Who was it?"

"He don't know," said Hatless. "He's a stranger in these parts."

"They held us up," the man went on, "and they told us to get out. There was just me and the girl riding back here and the driver up front. They let the driver stay up on the seat but they made me and the girl get out. It was just getting dusk and I couldn't see them good, but there were several of them, four or five, I'd say, and they wore masks and carried guns.

"One of them started toward the girl and made a move as if he was going to put his arm around her and she hauled off and slapped him. Hit him in the face and he cussed. The driver got up from the seat and started to jump down. Like he was going to come down and tangle with the fellow that the girl had hit. But he hadn't no more than got to his feet than somebody shot him. One of the fellows still sitting on his horse was the one that done it."

Ma yelled at him. "And you stood by . . ."

Hatless yelled at her. "You shut up and let this gent go on with his story."

The man pulled at his collar with trembling fingers. "When the driver was shot, the horses bolted. Guess they started the minute they felt the lines go slack. I turned around and jumped for the open door of the stage and made it. . . ."

He lifted his hands and let them drop. "I guess that's all," he said. "That's everything that happened."

Ma moved toward him threateningly. "I'd ought to skin you alive," she shouted at him. "A great big hulk of a man and you ran..."

Hatless put out a hand and jerked her back. "You leave him alone," he told her. "He was scared and he didn't think."

"I guess I didn't," said the man.

"Kidnaped," yelled Ma. "That's what it is. My little daughter kidnaped."

A heavy shouldered man pushed through the gaping crowd. "Maybe it isn't that at all, Mrs. Elden," he said. "Maybe they didn't take her. She may be out there along the trail."

Harrison saw that the heavy shouldered man was Dunham, of the Bar X spread.

"Well, then, why don't you get out there and see," yelled Ma. "What are you standing around for?"

Dunham stiffened. "We will, Ma'am, just as soon as I can get the boys together."

"Standing around!" shrieked Ma. "Standing around! That's all you're doing, every one of you... just standing around!"

The crowd shrank back before her belligerency, started to scatter.

For the first time Ma saw Harrison in the crowd. She moved toward him, put out a hand and grasped him by the arm.

"You're going to do something, ain't you, Johnny? You're going to do something to get her back...."

Harrison saw the faint gleam of tears in the flint-hard eyes. Cold inside, he nodded. "Sure thing, Ma. Sure thing."

Ma yelled at him. "Well, get going, then. Never saw anything like a man. Standing around, standing around..."

Harrison shook his head. "Look, Ma, I just thought of something. I'm not jumping a horse and riding out there on a wild goose chase. The others can do that as well as I can. And it wouldn't do any good. They got all creation to hunt in and not an idea where to look."

"Unless she's just out there, sitting along the road, waiting for someone to come along," said Hatless, hopefully.

"Not much chance of that," Harrison declared. "Ma's probably right when she figured it was a kidnaping. And I got a plan."

"I hope it works," Ma said, acidly, her very tone implying that some other plans of Harrison's hadn't worked at all.

"It's got to work," Harrison said grimly. "If it don't, I'm buzzard meat."

He stepped forward and grasped her shoulders, pulled her close and kissed her on the cheek.

"Well, I never . . ." gasped Ma Elden. She put up a gnarled, weathered hand, rubbed at her leathery cheek.

Harrison swung around and strode away, heading around the stage, back toward the street.

Rounding the stage, he came face to face with Marshal Haynes. The two men stopped dead in their tracks, not more than six feet apart, staring at one another.

The marshal's hands moved swiftly, driving for his gun-butts. Harrison knew his own hands were moving, streaking for his belt, but it was almost as if his hands were those of another person, acting independently, almost as if by instinct.

Steel rasped against leather and his hands were snapping the two guns into position.

Guns halfway out, Haynes froze, staring at the muzzles that were tilted at him.

"I wouldn't do it, Marshal," Harrison said, softly. "I would just put them back."

Haynes gulped, Adam's apple bobbing in his bull throat. His hands loosened and the guns slid back.

"Slow," said Harrison, and smugness crept into his voice even when he tried to keep it out. "Too slow to be a lawman."

For a long minute the two men stood facing one another.

"Someday," said Haynes. "Someday. . . ."

His tongue came out and licked dry lips.

Harrison nodded carelessly. "Yes, Haynes, someday, maybe. But not now. I got work to do. Get out of my way."

He motioned with the right gun-hand and the marshal moved, stepping swiftly to one side.

Harrison strode across the street, leaped to the board sidewalk. By the time he reached the Silver Dollar he was running. Behind him he heard the shouts of men forming the posse, heard the shrill voice of Ma Elden rising above the shouts and the pounding of hoofs.

By the time he had hitched up his team and driven the wagon onto the prairie stretching back of the town, Sundown was quiet. Sitting in the wagon-seat and listening, he could hear no sound. The posse apparently had ridden off. The buildings squatted, stolid, square match boxes dumped along the street.

Unhitching the team, he tied them to a wagon wheel, found a hammer in the wagon and headed for the row of dark, quiet buildings.

Back of the frame structure that served as the jail and marshal's office, he crouched in the darkness, ears strained for the sounds that did not come. The town was deathly quiet. Every man who was able to ride, he knew, was pounding out along the trail that the stage had taken, hunting for Carolyn.

He crept along the building, came to a halt beneath the window barred by heavy planking.

"Westman!" he whispered, softly.

The silence held.

Crouching against the building, Harrison felt the first chill of apprehension and doubt steal across his mind. Maybe he was wrong . . . maybe.

But somehow it all linked up. The men who had stopped him on the trail, the holdup of the stage, Dunham leading the posse, Carolyn's disappearance, Westman here in jail when he should be in the jail at Rattlesnake.

"Westman!" he called again.

Faint sounds of stirring came from inside and he heard the soft thud of feet crossing the floor toward the window.

A cautious voice came out of the darkness.

"That you, Spike?"

"Not Spike," said Harrison. "It's Johnny Harrison."

He saw the man's face faintly, a white smudge in the darkness behind the planking.

"Harrison!" The man's voice hissed through the night. "Say, you're the hombre . . ."

"Yes, I'm the one," said Harrison.

"You better keep out of that lawdog's way," warned Westman. "He's ripe to claw your guts out."

"He had a chance to just a while ago," said Harrison, "and he didn't do it."

"What you want?" asked Westman.

"Not a thing," said Harrison. "Figured maybe you'd like to get out of here."

Westman laughed softly, but he didn't answer.

"Got a hammer with me," Harrison told him. "Think I can get these planks off."

"What's the deal? Spike send you?"

"No one sent me," Harrison told him. "It's all my own idea. Need a place to do some hiding. Thought you could lead me to it."

"So that's it," Westman said.

Harrison waited, ears strained for any sound along the street. None came.

"All right," Westman said, finally. "Start ripping off them boards."

Harrison reached up with the hammer, worked the claws under the edge of the lower plank and pried. The spikes squealed faintly, protesting. Harrison tugged savagely, bearing down upon the hammer handle. The plank came free and hands from the inside reached out and pushed it away to clear the window.

"Just a minute," said Harrison. "I'll have another one."

"Don't bother," panted Westman. "This is big enough."

His hands gripped the window ledge and his head and shoulders came through, thrusting, struggling. Harrison dropped the hammer and reached out to help.

On the ground, Westman ran exploring hands over his body. "Skinned up some," he said, "but nothing serious. You got horses?"

"Team and wagon. You'll have to ride in that."

Westman made a motion of disgust. "We could pick up a couple."

Harrison shook his head. "Can't take the chance. You'll be safer in the wagon than in a saddle. No one would think of looking for you there."

Back at the wagon, Westman helped hitch up the team and climbed up on the seat. Harrison picked up the reins. "Which way?" he asked.

"Head for Rattlesnake," Westman told him and there was an ugliness in his voice that had not been there before.

Harrison clucked and the team started. The dry wheel squeaked.

Westman swore. "Can't you do something about that wheel?"

"Probably could," Harrison admitted, "but I never did get around to it. Just sit back and take it easy. Nothing's going to happen."

He headed north, striking across the prairie toward the trail that ran to Rattlesnake. A pale moon came up, a sickle in the sky playing hide and seek with clouds. The wind rustled the tall, dry grass and from some wooded ravine an owl complained. Half an hour later they struck the trail.

Westman stirred restlessly, eyes keeping watch on the faint, night horizon.

"Better split your guns with me," he suggested.

"The guns stay with me," Harrison told him, crisply.

Westman flared. "What the hell! I . . ."

"Just playing it close to my belt," said Harrison calmly. "You and I made a deal and I aim to see that you carry out your end of it."

The trail wound into broken ground, the level road giving way to steep pitches and sharp turns. Hills studded with scrub pine made a jigsaw skyline.

Westman fidgeted. "I heard something."

"Imagination," snapped Harrison.

"Like a horse."

Somewhere in the darkness a shod hoof struck a stone with ringing noise. Westman wheeled swiftly in the seat, hand clawing for Harrison's right hand gun.

"Hey!" yelled Harrison, but the man already was rising to his feet, gun gripped in his hand. With one, swift motion he was gone, leaping out and away from the wagon. A thud came out of the darkness and then the rustle of bushes.

A voice bellowed: "Stick 'em up!" Harrison pulled the team to a stop, slowly raised his hands, trying to make out the shadowy figure of the man and horse beside the trail.

Marshal Haynes sat the horse, a stolid, square-shouldered figure, teeth gleaming in his beard, moonlight shining on the gun he held.

"Lucky thing that I had to come back," he said. "Lucky thing no one thought to take along a lantern."

Another horse moved in the darkness, came alongside the marshal's.

The voice of Ben, the bartender, spoke: "Both of them here, marshal?"

The marshal roared at Harrison. "What did you do with Westman?"

Harrison pretended surprise. "Westman? You must be loco, marshal. I don't know any Westman."

"You helped him break out of jail," the marshal grated. "When I wouldn't let him out when you threatened me, you came back and let him out. Ben, here, heard that squeaky wheel of yours when you and Westman drove off."

"Didn't think nothing about it, at the time," said Ben. "But when Al here came steaming into the place yelling that Westman was gone, I remembered it."

"What did you do with him?" the marshal roared. "Where you got him hid?"

His gun arm leveled suddenly and the gun belched searing fire. The canvas cover of the wagon jerked and a pan clanged with the impact of the bullet. The gun bellowed again and yet again.

The marshal yelled. "You, Westman, come out of there. Ain't no use in hiding. If you don't . . ."

"Ah, hell," said Ben. "He ain't there. Let's just take Johnny back and hang him instead."

"You sure have run yourself up an awful bill with all that promiscuous shooting," Harrison told Haynes. "I'll tell you what it is soon as I figure up the damage."

The marshal's voice was icy with rage. "Smart-aleck, eh? I'll fix it so there won't be no bill."

Jangling bells of alarm rang in Harrison's brain . . . bells set off by the murderous intent that ran through the marshal's voice. He surged up out of the seat, hand going back to the left gun-butt. But he knew he'd never make it. Back in Sundown the marshal had had a head start and he'd beat him to the draw, but you can't beat a man who already has his fist wrapped around a gun.

A six-gun roared, stabbing with an orange finger through the dark and the marshal screamed in pain and rage as the gun flew from his hand.

Out of the darkness Westman's voice said: "Next time it'll be in the head instead of in the arm."

Harrison, his own gun out, swung it toward the bartender, who froze in the saddle and slowly raised his arms.

"You gents," commanded Harrison, "get down off them broncs. We're trading the team and wagon for them."

"And toss the gun away," Harrison told Ben. "Just reach down easy and let it drop. If you make a sudden move, I'll plug you."

Carefully the two got down off the horses, climbed into the wagon seat under the threat of Westman's gun. Harrison seized the bartender's horse, vaulted into the saddle.

The marshal's teeth were chattering with fear and rage. "I'll get you for this," he growled. "I'll get the both of you."

"You get that team turned around," snapped Westman, "and get started out of here."

Awkwardly, the marshal turned the team around, yelling at the horses. The wagon clattered at a fast clip back toward Sundown.

For a long moment Harrison sat his saddle, staring in the direction the wagon had taken. Harrison stiffened. Westman's gun was out, resting across the saddle, trained straight at his middle. And in the pale moonlight the man's face was twisted into something that might have been a grin, but probably wasn't.

"This," said Westman easily, "is as far as we go together."

For a second Harrison sat speechless, staring at the shining muzzle of the gun. Then he lifted his head, stirred slightly in the saddle.

"So you're backing out," he snapped. "You get me in a jam and you're backing out."

"And you played me for a sucker," snarled Westman. "You wanted to have me lead you someplace and you thought that I would do it if you got me out of jail."

He spat viciously. "Hell, I didn't need your help to get out of there. If you hadn't come along the boys would have been in in a day or two and yanked the place up by the roots to turn me loose plenty pronto!"

He motioned abruptly with the gun barrel. "Hit the dirt, tin horn. And don't try to follow me."

Harrison slowly swung his horse around. There was, he knew, no use of trying to argue. No use of doing anything. He'd gambled and he'd lost.

"I'll be watching," warned Westman, "and if you try to trail me, I'll waste a bullet on you . . . right between the eyes."

The horse paced slowly down the road . . . back toward Sundown.

But he couldn't go there, Harrison knew. He couldn't go anywhere.

"Damn fool," he told himself.

He switched around in the saddle and Westman still sat his horse in the middle of the road, a vague blot in the feeble moonlight.

I could pull my gun and shoot it out, Harrison told himself. I could . . .

But he'd gain nothing in a shoot-out with Westman, he realized. That wasn't the way to go about getting out of the jam . . . and what a jam, he thought. Assisting an accused murderer in escape, resisting a marshal, stealing a horse. . . .

"They'll hang me, sure," he said.

He shrugged and faced forward in the saddle, rocking with the slow plodding of the horse, head bent forward, thinking. There had to be a way to carry out the thing he had started to do. There had to be a way to find out where Carolyn had been taken, to find out why she had been taken. And Satan? There was Satan, too. Best horse he ever had.

Then, suddenly, he had it. Doc might help him. Doc would understand. Doc, with his legendary gold mine, with his riding off and coming back with money, Doc with his cold wry humor and the crow's feet at the corners of his eyes, might be the friend he needed. Hours of darkness still remained. Time to go and see.

Doc might know something. . . . Doc might help him out.

Chapter Three
Trapper Bill Disappears

Squeezed tightly against the wall of the bank, Harrison stood motionless in the narrow alleyway between the bank and Smith's general store, listening for any sign of life out on the street. Back of the bank the horse he had taken from the bartender whickered softly and pawed at the ground.

"Damn the horse," thought Harrison. "He'll wake somebody up."

But the street apparently was clear. Over it and up and down its length hung the unnatural, breathless silence that comes in the dark hours just before dawn.

Satisfied, Harrison slipped out of the alleyway, ducked into the doorway that led upstairs over the bank to Doc Falconer's office and living quarters.

Light seeped from beneath the door of Doc's waiting room and Harrison hesitated, sudden fear gripping at his throat.

"Of course, he might have a light," he told himself. "He might leave one burning so if someone needed him...."

Carefully he approached the waiting room door, reached out and turned the knob.

Doc was slumped forward on top of the desk on which the lamp was burning, slumped not as a man would slump in sleep, but with his body twisted.

"Doc!" Harrison whispered hoarsely.

A knife hilt stuck out of Doc's back, just between the shoulder blades, a little low and to the left. The cheap rag rug was scuffed beneath his feet as if he'd tried to rise and then had fallen back.

Harrison moved across the room, stood beside the desk, hands hanging at his side. Doc was dead. There could be no doubt of that. The one man who might have been able to tell him some facts that he needed to know, *must* know.

Killed with a knife blow in the back as he sat writing at the desk. Harrison's eyes took in the pencil and the scattered sheets. Harrison stiffened, remembering back to the afternoon. Doc's words came back to him:

Wonder if you'd keep a letter for me and forget you ever saw it.

A letter that he said he might come back and get but if he didn't Harrison was to mail. Perhaps . . . perhaps this very letter.

Harrison stooped quickly to examine the desk, reaching out to shuffle the paper. But there was no letter. The sheets were blank and clean . . . no pencil strokes upon them.

Harrison's breath caught in his throat. Here was the letter . . . or at least a duplicate of the letter Doc had been writing. The pencil had been hard and the paper thin and the lines were lettered here, once the light caught the paper right, as legibly as they had been upon the sheet on which they had been written.

He bent closer to the sheet, adjusting it so that the light brought out the lines, and read:

U.S. Marshal,
Omaha
My dear sir:

You no doubt have received complaints of the horse thievery going on in this territory. Through diligent observance, not without danger to my person, I have ascertained that the gang is using Grizzly Valley as it headquarters. Few persons know the exact location of this valley and while I hope to be here to lead you and your party to it when you arrive, if such should not be the case, I would advise that you contact Trapper Bill, who has a cabin. . . .

A creaking board brought Harrison spinning around, right hand darting for his gun.

—

In the doorway stood the man with the flowered waistcoat who had come in with the stage. His lips were drawn back in a vicious snarl and one gold tooth gleamed dully in the lamplight. His hand, coming away from the inside pocket of his coat, held a snub-nosed gun.

The gun snicked viciously, like a tiny, yapping dog. The bullet slammed past his head and smashed into the window.

Harrison tilted up the muzzle of his own gun, hauled the trigger back savagely, too hurried for smooth shooting.

The little gun in the gold-toothed man's hand snarled again, but its tiny noise was drowned out by the bellow of the .45 in Harrison's fist. Something twitched at Harrison's left shoulder, a stinging blow that rocked him on his heels as he watched the man in front of him sag back against the door.

The man hit the door jamb and bounced forward, wilting as he bounced. The gun leaped from his fingers, skittered and slid, a spinning wheel of blue across the lamplit floor. The man slumped to his knees, hung for an instant, then pitched forward, fell on one elbow and rolled over, face up, limp jaw hanging open, eyes rolled back.

Slowly, cat-footed, Harrison moved back toward the window. His eyes switched from the dead man in the doorway to the dead man at the desk and for the first time he saw the soft gleam of the chain that hung from Doc's fingers. Stooping swiftly, he examined it . . . a gold watch chain, its fragile links snapped at both ends.

And as he looked at it, he knew why the man in the doorway had come back . . . knew whose hand had wielded the knife still sticking in Doc's back.

Swiftly, he went across the room, stooped over the dead man, saw the two ends of broken chain that hung from the pockets of the flowered waistcoat. A chain that Doc, rising in the moment before death had struck him down, had seized and broken as the knife-man backed away from his victim.

On the street below a door slammed open with a bang. Boots hit the steps. Harrison spun around, raced for the window shattered by the gold-toothed man's bullet, dived through it, crossed arms shielding his face. He landed on the lean-to roof and rolled. Sprawling on the ground, he scrambled to his feet. In front of him the tied horse snorted and reared. With one swift jerk, Harrison tore loose the reins from the post, leaped for the saddle.

From the window he'd just quitted a gun blasted in the night. The horse was spinning on dancing hind feet, forelegs reaching out. Harrison yelled and the animal came down with a jolt and ran. The gun spoke again and Harrison heard the whine of the bullet passing overhead.

Faint shouts came from the street. Harrison bent low on the horse's neck, the drum of hoofs beating in his head. The cool wind smelled of grass that had been drying in the sun. The sickle moon hung low above the western horizon.

For the first time, Harrison became aware of the stiffness in his left shoulder and when he put up a hand, he found that the shirt was soaked. Moving his arm, he knew no bones were broken. The stranger's bullet had no more than creased him, tearing through muscles.

Something rustled in his shirt pocket as he moved his arm. Taking it out, he saw that it was a wad of crumpled paper. The duplicate of the letter that Doc had started, the letter to the marshal back at Omaha.

Wonder if you'd keep a letter for me. . . .

Harrison crinkled his brow, thinking. There could be no doubt that this was the letter Doc had meant for him to keep. But why keep? If Doc had wanted to tip off the marshal, he could have mailed the letter himself. It was as simple as that. But he'd said that maybe he'd be back to pick it up. Did that mean that under certain circumstances he would not have mailed the letter?

Harrison shook his head. Carefully he smoothed the sheet of paper out and folded it, put it back into his pocket.

The man with the flowered waistcoat and the shiny gold tooth had killed Doc to get that letter. Had gotten it, in fact, and then came back to get the broken watch chain, knowing that it would be evidence that might convict him. Too rattled to take it the first time and coming back to get it. Or maybe not realizing that it had been broken until he'd left the place.

The man had come in on the stage and within the next few hours had plunged his knife into Doc's back and stolen the letter. That must mean the man had come to Sundown to do that very thing . . . and if such had been the case, he must have known that Doc intended to write the letter. Harrison frowned. But that was impossible, he told himself. Doc wasn't one to talk. He told no one his business and maybe that was part of the reason that nobody really liked him.

The gold-toothed man had come on the stagecoach to kill Doc and while he'd been on the stage someone had kidnaped Carolyn Elden. Maybe fancy waistcoat had had something to do with the kidnaping, too. Maybe things hadn't happened just the way he told them. He could have told any story that he wanted to, for there was no one to contradict him. Carolyn had been kidnaped and the driver of the stage was dead.

It linked somehow . . . what had happened to Carolyn and Doc, Doc's letter, Westman in jail, even Dunham riding with the posse. For Sundown wasn't Dunham's town. Rattlesnake was more to Dunhams's liking and Sundown seldom saw any of the Bar X men. Funny that Dunham should have been Johnny-at-the-rat-hole when the stage came in.

Harrison put his hand up to the shirt pocket and the letter crinkled under his touch. Grizzly Valley, the letter had said, and added that few folks knew its exact location. Harrison touched the letter again. Grizzly valley, one of those places you hear about once in a while, but where no one's ever been. But Trapper Bill would know, Trapper Bill, at his cabin out on the south edge of the badlands.

The horse had slowed to an easy lope and Harrison urged it to greater speed.

"Hoss," he said, "we're dropping in on Trapper Bill."

The sun was three hours up the sky when the horse and rider wound cautiously down the tortuous trail that led to the coulee where Trapper Bill's cabin huddled under the looming cliff of vari-colored clay.

Smoke rose lazily from the chimney of the shack and Trapper Bill lounged against the door, watching Harrison ride up. Two decrepit hounds came bellowing and escorted the rider in.

Trapper Bill took the pipe out of his whiskers, spat across the chopping block.

"Howdy, young feller," he said. "Where did you leave your wagon?"

"Back in town," Harrison told him, shortly.

Trapper Bill eyed him speculatively. "Been in a ruckus?"

"Little argument," Harrison explained. "Hombre shot me up a bit."

"You shot back, I reckon."

Harrison got down out of the saddle, stiffly. The horse stood with bowed head, sides heaving.

"Riding kind of hard," said Trapper.

Harrison nodded. "The marshal took a dislike to me."

Trapper snorted. "That there marshal don't have right good sense. Probably the feller needed a little shooting to make a Christian of him."

Harrison leaned against the other side of the doorway, took out papers and tobacco sack, began a cigarette.

"Tell me, Trapper. You know how to get to Grizzly valley?"

Trapper pulled the pipe out of his whiskers.

"Figuring on going there?"

Harrison nodded. "Ain't in your right mind," Trapper told him. "Ain't been there myself for ten years or more. Nothing to go for."

"Have to meet a fellow there," Harrison explained.

Trapper wagged his head. "Funny spot you pick for a meeting place. But if you're bound set on getting there...."

He squatted on the ground, traced with his finger in the dust.

"You go straight north until you hit Cow Canyon...."

His voice mumbled on, his finger tracing the map.

"Figure you got it fixed square in your mind?" he asked.

Harrison nodded. Trapper smoothed the dirt with his palm, arose.

"You look all beat out," he said.

"No sleep since yesterday morning," Harrison told him.

"Better come in and take a nap while I cook you up some coffee."

Harrison shook his head. "Got to be pushing on."

"Hell," said Trapper, "that marshal won't nohow find you here. He'll hit plumb for Rattlesnake. Figure that you streaked for there."

"Not this marshal, he won't," said Harrison. "You wouldn't catch this marshal dead ten miles in any direction from Rattlesnake."

Trapper puffed at his pipe. "Did hear the Rattlesnake and Sundown folks were plumb bitter about some little matter."

"Splitting a county," said Harrison.

"Wouldn't know," said Trapper. "Don't get around, myself. Just over to the Elden spread, once in a while. Sing Lee keeps me fixed up with panther juice. Making his own now. Got a still rigged up out of an old wash boiler. Figured maybe the stuff would poison me, but it ain't hurt me yet."

"Hatless Joe was telling me about it," said Harrison. "Claims it's got forty rod beat all hollow."

"Damn smart Chinaman," Trapper said. "Taking up reading now. Tried to talk me into it, too, but I ain't got the patience for it. Foolish way to spend a feller's time."

"Comes in handy, sometimes, though."

"Maybe it does," Trapper agreed, "but I got along without books and stuff for sixty years and I figure I can go another twenty."

He squinted at Harrison. "You look plumb tuckered out. You'll never make Grizzly in the shape you're in. Better come in and have a little nap. I'll wake you up in an hour or so."

Harrison weakened. Not until now had he realized how tired he was, tired and muscle-sore. And the shoulder where the bullet had flicked him was a dull, red hurt.

"Just an hour or so," he finally said. "You'll promise to wake me, then. Can't waste much time."

"Cross my heart," pledged Trapper, "and hope to stumble. Some sleep and bear meat under your belt and you're good for another day. I'll take care of your animal."

Harrison entered the door, made his way around the rickety table, sat down on the bunk. The place was filthy, filled with the odor of ill-cooked food, of sweaty, greasy clothing. But he scarcely noticed it.

His eyes closed as soon as his head hit the burlap pillow. In just a little while, said a hazy thought, I'll be on the way again. Grizzly valley. Carolyn. Maybe Satan, too.

He woke with a sudden start, sitting bolt upright, filled with the feeling that something had gone wrong.

For a moment he fought to recollect where he was and then it came with a sudden rush.

"Trapper!" he yelled, surging to his feet.

There was no answer. Sultry, summer silence hung upon the cabin. Somewhere a fly was buzzing, but there was no other sound.

Outside in the glaring sunlight the silence held. The sun was high . . . and that, he suddenly knew, was what was wrong. The sun had been a morning sun when he had gone to sleep and now it was after noon. Standing, spread-legged, staring at the sun, his hand went to his shirt pocket, tapping for the paper that should have been there. But there was no rustle, nothing there at all.

He stood for a moment, stupefied.

Trapper Bill had run out on him, had stolen the paper in his pocket and run out on him. But run to where? A horse nickered and Harrison wheeled around, hand driving for his gun.

Then he relaxed. For the horse was riderless and trotting toward him and he recognized it as the one he'd taken from the bartender and ridden to this place.

"Good hoss," he said. "Good hoss."

He moved swiftly forward. He was getting out, he told himself, as fast as the horse could travel.

Chapter Four
Johnny Holds Up the Boss

The man in the gray slouch hat stepped from behind a boulder and thrust forth the rifle.

"Where the hell do you think you're going?" he demanded.

Harrison reined up, sat limply in the saddle.

"I could have shot you," said the man, "when you was coming up the trail and I damn near done it. Just natural kindness that kept me from it."

"I came to see the boss," said Harrison.

"He ain't seeing no one," said the man. "Fact, he'd be sorer than hell if he knowed I didn't shoot you. Told me to. 'Plug anybody comes up the trail,' he said."

"I got a message from Doc Falconer," said Harrison.

The man's jaw dropped. "But, Doc . . ."

Then his mouth snapped shut and he jerked the rifle up.

Hoofs clattered from the opposite slope and the man, gun almost to his shoulder, hesitated.

The horseman rounded a bend below the pile of boulders, reined in his horse.

"Hello, Westman," said Harrison.

Westman sat his horse, staring at Harrison, then he spoke to Spike.

"Put down that gun," he said. "You might have killed the man."

Spike muttered feebly. "But the boss said to shoot anyone that came. . . ."

"Yes, sure, he said that. But he didn't know that Harrison was coming."

"You know this jasper?" asked Spike, in amazement.

"Know him! He's the man that broke me out of jail!"

Spike's face split into a grin. "Well, in that case, maybe it's different. Says he's bringing word from Doc. But I thought that Doc . . ."

Westman yelled at him savagely: "Shut up!"

"If you mean you thought that Doc was dead," Harrison told Spike, "you're right. I got there right after he was killed and I got the letter he was writing."

"But that man the boss. . . ."

"If the man was the gent with the daisies on his vest, I killed him."

He laughed at the two of them, Spike with the rifle dangling in his hand, Westman stiff and straight upon the horse.

"So, if you're figuring on fixing it so that something happens to me," said Harrison, "you better give it up. You can't afford to kill me."

Westman wheeled his horse, said brusquely: "Come on. You better see the boss."

"That," declared Harrison, "is what I come for."

They rode carefully down the rocky trail and ahead of them Harrison saw the spreading green of a hidden valley.

"The boss ain't going to be pleased about this," said Westman. "He's plenty sore to start with. Sore at me for getting out of jail. Figured on using me for bait, I guess. Wanted me to stay there so he could have an excuse to shoot hell out of the town."

"How do you feel about it?" asked Harrison.

Westman hesitated, as if debating his answer. "To tell you the truth, Harrison, I don't really know. My wife, Marie, she's all for you. Says the boss don't care what happens to me. She figures maybe that if I had got killed in the jail break the boss was stewing up it would of pleased him fine."

"Sounds like you and the boss don't get along."

"We've had our arguments," Westman said tersely.

The trail reached the valley and slanted across its greenness, heading for the group of buildings huddled under the western wall of a towering escarpment. They splashed through a ford in the river.

In front of one of the larger residences Westman swung in to the hitching rack. Two men sitting on the front steps got up and lounged against the porch railing, watching Westman and Harrison dismount.

"The boss in?" asked Westman.

One of the men jerked his thumb toward the door, said nothing. The other gave his attention to rolling a quirly. Harrison glanced quickly, closely at the man who had jerked his thumb. There was something hauntingly familiar about the man, about his bearing rather than his face.

"Come on," said Westman.

Harrison followed him into the house. At the door of a small room furnished as an office he stopped stock still, staring at the man with his feet cocked up on the desk.

Dunham! Dunham, of Bar X!

The big rancher took a cigar out of his mouth, spat at a cuspidor and missed.

"Don't look so damned astonished, Johnny," he said. "Who did you expect to find?"

Harrison paced forward a step. He understood now. "So this is why you don't want the county split."

Dunham waved his cigar, airily. "Let me tell you something, Johnny. She ain't going to be split, either. Me, I get along swell the way it is. The boys at Rattlesnake understand the situation, but that damn Sundown gang would be riding my tail all the time . . . all the time."

"Nothing strange about the Rattlesnake gang understanding you," Harrison said, blithely. "You practically hand pick them."

Dunham chuckled good naturedly.

"Ain't none of them damn Sundowners suspected me, not out loud, at least. Except maybe Ma Elden and she didn't peep about it. Figured, I guess, she wasn't sure enough. And now I got her where I want her. I got it fixed so she'll never crack a whisper."

"Carolyn," said Harrison, quietly.

Dunham put the cigar back in his mouth, leered around it. "You figure things out fast," he said. "When Ma gets the note the gal's going to send her, she'll get out and work against the county splitting. She'll do an about-face so fast it'll make her dizzy." He chuckled at the thought. "Imagine Ma Elden lining up with Rattlesnake!"

"Smart," said Harrison. "Smart operator, Dunham. You even were on hand to join the posse that went out hunting Carolyn."

"Sure," Dunham told him. "I think of everything."

"And rigged one of your buzzards all up in city togs to do a killing job on Doc. Or was it somebody you hired to come in and do the trick?"

"Someone I hired," said Dunham, easily, "but I played it safe. He doesn't even know who hired him."

"I hope you haven't paid him yet," said Harrison, "because he sure botched up the works."

Dunham's mouth flopped open and the cigar tumbled to the desk. His feet came down off the desk with a heavy thump.

"What's that!" he roared.

"The gent with the daisies killed Doc all right enough," said Harrison, "but I sort of interfered. I pegged your killing hombre with a hunk of lead and got the letter Doc was writing."

With an angry gesture, Dunham swept the burning cigar off the desk. His face was red and flushed.

"What letter?" he shouted.

Harrison laughed quietly. "Why, I thought you knew," he said. "The one to Omaha. To the marshal there. Doc must sort of hinted to you that he was going to write it."

Dunham's hand moved swiftly beneath the desk, came up with a heavy six-gun that leveled on Harrison's stomach.

"Pull that trigger," said Harrison, "and there's a noose around your neck. Doc had got quite a ways along in that letter. He had put in some names."

"Where is it?" Dunham asked, icily. "Hand it over to me."

"I left it with a friend of mine," Harrison told him, "and asked him to mail it if I didn't come and get it. Told him if I wasn't back by tomorrow morning to send it on to Omaha."

Dunham snarled. "I could get it out of you, you lousy wagon tramp. I could . . ."

"You can't do a thing," said Harrison, softly. "I've got you across a barrel and you know I have. Kill me and the letter goes to Omaha. Wait too long to make up your mind and it goes to Omaha. So you better put away the gun and let us talk some business."

The six-gun in Dunham's fist sagged.

"What do you want, Harrison?"

"How much did Doc hold you up for?"

Dunham hesitated. "Ten thousand," he said, finally, "and it was too damn much. If he'd asked four or five . . ."

"It's going to cost you more than that," Harrison told him, flatly.

Dunham smashed his fist against the desk. "I won't pay it," he shouted. "I'll . . ."

"It will cost you a woman and a horse," said Harrison.

"A woman and a . . ."

"Carolyn Elden and the black horse that one of your men stole from me."

Dunham looked relieved. A grin crept across his face.

"Now, Johnny, that's fine. You get me the letter and then you and the gal ride out on the horse and don't tell no one where you been."

He licked his lips, like a cat that had just lapped up a plate of cream. "No trouble at all, you see. We make the deal and everything's all right."

Harrison shook his head. "And you'd have men along the trail to bushwhack us before we'd gone a mile."

Dunham raised his hands in horror. "Never! I stick to my word. I'll shoot square . . ."

Boots pounded on the porch outside and the door squeaked open. Harrison spun on his heel, backed against the wall. The boots tramped across the outer room and the man came in the door.

At the sight of him, Harrison's hand slipped swiftly for his gun.

"Hello, marshal," said Dunham smoothly. "Don't mind Johnny over there. He's just sort of nervous."

Marshal Albert Haynes stood rigid, staring at the gun in Harrison's hand.

"Get them up," snapped Harrison. "All of you. You, too, Westman!"

He switched a quick glance at Dunham, still seated in the chair, but with his elbows on the desk and his hands lifted stiffly in the air.

"So you hired him, too," said Harrison.

Dunham grunted. "Bought him. Sundown don't pay its marshal much."

Still watching Harrison, Haynes spoke out of the corner of his mouth. "Got a letter for you, Dunham. Took it out of the pocket of the hombre you sent to kill Falconer."

Dunham chuckled heavily. "You made a good bluff, Johnny," he said, "but I guess it's run out now."

Chapter Five
Bare Fists vs. Three Guns

Harrison's brain spun, but his gun hand held steady and his face was grim. Dunham was right. His bluff had run out to nothing and he was on his own. A moment before Dunham would not have dared to lift a gun against him, but now he was fair game for any bullet that should come his way.

"Hold still," he told them. "Anyone that moves will get it in the guts."

Dunham laughed at him. "Better think fast, Johnny. You can't stand there all day. The next move is up to you."

And that, Harrison knew, was the bitter truth. Slowly, cautiously, he catfooted toward the door, slid into the doorway. His hand reached out and grasped the knob.

"Good luck, Johnny," said Dunham, and the man was laughing at him . . . laughing because he knew that Johnny couldn't make it, knew that he would die as soon as he reached the street.

"I'll shove that laugh right down your throat," said Harrison. "With bullets!"

He stepped back and slammed the door behind him, ran across the room, heading for the stairs that ran to the upper floor. Half way up them, he swung around to cover his back trail, but there was no one there. The door into the office still was closed, but someone was shouting out a window to someone in the street.

"Don't let him get out! Watch all the doors and windows!"

Trapped, Harrison told himself. Trapped here in this house, without a chance to win.

A soft voice came to him from above.

"Johnny! Johnny Harrison!"

He swung around, a cry surging in this throat.

"Carolyn!"

She stood there, at the top of the stairs, more beautiful than he had remembered her. She wore a dress that matched her eyes and her hair was done up in a way he'd never seen . . . piled on top of her head instead of being braided into pigtails. Half school girl of the east . . . half Ma Elden's daughter as he remembered her.

"I knew you'd find me, Johnny," she said, and her voice was soft. "I knew that you would come."

"Get back!" warned Harrison. "Get back out of sight!"

He sprang up the stairs toward her, dragged her back out of line of the room below.

"Trouble, Johnny?"

Harrison half groaned. "Up to my eyes," he said. "I thought I had them bluffed, but it didn't work."

There were shouts outside the house, the sound of running feet, men calling to one another, the rushing pound of hoofs.

"You here all alone?"

He nodded glumly, then asked: "How about you?"

"Marie was with me, but she went out and left me for a minute."

"Marie?"

"Jim Westman's wife. She's been with me all the time. They want me to write a note to Ma, telling her she had to work against the county splitting if she ever wants to see me."

"And you wouldn't write it."

She shook her head, stubbornly.

His arm around her tightened. "Good girl," he said.

From the room below a voice bellowed at them. "Better come down, Johnny. We got the whole house covered."

Harrison's hand tightened on the six-gun and he glanced at the girl.

"Go to hell," said Harrison. "If you want me, come and get me."

"Good boy," said Carolyn, with a smile.

In the room below a six-gun bellowed and a bullet smashed into the wall opposite the staircase. Harrison waited. The six-gun roared again and splinters leaped from the paneling of the wall.

Silence . . . deep and deadly silence. Then all at once something scraped outside, a sliding, grating noise.

Carolyn gasped. "A ladder! Someone's putting a ladder up to one of the windows!"

Harrison half turned toward the room from which had come the scraping noise, and then turned back. Black defeat welled within his brain. Licked, he told himself. Licked right down to the ground. Boxed in so he couldn't move. If he left the stairway to get at the men on the ladder, the gang downstairs would charge up and get him and if he waited here, the ladder-men would nail him.

Silence again . . . and then the silence was broken by a steady creaking, the protest of the ladder at the weight of a man upon it . . . a man who was climbing fast.

"Carolyn," said Harrison, huskily. "Carolyn, I . . ."

His words were drowned out by a human scream, a soaring note of pain and terror. And cutting through the scream came the distant spat of a high power rifle. The rifle spat again, an angry sound thinned by distance . . . and then again. Another man screamed shortly, as if the scream had started and then someone had grabbed him by the throat.

Carolyn was staring at him with wide eyes. "It's the men out at the ladder," she cried. "Someone is shooting at . . ."

He jerked erect and grabbed her by the wrist.

"Come on," he shouted.

He charged across the hall and into the room where the ladder had been placed. At the window, he saw that the ladder still was there, planted against the house, while at its foot two dead men lay, one spread-eagled on the ground where the bullet had stretched him, the other huddled grotesquely where he had fallen from the rungs.

He glanced upward at the towering cliff. The gun, he knew, must be up there on that cliff . . . the gun that had driven all of Dunham's men to cover.

Feet were pounding up the stairs and Harrison switched around. With one hand, he shoved Carolyn away, toward one corner of the room. In a single leap, he reached the doorway of the room.

His gun spat fire as a man's head and shoulders came into sight around the corner of the staircase, the hammer of the weapon shaking the tiny room like a thunderclap. The head and shoulders slammed against the railing and slid out of sight. Someone yelled and feet were going down the stairway, not coming up.

"Quick!" Harrison yelled at Carolyn. "Get out of the window and go down that ladder."

She hesitated, crouching in the corner of the room.

"Hurry!" he shouted at her. "While there's light whoever's on the cliff can cover us and the light won't hold for long."

With one long stride, he was at the window, jerking it open.

"Here," he said, and reaching out an arm, boosted her roughly through the sash.

"Hold on tight," he whispered. "But hurry, hurry . . ."

Terror was in her eyes as she looked up at him, but she moved swiftly, sure footed down the rungs. Carolyn had reached the bottom of the ladder and was running, heading for the shadows that lay like a rumpled blanket at the foot of the towering cliffs.

Recklessly, Harrison hurled himself down the ladder in great leaps. From a clump of grass to his left a six-gun opened up with a hacking cough and somewhere to the right a rifle talked with measured tones. He heard the hum of lead spinning past him, heard the sullen chugging of the bullets in the house, felt the twitch of jerking hands that wrenched at his vest and shirt.

Then he was stumbling, falling headlong, throwing up his arms to shield his face from the ground that was rushing at him. Far up the cliff the hidden rifle churned. Harrison clawed blindly to his feet and ran, ran with head bent low and with shoulders hunched, ran with a mind that forced him on.

The edge of the shadow at the cliff was close . . . he was almost there . . . and that's King's X, his tired mind told him. The shadow is King's X. Once you get there no bullet can touch you . . . none of those buzzing little bees whimpering in the grass and whining overhead.

Something moved in the shadow ahead of him. Carolyn! Carolyn, coming toward him!

"Go back!" he croaked. "Go back!"

A dark form rose out of the grass and clutched at the girl with ape-like arms. Harrison tried to scream a warning, but all that came out of his throat was a rasping sound. He half-raised his gun and something sliced across his skull, something that was a streak of light tumbling into blackness, something that was a whirling pinball of flaming red. And he was falling, tumbling head over heels into an inky pit.

He groped back out of the darkness, revived. His head was a throbbing pulse that rose and fell, that swelled and then collapsed. Slowly he moved one of his hands and put it to his head. It came away wet and sticky.

The first star was twinkling in the east and the haze was bluer, almost black. Harrison lay on his back, thoughts surging through his pulsing head.

He had been hit by a bullet as he'd raced from the house, as he'd raised his gun to shoot at the man who had risen out of the grass beside Carolyn.

His lips moved. "Carolyn," they said. "Carolyn . . ."

But it was all over now. Back in the office Dunham had laughed at him and said the bluff had run out. And now it had. Despite . . .

The rifle on the cliff! Someone had been up there. Someone still might be around. One gun that would not be raised against him.

Hope flared and then almost flickered out. One gun against the valley. He shook his head slowly. It simply wouldn't work.

His own gun? Carefully he hunted for it. But there was no gun, nothing but the grass. It must have fallen from his hand when he had been hit, probably had gone tumbling for many feet before it came to rest.

A faint rustling came to his ears and he tensed. The rustling came on. Carefully, he rolled over, got to his knees and waited. His hands clenched tight, then opened, clenched again. Bare hands, he thought. Bare hands are all I have.

A voice called softly. "Johnny!"

Carolyn! Carolyn calling for him. Swiftly an answer came to his lips and then it died, for there was another sound, the sound of the men that he had forgotten. Boots coming through the grass, heading straight toward him.

"Over this way," said one voice and he recognized it as that of the man who had worn the blue mask back there on the road when the three had stopped him yesterday. Was it only yesterday? Enough had happened for a lifetime.

A voice growled at the blue mask man. "You're loco, all you heard was just the wind."

"It was a voice," the man said stubbornly. "Sounded like the girl."

"It wasn't Harrison," said the other one. "Spike got him. Didn't you, Spike?"

"Sure," said the third voice. "Had a feeling when I saw him coming up the road this afternoon that I'd have to shoot him. Shoot him then and save a lot of trouble."

Cautiously, Harrison lifted his head, saw the three bearing down upon him, saw that the tall man in the center was the blue mask man, the man who had jerked his thumb when Westman had asked him if the boss was in.

"Nice horse you took from him," said the second man.

"Damn fool just picketed him out, then walked away and left him."

"Seems as how," declared Spike, "a man like that don't deserve a horse."

Harrison's hands clenched into fists and his body tightened. His head was clearer, but it still was jumpy and his body was one vast dull ache.

Nothing to fight with . . . and yet he had to fight. It was stark madness . . . one man with nothing but his hands against three armed men. His mind went back to Carolyn, crouching somewhere back there in the grass. Thank Lord, he told himself, she's heard them, too, and is keeping quiet.

He counted as they came, counting footsteps as they came. One, two, and one, two and one, two. They were no more than three paces away and that was close enough. Almost too close. Almost . . .

He heaved himself out of the grass, rising like a fighting grizzly rearing on his legs when he finally is cornered, and from his throat ripped out an involuntary cry . . .

His legs drove him forward in a surging leap and his right fist came whizzing from his boot-tops even as he sprang. A fist that was aimed with deadly accuracy at the blue-mask man.

For an instant, in the twilight, he saw their blank stares, the jaws that dropped with astonishment, then the hurried, instinctively pistoning of hands for gunbutts.

The blue-mask man started to duck, but he moved too late. Harrison's fist caught him beneath the jaw, snapped back his head with its brutal power, lifted him clear off his feet.

Like a cat, Harrison pivoted, saw Spike's leering face before him, saw the gun come flashing up, knew that he'd never beat the bullet.

"Got you. . . ." jeered Spike, and then the gurgle stopped him, the gurgle that came into his throat, the soft *splat!* of steel on flesh that sent him reeling back. Staggering, he dropped his gun and his hands went to his throat, grasping for the knife hilt that stood out against his neck.

Like a plummet, Harrison dived for Spike's dropped gun, half stumbling as he scooped it out of the grass, half by feel, half by luck.

The one remaining man of the bandit trio was dropping the six-gun for a snap shot and in something that was almost panic, Harrison squeezed the trigger of the gun he had scooped up.

The revolver in front of him gushed fire, but the gun in his own fist was dancing in his grasp. The man in front of him staggered back on fighting heels, gun arm coming up above his head. Back and back he stumbled and with grim ferocity, with a dull red anger, Harrison kept the trigger working, slamming bullet after bullet into the sagging body.

"Him all over dead," said a quiet sing-song voice out of the twilight. "No use to shoot him more."

Harrison let the gun drop to his side and swung around.

"Sing Lee!" he shouted.

"Come to pick up missy," explained the Chinese cook. "Take along a knife just in case."

"Then that was you," said Harrison. "That was you who stopped her from running back."

"That was me," said Sing Lee.

"I damn near shot you," Harrison told him.

He moved forward slowly. "Where is Carolyn? Where is . . ."

Then he saw her, standing to one side of Sing Lee. He strode toward her, but Sing Lee put out a hand and stopped him.

"We run like hell," he said. "Men hear shots and come."

Harrison glanced quickly over his shoulder, saw that the cook was right. Men were coming . . . and not men on foot this time, but mounted men, sweeping in toward them with their horses at a dead run.

"No time to run!" gasped Harrison. "We have to stand and fight. Get down! Get down in the grass and hide!"

He leaped back toward Spike's dead form, unfastened his cartridge belt. With trembling fingers, he fed new shells into the six-gun.

On one knee, Harrison brought up the gun, leveled it deliberately and fired. One of the foremost riders jerked stiffly, sailed out of the saddle. Six-guns cracked and the horses swung, fighting their bits, rearing, skidding around. Bullets chunked into the ground and the air whined with their whisper overhead. Dirt struck Harrison across the face as a slug plowed ground at his very feet. Swiftly he worked the trigger.

Out of the darkness behind him came the angry *spat* of a high power rifle, a hacking, angry rifle that talked in measured tones, unhurried, deliberate, vindictive.

Then there were other rifles and the shouts of men charging in, closing upon the milling horses of the bandit band.

The six-gun clicked on an empty shell and Harrison reached for the belt lying at his feet. A fitful flash flared through the twilit gloom . . . a flash that was not gunfire. Harrison jerked up his head, let the gun fall from his hands.

Flames were curling from the houses, flames that crawled and leaped and climbed into the sky. The firing had died down and across the grassland that lay between him and the houses, Harrison could hear the crackle of the flames.

Slowly, stiffly, he stood up, drew in a deep breath of air.

A tall figure stalked out of the gloom toward him, rifle slung across his arm.

"Wal," said Trapper Bill, "I guess that polishes off the varmints. All we had to do was sort of hole up and hold out until Ma got that note."

Harrison gasped. "What note?"

"Why the note that Sing Lee wrote her. Damn smart Chinaman, Sing Lee. Told you he was taking up reading and writing, didn't I?"

"Sure. But how did Sing Lee . . ."

"Just sort of lifted that paper you was carrying in your pocket," explained Trapper. "Figured maybe it was something I should know about. So I took it when you was a-snoozing and loped over to have Sing Lee take a look at it."

"But there wasn't nothing on it."

"Sure, there was. Sing Lee held it up to the light. Said it was the funniest writing he ever run across."

"So you left a note for Ma and then came on, the two of you. That was you up on the cliff."

"Dang tooting," said Trapper. "Sure kept them all denned up."

Grass rustled and Harrison swung about. Carolyn was running toward him with Sing Lee behind her. Swiftly, Harrison stepped forward, caught the girl close. She huddled against him for comfort.

"All done in," said Trapper.

"Missy all right," said Sing Lee. "Just happy, that's all."

Horses swept toward them, pulled to a stop. Ma Elden climbed down stiffly from the saddle, waddled toward the group, fingers hauling out the makings from her shirt pocket.

"Everybody all right?" she demanded.

"Everybody here," Sing Lee told her in his high sing-song. "Everybody happy."

"I'm plumb glad of that," said Ma. "Some other folks ain't. We got Dunham tied up and we found Haynes where he shouldn't be, so we just gathered him in to be on the safe side. Westman got away, but the boys still are hunting for him."

She snapped a match across her thumb, held up the light so she could look at Harrison.

"Well," she asked, "ain't you got a thing to say?"

"Was wondering," said Harrison, "if you'd still loan me that money to buy out the store."

"Bet your boots," said Ma.

She lit the cigarette, puffed thoughtfully.

"Maybe," she said, "we could make it a double wedding. Me and Hatless figure on getting hitched some time, and this is as good a time as any."

THE END

KINDERGARTEN

"Kindergarten" was originally published in the July 1953 issue of Galaxy Science Fiction. *The date is close enough to the end of World War II that I am led to wonder whether this story represents—in a different way than the City stories—a reaction to the horror and pessimism the war engendered in many for the future of the human race.*

In a number of stories written after this one, Cliff seemed to be saying that perhaps the race needs help—help from outside—to make it.

—*dww*

He went walking in the morning before the Sun was up, down past the old, dilapidated barn that was falling in upon itself, across the stream and up the slope of pasture ankle-deep with grass and summer flowers, when the world was wet with dew and the chill edge of night still lingered in the air.

He went walking in the morning because he knew he might not have too many mornings left; any day, the pain might close down for good and he was ready for it—he'd been ready for it for a long time now.

He was in no hurry. He took each walk as if it were his last and he did not want to miss a single thing on any of the walks—the turned-up faces of the pasture roses with the tears of dew running down their cheeks or the matins of the birds in the thickets that ran along the ditches.

He found the machine alongside the path that ran through a thicket at the head of a ravine. At first glance, he was irritated by it, for it was not only unfamiliar, but an incongruous thing as well, and he had no room in heart or mind for anything but the commonplace. It had been the commonplace, the expected, the basic reality of Earth and the life one lived on it which he had sought in coming to this abandoned farm seeking out a place where he might stand on ground of his own choosing to meet the final day.

He stopped in the path and stood there, looking at this strange machine, feeling the roses and the dew and the early morning bird song slip away from him, leaving him alone with this thing beside the path which looked for all the world like some fugitive from a home appliance shop. But as he looked at it, he began to see the little differences and he knew that here was nothing he'd ever seen before or heard of—that it most certainly was not a wandering automatic washer or a delinquent dehumidifier.

For one thing, it shone—not with surface metallic luster or the gleam of sprayed-on porcelain, but with a shine that was all the way through whatever it was made of. If you looked at it just right, you got the impression that you were seeing into it, though not clearly enough to be able to make out the shape of any of its innards. It was rectangular, at a rough guess three feet by four by two, and it was without knobs for one to turn or switches to snap on or dials to set—which suggested that it was not something one was meant to operate.

He walked over to it and bent down and ran his hand along its top, without thinking why he should reach out and touch it, knowing when it was too late that probably he should have left it alone. But it seemed to be all right to touch it, for nothing happened—not right away, at least. The metal, or whatever it was made of, was smooth to the hand and beneath the sleekness of its surface he seemed to sense a terrible hardness and a frightening strength.

He took his hand away and straightened up, stepped back.

The machine clicked, just once, and he had the distinct impression that it clicked not because it had to click to operate, not because it was turning itself on, but to attract attention, to let him know that it was an operating machine and that it had a function and was ready to perform it. And he got the impression that for whatever purpose it might operate, it would do so with high efficiency and a minimum of noise.

Then it laid an egg.

Why he thought of it in just that way, he never was able to explain, even later when he had thought about it.

But, anyhow, it laid an egg, and the egg was a piece of jade, green with milky whiteness running through it, and exquisitely carved with what appeared to be outré symbolism.

He stood there in the path, looking at the jade, for a moment forgetting in his excitement how it had materialized, caught up by the beauty of the jade itself and the superb workmanship that had wrought it into shape. It was, he told himself, the finest piece that he had ever seen and he knew exactly how its texture would feel beneath his fingers and just how expertly, upon close examination, he would find the carving had been done.

He bent and picked it up and held it lovingly between his hands, comparing it with the pieces he had known and handled for years in the museum. But now, even with the jade between his hands, the museum was a misty place, far back along the corridors of time, although it had been less than three months since he had walked away from it.

"Thank you," he said to the machine and an instant later thought what a silly thing to do, talking to a machine as if it were a person.

The machine just sat there. It did not click again and it did not move.

So finally he left, walking back to the old farmhouse on the slope above the barn.

In the kitchen, he placed the jade in the center of the table, where he could see it while he worked. He kindled a fire in the stove and fed in split sticks of wood, not too large, to make quick heat. He put the kettle on to warm and got dishes from the pantry and set his place. He fried bacon and drained it on paper toweling and cracked the last of the eggs into the skillet.

He ate, staring at the jade that stood in front of him, admiring once again its texture, trying to puzzle out the symbolism of its carving and finally wondering what it might be worth. Plenty, he thought—although, of all considerations, that was the least important.

The carving puzzled him. It was in no tradition that he had ever seen or of which he had ever read. What it was meant to represent, he could not imagine. And yet it had a beauty and a force, a certain character, that tagged it as no haphazard doodling, but as the product of a highly developed culture.

He did not hear the young woman come up the steps and walk across the porch, but first knew that she was there when she rapped upon the door frame. He looked up from the jade and saw her standing in the open kitchen doorway and at first sight of her he found himself, ridiculously, thinking of her in the same terms he had been thinking of the jade.

The jade was cool and green and she was crisp and white, but her eyes, he thought, had the soft look of this wondrous piece of jade about them, except that they were blue.

"Hello, Mr. Chaye," she said.

"Good morning," he replied.

She was Mary Mallet, Johnny's sister.

"Johnny wanted to go fishing," Mary told him. "He and the little Smith boy. So I brought the milk and eggs."

"I am pleased you did," said Peter, "although you should not have bothered. I could have walked over later. It would have done me good."

He immediately regretted that last sentence, for it was something he was thinking too much lately—that such and such an act or the refraining from an act would do him good when, as a matter of plain fact, there was nothing that would help him at all. The doctors had made at least that much clear to him.

He took the eggs and milk and asked her in and went to place the milk in the cooler, for he had no electricity for a refrigerator.

"Have you had breakfast?" he asked.

Mary said she had.

"It's just as well," he said wryly. "My cooking's pretty bad. I'm just camping out, you know."

And regretted that one, too.

Chaye, he told himself, quit being so damn maudlin.

"What a pretty thing!" exclaimed Mary. "Wherever did you get it?"

"The jade? Now, that's a funny thing. I found it."

She reached a hand out for it.

"May I?"

"Certainly," said Peter.

He watched her face as she picked it up and held it in both hands, carefully, as he had held it.

"You *found* this?"

"Well, I didn't exactly find it, Mary. It was given to me."

"A friend?"

"I don't know."

"That's a funny thing to say."

"Not so funny. I'd like to show you the—well, the character who gave it to me. Have you got a minute?"

"Of course I have," said Mary, "although I'll have to hurry. Mother's canning peaches."

They went down the slope together, past the barn, and crossed the creek to come into the pasture. As they walked up the pasture, he wondered if they would find it there, if it still was there—or ever had been there.

It was.

"What an outlandish thing!" said Mary.

"That's the word exactly," Peter agreed.

"What is it, Mr. Chaye?"

"I don't know."

"You said you were given the jade. You don't mean . . ."

"But I do," said Peter.

They moved closer to the machine and stood watching it. Peter noticed once again the shine of it and the queer sensation of being able to see into it—not very far, just part way, and not very well at that. But still the metal or whatever it was could be seen into, and that was somehow uncomfortable.

Mary bent over and ran her fingers along its top.

"It feels all right," she said. "Just like porcelain or—"

The machine clicked and a flagon lay upon the grass.

"For you," said Peter.

"For me?"

Peter picked up the tiny bottle and handed it to her. It was a triumph of glassblower's skill and it shone with sparkling prismatic color in the summer sunlight.

"Perfume would be my guess," he said.

She worked the stopper loose.

"Lovely," she breathed and held it out to him to smell.

It was all of lovely.

She corked it up again.

"But, Mr. Chaye . . ."

"I don't know," said Peter. "I simply do not know."

"Not even a guess?"

He shook his head.

"You just found it here."

"I was out for a walk—"

"And it was waiting for you."

"Well, now . . ." Peter began to object, but now that he

thought about it, that seemed exactly right—he had not found the machine; it had been waiting for him.

"It was, wasn't it?"

"Now that you mention it," said Peter, "yes, I guess it was waiting for me."

Not for him specifically, perhaps, but for anyone who might come along the path. It had been waiting to be found, waiting for a chance to go into its act, to do whatever it was supposed to do.

For now it appeared, as plain as day, that someone had left it there.

He stood in the pasture with Mary Mallet, farmer's daughter, standing by his side—with the familiar grasses and the undergrowth and trees, with the shrill of locust screeching across the rising heat of day, with the far-off tinkle of a cowbell—and felt the chill of the thought within his brain, the cold and terrible thought backgrounded by the black of space and the dim endlessness of time. And he felt, as well, a *reaching out* of something, of a chilly alien thing, towards the warmth of humanity and Earth.

"Let's go back," he said.

They returned across the pasture to the house and stood for a moment at the gate.

"Isn't there something we should do?" asked Mary. "Someone we should tell about it?"

He shook his head. "I want to think about it first."

"And do something about it?"

"There may be nothing that anyone can or should do."

He watched her go walking down the road, then turned away and went back to the house.

He got out the lawn mower and cut the grass. After the lawn was mowed, he puttered in the flowerbed. The zinnias were coming along fine, but something had gotten into the asters and they weren't doing well. And the grass kept creeping in, he thought.

No matter what he did, the grass kept creeping into the bed to strangle out the plants.

After lunch, he thought, maybe I'll go fishing. Maybe going fishing will do me—

He caught the thought before he finished it.

He squatted by the flowerbed, dabbing at the ground with the point of his gardening trowel, and thought about the machine out in the pasture.

I want to think about it, he'd told Mary, but what was there to think about?

Something that someone had left in his pasture—a machine that clicked and laid a gift like an egg when you patted it.

What did that mean?

Why was it here?

Why did it click and hand out a gift when you patted it?

Response? The way a dog would wag its tail?

Gratitude? For being noticed by a human?

Negotiation?

Friendly gesture?

Booby trap?

And how had it known he would have sold his soul for a piece of jade one-half as fine as the piece it had given him?

How had it known a girl would like perfume?

He heard the running footsteps behind him and swung around and there was Mary, running across the lawn.

She reached him and went down on her knees beside him and her hands clutched his arm.

"Johnny found it, too," she panted. "I ran all the way. Johnny and that Smith boy found it. They cut across the pasture coming home from fishing . . ."

"Maybe we should have reported it," said Peter.

"It gave them something, too. A rod and reel to Johnny and a baseball bat and mitt to little Augie Smith."

"Oh, good Lord!"

"And now they're telling everyone."

"It doesn't matter," Peter said. "At least, I don't suppose it matters."

"What is that thing out there? You said you didn't know. But you have some idea. Peter, you must have some idea."

"I think it's alien," Peter reluctantly and embarrassedly told her. "It has a funny look about it, like nothing I've ever seen or read about, and Earth machines don't give away things when you lay a hand on them. You have to feed them coins first. This isn't—isn't from Earth."

"From Mars, you mean?"

"Not from Mars," said Peter. "Not from this solar system. We have no reason to think another race of high intelligence exists in this solar system and whoever dreamed up that machine had plenty of intelligence."

"But . . . not from this solar system . . ."

"From some other star."

"The stars are so far away!" she protested.

So far away, thought Peter. So far out of the reach of the human race. Within the realm of dreams, but not the reach of hands. So far away and so callous and uncaring. And the machine—

"Like a slot machine," he said, "except it always pays in jackpots and you don't even need a coin. That is crazy, Mary. That's one reason it isn't of this Earth. No Earth machine, no Earth inventor, would do that."

"The neighbors will be coming," Mary said.

"I know they will. They'll be coming for their handouts."

"But it isn't very big. It could not carry enough inside it for the entire neighborhood. It does not have much more than room enough for the gifts it's already handed out."

"Mary, did Johnny want a rod and reel?"

"He'd talked of practically nothing else."

"And you like perfume?"

"I'd never had any good perfume. Just cheap stuff." She laughed a little nervously. "And you? Do you like jade?"

"I'm what you might call a minor expert on it. It's a passion with me."

"Then that machine . . ."

"Gives each one the thing he wants," Peter finished for her.

"It's frightening," said Mary.

And it seemed strange that anything at all could be frightening on such a day as this—a burnished summer day, with white clouds rimming the western horizon and the sky the color of pale blue silk, a day that had no moods, but was as commonplace as the cornfield earth.

After Mary had left, Peter went in the house and made his lunch. He sat by the window, eating it, and watched the neighbors come. They came by twos and threes, tramping across the pasture from all directions, coming to his pasture from their own farms, leaving the haying rigs and the cultivators, abandoning their work in the middle of the day to see the strange machine. They stood around and talked, tramping down the thicket where he had found the machine, and at times their high, shrill voices drifted across to him, but he could not make out what they said, for the words were flattened and distorted by the distance.

From the stars, he'd said. From some place among the stars.

And if that be fantasy, he said, I have a right to it.

First contact, he thought.

And clever!

Let an alien being arrive on Earth and the women would run screaming for their homes and the men would grab their rifles and there'd be hell to pay.

But a machine—that was a different matter. What if it was a little different? What if it acted a little strangely? After all, it was only a machine. It was something that could be understood.

And if it handed out free gifts, that was all the better.

After lunch, he went out and sat on the steps and some of the neighbors came and showed him what the machine had given them. They sat around and talked, all of them excited and mystified, but not a single one of them was scared.

Among the gifts were wrist-watches and floor lamps, typewriters and fruit juicers, sets of dishes, chests of silver, bolts of drapery materials, shoes, shotguns, carving sets, book ends, neckties, and many other items. One youngster had a dozen skunk traps and another had a bicycle.

A modern Pandora's box, thought Peter, made by an alien intelligence and set down upon the Earth.

Apparently the word was spreading, for now the people came in cars. Some of them parked by the road and walked down to the pasture and others came into the barnyard and parked there, not bothering to ask for permission.

After a time, they would come back loaded with their loot and drive away. Out in the pasture was a milling throng of people. Peter, watching it, was reminded of a county fair or a village carnival.

By chore-time, the last of them had gone, even the neighbors who had come to say a few words with him and to show him what they'd gotten, so he left the house and walked up the pasture slope.

The machine still was there and it was starting to build something. It had laid out around it a sort of platform of a stone that looked like marble, as if it were laying a foundation for a building. The foundation was about ten feet by twelve and was set level against the pasture's slope, with footings of the same sort of stone going down into the ground.

He sat down on a stump a little distance away and looked out over the peace of the countryside. It seemed more beautiful, more quiet and peaceful than it had ever seemed before, and he sat there contentedly, letting the evening soak into his soul.

The Sun had set not more than half an hour ago. The western sky was a delicate lemon fading into green, with here and there the pink of wandering cloud, while beneath the horizon the land lay in the haze of a blue twilight, deepening at the edges. The liquid evensong of birds ran along the hedges and the thickets and the whisper of swallows' wings came down from overhead.

This is Earth, he thought, the peaceful, human Earth, a landscape shaped by an agricultural people. This is the Earth of plum blossom and of proud red barns and of corn rows as straight as rifle barrels.

For millions of years, the Earth had lain thus, without interference; a land of soil and life, a local corner of the Galaxy engaged in its own small strivings.

And now?

Now, finally, there was interference.

Now, finally, someone or something had come into this local corner of the Galaxy and Earth was alone no longer.

To himself, he knew, it did not matter. Physically, there was no longer anything that possibly could matter to him. All that was left was the morning brightness and the evening peace and from each of these, from every hour of each day that was left to him, it was his purpose to extract the last bit of joy in being alive.

But to the others it would matter—to Mary Mallet and her brother Johnny, to the little Smith boy who had gotten the baseball bat and mitt, to all the people who had visited this pasture, and to all the millions who had not visited or even heard of it.

Here, in this lonely place in the midst of the great cornlands, had come, undramatically, a greater drama than the Earth had yet known. Here was the pivot point.

He said to the machine: "What do you intend with us?"

There was no answer.

He had not expected one.

He sat and watched the shadows deepen and the lights spring up in the farm houses that were sprinkled on the land. Dogs barked from far away and others answered them and the cowbells rang across the hills like tiny vesper notes.

At last, when he could see no longer, he walked slowly back to the house.

In the kitchen, he found a lamp and lit it. He saw by the kitchen clock that it was almost nine o'clock—time for the evening news.

He went into the living room and turned on the radio. Sitting in the dark, he listened to it.

There was good news.

There had been no polio deaths in the state that day and only one new case had been reported.

"It is too soon to hope, of course," the newscaster said, "but it definitely is the first break in the epidemic. Up to the time of broadcast, there have been no new cases for more than twenty hours. The state health director said . . ."

He went on to read what the health director said, which wasn't much of anything, just one of those public statements which pretty generally add up to nothing tangible.

It was the first day in almost three weeks, the newscaster had said, during which no polio deaths had been reported. But despite the development, he said, there still was need of nurses. If you are a nurse, he added, won't you please call this number? You are badly needed.

He went on to warm over a grand jury report, without adding anything really new. He gave the weather broadcast. He said the Emmett murder trial had been postponed another month.

Then he said: "Someone has just handed me a bulletin. Now let me see . . ."

You could hear the paper rustling as he held it to read it through, could hear him gasp a little.

"It says here," he said, "that Sheriff Joe Burns has just now been notified that a Flying Saucer has landed on the Peter Chaye farm out near Mallet Corners. No one seems to know too much about it. One report is that it was found this morning, but no one thought to notify the sheriff. Let me repeat—this is just a report. We don't know any more than what we've told you. We don't know if it is true or not. The sheriff is on his way there now. We'll let you know as soon as we learn anything. Keep tuned to this . . ."

Peter got up and turned off the radio. Then he went into the kitchen to bring in the lamp. He set the lamp on a table and sat down again to wait for Sheriff Burns.

He didn't have long to wait.

"Folks tell me," said the sheriff, "this here Flying Saucer landed on your farm."

"I don't know if it's a Flying Saucer, Sheriff."

"Well, what is it, then?"

"I wouldn't know," said Peter.

"Folks tell me it was giving away things."

"It was doing that, all right."

"If this is some cockeyed advertising stunt," the sheriff said, "I'll have someone's neck for it."

"I'm sure it's not an advertising stunt."

"Why didn't you notify me right off? What you mean by holding out on a thing like this?"

"I didn't think of notifying you," Peter told him. "I wasn't trying to hold out on anything."

"You new around here, ain't you?" asked the sheriff. "I don't recollect seeing you before. Thought I knew everyone."

"I've been here three months."

"Folks tell me you ain't farming the place. Tell me you ain't got no family. Live here all by yourself, just doing nothing."

"That's correct," said Peter.

The sheriff waited for the explanation, but Peter offered none. The sheriff looked at him suspiciously in the smoky lamplight.

"Can you show us this here Flying Saucer?"

By now Peter was a little weary of the sheriff, so he said, "I can tell you how to find it. You go down past the barn and cross the brook . . ."

"Why don't you come with us, Chaye?"

"Look, Sheriff, I was telling you how to find it. Do you want me to continue?"

"Why, sure," the sheriff said. "Of course I do. But why can't you . . ."

"I've seen it twice," said Peter. "I've been overrun by people all the afternoon."

"All right, all right," the sheriff said. "Tell me how to find it."

He told him and the sheriff left, followed by his two deputies.

The telephone rang.

Peter answered it. It was the radio station he'd been listening to.

"Say," asked the radio reporter, "you got a Saucer out there?"

"I don't think so," Peter said. "I do have something out here, though. The sheriff is going to take a look at it."

"We want to send out our mobile TV unit, but we wanted to be sure there was something there. It be all right with you if we send it out?"

"No objections. Send it along."

"You sure you got something there?"

"I told you that I had."

"Well, then, suppose you tell me . . ."

Fifteen minutes later, he hung up.

The phone rang again.

It was the Associated Press. The man at the other end of the wire was wary and skeptical.

"What's this I hear about a Saucer out there?"

Ten minutes later, Peter hung up.

The phone rang almost immediately.

"McClelland of the *Tribune*," said a bored voice. "I heard a screwball story..."

Five minutes.

The phone rang again.

It was the United Press.

"Hear you got a Saucer. Any little men in it?"

Fifteen minutes.

The phone rang.

It was an irate citizen.

"I just heard on the radio you got a Flying Saucer. What kind of gag you trying to pull? You know there ain't any Flying Saucers..."

"Just a moment, sir," said Peter.

He let the receiver hang by its cord and went out to the kitchen. He found a pair of clippers and came back. He could hear the irate citizen still chewing him out, the voice coming ghostlike out of the dangling receiver.

He went outside and found the wire and clipped it. When he came back in again, the receiver was silent. He hung it carefully on the hook.

Then he locked the doors and went to bed.

To bed, but not immediately to sleep. He lay beneath the covers, staring up into the darkness and trying to quiet the turmoil of speculation that surged within his brain.

He had gone walking in the morning and found a machine. He had put his hand upon it and it had given him a gift. Later on, it had given other gifts.

"A machine came, bearing gifts," he said into the darkness.

A clever, calculated, well-worked-out first contact.

Contact them with something they will know and recognize and need not be afraid of, something to which they can feel superior.

Make it friendly—and what is more friendly than handing out a gift?

What is it?
Missionary?
Trader?
Diplomat?
Or just a mere machine and nothing more?
Spy? Adventurer? Investigator? Surveyor?
Doctor? Lawyer? Indian chief?
And why, of all places, had it landed here, in this forsaken farmland, in this pasture on his farm?
And its purpose?

What had been the purpose, the almost inevitable motive, of those fictional alien beings who, in tales of fantasy, had landed on Earth?

To take over, of course. If not by force, then by infiltration or by friendly persuasion and compulsion; to take over not only Earth, but the human race as well.

The man from the radio station had been excited, the Associated Press man had been indignant that anyone should so insult his intelligence, the *Tribune* man had been bored and the United Press man flippant. But the citizen had been angry. He was being taken in by another Flying Saucer story and it was just too much.

The citizen was angry because he didn't want his little world disturbed. He wanted no interference. He had trouble enough of his own without things being messed up by a Saucer's landing. He had problems of his own—earning a living, getting along with his neighbors, planning his work, worrying about the polio epidemic.

Although the newscaster had said the polio situation seemed a little brighter—no new cases and no deaths. And that was a fine thing, for polio was pain and death and a terror on the land.

Pain, he thought.

For the first time in many days, there has been no pain.

He lay stiff and still beneath the covers, examining himself for pain. He knew just where it lurked, the exact spot in his anatomy where it lurked hidden out of sight. He lay and waited for it, fearful, now that he had thought of it, that he would find it there.

But it was not there.

He lay and waited for it, afraid that the very thought of it would conjure it up from its hiding place. It did not come. He dared it to come, he invited it to show itself, he hurled mental jibes at it to lure it out. It refused to be lured.

He relaxed and knew that for the moment he was safe. But safe only temporarily, for the pain still was there. It bided its time, waited for its moment, would come when the time was right.

With careless abandon, trying to wipe out the future and its threat, he luxuriated in life without the pain. He listened to the house—the slightly settling joists that made the floor boards creak, the thrum of the light summer wind against the weathered siding, the scraping of the elm branch against the kitchen roof.

Another sound. A knocking at the door. "Chaye! Chaye, where are you?"

"Coming," he called.

He found slippers and went to the door. It was the sheriff and his men.

"Light the lamp," the sheriff said.

"You got a match?" Peter asked.

"Yeah, here are some."

Groping in the dark, Peter found the sheriff's hand and the book of matches.

He located the table, slid his hand across the top and left the lamp. He lit it and looked at the sheriff from across the table.

"Chaye," the sheriff said, "that thing is building something."

"I know it is."

"What's the gag?"

"There's no gag."

"It gave me this," the sheriff said.

He threw the object on the table.

"A gun," said Peter.

"You ever see one like it?"

It was a gun, all right, about the size of a .45. But it had no trigger and the muzzle flared and the whole thing was made of some white, translucent substance.

Peter picked it up and found it weighed no more than half a pound or so.

"No," said Peter. "No, I've never seen one like it." He put it back on the table, gingerly. "Does it work?"

"It does," the sheriff said. "I tried it on your barn."

"There ain't no barn no more," said one of the deputies.

"No report, no flash, no nothing," the sheriff added.

"Just no barn," repeated the deputy, obsessed with the idea.

A car drove into the yard.

"Go out and see who's there," said the sheriff.

One of the deputies went out.

"I don't get it," complained the sheriff. "They said Flying Saucer, but I don't think it's any Saucer. A box is all it is."

"It's a machine," said Peter.

Feet stamped across the porch and men came through the door.

"Newspapermen," said the deputy who had gone out to see.

"I ain't got no statement, boys," the sheriff said.

One of them said to Peter: "You Chaye?"

Peter nodded.

"I'm Hoskins from the *Tribune*. This is Johnson from the AP. That guy over there with the sappy look is a photographer, name of Langly. Disregard him."

He pounded Peter on the back. "How does it feel to be sitting in the middle of the century's biggest news break? Great stuff, hey, boy?"

Langly said: "Hold it."

A flash bulb popped.

"I got to use the phone," said Johnson. "Where is it?"

"Over there," said Peter. "It's not working."

"How come at a time like this?"

"I cut the wire."

"Cut the wire! You crazy, Chaye?"

"There were too many people calling."

"Now," said Hoskins, "wasn't that a hell of a thing to do?"

"I'll fix her up," Langly offered. "Anyone got a pair of pliers?"

The sheriff said, "You boys hold on a minute."

"Hurry up and get into a pair of pants," Hoskins said to Peter. "We'll want your picture on the scene. Standing with your foot on it, like the guy that's just killed an elephant."

"You listen here," the sheriff said.

"What is it, Sheriff?"

"This here's important. Get it straight. You guys can't go messing around with it."

"Sure it's important," said Hoskins. "That is why we're here. Millions of people standing around with their tongues hanging out for news."

"Here are some pliers," someone remarked.

"Leave me at that phone," said Langly.

"What are we horsing around for?" asked Hoskins. "Let's go out and see it."

"I gotta make a call," said Johnson.

"Look here, boys," the sheriff insisted in confusion. "Wait—"

"What's it like, Sheriff? Figure it's a Saucer? How big is it? Does it make a clicking noise or something? Hey, Langly, take the sheriff's picture."

"Just a minute," Langly shouted from outside. "I'm fixing up this wire."

More feet came across the porch. A head was thrust into the door.

"TV truck," the head said. "This the place? How do we get out to the thing?"

The phone rang.

Johnson answered it.

"It's for you, Sheriff."

The sheriff lumbered across the room. They waited, listening.

"Sure, this is Sheriff Burns . . . Yeah, it's out there, all right . . . Sure, I know. I've seen it . . . No, of course, I don't know what it is . . . Yes, I understand . . . Yes, sir . . . Yes, sir. I'll see to it, sir."

He hung up the receiver and turned around to face them.

"That was military intelligence," he said. "No one is going out there. No one's moving from this house. This place is restricted as of this minute."

He looked from one to another of them ferociously.

"Them's orders," he told them.

"Oh, hell," said Hoskins.

"I came all the way out here," bawled the TV man. "I'm not going to come out here and not . . ."

"It isn't me that's doing the ordering," said the sheriff. "It's Uncle Sam. You boys take things easy."

Peter went into the kitchen and poked up the fire and set on the kettle.

"The coffee's there," he said to Langly. "I'll put on some clothes."

Slowly, the night wore on. Hoskins and Johnson phoned in the information they had jotted down on folded copy paper, their pencils stabbing cryptic signs as they talked to Peter and the sheriff. After some argument with the sheriff about letting him go, Langly left with his pictures. The sheriff paced up and down the room.

The radio blared. The phone banged constantly.

They drank coffee and smoked cigarettes, littering the floor with ground-out stubs. More newsmen pulled in, were duly warned by the sheriff, and settled down to wait.

Someone brought out a bottle and passed it around. Someone else tried to start a poker game, but nobody was interested.

Peter went out to get an armload of wood. The night was quiet, with stars.

He glanced toward the pasture, but there was nothing there to see. He tried to make out the empty place where the barn had disappeared. It was too dark to tell whether the barn was there or not.

Death watch or the last dark hour before the dawn—the brightest, most wonderful dawn that Man had ever seen in all his years of striving?

The machine was building something out there, building something in the night.

And what was it building?

Shrine?

Trading Post?

Mission House?

Embassy?

Fort?

There was no way of knowing, no way that one could tell.

Whatever it was building, it was the first known outpost ever built by an alien race on the planet Earth.

He went back into the house with the load of wood.

"They're sending troops," the sheriff told him.

"Tramp, tramp, tramp," said Hoskins, dead-pan, cigarette hanging negligently to his underlip.

"The radio just said so," the sheriff said. "They called out the guard."

Hoskins and Johnson did some more tramp-tramping.

"You guys better not horse around with them soldier boys," the sheriff warned. "They'll shove a bayonet . . ."

Hoskins made a noise like a bugle blowing the charge. Johnson grabbed two spoons and beat out galloping hoofs.

"The cavalry!" shouted Hoskins. "By God, boys, we're saved!"

Someone said wearily: "Can't you guys be your age?"

They sat around, as the night wore on, drinking coffee and smoking. They didn't do much talking.

The radio station finally signed off. Someone fooled around, trying to get another station, but the batteries were too weak to pull in anything. He shut the radio off. It had been some time now since the phone had rung.

Dawn was still an hour away when the guardsmen arrived, not marching, nor riding horses, but in five canvas-covered trucks.

The captain came in for just a moment to find out where this goddam obscenity Saucer was. He was the fidgety type. He wouldn't even stay for a cup of coffee. He went out yelling orders at the drivers.

Inside the house, the others waited and heard the five trucks growl away.

Dawn came and a building stood in the pasture, and it was a bit confusing, for you could see that it was being built in a way that was highly unorthodox. Whoever or whatever was building it had started on the inside and was building outward, so that you saw the core of the building, as if it were a building that was being torn down and someone already had ripped off the entire exterior.

It covered half an acre and was five stories high. It gleamed pink in the first light of the morning, a beautiful misty pink that made you choke up a little, remembering the color of the dress the little girl next door had worn for her seventh birthday party.

The guardsmen were ringed around it, the morning light spattering off their bayonets as they stood the guard.

Peter made breakfast—huge stacks of flapjacks, all the bacon he had left, every egg he could find, a gallon or two of oatmeal, more coffee.

"We'll send out and get some grub," said Hoskins. "We'll make this right with you."

After breakfast, the sheriff and the deputies drove back to the county seat. Hoskins took up a collection and went to town to buy groceries. The other newsmen stayed on. The TV truck got squared off for some wide-angle distance shots.

The telephone started jangling again. The newsmen took turns answering it.

Peter walked down the road to the Mallet farm to get eggs and milk.

Mary ran out to the gate to meet him. "The neighbors are getting scared," she said.

"They weren't scared yesterday," said Peter. "They walked right up and got their gifts."

"But this is different, Peter. This is getting out of hand. The building . . ."

And that was it, of course. The building.

No one had been frightened of an innocent-appearing machine because it was small and friendly. It shone so prettily and it clicked so nicely and it handed out gifts. It was something that could be superficially recognized and it had a purpose that was understandable if one didn't look too far.

But the building was big and might get bigger still and it was being erected inside out. And who in all the world had ever seen a structure built as fast as that one—five stories in one single night?

"How do they do it, Peter?" Mary asked in a hushed little voice.

"I don't know," he said. "Some principle that is entirely alien to us, some process that men have never even thought of, a way of doing things, perhaps, that starts on an entirely different premise than the human way."

"But it's just the kind of building that men themselves would build," she objected. "Not that kind of stone, perhaps—maybe there isn't any stone like that in the entire world—but in every other way there's nothing strange about it. It looks like a big high school or a department store."

"My jade was jade," said Peter, "and your perfume was perfume and the rod and reel that Johnny got was a regular rod and reel."

"That means they know about us. They know all there is to know. Peter, they've been watching us!"

"I have no doubt of it."

He saw the terror in her eyes and reached out a hand to draw her close and she came into his arms and he held her tightly and thought, even as he did so, how strange that he should be the one to extend comfort and assurance.

"I'm foolish, Peter."

"You're wonderful," he assured her.

"I'm not really scared."

"Of course you're not." He wanted to say, "I love you," but he knew that those words he could never say. Although the pain, he thought—the pain had not come this morning.

"I'll get the milk and eggs," said Mary.

"Give me all you can spare. I have quite a crowd to feed."

Walking back, he thought about the neighbors being frightened now and wondered how long it would be before the world got frightened, too—how long before artillery would be wheeling into line, how long before an atom bomb would fall.

He stopped on the rise of the hill above the house and for the first time noticed that the barn was gone. It had been sheared off as cleanly as if cut with a knife, with the stump of the foundation sliced away at an angle.

He wondered if the sheriff still had the gun and supposed he had. And he wondered what the sheriff would do with it and why it had been given him. For, of all the gifts that he had seen, it was the only one that was not familiar to Earth.

In the pasture that had been empty yesterday, that had been only trees and grass and old, grassed-over ditches, bordered by the wild plum thickets and the hazel brush and blackberry vine, rose the building. It seemed to him that it was bigger than when he had seen it less than an hour before.

Back at the house, the newspapermen were sitting in the yard, looking at the building.

One of them said to him, "The brass arrived. They're waiting in there for you."

"Intelligence?" asked Peter.

The newsman nodded. "A chicken colonel and a major."

They were waiting in the living-room. The colonel was a young man with gray hair. The major wore a mustache, very military.

The colonel introduced himself. "I'm Colonel Whitman. This is Major Rockwell."

Peter put down his eggs and milk and nodded acknowledgment.

"You found this machine," said the colonel.

"That is right."

"Tell us about it," said the colonel, so Peter told them about it.

"This jade," the colonel said. "Could we have a look at it?"

Peter went to the kitchen and got the jade. They passed it from one to the other, examining it closely, turning it over and over in their hands, a bit suspicious of it, but admiring it, although Peter could see they knew nothing about jade.

Almost as if he might have known what was in Peter's mind, the colonel lifted his eyes from the jade and looked at him.

"You know jade," the colonel said.

"Very well," said Peter.

"You've worked with it before?"

"In a museum."

"Tell me about yourself."

Peter hesitated—then told about himself.

"But why are you here?" the colonel asked.

"Have you ever been in a hospital, Colonel? Have you ever thought what it would be like to die there?"

The colonel nodded. "I can see your point. But here you'll have no—"

"I won't wait that long."

"Yes, yes," the colonel said. "I see."

"Colonel," said the major. "Look at this, sir, if you will. This symbolism is the same . . ."

The colonel snatched it from his hands and looked.

"The same as on the letterhead!" he shouted.

The colonel lifted his head and stared at Peter, as if it had been the first time he had seen him, as if he were surprised at seeing him.

There was, suddenly, a gun in the major's hand, pointing at Peter, its muzzle a cold and steady eye.

Peter tried to throw himself aside.

He was too late.

The major shot him down.

Peter fell for a million years through a wool-gray nothingness that screamed and he knew it must be a dream, an endless atavistic dream of falling, brought down through all the years from incredibly remote forebears who had dwelt in trees and had lived in fear of falling. He tried to pinch himself to awaken from the dream, but he couldn't do it, since he had no hands to pinch with, and, after a time, it became apparent that he had no body to pinch. He was a disembodied consciousness hurtling through a gulf which seemed to have no boundaries.

He fell for a million years through the void that seemed to scream at him. At first the screaming soaked into him and filled his soul, since he had no body, with a terrible agony that went on and on, never quite reaching the breaking point that would send him into the release of insanity. But he got used to it after a time and as soon as he did, the screaming stopped and he plunged down through space in a silence that was more dreadful than the screaming.

He fell forever and forever and then it seemed that forever ended, for he was at rest and no longer falling.

He saw a face. It was a face from incredibly long ago, a face that he once had seen and had long forgotten, and he searched back along his memory to try to identify it.

He couldn't see it too clearly, for it seemed to keep bobbing around so he couldn't pin it down. He tried and tried and couldn't and he closed his eyes to shut the face away.

"Chaye," a voice said. "Peter Chaye."

"Go away," said Peter.

The voice went away.

He opened his eyes again and the face was there, clearer now and no longer bobbing.

It was the colonel's face.

He shut his eyes again, remembering the steady eye of the gun the major had held. He'd jumped aside, or tried to, and he had been too slow. Something had happened and he'd fallen for a million years and here he was, with the colonel looking at him.

He'd been shot. That was the answer, of course. The major had shot him and he was in a hospital. But where had he been hit? Arm? Both arms seemed to be all right. Leg? Both legs were all right, too. No pain. No bandages. No casts.

The colonel said: "He came to for just a minute, Doc, and now he's off again."

"He'll be all right," said Doc. "Just give him time. You gave him too big a charge, that's all. It'll take a little time."

"We must talk to him."

"You'll have to wait."

There was silence for a moment.

Then: "You're absolutely sure he's human?"

"We've gone over every inch of him," said Doc. "If he isn't human, he's too good an imitation for us ever to find out."

"He told me he had cancer," the colonel said. "Claimed he was dying of cancer. Don't you see, if he wasn't human, if there was something wrong, he could always try to make it look . . ."

"He hasn't any cancer. Not a sign of it. No sign he ever had it. No sign he ever will."

Even with his eyes shut, Peter felt that he was agape with disbelief and amazement. He forced his eyes to stay closed, afraid that this was a trick.

"That other doctor," the colonel said, "told Peter Chaye four months ago he had six more months to live. He told him . . ."

Doc said, "Colonel, I won't even try to explain it. All I can tell you is that the man lying on that bed hasn't got cancer. He's as healthy a man as you would wish to find."

"It isn't Peter Chaye, then," the colonel stated in a dogged voice. "It's something that took over Peter Chaye or duplicated Peter Chaye or . . ."

Doc said, "Now, now, Colonel. Let's stick to what we know."

"You're sure he's a man, Doc?"

"I'm sure he's a human being, if that is what you mean."

"No little differences? Just one seemingly unimportant deviation from the human norm?"

"None," Doc said, "and even if there were, it wouldn't prove what you are after. There could be minor mutational difference in anyone. The human body doesn't always run according to a blueprint."

"There were differences in all that stuff the machine gave away. Little differences that came to light only on close examination—but differences that spelled out a margin between human and alien manufacture."

"All right, then, so there were differences. So those things were made by aliens. I still tell you this man is a human being."

"It all ties in so neatly," the colonel declared. "Chaye goes out and buys this place—this old, abandoned farm. He's eccentric as hell by the standards of that neighborhood. By the very fact of his eccentricity, he invites attention, which might be undesirable, but at the same time his eccentricity might be used to cover up and smooth over anything he did out of the ordinary. It would be just somebody like him who'd supposedly find a strange machine. It would be . . ."

"You're building up a case," said Doc, "without anything to go on. You asked for one little difference in him to base your cock-eyed theory on—no offense, but that's how I, as a doctor, see it. Well, now let's have one little fact—fact, mind you, not guess—to support this idea of yours."

"What was in that barn?" demanded the colonel. "That's what I want to know. Did Chaye build that machine in there? Was that why it was destroyed?"

"The sheriff destroyed the barn," the doctor said. "Chaye had nothing to do with it."

"But who gave the gun to the sheriff? Chaye's machine, that's who. And it would be an easy matter of suggestion, mind control, hypnotism, whatever you want to call it . . ."

"Let's get back to facts. You used an anesthetic gun on this man. You've held him prisoner. By your orders, he had been subjected to intensive examination, a clear invasion of his privacy. I hope to God he never brings you into court. He could throw the book at you."

"I know," the colonel admitted reluctantly. "But we have to bust this thing. We must find out what it is. We have got to get that bomb back!"

"The bomb's what worries you."

"Hanging up there," the colonel said, sounding as if he'd shuddered. "Just hanging up there!"

"I have to get along," replied the doctor. "Take it easy, Colonel."

The doctor's footsteps went out the door and down the corridor, fading away. The colonel paced up and down a while then sat down heavily in a chair.

Peter lay in bed, and one thought crashed through his brain, one thought again and again:

I'm going to live!
But he hadn't been.

He had been ready for the day when the pain finally became too great to bear.

He had picked his ground to spend his final days, to make his final stand.

And now he had been reprieved. Now, somehow, he had been given back his life.

He lay in the bed, fighting against excitement, against a growing tenseness, trying to maintain the pretense that he still was under the influence of whatever he'd been shot with.

An anesthetic gun, the doctor had said. Something new, something he had never heard of. And yet somewhere there was a hint of it. Something, he remembered, about dentistry—a new technique that dentists used to desensitize the gums, a fine stream of anesthetic sprayed against the gums. Something like that, only hundreds or thousands of times stronger?

Shot and brought here and examined because of some wild fantasy lurking in the mind of a G-2 colonel.

Fantasy? He wondered. Unwitting, unsuspecting, could he have played a part? It was ridiculous, of course. For he remembered nothing he had done or said or even thought which gave him a clue to any part he might have played in the machine's coming to the Earth.

Could cancer be something other than disease? Some uninvited guest, perhaps, that came and lived within a human body? A clever alien guest who came from far away, across the unguessed light-years?

And that, he knew, was fantasy to match the colonel's fantasy, a malignant nightmare of distrust that dwelt within the human mind, an instinctive defense mechanism that conditioned the race to expect the worst and to arm against it.

There was nothing feared so much as the unknown factor, nothing which one must guard against so much as the unexplained.

We have to bust this thing, the colonel had said. We must find out what it is.

And that, of course, was the terror of it—that they had no way of knowing what it was.

He stirred at last, very deliberately, and the colonel spoke.

"Peter Chaye," he said.

"Yes, what is it, Colonel?"

"I have to talk to you."

"All right, talk to me."

He sat up in the bed and saw that he was in a hospital room. It had the stark, antiseptic quality, the tile floor, the colorless walls, the utilitarian look—and the bed on which he lay was a hospital bed.

"How do you feel?" the colonel asked.

"Not so hot," confessed Peter.

"We were a little rough on you, but we couldn't take a chance. There was the letter, you see, and the slot machines and the stamp machines and all the other things and . . ."

"You said something about a letterhead."

"What do you know about that, Chaye?"

"I don't know a thing."

"It came to the President," said the colonel. "A month or so ago. And a similar one went to every other administrative head on the entire Earth."

"Saying?"

"That's the hell of it. It was written in no language known anywhere on Earth. But there was one line—one line on all the letters—that you could read. It said: 'By the time you have this deciphered, you'll be ready to act logically.' And that was all anybody could read—one line in the native language of every country that got a copy of the letter. The rest was in gibberish, for all we could make of it."

"You haven't deciphered it?"

He could see the colonel sweating. "Not even a single character, much less a word."

Peter reached out a hand to the bedside table and lifted the carafe, tipped it above the glass. There was nothing in it.

The colonel heaved himself out of his chair. "I'll get you a drink of water."

He picked up the glass and opened the bathroom door.

"I'll let it run a while and get it cold," he said.

But Peter scarcely heard him, for he was staring at the door. There was a bolt on it and if—

The water started running and the colonel raised his voice to be heard above it.

"That's about the time we started finding the machines," he said. "Can you imagine it? A cigarette-vending machine and you could buy cigarettes from it, but it was more than that. It was something watching you. Something that studied the people and the way they lived. And the stamp machines and the slot machines and all the other mechanical contrivances that we have set up. Not machines, but watchers. Watching all the time. Watching and learning . . ."

Peter swung his legs out of bed and touched the floor. He approached swiftly and silently on bare feet and slammed the door, then reached up and slid the bolt. It snicked neatly into place.

"Hey!" the colonel shouted.

Clothes?

They might be in the closet.

Peter leaped at it and wrenched the door open and there they were, hung upon the hangers.

He ripped off the hospital gown, snatched at his trousers and pulled them on.

Shirt, now! In a drawer.

And shoes? There on the closet floor. Don't take time to tie them.

The colonel was pushing and hammering at the door, not yelling yet. Later he would, but right now he was intent on saving all the face he could. He wouldn't want to advertise immediately the fact that he'd been tricked.

Peter felt through his pockets. His wallet was gone. So was everything else—his knife, his watch, his keys. More than likely they'd taken all of it and put it in the office safe when he'd been brought in.

No time to worry about any of them. The thing now was to get away.

He went out the door and down the corridor, carefully not going too fast. He passed a nurse, but she scarcely glanced at him.

He found a stairway door and opened it. Now he could hurry just a little more. He went down the stairs three at a time, shoelaces clattering.

The stairs, he told himself, were fairly safe. Almost no one would use them when there were the elevators. He stopped and bent over for a moment and tied the laces.

The floor numbers were painted above each of the doors, so he knew where he was. At the ground floor, he entered the corridor again. So far, there seemed to be no alarms, although any minute now the colonel would start to raise a ruckus.

Would they try to stop him at the door? Would there be someone to question him? Would—

A basket of flowers stood beside a door. He glanced up and down the corridor. There were several people, but they weren't looking at him. He scooped up the flowers.

At the door, he said to the attendant who sat behind the desk: "Mistake. Wrong flowers."

She smiled sourly, but made no move to stop him.

Outside, he put the flowers down on the steps and walked rapidly away.

An hour later, he knew that he was safe. He knew also that he was in a city thirty miles away from where he wanted to go and that he had no money and that he was hungry and his feet were sore from walking on the hard and unyielding concrete of the sidewalks.

He found a park and sat down on a bench. A little distance away, a group of old men were playing checkers at a table. A mother wheeled her baby. A young man sat on a nearby bench, listening to a tiny radio.

The radio said: ". . . apparently the building is completed. There has been no sign of it growing for the last eighteen hours. At the moment, it measures a thousand stories high and covers more than a hundred acres. The bomb, which was dropped two days ago, still floats there above it, held in suspension by some strange force. Artillery is standing by, waiting for the word to fire, but the word has not come through. Many think that since the bomb could not get through, shells will have no better chance, if any at all.

"A military spokesman, in fact, has said that the big guns are mere precautionary measures, which may be all right, but it certainly doesn't explain why the bomb was dropped. There is a rising clamor, not only in Congress, but throughout the world, to determine why an attempt was made at bombing. There has as yet been no hostile move directed from the building. The only damage so far reported has been the engulfment by the building of the farm home of Peter Chaye, the man who found the machine.

"All trace has been lost of Chaye since three days ago, when he suffered an attack of some sort and was taken from his home. It is believed that he may be in military custody. There is wide speculation on what Chaye may or may not know. It is entirely likely that he is the only man on Earth who can shed any light on what has happened on his farm.

"Meanwhile, the military guard has been tightened around the scene and a corridor of some eighteen miles in depth around it has been evacuated. It is known that two delegations of scientists have been escorted through the lines. While no official announcement has been made, there is good reason to believe they learned little from their visits. What the building is, who or what has engineered its construction, if you can call the inside-out process by which it grew construction, or what may be expected next are all fields of groundless speculation. There is plenty of that, naturally, but no one has yet come up with what might be called an explanation.

"The world's press wires are continuing to pile up reams of copy, but even so there is little actual, concrete knowledge—few facts that can be listed one, two, three right down the line.

"There is little other news of any sort and perhaps it's just as well, since there is no room at the moment in the public interest for anything else but this mysterious building. Strangely, however, there is little other news. As so often happens when big news breaks, all other events seem to wait for some other time to happen. The polio epidemic is rapidly subsiding; there is no major crime news. In the world's capitols, of course, all legislative action is at a complete standstill, with the governments watching closely the developments at the building.

"There is a rising feeling at many of these capitols that the building is not of mere national concern, that decisions regarding it must be made at an international level. The attempted bombing has resulted in some argument that we, as the nation most concerned, cannot be trusted to act in a calm, dispassionate way, and that an objective world viewpoint is necessary for an intelligent handling of the situation."

Peter got up from his bench and walked away. He'd been taken from his home three days ago, the radio had said. No wonder he was starved.

Three days—and in that time the building had grown a thousand stories high and now covered a hundred acres.

He went along, not hurrying too much now, his feet a heavy ache, his belly pinched with hunger.

He had to get back to the building—somehow he had to get back there. It was a sudden need, realized and admitted now, but the reason for it, the source of it, was not yet apparent. It was as if there had been something he had left behind and he had to go and find it. Something I left behind, he thought. What could he have left behind? Nothing but the pain and the knowledge that he walked with a dark companion and the little capsule that he carried in his pocket for the time when the pain grew too great.

He felt in his pocket and the capsule was no longer there. It had disappeared along with his wallet and his pocket knife and watch. No matter now, he thought. I no longer need the capsule.

He heard the hurrying footsteps behind him and there was an urgency about them that made him swing around.

"Peter!" Mary cried out. "Peter, I thought I recognized you. I was hurrying to catch you."

He stood and looked at her as if he did not quite believe it was she whom he saw.

"Where have you been?" she asked.

"Hospital," Peter said. "I ran away from them. But you . . ."

"We were evacuated, Peter. They came and told us that we had to leave. Some of us are at a camp down at the other end of the park. Pa is carrying on something awful and I can't blame him—having to leave right in the middle of haying and with the small grain almost ready to be cut."

She tilted back her head and looked into his face.

"You look all worn out," she said. "Is it worse again?"

"It?" he asked, then realized that the neighbors must have known—that the reason for his coming to the farm must have been general knowledge, for there were no such things as secrets in a farming neighborhood.

"I'm sorry, Peter," Mary said. "Terribly sorry. I shouldn't have..."

"It's all right," said Peter. "Because it's gone now, Mary. I haven't got it any more. I don't know how or why, but I've gotten rid of it in some way."

"The hospital?" she suggested.

"The hospital had nothing to do with it. It had cleared up before I went there. They just found out at the hospital, that is all."

"Maybe the diagnosis was wrong."

He shook his head. "It wasn't wrong, Mary."

Still, how could he be sure? How could he, or the medical world, say positively that it had been malignant cells and not something else—some strange parasite to which he had played the unsuspecting host?

"You said you ran away," she reminded him.

"They'll be looking for me, Mary. The colonel and the major. They think I had something to do with the machine I found. They think I might have made it. They took me to the hospital to find out if I was human."

"Of all the silly things!"

"I've got to get back to the farm," he said. "I simply have to get back there."

"You can't," she told him. "There are soldiers everywhere."

"I'll crawl on my belly in the ditches, if I have to. Travel at night. Sneak through the lines. Fight if I'm discovered and they try to prevent me. There is no alternative. I have to make a try."

"You're ill," she said, anxiously staring at his face.

He grinned at her. "Not ill. Just hungry."

"Come on then." She took his arm.

He held back. "Not to the camp. I can't have someone seeing me. In just a little while, I'll be a hunted man—if I'm not one already."

"A restaurant, of course."

"They took my wallet, Mary. I haven't any money."

"I have shopping money."

"No," he said. "I'll get along. There's nothing that can beat me now."

"You really mean that, don't you?"

"It just occurred to me," Peter admitted, confused and yet somehow sure that what he had said was not reckless bravado, but a blunt fact.

"You're going back?"

"I have to, Mary."

"And you think you have a chance?"

He nodded.

"Peter," she began hesitantly.

"Yes?"

"How much bother would I be?"

"You? How do you mean? A bother in what way?"

"If I went along."

"But you can't. There's no reason for you to."

She lifted her chin just a little. "There is a reason, Peter. Almost as if I were being called there. Like a bell ringing in my head—a school bell calling in the children..."

"Mary," he said, "that perfume bottle—there was a certain symbol on it, wasn't there?"

"Carved in the glass," she told him. "The same symbol, Peter, that was carved into the jade."

And the same symbol, he thought, that had been on the letterheads.

"Come on," he decided suddenly. "You won't be any bother."

"We'll eat first," she said. "We can use the shopping money."

They walked down the path, hand in hand, like two teen-age sweethearts.

"We have lots of time," said Peter. "We can't start for home till dark."

They ate at a small restaurant on an obscure street and after that went grocery shopping. They bought a loaf of bread and two rings of bologna and a slab of cheese, which took all of Mary's money, and for the change the grocer sold them an empty bottle in which to carry water. It would serve as a canteen.

They walked to the edge of the city and out through the suburbs and into the open country, not traveling fast, for there was no point in trying to go too far before night set in.

They found a stream and sat beside it, for all the world like a couple on a picnic. Mary took off her shoes and dabbled her feet in the water and the two of them felt disproportionately happy.

Night came and they started out. There was no Moon, but the sky was ablaze with stars. Although they took some tumbles and at other times wondered where they were, they kept moving on, staying off the roads, walking through the fields and pastures, skirting the farmhouses to avoid barking dogs.

It was shortly after midnight that they saw the first of the campfires and swung wide around them. From the top of a ridge, they looked down upon the camp and saw the outlines of tents and the dull shapes of the canvas-covered trucks. And, later on, they almost stumbled into an artillery outfit, but got safely away without encountering the sentries who were certain to be stationed around the perimeter of the bivouac.

Now they knew that they were inside the evacuated area, that they were moving through the outer ring of soldiers and guns which hemmed in the building.

They moved more cautiously and made slower time. When the first false light of dawn came into the east, they holed up in a dense plum thicket in the corner of a pasture.

"I'm tired," sighed Mary. "I wasn't tired all night or, if I was, I didn't know it—but now that we've stopped, I feel exhausted."

"We'll eat and sleep," Peter said.

"Sleep comes first. I'm too tired to eat."

Peter left her and crawled through a thicket to its edge.

In the growing light of morning stood the Building, a great blue-misted mass that reared above the horizon like a blunted finger pointing at the sky.

"Mary!" Peter whispered. "Mary, there it is!"

He heard her crawling through the thicket to his side.

"Peter, it's a long way off."

"Yes, I know it is. But we are going there."

They crouched there watching it.

"I can't see the bomb," said Mary. "The bomb that's hanging over it."

"It's too far off to see."

"Why is it us? Why are we the ones who are going back? Why are we the only ones who are not afraid?"

"I don't know," said Peter, frowning puzzledly. "No actual reason, that is. I'm going back because I want to—no, because I have to. You see, it was the place I chose. The dying place. Like the elephants crawling off to die where all other elephants die."

"But you're all right now, Peter."

"That makes no difference—or it doesn't seem to. It was where I found peace and an understanding."

"And there were the symbols, Peter. The symbols on the bottle and the jade."

"Let's go back," he said. "Someone will spot us here."

"Our gifts were the only ones that had the symbols," Mary persisted. "None of the others had any of them. I asked around. There were no symbols at all on the other gifts."

"There's no time to wonder about that. Come on."

They crawled back to the center of the thicket.

The Sun had risen above the horizon now and sent level shafts of light into the thicket and the early morning silence hung over them like a benediction.

"Peter," said Mary, "I just can't stay awake any longer. Kiss me before I go to sleep."

He kissed her and they clung together, shut from the world by the jagged, twisted, low-growing branches of the plum trees.

"I hear the bells," she breathed. "Do you hear them, too?"

Peter shook his head.

"Like school bells," she said. "Like bells on the first day of school—the first day you ever went."

"You're tired," he told her.

"I've heard them before. This is not the first time."

He kissed her again. "Go to sleep," he said and she did, almost as soon as she lay down and closed her eyes.

He sat quietly beside her and his mind retreated to his own hidden depths, searching for the pain within him. But there was no pain. It was gone forever.

The pain was gone and the incidence of polio was down and it was a crazy thing to think, but he thought it, anyhow:

Missionary!

When human missionaries went out to heathen lands, what were the first things that they did?

They preached, of course, but there were other things as well. They fought disease and they worked for sanitation and labored to improve the welfare of the people and tried to educate them to a better way of life. And in this way they not only carried out their religious precepts, but gained the confidence of the heathen folk as well.

And if an alien missionary came to Earth, what would be among the first things that he was sure to do? Would it not be reasonable that he, too, would fight disease and try to improve the welfare of his chosen charges? Thus he would gain their confidence. Although he could not expect to gain too much at first. He could expect hostility and suspicion. Only a pitiful handful would not resent him or be afraid of him.

And if the missionary—

And if THIS missionary—

Peter fell asleep.

The roar awakened him and he sat upright, sleep entirely wiped from his mind.

The roar still was there, somewhere outside the thicket, but it was receding.

"Peter! Peter!"

"Quiet, Mary! There is something out there!"

The roar turned around and came back again, growing until it was the sound of clanking thunder and the Earth shook with the sound. It receded again.

The midday sunlight came down through the branches and made of their hiding place a freckled spot of Sun and shade. Peter could smell the musky odor of warm soil and wilted leaf.

They crept cautiously through the thicket and when they gained its edge, where the leaves thinned out, they saw the racing tank far down the field. Its roar came to them as it tore along, bouncing and swaying to the ground's unevenness, the great snout of its cannon pugnaciously thrust out before it, like a stiff-arming football player.

A road ran clear down the field—a road that Peter was sure had not been there the night before. It was a straight road, absolutely straight, running toward the building, and it was of some metallic stuff that shimmered in the Sun.

And far off to the left was another road and to the right another, and in the distance the three roads seemed to draw together, as the rails seem to converge when one looks down a railroad track.

Other roads running at right angles cut across the three roads, intersecting them so that one gained the impression of three far-reaching ladders set tightly side by side.

The tank raced toward one of the intersecting roads, a tank made midget by the distance, and its roar came back to them no louder than the humming of an angry bee.

It reached the road and skidded off, whipping around sidewise and slewing along, as if it had hit something smooth and solid that it could not get through, as if it might have struck a soaped metallic wall. There was a moment when it tipped and almost went over, but it stayed upright and finally backed away, then swung around to come lumbering down the field, returning toward the thicket.

Halfway down the field, it pivoted around and halted, so that the gun pointed back toward the intersecting road.

The gun's muzzle moved downward and flashed and, at the intersecting road, the shell exploded with a burst of light and a puff of smoke. The concussion of the shot slapped hard against the ear.

Again and again the gun belched out its shells point blank. A haze of smoke hung above the tank and road—and the shells still exploded at the road—this side of the road and not beyond it.

The tank clanked forward once more until it reached the road. It approached carefully this time and nudged itself along, as if it might be looking for a way to cross.

From somewhere a long distance off came the crunching sound of artillery. An entire battery of guns seemed to be firing. They fired for a while, then grudgingly quit.

The tank still nosed along the road like a dog sniffing beneath a fallen tree for a hidden rabbit.

"There's something there that's stopping them," said Peter.

"A wall," Mary guessed. "An invisible wall of some sort, but one they can't get through."

"Or shoot through, either. They tried to break through with gunfire and they didn't even dent it."

He crouched there, watching as the tank nosed along the road. It reached the point where the road to the left came down to intersect the cross road. The tank sheered off to follow the left-hand one, bumping along with its forward armor shoved against the unseen wall.

Boxed in, thought Peter—those roads have broken up and boxed in all the military units. A tank in one pen and a dozen tanks in another, a battery of artillery in another, the motor pool in yet another. Boxed in and trapped; penned up and useless.

And we, he wondered—are we boxed in as well?

A group of soldiers came tramping down the right-hand road. Peter spotted them from far off, black dots moving down the road, heading east, away from the building. When they came closer, he saw that they carried no guns and slogged along with the slightest semblance of formation and he could see from the way they walked that they were dog-tired.

He had not been aware that Mary had left his side until she came creeping back again, ducking her head to keep her hair from being caught in the low-hanging branches.

She sat down beside him and handed him a thick slice of bread and a chunk of bologna. She set the bottle of water down between them.

"It was the building," she said, "that built the roads."

Peter nodded, his mouth full of bread and meat.

"They want to make it easy to get to the building," Mary said. "The building wants to make it easy for people to come and visit it."

"The bells again?" he asked.

She smiled and said, "The bells."

The soldiers now had come close enough to see the tank. They stopped and stood in the road, looking at it.

Then four of them turned off the road and walked out into the field, heading for the tank. The others sat down and waited.

"The wall only works one way," said Mary.

"More likely," Peter told her, "it works for tanks, but doesn't work for people."

"The building doesn't want to keep the people out."

The soldiers crossed the field and the tank came out to meet them. It stopped and the crew crawled out of it and climbed down. The soldiers and the crew stood talking and one of the soldiers kept swinging his arms in gestures, pointing here and there.

From far away came the sound of heavy guns again.

"Some of them," said Peter, "still are trying to blast down the walls."

Finally the soldiers and the tank crew walked back to the road, leaving the tank deserted in the field.

And that must be the way it was with the entire military force which had hemmed in the building, Peter told himself. The roads and walls had cut it into bits, had screened it off—and now the tanks and the big guns and the planes were just so many ineffective toys of an infant race, lying scattered in a thousand playpens.

Out on the road, the foot soldiers and the tank crew slogged eastward, retreating from the siege which had failed so ingloriously.

In their thicket, Mary and Peter sat and watched the Building.

"You said they came from the stars," said Mary. "But why did they come here? Why did they bother with us? Why did they come at all?"

"To save us," Peter offered slowly. "To save us from ourselves. Or to exploit and enslave us. Or to use our planet as a military base. For any one of a hundred reasons. Maybe for a reason we couldn't understand even if they told us."

"You don't believe those other reasons, the ones about enslaving us or using Earth as a military base. If you believed that, we wouldn't be going to the building."

"No, I don't believe them. I don't because I had cancer and I haven't any longer. I don't because the polio began clearing up on the same day that they arrived. They're doing good for us, exactly the same as the missionaries did good among the primitive, disease-ridden people to whom they were assigned. I hope—"

He sat and stared across the field, at the trapped and deserted tank, at the shining ladder of the roads.

"I hope," he said, "they don't do what some of the missionaries did. I hope they don't destroy our self-respect with alien Mother

Hubbards. I hope they don't save us from ringworm and condemn us to a feeling of racial inferiority. I hope they don't chop down the coconuts and hand us—"

But they know about us, he told himself. They know all there is to know. They've studied us for—how long? Squatting in a drugstore corner, masquerading as a cigarette machine. Watching us from the counter in the guise of a stamp machine.

And they wrote letters—letters to every head of state in all the world. Letters that might, when finally deciphered, explain what they were about. Or that might make certain demands. Or that might, just possibly, be no more than applications for permits to build a mission or a church or a hospital or a school.

They know us, he thought. They know, for example, that we're suckers for anything that's free, so they handed out free gifts—just like the quiz shows and contests run by radio and television and Chambers of Commerce, except that there was no competition and everybody won.

Throughout the afternoon, Peter and Mary watched the road and during that time small groups of soldiers had come limping down it. But now, for an hour or more, there had been no one on the road.

They started out just before dark, walking across the field, passing through the wall-that-wasn't-there to reach the road. And they headed west along the road, going toward the purple cloud of the building that reared against the redness of the sunset.

They travelled through the night and they did not have to dodge and hide, as they had that first night, for there was no one on the road except the one lone soldier they met.

By the time they saw him, they had come far enough so that the great shaft of the building loomed halfway up the sky, a smudge of misty brightness in the bright starlight.

The soldier was sitting in the middle of the road and he'd taken off his shoes and set them neatly beside him.

"My feet are killing me," he said by way of greeting.

So they sat down with him to keep him company and Peter took out the water bottle and the loaf of bread and the cheese and bologna and spread them on the pavement with wrapping paper as a picnic cloth.

They ate in silence for a while and finally the soldier said, "Well, this is the end of it."

They did not ask the question, but waited patiently, eating bread and cheese.

"This is the end of soldiering," the soldier told them. "This is the end of war."

He gestured out toward the pens fashioned by the roads and in one nearby pen were three self-propelled artillery pieces and in another was an ammunition dump and another pen held military vehicles.

"How are you going to fight a war," the soldier asked, "if the things back there can chop up your armies into checkerboards? A tank ain't worth a damn guarding ten acres, not when it isn't able to get out of those ten acres. A big gun ain't any good to you if you can't fire but half a mile."

"You think they would?" asked Mary. "Anywhere, I mean?"

"They done it here. Why not somewhere else? Why not any place that they wanted to? They stopped us. They stopped us cold and they never shed a single drop of blood. Not a casualty among us."

He swallowed the bit of bread and cheese that was in his mouth and reached for the water bottle. He drank, his Adam's apple bobbing up and down.

"I'm coming back," he said. "I'm going out and get my girl and we both are coming back. The things in that building maybe need some help and I'm going to help them if there's a way of doing it. And if they don't need no help, why, then I'm going to figure out some way to let them know I'm thankful that they came."

"Things? You saw some things?"

The soldier stared at Peter. "No, I never saw anything at all."

"But this business of going out to get your girl and both of you coming back? How did you get that idea? Why not go back right now with us?"

"It wouldn't be right," the soldier protested. "Or it doesn't seem just right. I got to see her first and tell her how I feel. Besides, I got a present for her."

"She'll be glad to see you," Mary told him softly. "She'll like the present."

"She sure will." The soldier grinned proudly. "It was something that she wanted."

He reached in his pocket and took out a leather box. Fumbling with the catch, he snapped it open. The starlight blazed softly on the necklace that lay inside the box.

Mary reached out her hand. "May I?" she asked.

"Sure," the soldier said. "I want you to take a look at it. You'd know if a girl would like it."

Mary lifted it from the box and held it in her hand, a stream of starlit fire.

"Diamonds?" asked Peter.

"I don't know," the soldier said. "Might be. It looks real expensive. There's a pendant, sort of, at the bottom of it, of green stone that doesn't sparkle much, but—"

"Peter," Mary interrupted, "have you got a match?"

The soldier dipped his hand into a pocket. "I got a lighter, Miss. That thing gave me a lighter. A beaut!"

He snapped it open and the flame blazed out. Mary held the pendant close.

"It's the symbol," she said. "Just like on my bottle of perfume."

"That carving?" asked the soldier, pointing. "It's on the lighter, too."

"Something gave you this?" Peter urgently wanted to know.

"A box. Except that it really was more than a box. I reached down to put my hand on it and it coughed up a lighter and when it did, I thought of Louise and the lighter she had given me. I'd lost it and I felt bad about it, and here was one just like it except for the carving on the side. And when I thought of Louise, the box made a funny noise and out popped the box with the necklace in it."

The soldier leaned forward, his young face solemn in the glow from the lighter's flame.

"You know what I think?" he said. "I think that box was one of them. There are stories, but you can't believe everything you hear . . ."

He looked from one to the other of them. "You don't laugh at me," he remarked wonderingly.

Peter shook his head. "That's about the last thing we'd do, Soldier."

Mary handed back the necklace and the lighter. The soldier put them in his pocket and began putting on his shoes.

"I got to get on," he said. "Thanks for the chow."

"We'll be seeing you," said Peter.

"I hope so."

"I know we will," Mary stated positively.

They watched him trudge away, then walked on in the other direction.

Mary said to Peter, "The symbol is the mark of them. The ones who get the symbol are the ones who will go back. It's a passport, a seal of approval."

"Or," Peter amended, "the brand of ownership."

"They'd be looking for certain kinds of people. They wouldn't want anybody who was afraid of them. They'd want people who had some faith in them."

"What do they want us for?" Peter fretted. "That's what bothers me. What use can we be to them? The soldier wants to help them, but they don't need help from us. They don't need help from anyone."

"We've never seen one of them," said Mary. "Unless the box was one of them."

And the cigarette machines, thought Peter. The cigarette machines and God knows what else.

"And yet," said Mary, "they know about us. They've watched us and studied us. They know us inside out. They can reach deep within us and know what each of us might want and then give it to us. A rod and reel for Johnny and a piece of jade for you. And the rod and reel were a *human* rod and reel and the jade was Earth jade. They even know about the soldier's girl. They knew she would like a shiny necklace and they knew she was the kind of person that they wanted to come back again and . . ."

"The Saucers," Peter said. "I wonder if it was the Saucers, after all, watching us for years, learning all about us."

How many years would it take, he wondered, from a standing start, to learn all there was to know about the human race? For it would be from a standing start; to them, all of humanity would have been a complex alien race and they would have had to feel their way along, learning one fact here and another there. And they would make mistakes; at times their deductions would be wrong, and that would set them back.

"I don't know," said Peter. "I can't figure it out at all."

They walked down the shiny metal road that glimmered in the starlight, with the building growing from a misty phantom to a gigantic wall that rose against the sky to blot out the stars. A thousand stories high and covering more than a hundred acres, it was a structure that craned your head and set your neck to aching and made your brain spin with its glory and its majesty.

And even when you drew near it, you could not see the dropped and cradled bomb, resting in the emptiness above it, for the bomb was too far away for seeing.

But you could see the little cubicles sliced off by the roads and, within the cubicles, the destructive toys of a violent race, deserted now, just idle hunks of fashioned metal.

They came at last, just before dawn, to the great stairs that ran up to the central door. As they moved across the flat stone approach to the stairs, they felt the hush and the deepness of the peace that lay in the building's shadow.

Hand in hand, they went up the stairs and came to the great bronze door and there they stopped. Turning around, they looked back in silence.

The roads spun out like wheel spokes from the building's hub as far as they could see, and the crossing roads ran in concentric circles so that it seemed they stood in the center of a spider's web.

Deserted farm houses, with their groups of buildings—barns, granaries, garages, silos, hog pens, machine sheds—stood in the sectors marked off by the roads, and in other sectors lay the machines of war, fit now for little more than birds' nests or a hiding place for rabbits. Bird songs came trilling up from the pastures and the fields and you could smell the freshness and the coolness of the countryside.

"It's good," said Mary. "It's our country, Peter."

"It was our country," Peter corrected her. "Nothing will ever be quite the same again."

"You aren't afraid, Peter?"

"Not a bit. Just baffled."

"But you seemed so sure before."

"I still am sure," he said. "Emotionally, I am as sure as ever that everything's all right."

"Of course everything's all right. There was a polio epidemic and now it has died out. An army has been routed without a single death. An atomic bomb was caught and halted before it could go off. Can't you see, Peter, they're already making this a better world. Cancer and polio gone—two things that Man had fought for years and was far from conquering. War stopped, disease stopped, atomic bombs stopped—things we couldn't solve for ourselves that were solved for us."

"I know all that," said Peter. "They'll undoubtedly also put an end to crime and graft and violence and everything else that has been tormenting and degrading mankind since it climbed down out of the trees."

"What more do you want?"

"Nothing more, I guess—it's just that it's circumstantial. It's not real evidence. All that we know, or think we know, we've learned from inference. We have no proof—no actual, solid proof."

"We have faith. We must have faith. If you can't believe in someone or something that wipes out disease and war, what can you believe in?"

"That's what bothers me."

"The world is built on faith," said Mary. "Faith in God and in ourselves and in the decency of mankind."

"You're wonderful," exclaimed Peter.

He caught her tight and kissed her and she clung against him and when finally they let each other go, the great bronze door was opening.

Silently, they walked across the threshold with arms around each other, into a foyer that arched high overhead. There were murals on the high arched ceiling, and others paneled in the walls, and four great flights of stairs led upward.

But the stairways were roped off by heavy velvet cords. Another cord, hooked into gleaming standards, and signs with pointing arrows showed them which way to go.

Obediently, walking in the hush that came close to reverence, they went across the foyer to the single open door.

They stepped into a large room, with great, tall, slender windows that let in the morning sunlight, and it fell across the satiny newness of the blackboards, the big-armed class chairs, the heavy reading tables, case after case of books, and the lectern on the lecture platform.

They stood and looked at it and Mary said to Peter: "I was

right. They were school bells, after all. We've come to school, Peter. The first day we ever went to school."

"Kindergarten," Peter said, and his voice choked as he pronounced the word.

It was just right, he thought, so humanly right: the sunlight and the shadow, the rich bindings of the books, the dark patina of the wood, the heavy silence over everything. It was an Earthly classroom in the most scholarly tradition. It was Cambridge and Oxford and the Sorbonne and an Eastern ivy college all rolled into one.

The aliens hadn't missed a bet—not a single bet.

"I have to go," said Mary. "You wait right here for me."

"I'll wait right here," he promised.

He watched her cross the room and open a door. Through it, he saw a corridor that went on for what seemed miles and miles. Then she shut the door and he was alone.

He stood there for a moment, then swung swiftly around. Almost running across the foyer, he reached the great bronze door. But there was no door, or none that he could see. There was not even a crack where a door should be. He went over the wall inch by inch and he found no door.

He turned away from the wall and stood in the foyer, naked of soul, and felt the vast emptiness of the building thunder in his brain.

Up there, he thought, up there for a thousand stories, the building stretched into the sky. And down here was kindergarten and up on the second floor, no doubt, first grade, and you'd go up and up and what would be the end—and the purpose of that end?

When did you graduate?

Or did you ever graduate?

And when you graduated, what would you be?

What would you be? he asked.

Would you be human still?

They would be coming to school for days, the ones who had been picked, the ones who had passed the strange entrance examination that was necessary to attend this school. They'd come down the metal roads and climb the steps and the great bronze door would open and they would enter. And others would come, too, out of curiosity, but if they did not have the symbol, the doors would not open for them.

And those who did come in, when and if they felt the urge to flee, would find there were no doors.

He went back into the classroom and stood where he had stood before.

Those books, he wondered. What was in them? In just a little while, he'd have the courage to pick one out and see. And the lectern? What would stand behind the lectern?

What, not *who*.

The door opened and Mary came across the room to him.

"There are apartments out there," she said. "The cutest apartments you have ever seen. And one of them has our names on it and there are others that have other names and some that have no names at all. There are other people coming, Peter. We were just a little early. We were the ones who started first. We got here before the school bell rang."

Peter nodded. "Let's sit down and wait," he said.

Side by side, they sat down, waiting for the Teacher.

REUNION ON GANYMEDE

Written as part of the first wave of stories that Clifford D. Simak wrote for Astounding Science Fiction *after John W. Campbell Jr. was appointed that magazine's new editor, "Reunion on Ganymede" represents Cliff's desire to write science fiction stories that featured ordinary people—in this case, an elderly veteran with striking similarities to Gramp Stevens, the first character to appear in "City," written just a short time after this story.*

This story was first published in the November 1938 issue of Campbell's magazine.

—dww

I

"By cracky," shouted Gramp Parker, "you're tryin' to mess up all my plans. You're tryin' to keep me from goin' to this reunion."

"You know that isn't true, pa," protested his daughter, Celia. "But I declare, you are a caution. I'll worry every minute you are gone."

"Who ever heard of a soldier goin' any place without his side arms?" stormed Gramp. "If I can't wear those side arms I'm not goin'. All the other boys will have 'em."

His daughter argued. "You know what happened when you tried to show Harry how that old flame pistol worked," she reminded him. "It's a wonder both of you weren't killed."

"I ain't goin' to do no shootin' with 'em," declared Gramp. "I just want to wear 'em with my uniform. Don't feel dressed without 'em."

His daughter gave up. She knew the argument might go on all day. "All right, pa," she said, "but you be careful."

She got up and went into the house. Gramp stretched his old bones in the sun. It was pleasant here of a June morning on a bench in front of the house.

Little Harry came around the corner and headed for the old man. "What you doing, grandpa?" he demanded.

"Nothin'," Gramp told him.

The boy climbed onto the bench. "Tell me about the war," he begged.

"You go on and play," Gramp told him.

"Aw, grandpa, tell me about that big battle you was in!"

"The battle of Ganymede?" asked Gramp.

Harry nodded. "Uh-huh, that's the one."

"Well," said Gramp, "I can remember it just as if it was yesterday. And it was forty years ago, forty years ago the middle of next month. The Marshies were gettin' their big fleet together out there on Ganymede, figurin' to sneak up on us when we wasn't expectin' 'em around—"

"Who was the Marshies?" asked the boy.

"The Marshies?" said Gramp. "Why that's what we called the Martians. Kind of a nickname for 'em."

"You was fighting them?"

Gramp chuckled. "You're dog-gone right we fit 'em. We fit 'em to a stand-still and then we licked 'em, right there at Ganymede. After that the peace was signed and there hasn't been any war since then."

"And that's where you are going?" demanded the boy.

"Sure, they're havin' a big reunion out on Ganymede. First one. Maybe they'll have one every year or two from now on."

"And will the Martian soldiers that you whipped be there, too?"

Gramp scowled fiercely. "They been asked to come," he said. "I don't know why. They ain't got no right to be there. We licked 'em and they ain't got no right to come."

"Harry!" came the voice of the boy's mother.

The boy hopped off the bench and trotted toward the house.

"What have you been doing?" asked his mother.

"Grandpa's been telling me about the war."

"You come right in here," his mother shouted. "If your grandpa don't know better than to tell you about the war, you should know better than to listen. Haven't I told you not to ask him to tell you about it?"

Gramp writhed on the bench.

"Dog-gone," he said. "A hero don't get no honor any more at all."

"You don't need to worry," Garth Mitchell, salesman for Robots, Inc., assured Pete Dale, secretary for the Ganymede Chamber of Commerce. "We make robots that are damn near alive. We can fill the bill exactly. If you want us to manufacture you a set of beasts that are just naturally so ornery they will chew one another up on sight, we can do it. We'll ship you the most bloodthirsty pack of nightmares you ever clapped your eyes on."

Pete leveled a pencil at the salesman.

"I want to be sure," he said. "I'm using this big sham battle we are planning for a big promotion. I want it to live up to what we promise. We want to make it the biggest show in the whole damn system. When we turn those robots of yours out in the arena, I want to be sure they will go for one another like a couple of wildcats on top of a red-hot stove. "And I don't want them to quit until they're just hunks of broken-down machinery. We want to give the reunion crowd a fight that will put the real Battle of Ganymede in the shade."

"Listen," declared Mitchell, "we'll make them robots so mean they'll hate themselves. It's a secret process we got and we aren't letting anyone in on it. We use a radium brain in each one of the robots and we know how to give them personality. Most of our orders are for gentle ones or hard workers, but if you want them mean, we'll make them mean for you."

"Fine," said Pete. "Now that that's settled, I want to be sure you understand exactly what we want. We want robots representing every type of ferocious beast in the whole system. I got a list here."

He spread out a sheet of paper.

"They're from Mars and Earth and Venus and a few from Titan out by Saturn. If you can think of any others, throw them in. We want them to represent the real beasts just as closely as possible and I want them ornery mean. We're advertising this as the greatest free-for-all, catch-as-catch-can wild animal fight in history. The idea is from the Roman arenas way back in Earth history when they used to turn elephants and lions and tigers and men all into the same arena and watch what they did to one another. Only here we are using robots instead of the real article, and if your robots are as good as you say they are, they'd ought to put on a better show."

Mitchell grinned and strapped up his brief case.

"Just forget about it, Mr. Dale," he counseled. "We'll make them in our factory on Mars and get them to you in plenty of time. There's still six weeks left before the reunion and that will give us time to do a fancy job."

The two shook hands and Mitchell left.

Pete leaned back in his chair and looked out through the yard-thick quartz of the dome which enclosed Satellite City, Ganymede's only place of habitation. That is, if one didn't consider Ganymede prison, which, technically speaking, probably was a place of habitation. Other than for the dome which enclosed Satellite City and the one which enclosed the prison, however, there was no sign of life on the entire moon, a worthless, lifeless globe only slightly smaller than the planet Mars.

He could see the top of the prison dome, just rising above the western horizon. To that Alcatraz of Space were sent only the most desperate of the Solar System's criminals. The toughest prison in the entire system, its proud tradition was that not a single prisoner had escaped since its establishment twenty years before. Why risk escape, when only misery and death lurked outside the dome?

The Chamber of Commerce offices were located in the peak of the city's dome and from his outer office, against the quartz, Pete had a clear view of the preparations going forward for the reunion which was to celebrate the fortieth anniversary of the Battle of Ganymede.

Far below, at the foot of the magnetically anchored dome, work was progressing on the vast outdoor arena, which would be enclosed in a separate dome, with heat and atmosphere pumped from the larger dome.

On one of the higher snow-swept hills, a short distance from the arena, reared a massive block of marble, swarming with space-armored sculptors. That was the Battle Monument, to be dedicated in the opening ceremonies.

Drift snow, driven by the feeble winds which always stirred restlessly over the surface of this satellite from which the atmosphere was nearly gone, swept over the brown, rolling hills and eddied around the dome. It was cold out there. Pete shivered involuntarily. Down close to 180 degrees below, Fahrenheit. The snow was frozen carbon dioxide.

An inhospitable place to live, but Satellite City was one of the greatest resorts in the entire System. To it, each year, came thousands of celebrities, tens of thousands of common tourists. The guest lists of the better hotels read like the social register and every show house and cafe, every night club, every concession, every dive was making money.

And now the Ganymede reunion!

That had been a clever idea. It had taken some string-pulling back in London to get the Solar Congress to pass the resolution calling the reunion and to appropriate the necessary money. But that had not been too hard to do. Just a little ballyhoo about cementing Earth-Mars friendship for all eternity. Just a little clever work out in the lobbies.

This year Satellite City would pack them in, would get System-wide publicity, would become a household word on every planet.

He tilted farther back in his chair and stared at the sky. The greatest sight in the entire Solar System! Tourists came millions of miles to gaze in wonder at that sky.

Jupiter rode there against the black of space, a giant disk of orange and red, flattened at the poles, bulging at the equator. To the right of Jupiter was the sun, a small globe of white, its searing light and tremendous heat enfeebled by almost 500 million miles of space. Neither Io nor Europa were in sight, but against the velvet curtain of space glittered the brilliant, cold pin-points of distant stars.

Pete rocked back and forth in his chair, rubbing his hands gleefully.

"We'll put Ganymede on the map this year," he exulted.

II

"But I don't want to go to Ganymede," protested Senator Sherman Brown. "I hate space travel. Always get sick."

Izzy Newman almost strangled in exasperation.

"Listen, senator," he pleaded, "don't be a damn fool all your life. We're running you for president two years from now and you need them Martian votes. You can pick up plenty of them by going out to Ganymede and dedicating this battle monument. You can say some nice things about the Martians and then, quick, before the Earth boys get mad at you, you can say something nice about the Earth. And then you can praise the bravery of the men who fought in the battle and then, just to quiet down the pacifists, praise the forty years of peace we've had. And if you do that you'll make everybody happy and everyone will think you are on their side. You'll get a lot of votes."

"But I don't want to go," protested the senator. "I won't go. You can't bulldoze me."

Izzy spread his hands.

"Listen, senator," he said. "I'm your manager, ain't I? Have I ever given you the wrong steer yet? Have I ever done anything but good for you? Didn't I take you out of a one-horse county seat and make you one of the biggest men of your day?"

"Well," said the senator, "I have done well by myself, if I do say so. And part of the credit goes to you. I hate to go to Ganymede. But if you think I should make—"

"Fine," said Izzy, rubbing his hands together. "I'll fix it all up for you. I'll give the newspaper boys some interviews. I'll have the best ghost writer fix you up a speech. We'll get a half million votes out of this trip."

He eyed Senator Brown sternly.

"There's just two things you've got to do," he warned.

"What's that?"

"Learn your speech. I don't want you forgetting it like you did the time you dedicated the communications building on the moon. And leave that damn candid camera at home."

Senator Brown looked unhappy.

Ganymede was plunging into Jupiter's shadow. For a time "night" would fall upon the satellite. Part of the time Europa would be in the sky, but Europa's light would do little more than make the shadows of the surface deeper and darker.

"Spike" Cardy waited for Ganymede to swing into the shadow. For Spike was going to do something that no man had ever done before. He was going to escape from Ganymede prison, from this proud Alcatraz of Space, whose warden boasted that no man had ever left its dome alive until his time was served.

But Spike was leaving before his time was served. He was going to walk out the northwest port and disappear into the Ganymedean night as completely as if he had been wiped out of existence. It was all planned. The planning had been careful and had taken a long time. Spike had waited until he was sure there was no chance for a slip-up.

The plan had cost money, had called for pressure being exerted in the right spots, had called for outside assistance that was hard to get. But what others had failed to do, Spike Cardy had done. For was he not the old Spike Cardy of space-racket fame? Had he not for years levied toll upon the interplanetary lines? Were not his men still levying toll on the ships of space? Spike Cardy was tops in gangdom and even now his word was law to many men.

Spike waited until the guard paced past his cell. Then he moved swiftly to his bunk, mounted it and grasped the almost invisible wire of thin spun glass which was tied to one of the ventilator grids. Swiftly, but carefully, he hauled in the wire, taking care to make no noise. At the end of the wire, where it had hung down the ventilator pipe, was a flame pistol.

Like a cat stalking for a kill, Spike moved to the heavily barred cell door. He thrust the pistol inside his shirt and slumped against the bars. He heard the guard returning on his beat.

Spike whimpered softly, as if he were in great pain. The guard heard the sound, his footsteps quickened.

"What's the matter, Cardy? You sick?" asked the guard.

The gangster chief reached a feeble hand through the bars, clutching wildly at the guard's shoulder. The guard leaned nearer. Cardy's left hand moved like a striking snake, the steel fingers closing around the man's throat. At the same instant the flame pistol, its charge screwed down to low power and a pencil point in diameter, flashed across the space between Cardy's shirt and the guard's heart. Just one little burst of white-hot flame, expertly aimed. Just one little chuckle out of the heat gun, like a man might chuckle at a joke. That was all.

The guard slumped closer against the bars. The death-clutch on his throat had throttled down his outcry. Anyone looking at the scene would have thought he was talking to the prisoner.

Cardy worked swiftly. It was all planned out. He knew just what to do.

His right hand tore the ring of keys from the dead man's belt. His fingers found the correct key, inserted it in the lock. The cell door swung open.

Now was the one dangerous point in the whole plan. But Cardy did not falter.

Swiftly he swung the door open and dragged the guard inside. He would have to take the chance no one would see.

Working deftly, he stripped the dead man's trousers off, slipped them on; ripped the coat from his back and donned it. The cap next and the guard's flame pistol.

Cardy stepped outside, closed and locked his cell door, walked along the cell-block cat-walk. His heart sang with exultation. The hard part was over. But his lips were set in grim, hard lines; his eyes were squinted, alert for danger, ready for action.

Only by stern iron will did he keep his pace to a walk. The guard in the next block saw him, looked at him for a moment and then whirled about and started his march back along the block again.

Only when the guard was out of sight did Spike quicken his pace.

Down the flight of stairs to the ground floor, across the floor and out of the cell sections into the exercise yard and to the northwest port.

A dim light burned in the guard house at the port.

Cardy rapped on the door.

The guard opened the door.

"A space suit," said Cardy. "I'm going out."

"Where's your pass?" asked the guard.

"Here," said Cardy, leveling a flame gun.

The guard's hand darted toward the holster at his side, but he didn't have a chance. Spike's gun flared briefly and the guard slumped.

Scarcely glancing at the body, Spike lifted a space suit from its hanger, donned it, and stepped out to the port. Inside the port, he closed the inner lock behind him, spun the outer lock. It swung open and Spike stepped outside.

In great, soaring leaps, thankful for the lesser gravity, he hurried away. To the east he saw the shining dome of Satellite City. To the northwest loomed the dark, shadow-blackened hills.

Spike disappeared toward the hills.

III

Senator Sherman Brown was happy. Also slightly drunk.

He had eluded Izzy Newman and now here he was, squatting on the floor in the Jupiter Lantern, one of the noisiest night clubs in all of Satellite City, taking pictures of two old veterans engaged in an argument over the Battle of Ganymede.

A crowd had gathered to take in the argument. It was one that stirred imagination and there was always a chance it might develop into a fight.

Senator Brown plastered the view-finder of his candid camera against his eye and worked joyfully. Here was a series of pictures that would do justice to his albums.

Gramp Parker pounded the table with his fist.

"We fit you and we licked you," he yelled, "and I don't give a 'tarnal dang how we come to do it. If your generals had been so all-fired smart, how come we licked the stuffin' out of you?"

Jurg Tec, a doddering old Martian, pounded the table back at Gramp.

"You Earthians won that battle by pure luck," he squeaked, and his squeak was full of honest rage. "You had no right to win. By all the rules of warfare you were beaten from the start. Your strategy was wrong. Your space division was wrong, your timing was wrong. Alexander, when he brought his cruisers down to attack our camp, should have been wiped out."

"But he wasn't," Gramp yelped.

"Just luck," Jurg Tec squeaked back. "Fight that battle over again and the Martians would win. Something went wrong. Something that historians can't explain. Work it out on paper and Mars wins every time."

Gramp pounded the table with both fists. His beard twitched belligerently.

"But dang your ornery hide," he screamed, "battles ain't fit on paper. They're fit with men and ships and guns. And men count most. The men with guts are the ones who win. And battles ain't fit over, neither. There ain't no second chance in war. You either win or lose and there ain't no rain checks handed out."

The Martian seemed to be choking with rage. He sputtered in an attempt to find his voice.

Gramp gloated like a cat that has just polished off a canary.

"Same as I was tellin' you," he asserted. "One good Earthman can lick ten Marshies any time of day or night."

Jurg Tec sputtered in helpless anger.

Gramp improved upon his boast. "Any time of day or night," he said, "blindfolded and with one hand tied behind him."

Jurg Tec's fist lashed out without warning and caught Gramp square on the beard. Gramp staggered and then let out a bellowing howl and made for the Martian. The crowd yelled encouragement.

Jurg Tec, retreating before Gramp's flailing fists, staggered over the kneeling Senator Brown. Gramp leaped at him at the same instant and the three were tangled on the floor in a flurry of lashing arms and legs.

"Take that," yelled Gramp.

"Hey, look out for my camera," shrieked the senator.

The Martian said nothing, but he hung a beauty on the senator's left eye. He had aimed it at Gramp.

A table toppled with a crash. The crowd hooted in utter delight.

The senator glimpsed his camera on the floor, reached out and grabbed it. Someone stepped on his hand and he yelled. Jurg Tec grabbed Gramp by the beard.

"Cut it out," boomed a voice and two policemen came charging through the crowd. They jerked Gramp and Jurg Tec to their feet. The senator got up by himself.

"What you fellows fighting about?" asked the big policeman.

"He's a dog-gone Marshy," yelled Gramp.

"He said one Earthy could lick ten Martians," squeaked Jurg Tec.

The big policeman eyed the senator. "What have you got to say for yourself?" he asked.

The senator was suddenly at a loss for words. "Why, nothing, officer, nothing at all," he stammered.

"I don't suppose you were down there rolling around with them?" snarled the policeman.

"Why, you see, it was this way, officer," the senator explained. "I tried to separate them. Tried to make them quit fighting. And one of them hit me."

The policeman chuckled. "Peacemaker, eh?" he said.

The senator nodded, miserably.

The officer turned his attention toward Gramp and Jurg Tec.

"Fighting the war over again," he said. "Can't you fellows forget it? The war was over forty years ago."

"He insulted me," Jurg Tec squeaked.

"Sure, I know," said the officer, "and you were insulted pretty easy."

"Listen here, officer," said the senator. "If I take these two boys and promise you they won't make any more disturbance, will you just forget about this?"

The big policeman looked at the little policeman.

"Who are *you*?" the little policeman asked.

"Why, I'm—I'm Jack Smith. I know these two boys. I was sitting talking with them before this happened."

The two policemen looked at one another again.

Then they both looked at the senator.

"Why, I guess it would be all right," agreed the little policeman. "But you see they keep peaceable or we'll throw all three of you in the jug."

They eyed him sternly. The senator shifted uneasily. Then he stepped forward and took Gramp and Jurg Tec by the arm.

"Come on, boys, let's have a drink," he suggested.

"I still say," protested Gramp, "that one Earthman can lick ten Marshies—"

"Here, here," warned the senator, "you pipe down. I promised the police you two would be friends."

"Friends with him?" asked Gramp.

"Why not?" asked the senator. "After all, this reunion is for the purpose of demonstrating the peace and friendship which exists between Mars and Earth. Out of the dust and roar of battle rises a newer and clearer understanding. An understanding which will lead to an everlasting peace—"

"Say," said Gramp, "danged if you don't sound like you was makin' a speech."

"Huh," said the senator.

"Like you was makin' a speech," said Gramp. "Like you was one of them political spellbinders that are out gettin' votes."

"Well," said the senator, "maybe I am."

"With that eye of yourn," Gramp pointed out, "you ain't in no shape to make any speech."

Senator Brown strangled on his drink. He set down his glass and coughed.

"What's the matter with you?" asked Jurg Tec.

"I forgot something," the senator explained. "Something very important."

"It can wait," Jurg Tec said. "I'll buy the next round."

"Sure," agreed Gramp, "ain't nothin' so important you can't have another drink."

"You know," said the senator, "I *was* going to make a speech."

The two old soldiers stared at him in disbelief.

"It's a fact," the senator told them, "but I can't with this eye. And will I catch hell for not making that speech! That's what I get for sneaking out with my camera."

"Maybe we can help you out," suggested Gramp. "Maybe we could square things for you."

"Maybe we could," squeaked the Martian.

"Listen, boys," said the senator, "if I were to go out in a ship for a tour of the surface and if the ship broke down and I couldn't get back in time to make my speech, nobody would blame me for that, would they?"

"You're dang right they wouldn't," said Gramp.

"How about the eye?" asked Jurg Tec.

"Shucks," said Gramp, "we could say he run into somethin'."

"Would you boys like to come along with me?" asked the senator.

"Bet your life," said Gramp.

Jurg Tec nodded.

"There's some old battle hulls out there I'd like to see," he said. "Ships that were shot down during the battle and just left there.

Shot up too bad to salvage. The pilot probably would land and let us look at one or two of them."

"Better take along your camera," suggested Gramp. "You'd ought to get some crackin' good pictures on one of 'em old tubs."

IV

The navigator tore open the door of the control room, slammed it behind him and leaned against it. His coat was ripped and blood dripped from an ugly gash across his forehead.

The pilot started from his controls.

"The robots!" screamed the navigator. "The robots are loose!"

The pilot blanched. "Loose!" he screamed back.

The navigator nodded, panting.

In the little silence they could hear the scraping and clashing of steel claws throughout the ship.

"They got the crew," the navigator panted. "Tore them apart, back in the engine room."

The pilot looked through the glass. The surface of Ganymede was just below. He had been leveling off with short, expert rocket blasts, for an easy coast into Satellite City.

"Get a gun!" he shouted. "Hold them off! Maybe we can make it."

The navigator leaped for the rack where the heavy flame rifles hung. But he was too late.

The door buckled beneath a crushing weight. Savage steel claws caught it and ripped it asunder.

The pilot, glancing over his shoulder, saw a nightmare of mad monsters clawing into the control room. Monsters manufactured at the Robots, Inc., plant on Mars, enroute to Satellite City for the show at the Ganymede Battle reunion.

The flame rifle flared, fusing the hideous head of one monster, but the tentacles of another whipped out, snared the pilot with uncanny ease. The pilot screamed, once—a scream chopped short by choking bands of steel.

Then the ship spun crazily, out of control, toward the surface.

"An old cruiser hull is right over that ridge," the pilot told the senator. "It's in pretty good condition, but the nose was driven into the ground by the impact of its fall, wedged tight into the rock, so that all hell and high water couldn't move it."

"Earthian or Marshy?" asked Gramp.

The pilot shook his head. "I'm not sure," he said. "Earth, I think."

The senator was struggling into his space suit.

"You remember the deal we made?" he asked the pilot. "You're to say your ship broke down. You'll know how to explain it. So you couldn't get me back in time to make the speech."

The pilot grinned. "Sure do, senator," he said.

Gramp paused with his helmet poised above his head. "Senator!" he shouted.

He looked at the senator.

"Just who in tarnation are you?" he asked.

"I'm Senator Sherman Brown," the senator told him. "Supposed to dedicate the battle monument."

"Well, I'll be a freckled frog!" said Gramp.

Jurg Tec chuckled.

Gramp whirled on him. "No wisecracks, Marshy," he warned.

"Here, here," shouted the senator. "You fellows quiet down. No more fighting."

Space-armored, the four of them left the ship and tramped up the hill toward the ridge top.

Faintly in his helmet-phones, Gramp heard the crunch of carbon dioxide snow beneath their feet, its hiss against the space suits.

Jupiter was setting, a huge red and orange ball with a massive scallop gnawed from its top half. Against this darkened, unseen segment of the primary rode the quarter moon of tiny Io, while just above, against the black of space, hung the shining sickle of Europa.

The sun had set many hours before.

"Pretty as a Christmas tree," Gramp said.

"Them tourists go nutty over it," the pilot declared. "That taxi of mine has been worked to death ever since the season started. There's something about old Jupiter that gets them."

"I remember," Jurg Tec said, "that it was just like this before the battle. My pal and I walked out of camp to look at it."

"I didn't know you Marshies ever got to be pals," said Gramp. "Figured you were too danged mean."

"My pal," said Jurg Tec, "was killed the next day."

"Oh," said Gramp.

They walked in silence for a moment.

"I'm right sorry about your pal," Gramp told the Martian then.

They topped the ridge.

"There she is," said the pilot, pointing.

Below them lay the dark shape of a huge space ship, resting crazily on the surface, with the stern tilted at a grotesque angle, the nose buried in the rock-hard soil.

"Earth, all right," said Gramp.

They walked down the hillside toward the ship.

In the derelict's side was a great hole, blasted by a shot of long ago, a shot that echoed in dim memory of that battle forty years before.

"Let's go in," said the senator. "I want to take some pictures. Brought some night equipment along. Take pictures in pitch black."

Something moved inside the ship, something that glinted and shone redly in the light of setting Jupiter.

Astonished, the four fell back a step.

A space-armored man stood just inside the ship, half in shadow, half in light. He held two flame pistols in his hands and they were leveled at Gramp and the other three.

"All right," said the man, and his voice was savage, vicious, with just a touch of madness in it. "I got you covered. Just hoist out your guns and let them drop."

They did not move, astounded, scarcely believing what they saw.

"Didn't you hear me!" bellowed the man. "Drop your guns onto the ground."

The pilot went for his flame pistol, in a swift blur of motion that almost tricked the eye.

But the gun was only half out of its holster when one of the guns in the hands of the man inside the ship blasted with a lurid jet of flame. The charge struck the pilot's space suit, split it open with the fury of its energy. The pilot crumpled and rolled, with arms flapping weirdly, down the hill, to come to rest against the old space derelict. His suit glowed cherry-red.

"Maybe now you know I ain't fooling," said the man.

Gramp, with one finger, carefully lifted his pistol from its holster and let it drop to the ground. Jurg Tec and the senator did likewise. There was no use being foolish. Not when a killer had you covered with two guns.

The man stepped carefully out of the ship and waved them back. He holstered one of his guns, stooped and scooped up the three weapons on the ground.

"What's the meaning of this?" demanded the senator.

The man chuckled.

"I'm Spike Cardy," he said. "Maybe you heard of me. Only man to escape from Ganymede prison. Said nobody could break that crib. But Spike Cardy did."

"What are you going to do with us?" asked the senator.

"Leave you here," said Spike. "I'm going to take your ship and leave you here."

"But that's murder," shouted the senator. "We'll die. We only have about four hours' air."

Spike chuckled again. "Now," he said, "ain't that just too damn bad."

Jurg Tec spoke.

"But you lived here somehow. It's been three weeks since you escaped. You haven't been in a space suit all that time. You haven't had enough air tanks to hold out that long."

"What are you getting at?" asked Spike.

"Why," said Jurg Tec, "just this. Why don't you give us a chance to live? Why don't you tell us how you did it? We might be able to do the same, keep alive until somebody found us. After all, you are taking our ship. It won't serve any purpose to kill us. We haven't done anything against you."

"Now," said Spike, "there's some reason to that. And I'll tell you. Friends of mine fixed up a part of this old ship, walled it off and installed a lock and a small atmosphere generator. Atmosphere condenser, rather. 'Cause there's air enough here, only it ain't thick enough. When I made my getaway I came out here and waited for a ship that was supposed to pick me up. But the ship didn't come. Something went wrong and it didn't come. So I'm taking yours."

"That's sporting of you," said the senator. "Would you mind telling us whereabouts in the ship you've got this hideaway?"

"Why, no," said Spike. "Glad to. Anything to help you out."

But there was something about the way he said it, the ugly twist to his mouth, the mockery in his words, that Gramp didn't like.

"Just go down into the nose of the ship," said Spike. "You can't miss it."

An evil smile tugged at Spike's mouth.

"Only," he said, "it won't do you a damn bit of good. Because the condenser broke down about half an hour ago. It can't be fixed. I tried. I was getting ready to try to make it back to Satellite City and take my chances there when you showed up."

"It can't be fixed?" asked the senator.

Spike shook his head inside his space suit.

"Nope," he said, cheerfully, "there's a couple of parts broke.

I tried to weld them with my flame gun, but it didn't work. I ruined them entirely."

V

Spike backed away, toward the top of the ridge.

"Stay back," he warned, with his gun still leveled. "Don't try to follow. I'll let you have it if you do."

"But," shrieked the senator, "you don't mean to leave us here, do you? We'll die!"

The bandit waved his pistol toward the southeast.

"Satellite City is over that way. You can make it on four hours of air. I did."

His laugh boomed in their helmets.

"But you won't. Not creaking old scarecrows like you."

Then he was gone over the ridge.

Gramp, suddenly galvanized into action, leaped toward the lifeless body of the pilot. He tugged the space-suited figure over and his hand reached out and jerked the flame pistol free.

One swift glance told him it was undamaged.

"You can't do that!" Jurg Tec yelled at him.

"Get outta my way, Marshy," yelped Gramp. "I'm goin' after him."

Gramp started up the hill.

Topping the ridge, he saw Spike halfway to the ship.

"Come back and fight," Gramp howled, waving his gun. "Come back and fight, you ornery excuse for a polecat."

Spike swung about, snapped a wild burst of flame along his backtrail and then fled, in ludicrous hops, toward the space ship.

Gramp halted, aimed the flame pistol carefully and fired. Spike turned a somersault in mid-air and sprawled on the ground. Gramp saw the guns Spike had taken from them flash redly in the Jupiter-light as the flame struck home.

"He dropped the guns!" Gramp yelled.

But Spike was up again and running, although his left arm hung limply from the shoulder, swinging freely as he hopped over the surface.

"Too far away," grunted Jurg Tec, overtaking Gramp.

"I had 'im dead center," Gramped yelled, "but it was a mite long range."

Spike reached the ship and leaped into the port.

Cursing, Gramp laid down a blast of flame against the ship as the bandit swung in the outer lock.

"Dang it," shrieked Gramp, "he got away."

Dejectedly the two old veterans stood and stared at the ship.

"I guess this ends it for us," said Jurg Tec.

"Not by a dang sight," declared Gramp. "We'll make it back to Satellite City easy."

But he didn't believe it. He knew they wouldn't.

He heard the sound of footsteps coming down the hill and turned. The senator was hurrying toward them.

"What happened to you?" demanded Jurg Tec.

"I fell and twisted my ankle," the senator explained.

"Sure," said Gramp, "it's plumb easy for a feller to sprain his ankle. Especially at a time like this."

The ground shuddered under their feet as the ship leaped out into space with rockets blasting.

Gramp plodded doggedly along. He heard the hissing of the snow against his space suit. Heard it crunching underfoot. Heard the stumbling footsteps of the other two behind him.

Jupiter was lower in the sky. Io had moved away from its position against the darkened segment of the primary, was swinging free in space.

Before him Gramp saw the bitter hills, covered with drift snow, tinted a ghastly red by the flood of Jupiter-light.

One foot forward and now another. That was the way to do it. Keep plugging away.

But he knew it wasn't any use. He knew that he would die on Ganymede.

"Forty years ago I fit here and came through without a scratch," he told himself. "And now I come back to die here."

He remembered that day of forty years before. Remembered how the sky was laced with fiery flame-ribbons and stabbing ray-beams. How ships, their guns silenced, rammed enemy craft and took them with them to the surface.

"We'll never make it," moaned the senator.

Gramp swung on him savagely; a steel-sheathed fist lifted menacingly.

"You stop your bawlin'," he shouted. "You sound like a sick calf. I'll smack you down if I hear one more peep out of you."

"But what's the use of fooling ourselves?" the senator cried. "Our air is nearly gone. We don't even know if we're going in the right direction."

Gramp roared at him.

"Buck up, you spineless jackass. You're a big man. A senator. Remember that. You gotta get back. Who'd they get to make all 'em speeches if you didn't get back?"

Jurg Tec's voice hissed in Gramp's helmet. "Listen!"

Gramp stood still and listened.

But there was nothing to hear. Just the hiss of the snow against his suit.

"I don't hear nothin'," Gramp said.

And then he heard it—a weird thunder that seemed to carry with it an indefinable threat of danger. A thunder like the stamping of many feet, like the measured march of hoofs.

"Ever hear anything like that, Earthy?" asked the Martian.

"It isn't anything," shrieked the senator. "Nothing at all. We just imagine it. We all are going crazy."

The thunder sounded nearer and nearer—clearer and clearer.

"There ain't supposed to be a livin' thing on Ganymede," said Gramp. "But there's somethin' out there. Somethin' alive."

He felt prickles of fear run up his spine and ruffle the hair at the base of his skull.

A long line of things moved out of the horizon haze and into indistinct vision—a nightmare line of things that shone and glittered in the rays of Jupiter.

"My Lord," said Gramp, "what are they?"

He glanced around.

To their left was a deep cut-bank, where erosion of long past ages had scooped out a deep, but narrow, depression in the hillside.

"This way," Gramp yelled and leaped away, heading for the cut-bank.

The line of charging horrors was nearer when they reached the natural fortress.

Gramp looked at Jurg Tec.

"Marshy," he croaked, "if you never fit before, get ready for it now."

Jurg Tec nodded grimly, his flame pistol in his fist.

The senator whimpered.

Gramp swung on him, drew back his fist and let drive a blow that caught the senator in the center of his breast-plate and sent him sprawling.

Gramp snarled at him.

"Get out your gun, dang you," he shrieked, "and pretend you are a man."

The bunched monsters were closing in—a leaping, frightful mass of beasts that gleamed weirdly in the moon-and-primary light. Massive jaws and cruel, taloned claws and whipping tentacles.

Gramp leveled his flame gun.

"Now," he shouted, "let 'em have it." From the jaws of the cut-bank leaped a blast of withering fire that swept the monsters as they charged and seemed to melt them down. But those behind climbed over and charged through the ones the flame had stopped and came on, straight toward the men who crouched in the shadow of the hill.

Gramp's gun was getting hot. He knew that in a moment it would be a warped and useless thing. That it might even explode in his hand and kill all three of them. For the flame gun is not built to stand continuous fire.

And still the things came on.

Before the cut-bank lay a pile of bodies that glowed metal-red where the pistol flames had raked them.

Gramp dropped his gun and backed away toward the wall of the cut-bank.

Jurg Tec still crouched and worked his pistol with short, sharp, raking jabs, trying to keep it from over-heating.

In a smaller recess crouched the whimpering senator, his gun still in its holster.

Cursing him, Gramp leaped at him, hauled out the flame gun and shoved the senator to one side.

"Let your gun cool, Marshy," Gramp yelled.

He aimed the new weapon at a shambling thing that crawled over the barricade of bodies. Calmly he blasted it straight between the eyes.

"We'll need your gun later," Gramp yelled at Jurg Tec.

A shadowy something, with spines around its face and with a cruel beak just below its eyes, charged over the barricade and Gramp blasted it with one short burst.

The attack was thinning out.

Gramp held his pistol ready and waited for more. But no more came.

"What are 'em dog-gone things?" asked Gramp, jerking his pistol toward the pile of bodies.

"Don't know," said the Martian. "There aren't supposed to be any beasts on Ganymede."

"They acted dog-gone funny," Gramp declared. "Not exactly like animals. Like something you wind up and put down on the floor. Like toys. Like the toy animals I got my grandson for Christmas a year or two ago. You wind 'em up and the little rascals run around in circles."

Jurg Tec stepped outside the cut-bank, nearer to the pile of bodies.

"You be careful, Marshy," Gramp called out.

"Look here, Earthy," yelled the Martian.

Gramp strode forward and looked. And what he saw—instead of flesh and bone, instead of any animal structure—were metal plates and molten wire and cogs of many shapes and sizes.

"Robots," he said. "I'll be a bowlegged Marshy if that ain't what they are. Nothin' but dog-gone robot animals."

The two old soldiers looked at one another.

"It was a tight squeeze at that," said Jurg Tec.

"We sure licked hell out of 'em," Gramp exulted.

"Say," said Jurg Tec, "they were supposed to have a robot wild-animal fight at Satellite City. You don't suppose these things were the robots? Got loose some way?"

"By cracky," said Gramp, "maybe that explains it."

He straightened from his examination of the heap of twisted, flame-scarred metal and looked at the sky. Jupiter was almost gone.

"We better get goin'," Gramp decided.

VI

"That must be them," said the pilot.

He pointed downward and Izzy Newman looked where he pointed.

He saw two figures.

One of them was erect, but staggering as it marched along.

Beside it limped another, with its arm thrown across the shoulders of the first to keep from falling.

"But there's only two," said Izzy.

"No, there's three," declared the pilot. "That one fellow is holding the second one up and he's dragging the third fellow along by his arm. Look at him. Just skidding along the ground like a sled."

The pilot dove the plane, struck the ground and taxied close.

Gramp, seeing the plane, halted. He let go of the senator's arm and eased Jurg Tec to the ground. Then, tottering on his feet, gasping for what little air remained within his oxygen tank, he waited.

Two men came out of the plane. Gramp staggered to meet them.

They helped him in and brought in the other two.

Gramp tore off his helmet and breathed deeply. He helped Jurg Tec to remove his helmet. The senator, he saw, was coming around.

"Dog-gone," said Gramp, "I did somethin' today I swore I'd never do."

"What's that?" asked Jurg Tec.

"I swore," said Gramp, "that if I ever had a chance to help a Marshy, I wouldn't lift a finger. I'd just stand by and watch him kick the bucket."

Jurg Tec smiled.

"You must have forgot yourself," he said.

"Dog-gone," said Gramp, "I ain't got no will power left, that's what's the matter with me."

The reunion was drawing to a close. Meeting in extraordinary convention, the veterans had voted to form an Earth-Mars Veterans' Association. All that remained was to elect the officers.

Jurg Tec had the floor.

"Mr. Chairman," he said, "I won't make a speech. I'm just

going to move a nomination for commander. No speech is necessary."

He paused dramatically and the hall was silent.

"I nominate," said Jurg Tec, "Captain Johnny Parker, better known as Gramp."

The hall exploded in an uproar. The chairman pounded for order, but the thumping of his gavel was scarcely a whisper in the waves of riotous sound that swept and reverberated in the room.

"Gramp!" howled ten thousand throats. "We want Gramp."

Hands lifted a protesting Gramp and bore him to the platform.

"Cut it out, dog-gone you," yelled Gramp, but they only pounded him on the back and yelled at him and left him standing there, all alone beside the chairman's table.

Before him the convention hall rocketed and weaved in uproar. Bands played and their music did no more than form a background for the boisterous cheering. Newsmen popped up and down, taking pictures. The man beside the microphone crooked a finger at the old man and Gramp, hardly knowing why he did it, stumbled forward, to stand before the mike.

He couldn't see the crowd so well. There was something the matter with his eyes. Sort of misted up. Funny way for them to act. And his heart was pounding. Too much excitement. Bad for the heart.

"Speech!" roared the ten thousand down below. "Speech! Speech!"

They wanted him to make a speech! They wanted old Gramp Parker to talk into the mike so they could hear what he had to say. He'd never made a speech before in all his life. He didn't know how to make a speech and he was scared.

Gramp wondered, dimly, what Celia would think of all these goings-on. Hoppin' mad, probably. And little Harry. But Harry would think his grandpa was a hero. And the bunch down at Grocer White's store.

"Speech," thundered the convention hall.

Out of the mist of faces Gramp picked one face—one he could see as plain as day. Jurg Tec, smiling at him, smiling that crooked way the Martians smile. Jurg Tec, his friend. A dog-gone Marshy. A Marshy who had stood shoulder to shoulder with him out on the surface. A Marshy who had stood with him against the metal beasts. A Marshy who had slogged those bitter miles beside him.

There was a word for it. Gramp knew there was a word. He groped madly in his brain for the single word that would tell the story.

And then he had it. It was a funny word. Gramp whispered it. It didn't sound right. Not the kind of word he'd say. Not what anyone would expect old Gramp Parker to say. A word that would fit better in the mouth of Senator Sherman Brown.

Maybe they'd laugh at him for saying it. Maybe they'd think he was just a damn old fool.

He moved closer to the mike and the uproar quieted, waiting.

"Comrades—" Gramp began and then he stopped.

That was the word. They were comrades now. Marshies and Earthies. They'd fought in bitter hatred, each for what he thought was right. Maybe they had to fight. Maybe that war was something that was needed. But it was forty years ago and all its violence was a whisper in the wind—a dim, old memory blowing from a battlefield where hatred and violence had burned itself out in one lurid blast of strength.

But they were waiting. And they hadn't laughed.

GALACTIC CHEST

Perhaps providing us with a satirical portrait of the workings of a big-city newspaper of six decades ago, this story was rejected by editors H. F. Gold, John W. Campbell Jr., Anthony Boucher, and Leo Margulies before finally being purchased by Robert A. W. Lowndes more than a year later after it was first submitted in January 1955. It then saw its first publication in the September 1956 issue of Science Fiction Stories.

It's a lightweight story, no doubt, but there is value to be found in it, not least in its evocation of Cold War–era America (something Cliff viewed with regret, even alarm, in a number of stories written during that period). But I always chuckle a little as Cliff—as he did in several earlier stories—reprises a journalistic tradition of giving the nickname "Lightning" to the paper's copy boy.

—dww

I had just finished writing the daily Community Chest story, and each day I wrote that story I was sore about it; there were plenty of punks in the office who could have ground out that kind of copy. Even the copy boys could have written it and no one would have known the difference; no one ever read it—except maybe some of the drive chairmen, and I'm not even sure about them reading it.

I had protested to Barnacle Bill about my handling the Community Chest for another year. I had protested loud. I had said:

"Now, you know, Barnacle, I been writing that thing for three or four years. I write it with my eyes shut. You ought to get some new blood into it. Give one of the cubs a chance; they can breathe some life into it. Me, I'm all written out on it."

But it didn't do a bit of good. The Barnacle had me down on the assignment book for the Community Chest, and he never changed a thing once he put it in the book.

I wish I knew the real reason for that name of his. I've heard a lot of stories about how it was hung on him, but I don't think there's any truth in them. I think he got it simply from the way he can hang on to a bar.

I had just finished writing the Community Chest story and was sitting there, killing time and hating myself, when along came Jo Ann. Jo Ann was the sob sister on the paper; she got some lousy yarns to write, and that's a somber fact. I guess it was because I am of a sympathetic nature, and took pity on her, and let her cry upon my shoulder that we got to know each other so well. By now, of course, we figure we're in love; off and on we talk about getting married, as soon as I snag that foreign correspondent job I've been angling for.

"Hi, kid," I said.

And she says, "Do you know, Mark, what the Barnacle has me down for today?"

"He's finally ferreted out a one-armed paperhanger," I guessed, "and he wants you to do a feature. . . ."

"It's worse than that," she moans. "It's an old lady who is celebrating her one hundredth birthday."

"Maybe," I said, "she will give you a piece of her birthday cake."

"I don't see how even you can joke about a thing like this," Jo Ann told me. "It's positively ghastly."

Just then the Barnacle let out a bellow for me. So I picked up the Community Chest story and went over to the city desk.

—

Barnacle Bill is up to his elbows in copy; the phone is ringing and he's ignoring it, and for this early in the morning he has worked himself into more than a customary lather. "You remember old Mrs. Clayborne?"

"Sure, she's dead. I wrote the obit on her ten days or so ago."

"Well, I want you to go over to the house and snoop around a bit."

"What for?" I asked. "She hasn't come back, has she?"

"No, but there's some funny business over there. I got a tip that someone might have hurried her a little."

"This time," I told him, "you've outdone yourself. You've been watching too many television thrillers."

"I got it on good authority," he said and turned back to his work.

So I went and got my hat and told myself it was no skin off my nose how I spent the day; I'd get paid just the same!

But I was getting a little fed up with some of the wild-goose chases to which the Barnacle was assigning not only me, but the rest of the staff as well. Sometimes they paid off; usually, they didn't. And when they didn't, Barnacle had the nasty habit of making it appear that the man he had sent out, not he himself, had dreamed up the chase. His "good authority" probably was no more than some casual chatter of someone next to him at the latest bar he'd honored with his cash.

Old Mrs. Clayborne had been one of the last of the faded gentility which at one time had graced Douglas Avenue. The family had petered out, and she was the last of them; she had died in a big and lonely house with only a few servants, and a nurse in attendance on her, and no kin close enough to wait out her final hours in person.

It was unlikely, I told myself, that anyone could have profited by giving her an overdose of drugs, or otherwise hurrying her death. And even if it was true, there'd be little chance that it could be proved; and that was the kind of story you didn't run unless you had it down in black and white.

I went to the house on Douglas Avenue. It was a quiet and lovely place, standing in its fenced-in yard among the autumn-colored trees.

There was an old gardener raking leaves, and he didn't notice me when I went up the walk. He was an old man, pottering away and more than likely mumbling to himself, and I found out later that he was a little deaf.

I went up the steps, rang the bell and stood waiting, feeling cold at heart and wondering what I'd say once I got inside. I couldn't say what I had in mind; somehow or other I'd have to go about it by devious indirection.

A maid came to the door.

"Good morning, ma'am," I said. "I am from the *Tribune*. May I come in and talk?"

She didn't even answer; she looked at me for a moment and then slammed the door. I told myself I might have known that was the way it would be.

I turned around, went down the steps, and cut across the grounds to where the gardener was working. He didn't notice me until I was almost upon him; when he did see me, his face sort of lit up. He dropped the rake, and sat down on the wheelbarrow. I suppose I was as good an excuse as any for him to take a breather.

"Hello," I said to him.

"Nice day," he said to me.

"Indeed it is."

"You'll have to speak up louder," he told me; "I can't hear a thing you say."

"Too bad about Mrs. Clayborne," I told him.

"Yes, yes," he said. "You live around here? I don't recall your face."

I nodded; it wasn't much of a lie, just twenty miles or so.

"She was a nice old lady. Worked for her almost fifty years. It's a blessing she is gone."

"I suppose it is."

"She was dying hard," he said.

He sat nodding in the autumn sun and you could almost hear his mind go traveling back across those fifty years. I am certain that, momentarily, he'd forgotten I was there.

"Nurse tells a funny story," he said finally, speaking to himself more than he spoke to me. "It might be just imagining; Nurse was tired, you know."

"I heard about it," I encouraged him.

"Nurse left her just a minute and she swears there was something in the room when she came back again. Says it went out the window, just as she came in. Too dark to see it good, she says. I told her she was imagining. Funny things happen, though; things we don't know about."

"That was her room," I said, pointing at the house. "I remember, years ago . . ."

He chuckled at having caught me in the wrong. "You're mistaken, sonny. It was the corner one; that one over there."

He rose from the barrow slowly and took up the rake again.

"It was good to talk with you," I said. "These are pretty flowers you have. Mind if I walk around and have a look at them?"

"Might as well. Frost will get them in a week or so."

So I walked around the grounds, hating myself for what I had to do, and looking at the flowers, working my way closer to the corner of the house he had pointed out to me.

There was a bed of petunias underneath the window and they were sorry-looking things. I squatted down and pretended I was admiring them, although all the time I was looking for some evidence that someone might have jumped out the window.

I didn't expect to find it, but I did.

There, in a little piece of soft earth where the petunias had petered out, was a footprint—well, not a footprint, either, maybe, but anyhow a print. It looked something like a duck track—except that the duck that made it would have had to be as big as a good-sized dog.

I squatted on the walk, staring at it and I could feel spiders on my spine. Finally I got up and walked away, forcing myself to saunter when my body screamed to run.

Outside the gate I *did* run.

I got to a phone as fast as I could, at a corner drugstore, and sat in the booth a while to get my breathing back to normal before I put in a call to the city desk.

The Barnacle bellowed at me. "What you got?"

"I don't know," I said. "Maybe nothing. Who was Mrs. Clayborne's doctor?"

He told me. I asked him if he knew who her nurse had been, and he asked how the hell should he know, so I hung up.

I went to see the doctor and he threw me out.

I spent the rest of the day tracking down the nurse; when I finally found her she threw me out too. So there was a full day's work gone entirely down the drain.

It was late in the afternoon when I got back to the office. Barnacle Bill pounced on me at once. "What did you get?"

"Nothing," I told him. There was no use telling him about that track underneath the window. By that time, I was beginning to doubt I'd ever seen it, it seemed so unbelievable.

"How big do ducks get?" I asked him. He growled at me and went back to his work.

I looked at the next day's page in the assignment book. He had me down for the Community Chest, and: *See Dr. Thomas at Univ.—magnetism.*

"What's this?" I asked. "This magnetism business?"

"Guy's been working on it for years," said the Barnacle. "I got it on good authority he's set to pop with something."

There was that "good authority" again. And just about as hazy as the most of his hot tips.

And anyhow, I don't like to interview scientists. More often than not, they're a crochety set and are apt to look down their noses at newspapermen. Ten to one the newspaperman is earning more than they are—and in his own way, more than likely, doing just as good a job and with less fumbling.

I saw that Jo Ann was getting ready to go home, so I walked over to her and asked her how it went.

"I got a funny feeling in my gizzard, Mark," she told me. "Buy me a drink and I'll tell you all about it."

So we went down to the corner bar and took a booth way in the back.

Joe came over and he was grumbling about business, which was unusual for him. "If it weren't for you folks over at the paper," he said, "I'd close up and go home. That must be what all my customers are doing; they sure ain't coming here. Can you think of anything more disgusting than going straight home from your job?"

We told him that we couldn't, and to show that he appreciated our attitude he wiped off the table—a thing he almost never did.

He brought the drinks and Jo Ann told me about the old lady and her hundredth birthday. "It was horrible. There she sat in her rocking chair in that bare living room, rocking back and forth, gently, delicately, the way old ladies rock. And she was glad to see me, and she smiled so nice and she introduced me all around."

"Well, that was fine," I said. "Were there a lot of people there?"

"Not a soul."

I choked on my drink. "But you said she introduced . . ."

"She did. To empty chairs."

"Good Lord!"

"They all were dead," she said.

"Now, let's get this straight . . ."

"She said, 'Miss Evans, I want you to meet my old friend, Mrs. Smith. She lives just down the street. I recall the day she moved into the neighborhood, back in '33. Those were hard times, I tell you.' Chattering on, you know, like most old ladies do. And me, standing there and staring at an empty chair, wondering what to do. And, Mark, I don't know if I did right or not, but I said, 'Hello, Mrs. Smith. I am glad to know you.' And do you know what happened then?"

"No," I said. "How could I?"

"The old lady said, just as casually as could be—just conversationally, as if it were the most natural thing in all the world—'You know, Miss Evans, Mrs. Smith died three years ago. Don't you think it's nice she dropped in to see me?'"

"She was pulling your leg," I said. "Some of these old ones sometimes get pretty sly."

"I don't think she was. She introduced me all around; there were six or seven of them, and all of them were dead."

"She was happy, thinking they were there. What difference does it make?"

"It was horrible," said Jo Ann.

So we had another drink to chase away the horror.

Joe was still down in the mouth. "Did you ever see the like of it? You could shoot off a cannon in this joint and not touch a single soul. By this time, usually, they'd be lined up against the bar, and it'd be a dull evening if someone hadn't taken a poke at someone else—although you understand I run a decent place."

"Sure you do," I said. "Sit down and have a drink with us."

"It ain't right that I should," said Joe. "A bartender should never take a drink when he's conducting business. But I feel so low that if you don't mind, I'll take you up on it."

He went back to the bar and got a bottle and a glass and we had quite a few.

The corner, he said, had always been a good spot—steady business all the time, with a rush at noon and a good crowd in the evening. But business had started dropping off six weeks before, and now was down to nothing.

"It's the same all over town," he said, "some places worse than others. This place is one of the worst; I just don't know what's gotten into people."

We said we didn't, either. I fished out some money and left it for the drinks, and we made our escape.

Outside I asked Jo Ann to have dinner with me, but she said it was the night her bridge club met, so I drove her home and went on to my place.

I take a lot of ribbing at the office for living so far out of town, but I like it. I got the cottage cheap, and it's better than living in a couple of cooped-up rooms in a third-rate resident hotel—which would be the best I could afford if I stayed in town.

After I'd fixed up a steak and some fried potatoes for supper, I went down to the dock and rowed out into the lake a ways. I sat there for a while, watching the lighted windows winking all around the shore and listening to the sounds you never hear in daytime—the muskrat swimming and the soft chuckling of the ducks and the occasional slap of a jumping fish.

It was a bit chilly and after a little while I rowed back in again, thinking there was a lot to do before winter came. The boat should be caulked and painted; the cottage itself could take a coat of paint, if I could get around to it. There were a couple of storm windows that needed glass replaced, and by rights I should putty all of them. The chimney needed some bricks to replace the ones that had blown off in a windstorm earlier in the year, and the door should have new weatherstripping.

I sat around and read a while and then I went to bed. Just before I went to sleep I thought some about the two old ladies—one of them happy and the other dead.

The next morning I got the Community Chest story out of the way, first thing; then I got an encyclopedia from the library and did some reading on magnetism. I figured that I should know something about it, before I saw this whiz-bang at the university.

But I needn't have worried so much; this Dr. Thomas turned out to be a regular Joe. We sat around and had quite a talk. He told me about magnetism, and when he found out I lived at the lake he talked about fishing; then we found we knew some of the same people, and it was all right.

Except he didn't have a story.

"There may be one in another year or so," he told me. "When there is, I'll let you in on it."

I'd heard that one before, of course, so I tried to pin him down.

"It's a promise," he said; "you get it first, ahead of anyone."

I let it go at that. You couldn't ask the man to sign a contract on it.

I was watching for a chance to get away, but I could see he still had more to say. So I stayed on; it's refreshing to find someone who wants to talk to you.

"I think there'll be a story," he said, looking worried, as if he were afraid there mightn't be. "I've worked on it for years. Magnetism is still one of the phenomena we don't know too much about. Once we knew nothing about electricity, and even now we do not entirely understand it; but we found out about it, and when we knew enough about it, we put it to work. We could do the same with magnetism, perhaps—if we only could determine the first fundamentals of it."

He stopped and looked straight at me. "When you were a kid, did you believe in brownies?"

That one threw me and he must have seen it did.

"You remember—the little helpful people. If they liked you, they did all sorts of things for you; and all they expected of you was that you'd leave out a bowl of milk for them."

I told him I'd read the stories, and I supposed that at one time I must have believed in them—although right at the moment I couldn't swear I had.

"If I didn't know better," he said, "I'd think I had brownies in this lab. Someone—or something—shuffled my notes for me.

I'd left them on the desktop held down with a paperweight; the next morning they were spread all over, and part of them dumped onto the floor."

"A cleaning woman," I suggested.

He smiled at my suggestion. "I'm the cleaning woman here."

I thought he had finished and I wondered why all this talk of notes and brownies. I was reaching for my hat when he told me the rest of it.

"There were two sheets of the notes still underneath the paperweight," he said. "One of them had been folded carefully. I was about to pick them up, and put them with the other sheets so I could sort them later, when I happened to read what was on those sheets beneath the paperweight."

He drew a long breath. "They were two sections of my notes that, if left to myself, I probably never would have tied together. Sometimes we have strange blind spots; sometimes we look so closely at a thing that we are blinded to it. And there it was—two sheets laid there by accident. Two sheets, one of them folded to tie up with the other, to show me a possibility I'd never have thought of otherwise. I've been working on that possibility ever since; I have hopes it may work out."

"When it does . . ." I said.

"It is yours," he told me.

I got my hat and left.

And I thought idly of brownies all the way back to the office.

I had just got back to the office, and settled down for an hour or two of loafing, when old J. H.—our publisher—made one of his irregular pilgrimages of good will out into the newsroom. J. H. is a pompous windbag, without a sincere bone in his body; he knows we know this and we know he knows—but he, and all the rest of us, carry out the comedy of good fellowship to its bitter end.

He stopped beside my desk, clapped me on the shoulder, and said in a voice that boomed throughout the newsroom: "That's a tremendous job you're doing on the Community Chest, my boy."

Feeling a little sick and silly, I got to my feet and said, "Thank you, J. H.; it's nice of you to say so."

Which was what was expected of me. It was almost ritual.

He grabbed me by the hand, put the other hand on my shoulder, shook my hand vigorously and squeezed my shoulder hard. And I'll be damned if there weren't tears in his eyes as he told me, "You just stick around, Mark, and keep up the work. You won't regret it for a minute. We may not always show it, but we appreciate good work and loyalty and we're always watching what you do out here."

Then he dropped me like a hot potato and went on with his greetings.

I sat down again; the rest of the day was ruined for me. I told myself that if I deserved any commendation I could have hoped it would be for something other than the Community Chest stories. They were lousy stories; I knew it, and so did the Barnacle and all the rest of them. No one blamed me for their being lousy—you can't write anything but a lousy story on a Community Chest drive. But they weren't cheering me.

And I had a sinking feeling that, somehow, old J. H. had found out about the applications I had planted with a half dozen other papers and that this was his gentle way of letting me know he knew—and that I had better watch my step.

Just before noon, Steve Johnson—who handles the medical run along with whatever else the Barnacle can find for him to do—came over to my desk. He had a bunch of clippings in his hand and he was looking worried. "I hate to ask you this, Mark," he said, "but would you help me out?"

"Sure thing, Steve."

"It's an operation. I have to check on it, but I won't have the time. I got to run out to the airport and catch an interview."

He laid the clips down on my desk. "It's all in there."

Then he was off for his interview.

I picked up the clippings and read them through; it was a story that would break your heart.

There was this little fellow, about three years old, who had to have an operation on his heart. It was a piece of surgery that had been done only a time or two before, and then only in big Eastern hospitals by famous medical names—and never on one as young as three.

I hated to pick up the phone and call; I was almost sure the kind of answer I would get.

But I did, and naturally I ran into the kind of trouble you always run into when you try to get some information out of a hospital staff—as if they were shining pure and you were a dirty little mongrel trying to sneak in. But I finally got hold of someone who told me the boy seemed to be okay and that the operation appeared to be successful.

So I called the surgeon who had done the job. I must have caught him in one of his better moments, for he filled me in on some information that fit into the story.

"You are to be congratulated, Doctor," I told him and he got a little testy.

"Young man," he told me, "in an operation such as this the surgeon is no more than a single factor. There are so many other factors that no one can take credit."

Then suddenly he sounded tired and scared. "It was a miracle," he said.

"But don't you quote me on that," he fairly shouted at me.

"I wouldn't think of it," I told him.

Then I called the hospital again, and talked to the mother of the boy.

It was a good story. We caught the home edition with it, a four-column head on the left side of page one, and the Barnacle slipped a cog or two and gave me a byline on it.

After lunch I went back to Jo Ann's desk; she was in a tizzy. The Barnacle had thrown a church convention program at her and she was in the midst of writing an advance story, listing all the speakers and committee members and special panels and events. It's the deadliest kind of a story you can be told to write; it's worse, even, than the Community Chest.

I listened to her being bitter for quite a while; then I asked her if she figured she'd have any strength left when the day was over.

"I'm all pooped out," she said.

"Reason I asked," I told her, "is that I want to take the boat out of the water and I need someone to help me."

"Mark," she said, "if you expect me to go out there and horse a boat around . . ."

"You wouldn't have to lift," I told her. "Maybe just tug a little. We'll use a block and tackle to lift it on the blocks so that I can paint it later. All I need is someone to steady it while I haul it up."

She still wasn't sold on it, so I laid out some bait.

"We could stop downtown and pick up a couple of lobsters," I told her. "You are good at lobsters. I could make some of my Roquefort dressing, and we could have a . . ."

"But without the garlic," she said. So I promised to forego the garlic and she agreed to come.

Somehow or other, we never did get that boat out of the water; there were so many other things to do.

After dinner we built a fire in the fireplace and sat in front of it. She put her head on my shoulder and we were comfortable and cozy. "Let's play pretend," she said. "Let's pretend you have that job you want. Let's say it is in London, and this is a lodge in the English fens . . ."

"A fen," I said, "is a hell of a place to have a lodge."

"You always spoil things," she complained. "Let's start over again. Let's pretend you have that job you want . . ."

And she stuck to her fens.

Driving back to the lake after taking her home, I wondered if I'd ever get that job. Right at the moment it didn't look so rosy. Not that I couldn't have handled it, for I knew I could. I had racks of books on world affairs, and I kept close track of what was going on. I had a good command of French, a working knowledge of German, and off and on I was struggling with Spanish. It was something I'd wanted all my life—to feel that I was part of that fabulous newspaper fraternity which kept check around the world.

I overslept, and was late to work in the morning. The Barnacle took a sour view of it. "Why did you bother to come in at all?" he growled at me. "Why do you ever bother to come in? Last two days I sent you out on two assignments, and where are the stories?"

"There weren't any stories," I told him, trying to keep my temper. "They were just some more pipe dreams you dug up."

"Some day," he said, "when you get to be a real reporter, you'll dig up stories for yourself. That's what's the matter with this staff," he said in a sudden burst of anger. "That's what's wrong with you. No initiative; sit around and wait; wait until I dig up something I can send you out on. No one ever surprises me and brings in a story I haven't sent them out on."

He pegged me with his eyes. "Why don't you just once surprise me?"

"I'll surprise you, buster," I said and walked over to my desk.

I sat there thinking. I thought about old Mrs. Clayborne, who had been dying hard—and then suddenly had died easy. I remembered what the gardener had told me, and the footprint I had found underneath the window. I thought of that other old lady who had been a hundred years old, and how all her old, dead friends had come visiting. And about the physicist who had brownies in his lab. And about the boy and his successful operation.

And I got an idea.

I went to the files and went through them three weeks back, page by page. I took a lot of notes and got a little scared, but told myself it was nothing but coincidence.

Then I sat down at my typewriter and made half a dozen false starts, but finally I had it.

The brownies have come back again, I wrote.

You know, those little people who do all sorts of good deeds for you, and expect nothing in return except that you set out a bowl of milk for them.

At the time I didn't realize that I was using almost the exact words the physicist had said.

I didn't write about Mrs. Clayborne, or the old lady with her visitors, or the physicist, or the little boy who had the operation; those weren't things you could write about with your tongue in cheek, and that's the way I wrote it.

But I did write about the little two and three paragraph items I had found tucked away in the issues I had gone through—the good luck stories; the little happy stories of no consequence, except for the ones they had happened to—about people finding things they'd lost months or years ago, about stray dogs coming home, and kids winning essay contests, and neighbor helping neighbor. All the kindly little news stories that we'd thrown in just to fill up awkward holes.

There were a lot of them—a lot more, it seemed to me, than you could normally expect to find. *All these things happened in our town in the last three weeks*, I wrote at the end of it.

And I added one last line: *Have you put out that bowl of milk?*

After it was finished, I sat there for a while, debating whether I should hand it in. And thinking it over, I decided that the Barnacle had it coming to him, after the way he'd shot off his mouth.

So I threw it into the basket on the city desk and went back to write the Community Chest story.

The Barnacle never said a thing to me and I didn't say a thing to him; you could have knocked my eyes off with a stick when the kid brought the papers up from the pressroom, and there was my brownie story spread across the top of page one in an eight-column feature strip.

No one mentioned it to me except Jo Ann, who came along and patted me on the head and said she was proud of me—although God knows why she should have been.

Then the Barnacle sent me out on another one of his wild-goose chases concerning someone who was supposed to be building a homemade atomic pile in his back yard. It turned out that this fellow is an old geezer who, at one time, had built a perpetual motion machine that didn't work. Once I found that out, I was so disgusted that I didn't even go back to the office, but went straight home instead.

I rigged up a block and tackle, had some trouble what with no one to help me, but I finally got the boat up on the blocks. Then I drove to a little village at the end of the lake and bought paint not only for the boat, but the cottage as well. I felt pretty good about making such a fine start on all the work I should do that fall.

The next morning when I got to the office, I found the place in an uproar. The switchboard had been clogged all night and it still looked like a Christmas tree. One of the operators had passed out, and they were trying to bring her to.

The Barnacle had a wild gleam in his eye, and his necktie was all askew. When he saw me, he took me firmly by the arm and led me to my desk and sat me down. "Now, damn you, get to work!" he yelled and he dumped a bale of notes down in front of me.

"What's going on?" I asked.

"It's that brownie deal of yours," he yelled. "Thousands of people are calling in. All of them have brownies; they've been helped by brownies; some of them have even seen brownies."

"What about the milk?" I asked.

"Milk? What milk?"

"Why, the milk they should set out for them."

"How do I know?" he said. "Why don't you call up some of the milk companies and find out?"

That is just what I did—and, so help me Hannah, the milk companies were slowly going crazy. Every driver had come racing back to get extra milk, because most of their customers were ordering an extra quart or so. They were lined up for blocks outside the stations waiting for new loads and the milk supply was running low.

There weren't any of us in the newsroom that morning who did anything but write brownie copy. We filled the paper with it—all sorts of stories about how the brownies had been helping people. Except, of course, they hadn't known it was brownies helping them until they read my story. They'd just thought that it was good luck.

When the first edition was in, we sat back and sort of caught our breath—although the calls still were coming in—and I swear my typewriter still was hot from the copy I'd turned out.

The papers came up, and each of us took our copy and started to go through it, when we heard a roar from J. H.'s office. A second later, J. H. came out himself, waving a paper in his fist, his face three shades redder than a brand-new fire truck.

He practically galloped to the city desk and he flung the paper down in front of the Barnacle and hit it with his fist. "What do you mean?" he shouted. "Explain yourself. Making us ridiculous!"

"But, J. H., I thought it was a good gag and—"

"Brownies!" J. H. snorted.

"We got all those calls," said Barnacle Bill. "They still are coming in. And—"

"That's enough," J. H. thundered. "You're fired!"

He swung around from the city desk and looked straight at me. "You're the one who started it," he said. "You're fired, too."

I got up from my chair and moved over to the city desk. "We'll be back a little later," I told J. H., "to collect our severance pay."

He flinched a little at that, but he didn't back up any.

The Barnacle picked up an ash tray off his desk and let it fall. It hit the floor and broke. He dusted off his hands. "Come on, Mark," he said; "I'll buy you a drink."

—

We went over to the corner. Joe brought us a bottle and a couple of glasses, and we settled down to business.

Pretty soon some of the other boys started dropping in. They'd have a drink or two with us and then go back to work. It was their way of showing us they were sorry the way things had turned out. They didn't say anything, but they kept dropping in. There never was a time during the entire afternoon when there wasn't someone drinking with us. The Barnacle and I took on quite a load.

We talked over this brownie business and at first we were a little skeptical about it, laying the situation more or less to public gullibility. But the more we thought about it, and the more we drank, the more we began to believe there might really be brownies. For one thing, good luck just doesn't come in hunks the way it appeared to have come to this town of ours in the last few weeks. Good luck is apt to scatter itself around a bit—and while it may run in streaks, it's usually pretty thin. But here it seemed that hundreds—if not thousands—of persons had been visited by good luck.

By the middle of the afternoon, we were fairly well agreed there might be something to this brownie business. Then, of course, we tried to figure out who the brownies were, and why they were helping people.

"You know what I think," said Barnacle. "I think they're aliens. People from the stars. Maybe they're the ones who have been flying all these saucers."

"But why would aliens want to help us?" I objected. "Sure, they'd want to watch us and find out all they could; and after a while, they might try to make contact with us. They might even be willing to help us, but if they were they'd want to help us as a race, not as individuals."

"Maybe," the Barnacle suggested, "they're just busybodies. There are humans like that. Psychopathic do-gooders, always sticking in their noses, never letting well enough alone."

"I don't think so," I argued back at him. "If they are trying to help us, I'd guess it's a religion with them. Like the old friars who wandered all over Europe in the early days. Like the Good Samaritan. Like the Salvation Army."

But he wouldn't have it that way. "They're busybodies," he insisted. "Maybe they come from a surplus economy, a planet where all the work is done by machines and there is more than enough of everything for everyone. Maybe there isn't anything left for anyone to do—and you know yourself that a man has to have something to keep him occupied, something to do so he can think that he is important."

Then along about five o'clock Jo Ann came in. It had been her day off and she hadn't known what had happened until someone from the office phoned her. So she'd come right over.

She was plenty sore at me, and she wouldn't listen to me when I tried to explain that at a time like this a man had to have a drink or two. She got me out of there and out back to my car and drove me to her place. She fed me black coffee and finally gave me something to eat and along about eight o'clock or so she figured I'd sobered up enough to try driving home.

I took it easy and I made it, but I had an awful head and I remembered that I didn't have a job. Worst of all, I was probably tagged for life as the man who had dreamed up the brownie hoax. There was no doubt that the wire services had picked up the story, and that it had made front page in most of the papers coast to coast. No doubt, the radio and television commentators were doing a lot of chuckling at it.

My cottage stands up on a sharp little rise above the lake, a sort of hog's back between the lake and road, and there's no road up to it. I had to leave my car alongside the road at the foot of the rise, and walk up to the place.

I walked along, my head bent a little so I could see the path in the moonlight, and I was almost to the cottage before I heard a sound that made me raise my head.

And there they were.

They had rigged up a scaffold and there were four of them on it, painting the cottage madly. Three of them were up on the roof replacing the bricks that had been knocked out of the chimney. They had storm windows scattered all over the place and were furiously applying putty to them. And you could scarcely see the boat, there were so many of them slapping paint on it.

I stood there staring at them, with my jaw hanging on my breastbone, when I heard a sudden *swish* and stepped quickly to one side. About a dozen of them rushed by, reeling out the hose, running down the hill with it. Almost in a shorter time than it takes to tell it, they were washing the car.

They didn't seem to notice me. Maybe it was because they were so busy they didn't have the time to—or it might have been just that it wasn't proper etiquette to take notice of someone when they were helping him.

They looked a lot like the brownies that you see pictured in the children's books, but there were differences. They wore pointed caps, all right, but when I got close to one of them who was busy puttying, I could see that it was no cap at all. His head ran up to a point, and the tassle on the top of it was no tassle of a cap, but a tuft of hair or feathers—I couldn't make out which. They wore coats with big fancy buttons on them, but I got the impression— I don't know how—that they weren't buttons, but something else entirely. And instead of the big sloppy clown-type shoes they're usually shown as wearing, they had nothing on their feet.

They worked hard and fast; they didn't waste a minute. They didn't walk, but ran. And there were so many of them.

Suddenly they were finished. The boat was painted, and so was the cottage. The puttied, painted storm windows were leaned against the trees. The hose was dragged up the hill and neatly coiled again.

I saw that they were finishing and I tried to call them all together so that I could thank them, but they paid no attention to me. And when they were finished, they were gone. I was left standing, all alone—with the newly painted cottage shining in the moonlight and the smell of paint heavy in the air.

I suppose I wasn't exactly sober, despite the night air and all the coffee Jo Ann had poured into me. If I had been cold, stone sober I might have done it better; I might have thought of something. As it was, I'm afraid I bungled it.

I staggered into the house, and the outside door seemed a little hard to shut. When I looked for the reason, I saw it had been weather-stripped.

With the lights on, I looked around—and in all the time I'd been there the place had never been so neat. There wasn't a speck of dust on anything and all the metal shone. All the pots and pans were neatly stacked in place; all the clothing I had left strewn around had been put away; all the books were lined straight within the shelves, and the magazines were where they should be instead of just thrown anywhere.

I managed to get into bed, and I tried to think about it; but someone came along with a heavy mallet and hit me on the head and that was the last I knew until I was awakened by a terrible racket.

I got to it as fast as I could.

"What is it now?" I snarled, which is no way to answer a phone, but was the way I felt.

It was J. H. "What's the matter with you?" he yelled. "Why aren't you at the office? What do you mean by . . ."

"Just a minute, J. H.; don't you remember? You canned me yesterday."

"Now, Mark," he said, "you wouldn't hold that against me, would you? We were all excited . . ."

"*I* wasn't excited," I told him.

"Look," he said, "I need you. There's someone here to see you."

"All right," I said and hung up.

I didn't hurry any; I took my time. If J. H. needed me, if there was someone there to see me, both of them could wait. I turned on the coffee maker and took a shower; after the shower and coffee, I felt almost human.

I was crossing the yard, heading for the path down to the car, when I saw something that stopped me like a shot.

There were tracks in the dust, tracks all over the place—exactly the kind of tracks I'd seen in the flower bed underneath the window at the Clayborne estate. I squatted down and looked closely at them to make sure there was no mistake and there couldn't be. They were the self-same tracks.

They were brownie tracks!

I stayed there for a long time, squatting beside the tracks and thinking that now it was all believable because there was no longer any room for disbelief.

The nurse had been right; there had been something in the room that night Mrs. Clayborne died. It was a mercy, the old gardener said, his thoughts and speech all fuzzed with the weariness and the basic simplicity of the very old. An act of mercy, a good deed, for the old lady had been dying hard, no hope for her.

And if there were good deeds in death, there were as well in life. In an operation such as this, the surgeon had told me, there are so many factors that no one can take the credit. It was a miracle, he'd said, but don't you quote me on it.

And someone—no cleaning woman, but someone or something else—had messed up the notes of the physicist and in the messing of them had put together two pages out of several hundred—two pages that tied together and made sense.

Coincidence? I asked myself. Coincidence that a woman died and that a boy lived, and that a researcher got a clue he'd otherwise have missed? No, not coincidence when there was a track beneath a window and papers scattered from beneath a paperweight.

And—I'd almost forgotten—Jo Ann's old lady who sat rocking happily because all her old dead friends had come to visit her. There were even times when senility might become a very kindness.

I straightened up and went down to the car. As I drove into town I kept thinking about the magic touch of kindness from the stars or if, perhaps, there might be upon this earth, coexistent with the human race, another race that had a different outlook and a different way of life. A race, perhaps, that had tried time and time again to ally itself with the humans and each time had been rejected and driven into hiding—sometimes by ignorance and superstition and again by a too-brittle knowledge of what was impossible. A race, perhaps, that might be trying once again.

J. H. was waiting for me, looking exactly like a cat sitting serenely inside a bird cage, with feathers on his whiskers. With him was a high brass flyboy, who had a rainbow of decorations spread across his jacket and eagles on his shoulders. They shone so bright and earnestly that they almost sparkled.

"Mark, this is Colonel Duncan," said J. H. "He'd like to have a word with you."

The two of us shook hands and the colonel was more affable than one would have expected him to be. Then J. H. left us in his office and shut the door behind him. The two of us sat down and each of us sort of measured up the other. I don't know how the colonel felt, but I was ready to admit I was uncomfortable. I wondered what I might have done and what the penalty might be.

"I wonder, Lathrop," said the colonel, "if you'd mind telling me exactly how it happened. How you found out about the brownies?"

"I didn't find out about them, Colonel; it was just a gag."

I told him about the Barnacle shooting off his mouth about no one on the staff ever showing any initiative, and how I'd dreamed up the brownie story to get even with him. And how the Barnacle had got even with me by running it.

But that didn't satisfy the colonel. "There must be more to it than that," he said.

I could see that he'd keep at me until I'd told it, anyhow; and while he hadn't said a word about it, I kept seeing images of the Pentagon, and the chiefs of staff, and Project Saucer—or whatever they might call it now—and the FBI, and a lot of other unpleasant things just over his left shoulder.

So I came clean with him. I told him all of it and a lot of it, I granted, sounded downright silly.

But he didn't seem to think that it was silly. "And what do you think about all this?"

"I don't know," I told him. "They might come from outer space, or . . ."

He nodded quietly. "We've known for some time now that there have been landings. This is the first time they've ever deliberately called attention to themselves."

"What do they want, Colonel? What are they aiming at?"

"I wish I knew."

Then he said very quietly, "Of course, if you should write anything about this, I shall simply deny it. That will leave you in a most peculiar position at best."

I don't know how much more he might have told me—maybe quite a bit. But right then the phone rang. I picked it up and answered; it was for the colonel.

He said "Yes," and listened. He didn't say another word. He got a little white around the gills; then he hung up the phone.

He sat there, looking sick.

"What's the matter, Colonel?"

"That was the field," he told me. "It happened just a while ago. They came out of nowhere and swarmed all over the plane—polished it and cleaned it and made it spic and span, both inside and out. The men couldn't do a thing about it. They just had to stand and watch."

I grinned. "There's nothing bad about that, Colonel. They were just being good to you."

"You don't know the half of it," he said. "When they got it all prettied up, they painted a brownie on the nose."

That's just about all there's to it as far as the brownies are concerned. The job they did on the colonel's plane was, actually, the sole public appearance that they made. But it was enough to serve their purpose if publicity was what they wanted—a sort of visual clincher, as it were. One of our photographers—a loopy character by the name of Charles, who never was where you wanted him when you wanted him, but nevertheless seemed to be exactly on the spot when the unusual or disaster struck—was out at the airport that morning. He wasn't supposed to be there; he was supposed to be covering a fire, which turned out luckily to be no more than a minor blaze. How he managed to wind up at the airport even he, himself, never was able to explain. But he was there and he got the pictures of the brownies polishing up the plane—not only one or two pictures, but a couple dozen of them, all the plates he had. Another thing—he got the pictures with a telescopic lens. He'd put it in his bag that morning by mistake; he'd never carried it before. After that one time he never was without it again and, to my knowledge, never had another occasion where he had to use it.

Those pictures were a bunch of lulus. We used the best of them on page one—a solid page of them—and ran two more pages of the rest inside. The AP got hold of them, transmitted them, and a number of other member papers used them before someone at the Pentagon heard about it and promptly blew his stack. But no matter what the Pentagon might say, the pictures had been run and whatever harm—or *good*—they might have done could not be recalled.

I suppose that if the colonel had known about them, he'd have warned us not to use them and might have confiscated them. But no one knew the pictures had been taken until the colonel was out of town, and probably back in Washington. Charlie got waylaid somehow—at a beer joint most likely—and didn't get back to the office until the middle of the afternoon.

When he heard about it, J. H. paced up and down and tore his hair and threatened to fire Charlie; but some of the rest of us got him calmed down and back into his office. We caught the pictures in our final street edition, picked the pages up for the early runs next day, and the circulation boys were pop-eyed for days at the way those papers sold.

The next day, after the worst of the excitement had subsided, the Barnacle and I went down to the corner to have ourselves a couple. I had never cared too much for the Barnacle before, but the fact that we'd been fired together established a sort of bond between us; and he didn't seem to be such a bad sort, after all.

Joe was as sad as ever. "It's them brownies," he told us, and he described them in a manner no one should ever use when talking of a brownie. "They've gone and made everyone so happy they don't need to drink no more."

"Both you and me, Joe," said the Barnacle; "they ain't done nothing for me, either."

"You got your job back," I told him.

"Mark," he said, solemnly, pouring out another. "I'm not so sure if that is good or not."

It might have developed into a grade-A crying session if Lightning, our most up-and-coming copy boy, had not come shuffling in at that very moment.

"Mr. Lathrop," he said, "there's a phone call for you."

"Well, that's just fine."

"But it's from New York," said the kid.

That did it. It's the first time in my life I ever left a place so fast that I forgot my drink.

The call was from one of the papers to which I had applied, and the man at the New York end told me there was a job opening in the London staff and that he'd like to talk with me about it. In itself, it probably wasn't any better than the job I had, he said, but it would give me a chance to break in on the kind of work I wanted.

When could I come in? he asked, and I said tomorrow morning.

I hung up and sat back and the world all at once looked rosy. I knew right then and there those brownies still were working for me.

I had a lot of time to think on the plane trip to New York; and while I spent some of it thinking about the new job and London, I spent a lot of it thinking about the brownies, too.

They'd come to Earth before, that much at least was clear. And the world had not been ready for them. It had muffled them in a fog of folklore and superstition, and had lacked the capacity to use what they had offered it. Now they tried again. This time we must not fail them, for there might not be a third time.

Perhaps one of the reasons they had failed before—although not the only reason—had been the lack of a media of mass communications. The story of them, and of their deeds and doings, had gone by word of mouth and had been distorted in the telling. The fantasy of the age attached itself to the story of the brownies until they became no more than a magic little people who were very droll, and on occasion helpful, but in the same category as the ogre, or the dragon, and others of their ilk.

Today it had been different. Today there was a better chance the brownies would be objectively reported. And while the entire story could not be told immediately, the people could still guess.

And that was important—the publicity they got. People must know they were back again, and must believe in them and trust them.

And why, I wondered, had one medium-sized city in the midwest of America been chosen as the place where they would make known their presence and demonstrate their worth? I puzzled a lot about that one, but I never did get it figured out, not even to this day.

—

Jo Ann was waiting for me at the airport when I came back from New York with the job tucked in my pocket. I was looking for her when I came down the ramp and I saw that she'd got past the gate and was running toward the plane. I raced out to meet her and I scooped her up and kissed her and some damn fool popped a flash bulb at us. I wanted to mop up on him, but Jo Ann wouldn't let me.

It was early evening and you could see some stars shining in the sky, despite the blinding floodlights; from way up, you could hear another plane that had just taken off; and up at the far end of the field, another one was warming up. There were the buildings and the lights and the people and the great machines and it seemed, for a long moment, like a table built to represent the strength and swiftness, the competence and assurance of this world of ours.

Jo Ann must have felt it, too, for she said suddenly: "It's nice, Mark. I wonder if they'll change it."

I knew who she meant without even asking.

"I think I know what they are," I told her; "I think I got it figured out. You know that Community Chest drive that's going on right now. Well, that's what they are doing, too—a sort of Galactic Chest. Except that they aren't spending money on the poor and needy; their kind of charity is a different sort. Instead of spending money on us, they're spending love and kindness, neighborliness and brotherhood. And I guess that it's all right. I wouldn't wonder but that, of all the people in the universe, we are the ones who need it most. They didn't come to solve all our problems for us—just to help clear away some of the little problems that somehow keep us from turning our full power on the important jobs, or keep us from looking at them in the right way."

That was more years ago than I like to think about, but I still can remember just as if it were yesterday.

Something happened yesterday that brought it all to mind again.

I happened to be in Downing Street, not too far from No. 10, when I saw a little fellow I first took to be some sort of dwarf. When I turned to look at him, I saw that he was watching me; he raised one hand in an emphatic gesture, with the thumb and first finger made into a circle—the good, solid American signal that everything's okay.

Then he disappeared. He probably ducked into an alley, although I can't say for a fact I actually saw him go.

But he was right. Everything's okay.

The world is bright, and the cold war is all but over. We may be entering upon the first true peace the human race has ever known.

Jo Ann is packing, and crying as she packs, because she has to leave so many things behind. But the kids are goggle-eyed about the great adventure just ahead. Tomorrow morning we leave for Peking, where I'll be the first accredited American correspondent for almost thirty years.

And I can't help but wonder if, perhaps, somewhere in that ancient city—perhaps in a crowded, dirty street; perhaps along the imperial highway; maybe some day out in the country beside the Great Wall, built so fearsomely so many years ago—I may not see another little man.

DEATH SCENE

This story ended up being published for the first time in the October 1957 issue of Infinity Science Fiction, *which was being edited by Larry Shaw at the time, but that only happened because the story had been rejected by H. F. Gold, John W. Campbell Jr., and Anthony Boucher (in his journal, Cliff tended to identify his markets by the names of their editors—perhaps an indication of the importance he placed on personal relations).*

This is a story about the world finding a way to achieve total peace—but at the cost of it becoming a world different from the one everybody knew. And it's sobering to ponder how a person could handle that transition. Would you be willing to pay any price for such a world?

—*dww*

She was waiting on the stoop of the house when he turned into the driveway and as he wheeled the car up the concrete and brought it to a halt he was certain she knew, too.

She had just come from the garden and had one arm full of flowers and she was smiling at him just a shade too gravely.

He carefully locked the car and put the keys away in the pocket of his jacket and reminded himself once again, "Matter-of-factly, friend. For it is better this way."

And that was the truth, he reassured himself. It was much better than the old way. It gave a man some time.

He was not the first and he would not be the last and for some of them it was rough, and for others, who had prepared themselves, it was not so rough and in time, perhaps, it would become a ritual so beautiful and so full of dignity one would look forward to it. It was more civilized and more dignified than the old way had been and in another hundred years or so there could be no doubt that it would become quite acceptable. All that was wrong with it now, he told himself, was that it was too new. It took a little time to become accustomed to this way of doing things after having done them differently through all of human history.

He got out of the car and went up the walk to where she waited for him. He stooped and kissed her and the kiss was a little longer than was their regular custom—and a bit more tender. And as he kissed her he smelled the summer flowers she carried, and he thought how appropriate it was that he should at this time smell the flowers from the garden they both loved.

"You know," he said and she nodded at him.

"Just a while ago," she said. "I knew you would be coming home. I went out and picked the flowers."

"The children will be coming, I imagine."

"Of course," she said, "They will come right away."

He looked at his watch, more from force of habit than a need to know the time. "There is time," he said. "Plenty of time for all of them to get here. I hope they bring the kids."

"Certainly they will," she said. "I went to phone them once, then I thought how silly."

He nodded. "We're of the old school, Florence. It's hard even yet to accept this thing—to know the children will know and come almost as soon as we know. It's still a little hard to be sure of a thing like that."

She patted his arm. "The family will be all together. There'll be time to talk. We'll have a splendid visit."

"Yes, of course," he said.

He opened the door for her and she stepped inside.

"What pretty flowers," he said.

"They've been the prettiest this year that they have ever been."

"That vase," he said. "The one you got last birthday. The blue and gold. That's the one to use."

"That's exactly what I thought. On the dining table."

She went to get the vase and he stood in the living room and thought how much he was a part of this room and this room a part of him. He knew every inch of it and it knew him as well and it was a friendly place, for he'd spent years making friends with it.

Here he'd walked the children of nights when they had been babies and been ill of cutting teeth or croup or colic, nights when the lights in this room had been the only lights in the entire block. Here the family had spent many evening hours in happiness and peace—and it had been a lovely thing, the peace. For he could remember the time when there had been no peace, nowhere in the world, and no thought or hope of peace, but in its place the ever-present dread and threat of war, a dread that had been so commonplace that you scarcely noticed it, a dread you came to think was a normal part of living.

Then, suddenly, there had been the dread no longer, for you could not fight a war if your enemy could look ahead an entire day and see what was about to happen. You could not fight a war and you could not play a game of baseball or any sort of game, you could not rob or cheat or murder, you could not make a killing in the market. There were a lot of things you could no longer do and there were times when it spoiled a lot of fun, for surprise and anticipation had been made impossible. It took a lot of getting used to and a lot of readjustment, but you were safe, at least, for there could be no war—not only at the moment, but forever and forever, and you knew that not only were you safe, but your children safe as well and their children and your children's children's children and you were willing to pay almost any sort of price for such complete assurance.

It is better this way, he told himself, standing in the friendly room. It is much better this way. Although at times it's hard.

He walked across the room and through it to the porch and stood on the porch steps looking at the flowers. Florence was right, he thought; they were prettier this year than any year before. He tried to remember back to some year when they might have been prettier, but he couldn't quite be sure. Maybe the autumn when young John had been a baby, for that year the mums and asters had been particularly fine. But that was unfair, he told himself, for it was not autumn now, but summer. It was impossible to compare summer flowers with autumn. Or the year when Mary had been ill so long—the lilacs had been so deeply purple and had smelled so sweet; he remembered bringing in great bouquets of them each evening because she loved them so. But that was no comparison, for the lilacs bloomed in spring.

A neighbor went past on the sidewalk outside the picket fence and he spoke gravely to her: "Good afternoon, Mrs. Abrams."

"Good afternoon, Mr. Williams," she said and that was the way it always was, except on occasions she would stop a moment and they'd talk about the flowers. But today she would not stop unless he made it plain he would like to have her stop, for otherwise she would not wish to intrude upon him.

That was the way it had been at the office, he recalled.

He'd put away his work with sure and steady hands—as sure and steady as he could manage them. He'd walked to the rack and got down his hat and no one had spoken to him, not a single one of them had kidded him about his quitting early, for all had guessed—or known—as well as he. You could not always tell, of course, for the foresight ability was more pronounced in some than it was in others, although the lag in even the least efficient of them would not be more than a quarter-hour at most.

He'd often wished he could understand how it had been brought about, but there were factors involved he could not even remotely grasp. He knew the story, of course, for he could remember the night that it had happened and the excitement there had been—and the consternation. But knowing how it came about and the reason for it was quite a different thing from understanding it.

It had been an ace in the hole, a move of desperation to be used only as a last resort. The nation had been ready for a long time with the transmitters all set up and no one asking any questions because everyone had taken it for granted they were a part of the radar network and, in that case, the less said of them the better.

No one had wanted to use those transmitters, or at least that had been the official explanation after they'd been used—but anything was better than another war.

So the time had come, the time of last resort, the day of desperation, and the switches had been flicked, blanketing the nation with radiations that did something to the brain—"stimulating latent abilities" was as close a general explanation as anyone had made—and all at once everyone had been able to see twenty-four hours ahead.

There'd been hell to pay, of course, for quite a little while, but after a time it simmered down and the people settled down to make the best of it, to adapt and live with their strange new ability.

The President had gone on television to tell the world what had happened and he had warned potential enemies that we'd know twenty-four hours ahead of time exactly what they'd do. In consequence of which they did exactly nothing except to undo a number of incriminating moves they had already made—some of which the President had foretold that they would undo, naming the hour and place and the manner of their action.

He had said the process was no secret and that other nations were welcome to the know-how if they wanted it, although it made but little difference if they did or not, for the radiations in time would spread throughout the entire world and would affect all people. It was a permanent change, he said, for the ability was inheritable and would be passed on from one generation to the next, and never again, for good or evil, would the human race be blind as it had been in the past.

So finally there had been peace, but there'd been a price to pay. Although, perhaps, not too great a price, Williams told himself. He'd liked baseball, he recalled, and there could be no baseball now, for it was a pointless thing to play a game the outcome of which you'd know a day ahead of time. He had liked to have the boys in occasionally for a round of poker—but poker was just as pointless now and as impossible as baseball or football or horse racing or any other sport.

There had been many changes, some of them quite awkward. Take newspapers, for example, and radio and television reporting of the news. Political tactics had been forced to undergo a change, somewhat for the better, and gambling and crime had largely disappeared.

Mostly, it had been for the best. Although even some of the best was a little hard at first—and some of it would take a long time to become completely accustomed to.

Take his own situation now, he thought.

A lot more civilized than in the old days, but still fairly hard to take. Hard especially on Florence and the children, forcing them into a new and strange attitude that in time would harden into custom and tradition, but now was merely something new and strange. But Florence was standing up to it admirably, he thought. They'd often talked of it, especially in these last few years, and they had agreed that no matter which of them it was they would keep it calm and dignified, for that was the only way to face it. It was one of the payments that you made for peace, although sometimes it was a little hard to look at it that way.

But there were certain compensations. Florence and he could have a long talk before the children arrived. There'd be a chance to go over certain final details—finances and insurance and other matters of like nature. Under the old way there would have been, he told himself, no chance at all for that. There'd be the opportunity to do all the little worthwhile things, all the final sentimental gestures, that except for the foresight ability would have been denied.

There'd be talk with the children and the neighbors bringing things to eat and the big bouquet of flowers the office gang would send—the flowers that under other circumstances he never would have seen. The minister would drop in for a moment and manage to get in a quiet word or two of comfort, all the time making it seem to be no more than a friendly call. In the morning the mail would bring many little cards and notes of friendship sent by people who wanted him to know they thought of him and would have liked to have been with him if there had been the time. But they would not intrude, for the time that was left was a family time.

The family would sit and talk, remembering the happy days—the dog that Eddie had and the time John had run away from home for an hour or two and the first time Mary had ever had a date and the dress she wore. They'd take out the snapshot albums and look at the pictures, recalling all the days of bittersweetness and would know that theirs had been a good life—and especially he would know. And through it all would run the happy clatter of grandchildren playing in the house, climbing up on Granddad's knee to have him tell a story.

All so civilized, he thought.

Giving all of them a chance to prove they were civilized. He'd have to go back inside the house now, for he could hear Florence arranging the flowers in the birthday vase that was blue and gold. And they had so much to say to one another—even after forty years they still had so much to say to one another.

He turned and glanced back at the garden.

Most beautiful flowers, he thought, that they had ever raised.

He'd go out in the morning, when the dew was on them, when they were most beautiful, to bid them all good-bye.

CENSUS

Sent to Astounding Science Fiction *in January 1944, "Census," the third story in the series that became the City cycle, was returned to the author "to be resubmitted"—presumably after revision. It was indeed resubmitted, early in April, and it was purchased later that month for $175 and published in the September 1944 issue. It is the story that set up the themes that would form the basis for the City cycle; and that may explain the length of time—very unusual for Cliff Simak—taken to make his revisions.*

There have been those who have opined that "Census" was so important a story as to have been worthy of a retroactive Hugo. But, for me, the story is stolen, within its first page, by a little black dog who makes me smile whenever I think of him.

—dww

Richard Grant was resting beside the little spring that gushed out of the hillside and tumbled in a flashing stream across the twisting trail when the squirrel rushed past him and shinnied up a towering hickory tree. Behind the squirrel, in a cyclone of churning autumn-fallen leaves, came the little black dog.

When he saw Grant the dog skidded to a stop, stood watching him, tail wagging, eyes a-dance with fun.

Grant grinned. "Hello, there," he said.

"Hi," said the dog.

Grant jerked out of his easy slouch, jaw hanging limp. The dog laughed back at him, red dish rag of a tongue lolling from its mouth.

Grant jerked a thumb at the hickory. "Your squirrel's up there."

"Thanks," said the dog. "I know it. I can smell him."

Startled, Grant looked swiftly around, suspecting a practical joke. Ventriloquism, maybe. But there was no one in sight. The woods were empty except for himself and the dog, the gurgling spring, the squirrel chattering in the tree.

The dog walked closer.

"My name," he said, "is Nathaniel."

The words were there. There was no doubt of it. Almost like human speech, except they were pronounced carefully, as one who was learning the language might pronounce them. And a brogue, an accent that could not be placed, a certain eccentricity of intonation.

"I live over the hill," declared Nathaniel, "with the Websters."

He sat down, beat his tail upon the ground, scattering leaves. He looked extremely happy.

Grant suddenly snapped his fingers.

"Bruce Webster! Now I know. Should have thought of it before. Glad to meet you, Nathaniel."

"Who are you?" asked Nathaniel.

"Me? I'm Richard Grant, enumerator."

"What's an enum . . . enumer—"

"An enumerator is someone who counts people," Grant explained. "I'm taking a census."

"There are lots of words," said Nathaniel, "that I can't say."

He got up and walked over to the spring, lapped noisily. Finished, he plunked himself down beside the man.

"Want to shoot the squirrel?" he asked.

"Want me to?"

"Sure thing," said Nathaniel.

But the squirrel was gone. Together they circled the tree, searching its almost bare branches. There was no bushy tail sticking out from behind the boll, no beady eyes staring down at them. While they had talked, the squirrel had made his getaway.

Nathaniel looked a bit crestfallen, but he made the best of it.

"Why don't you spend the night with us?" he invited. "Then, come morning, we could go hunting. Spend all day at it."

Grant chuckled. "I wouldn't want to trouble you. I am used to camping out."

Nathaniel insisted. "Bruce would be glad to see you. And Grandpa wouldn't mind. He don't know half what goes on, anyway."

"Who's Grandpa?"

"His real name is Thomas," said Nathaniel, "but we all call him Grandpa. He is Bruce's father. Awful old now. Just sits all day and thinks about a thing that happened long ago."

Grant nodded. "I know about that, Nathaniel. Juwain."

"Yeah, that's it," agreed Nathaniel. "What does it mean?"

Grant shook his head. "Wish I could tell you, Nathaniel. Wish I knew."

He hoisted the pack to his shoulder, stooped and scratched the dog behind the ear. Nathaniel grimaced with delight.

"Thanks," he said, and started up the path.

Grant followed.

Thomas Webster sat in his wheel chair on the lawn and stared out across the evening hills.

I'll be eighty-six tomorrow, he was thinking. Eighty-six. That's a hell of a long time for a man to live. Maybe too long. Especially when he can't walk any more and his eyes are going bad.

Elsie will have a silly cake for me with lots of candles on it and the robots all will bring me a gift and those dogs of Bruce's will come in and wish me happy returns of the day and wag their tails at me. And there will be a few televisor calls—although not many, perhaps. And I'll pound my chest and say I'm going to live to be one hundred and everyone will grin behind their hands and say "listen to the old fool."

Eighty-six years and there were two things I meant to do. One of them I did and the other one I didn't.

A cawing crow skimmed over a distant ridge and slanted down into the valley shadow. From far away, down by the river, came the quacking of a flock of mallards.

Soon the stars would be coming out. Came out early this time of year. He liked to look at them. The stars! He patted the arms of the chair with fierce pride. The stars, by Lord, were his meat. An obsession? Perhaps—but at least something to wipe out that stigma of long ago, a shield to keep the family from the gossip of historic busybodies. And Bruce was helping, too. Those dogs of his—

A step sounded in the grass behind him.

"Your whiskey, sir," said Jenkins.

Thomas Webster stared at the robot, took the glass off the tray.

"Thank you, Jenkins," he said.

He twirled the glass between his fingers. "How long, Jenkins, have you been lugging drinks to this family?"

"Your father, sir," said Jenkins. "And his father before him."

"Any news?" asked the old man.

Jenkins shook his head. "No news."

Thomas Webster sipped the drink. "That means, then, that they're well beyond the solar system. Too far out even for the Pluto station to relay. Halfway or better to Alpha Centauri. If only I live long enough—"

"You will, sir," Jenkins told him. "I feel it in my bones."

"You," declared the old man, "haven't any bones."

He sipped the drink slowly, tasting it with expert tongue. Watered too much again. But it wouldn't do to say anything. No use flying off the handle at Jenkins. That doctor. Telling Jenkins to water it a bit more. Depriving a man of proper drinking in his final years—

"What's that down there?" he asked, pointing to the path that straggled up the hill.

Jenkins turned to look.

"It appears, sir," he said, "that Nathaniel's bringing someone home."

The dogs had trooped in to say goodnight, had left again.

Bruce Webster grinned after them.

"Great gang," he said.

He turned to Grant. "I imagine Nathaniel gave you quite a start this afternoon."

Grant lifted the brandy glass, squinted through it at the light.

"He did," he said. "Just for a minute. And then I remembered things I'd read about what you're doing here. It isn't in my line, of course, but your work has been popularized, written up in more or less nontechnical language."

"Your line?" asked Webster. "I thought—"

Grant laughed. "I see what you mean. A census taker. An enumerator. All of that, I grant you."

Webster was puzzled, just a bit embarrassed. "I hope, Mr. Grant, that I haven't—"

"Not at all," Grant told him. "I'm used to being regarded as someone who writes down names and ages and then goes on to the next group of human beings. That was the old idea of a census, of course. A nose counting, nothing more. A matter of statistics. After all, the last census was taken more than three hundred years ago. And times have changed."

"You interest me," said Webster. "You make this nose counting of yours sound almost sinister."

"It isn't sinister," protested Grant. "It's logical. It's an evaluation of the human population. Not just how many of them there are, but what are they really like, what are they thinking and doing?"

Webster slouched lower in his chair, stretching his feet out toward the fire upon the hearth. "Don't tell me, Mr. Grant, that you intend to psychoanalyze me?"

Grant drained the brandy glass, set it on the table. "I don't need to," he said. "The World Committee knows all it needs to know about the folks like you. But it is the others—the ridge runners, you call them here. Up north they're jackpine savages. Farther south they're something else. A hidden population—an almost forgotten population. The ones who took to the woods. The ones who scampered off when the World Committee loosened the strings of government."

Webster grunted. "The governmental strings had to be loosened," he declared. "History will prove that to anyone. Even before the World Committee came into being the governmental setup of the world was burdened by oxcart survivals. There was no more reason for the township government three hundred years ago than there is for a national government today."

"You're absolutely right," Grant told him, "and yet when the grip of government was loosened, its hold upon the life of each man was loosened. The man who wanted to slip away and live outside his government, losing its benefits and escaping its obligations, found it an easy thing to do. The World Committee didn't mind. It had more things to worry over than the irresponsibles and malcontents. And there were plenty of them. The farmers, for instance, who lost their way of life with the coming of hydroponics. Many of them found it hard to fit into industrial life. So what? So they slipped away. They reverted to a primitive life. They raised a few crops, they hunted game, they trapped, they cut wood, did a little stealing now and then. Deprived of a livelihood, they went back to the soil, all the way back, and the soil took care of them."

"That was three hundred years ago," said Webster. "The World Committee didn't mind about them then. It did what it could, of course, but as you say, it didn't really mind if a few slipped through its fingers. So why this sudden interest now?"

"Just, I guess," Grant told him, "that they've got around to it."

He regarded Webster closely, studying the man. Relaxed before the fire, his face held power, the shadows of the leaping flames etching planes upon his features, turning them almost surrealistic.

Grant hunted in his pocket, found his pipe, jammed tobacco in the bowl.

"There is something else," he said.

"Eh," asked Webster.

"There is something else about this census. They'd take it anyhow, perhaps, because a picture of Earth's population must always be an asset, a piece of handy knowledge. But that isn't all."

"Mutants," said Webster.

Grant nodded. "That's right. I hardly expected anyone to guess it."

"I work with mutants," Webster pointed out. "My whole life is bound up with mutations."

"Queer bits of culture have been turning up," said Grant. "Stuff that has no precedent. Literary forms which bear the unmistakable imprint of fresh personalities. Music that has broken away from traditional expression. Art that is like nothing ever seen before. And most of it anonymous or at least hidden under pseudonyms."

Webster laughed. "Such a thing, of course, is utter mystery to the World Committee."

"It isn't that so much as something else," Grant explained. "The Committee is not so concerned with art and literature as it is with other things—things that don't show up. If there is a backwoods renaissance taking place, it would first come to notice, naturally, through new art and literary forms. But a renaissance is not concerned entirely with art and literature."

Webster sank even lower in his chair, cupped his hands beneath his chin.

"I think I see," he said, "what you are driving at."

—

They sat for long minutes in silence broken only by the crackling of the fire, by the ghostly whisper of an autumn wind in the trees outside.

"There was a chance once," said Webster, almost as if he were speaking to himself. "A chance for new viewpoints, for something that might have wiped out the muddle of four thousand years of human thought. A man muffed that chance."

Grant stirred uncomfortably, then sat rigid, afraid Webster might have seen him move.

"That man," said Webster, "was my grandfather."

Grant knew he must say something, that he could not continue to sit there, unspeaking.

"Juwain may have been wrong," he said. "He might not have found a new philosophy."

"That is a thought," declared Webster, "we have used to console ourselves. And yet, it is unlikely. Juwain was a great Martian philosopher, perhaps the greatest Mars had ever known. If he could have lived, there is no doubt in my mind he would have developed that new philosophy. But he didn't live. He didn't live because my grandfather couldn't go to Mars."

"It wasn't your grandfather's fault," said Grant. "He tried to. Agoraphobia is a thing that a man can't fight—"

Webster waved the words aside. "That is over and done with. It is a thing that cannot be recaptured. We must accept that and go on from there. And since it was my family, since it was grandfather—"

Grant stared, shaken by the thought that occurred to him. "The dogs! That's why—"

"Yes, the dogs," said Webster.

From far away, in the river bottoms, came a crying sound, one with the wind that talked in the trees outside.

"A raccoon," said Webster. "The dogs will hear him and be rearing to get out."

The cry came again, closer it seemed, although that must have been imagination.

Webster had straightened in the chair, was leaning forward, staring at the flames.

"After all, why not?" he asked. "A dog has a personality. You can sense that in every one you meet. No two are exactly alike in mood and temperament. All of them are intelligent, in varying degrees. And that is all that's needed, a conscious personality and some measure of intelligence.

"They didn't get an even break, that's all. They had two handicaps. They couldn't talk and they couldn't walk erect and because they couldn't walk erect they had no chance to develop hands. But for speech and hands, we might be dogs and dogs be men."

"I'd never thought of it like that," said Grant. "Not of your dogs as a thinking race—"

"No," said Webster, and there was a trace of bitterness running in his words. "No, of course, you didn't. You thought of them as most of the rest of the world still thinks of them. As curiosities, as sideshow animals, as funny pets. Pets that can talk with you.

"But it's more than that, Grant. I swear to you it is. Thus far Man has come alone. One thinking, intelligent race all by itself. Think of how much farther, how much faster it might have gone had there been two races, two thinking, intelligent races, working together. For, you see, they would not think alike. They'd check their thoughts against one another. What one couldn't think of, the other could. The old story of two heads.

"Think of it, Grant. A different mind than the human mind, but one that will work with the human mind. That will see and understand things the human mind cannot, that will develop, if you will, philosophies the human mind could not."

He spread his hands toward the fire, long fingers with bone-hard, merciless knuckles.

"They couldn't talk and I gave them speech. It was not easy, for a dog's tongue and throat are not designed to speak. But surgery did it . . . an expedient at first . . . surgery and grafting. But now . . . now, I hope, I think… it is too soon to say—"

Grant was leaning forward, tensed.

"You mean the dogs are passing on the changes you have made. That there are hereditary evidences of the surgical corrections?"

Webster shook his head. "It is too soon to say. Another twenty years, maybe I can tell you."

He lifted the brandy bottle from the table, held it out.

"Thanks," said Grant.

"I am a poor host," Webster told him. "You should have helped yourself."

He raised the glass against the fire. "I had good material to work with. A dog is smart. Smarter than you think. The ordinary, run of the mill dog recognizes fifty words or more. A hundred is not unusual. Add another hundred and he has a working vocabulary. You noticed, perhaps, the simple words that Nathaniel used. Almost basic English."

Grant nodded. "One and two syllables. He told me there were a lot of words he couldn't say."

"There is much more to do," said Webster. "So much more to do. Reading, for example. A dog doesn't see as you and I do. I have been experimenting with lenses—correcting their eyesight so they can see as we do. And if that fails, there's still another way. Man must visualize the way a dog sees—learn to print books that dogs can read."

"The dogs," asked Grant, "what do they think of it?"

"The dogs?" said Webster. "Believe it or not, Grant, they're having the time of their merry lives."

He stared into the fire.

"God bless their hearts," he said.

Following Jenkins, Grant climbed the stairs to bed, but as they passed a partially opened door a voice hailed them.

"That you, stranger?"

Grant stopped, jerked around.

Jenkins said, in a whisper, "That's the old gentleman, sir. Often he cannot sleep."

"Yes," called Grant.

"Sleepy?" asked the voice.

"Not very," Grant told him.

"Come in for a while," the old man invited.

Thomas Webster sat propped up in bed, striped nightcap on his head. He saw Grant staring at it.

"Getting bald," he rasped. "Don't feel comfortable unless I got something on. Can't wear my hat to bed."

He shouted at Jenkins. "What you standing there for? Don't you see he needs a drink?"

"Yes, sir," said Jenkins, and disappeared.

"Sit down," said Thomas Webster. "Sit down and listen for a while. Talking will help me go to sleep. And, besides, we don't see new faces every day."

Grant sat down.

"What do you think of that son of mine?" the old man asked.

Grant started at the unusual question. "Why, I think he's splendid. The work he's doing with the dogs—"

The old man chuckled. "Him and his dogs! Ever tell you about the time Nathaniel tangled with a skunk? Of course, I haven't. Haven't said more than a word or two to you."

He ran his hands along the bed covering, long fingers picking at the fabric nervously.

"Got another son, you know. Allen. Call him Al. Tonight he's the farthest from Earth that Man has ever been. Heading for the stars."

Grant nodded. "I know. I read about it. The Alpha Centauri expedition."

"My father was a surgeon," said Thomas Webster. "Wanted me to be one, too. Almost broke his heart, I guess, when I didn't take to it. But if he could know, he'd be proud of us tonight."

"You mustn't worry about your son," said Grant. "He—"

The old man's glare silenced him. "I built that ship myself. Designed it, watched it grow. If it's just a matter of navigating space, it'll get where it is going. And the kid is good. He can ride that crate through hell itself."

He hunched himself straighter in the bed, knocking his nightcap askew against the piled-up pillows.

"And I got another reason to think he'll get there and back. Didn't think much about it at the time, but lately I've been recalling it, thinking it over, wondering if it mightn't mean . . . well, if it might not be—"

He gasped a bit for breath. "Mind you, I'm not superstitious."

"Of course you're not," said Grant.

"You bet I'm not," said Webster.

"A sign of some sort, perhaps," suggested Grant. "A feeling. A hunch."

"None of those," declared the old man. "An almost certain knowledge that destiny must be with me. That I was meant to build a ship that would make the trip. That someone or something decided it was about time Man got out to the stars and took a hand to help him along a bit."

"You sound as if you're talking about an actual incident," said Grant. "As if there were some positive happening that makes you think the expedition will succeed."

"You bet your boots," said Webster. "That's just exactly what I mean. It happened twenty years ago, out on the lawn in front of this very house."

He pulled himself even straighter, gasped for breath, wheezing.

"I was stumped, you understand. The dream was broken. Years spent for nothing. The basic principle I had evolved to get the speed necessary for interstellar flight simply wouldn't work. And the worst of it was, I knew it was almost right. I knew there was just one little thing, one theoretical change that must be made. But I couldn't find it.

"So I was sitting out there on the lawn, feeling sorry for

myself, with a sketch of the plan in front of me. I lived with it, you see. I carried it everywhere I went, figuring maybe that by just looking at it, the thing that was wrong would pop into my mind. You know how it does, sometimes."

Grant nodded.

"While I was sitting there a man came along. One of the ridge runners. You know what a ridge runner is?"

"Sure," said Grant.

"Well, this fellow came along. Kind of limber-jointed chap, ambling along as if he didn't have a trouble in the world. He stopped and looked over my shoulder and asked me what I had.

"'Spaceship drive,' I told him.

"He reached down and took it and I let him have it. After all, what was the use? He couldn't understand a thing about it and it was no good, anyhow.

"And then he handed it back to me and jabbed his finger at one place. 'That's your trouble,' he said. And then he turned and galloped off and I sat staring after him, too done in to say a single word, to even call him back."

The old man sat bolt upright in the bed, staring at the wall, nightcap canted crazily. Outside the wind sucked along the eaves with hollow hooting. And in that well-lighted room, there seemed to be shadows, although Grant knew there weren't any.

"Did you ever find him?" asked Grant.

The old man shook his head. "Hide nor hair," he said.

Jenkins came through the door with a glass, set it on the bedside table.

"I'll be back, sir," he said to Grant, "to show you to your room."

"No need of it," said Grant. "Just tell me where it is."

"If you wish, sir," said Jenkins. "It's the third one down. I'll turn on the light and leave the door ajar."

They sat, listening to the robot's feet go down the hall.

The old man glanced at the glass of whiskey, cleared his throat.

"I wish now," he said, "I'd had Jenkins bring me one."

"Why, that's all right," said Grant. "Take this one. I don't really need it."

"Sure you don't?"

"Not at all."

The old man stretched out his hand, took a sip, sighed gustily.

"Now that's what I call a proper mix," he said. "Doctor makes Jenkins water mine."

There was something in the house that got under one's skin. Something that made one feel like an outsider—uncomfortable and naked in the quiet whisper of its walls.

Sitting on the edge of his bed, Grant slowly unlaced his shoes, dropped them on the carpet.

A robot who had served the family for four generations, who talked of men long dead as if he had brought them a glass of whiskey only yesterday. An old man who worried about a ship that slid through the space-darkness beyond the solar system. Another man who dreamed of another race, a race that might go hand in paw with man down the trail of destiny.

And over it all, almost unspoken and yet unmistakable, the shadow of Jerome A. Webster—the man who had failed a friend, a surgeon who had failed his trust.

Juwain, the Martian philosopher, had died, on the eve of a great discovery, because Jerome A. Webster couldn't leave this house, because agoraphobia chained him to a plot a few miles square.

On stockinged feet, Grant crossed to the table where Jenkins had placed his pack. Loosening the straps, he opened it, brought out a thick portfolio. Back at the bed again, he sat down and hauled out sheafs of papers, thumbed through them.

Records, hundreds of sheets of records. The story of hundreds of human lives set down on paper. Not only the things they told him or the questions that they answered, but dozens of other little things—things he had noted down from observation, from sitting and watching, from living with them for an hour or day.

For the people that he ferreted out in these tangled hills accepted him. It was his business that they should accept him. They accepted him because he came on foot, briar-scratched and weary, with a pack upon his shoulder. To him clung none of the modernity that would have set him apart from them, made them suspicious of him. It was a tiresome way to make a census, but it was the only way to make the kind the World Committee wanted—and needed.

For somewhere, sometime, studying sheets like these that lay upon the bed, some man like him would find a thing he sought, would find a clue to some life that veered from the human pattern. Some betraying quirk of behaviorism that would set out one life against all the others.

Human mutations were not uncommon, of course. Many of them were known, men who held high position in the world. Most of the World Committee members were mutants, but, like the others, their mutational qualities and abilities had been modified and qualified by the pattern of the world, by unconscious conditioning that had shaped their thoughts and reactions into some conformity with other fellow men.

There had always been mutants, else the race would not have advanced. But until the last hundred years or so they had not been recognized as such. Before that they had merely been great businessmen or great scientists or great crooks. Or perhaps eccentrics who had gained no more than scorn or pity at the hands of a race that would not tolerate divergence from the norm.

Those who had been successful had adapted themselves to the world around them, had bent their greater mental powers into the pattern of acceptable action. And this dulled their usefulness, limited their capacity, hedged their ability with restrictions set up to fit less extraordinary people.

Even as today the known mutant's ability was hedged, unconsciously, by a pattern that had been set—a groove of logic that was a terrible thing.

But somewhere in the world there were dozens, probably hundreds, of other humans who were just a little more than human—persons whose lives had been untouched by the rigidity of complex human life. Their ability would not be hedged, they would know no groove of logic.

From the portfolio Grant brought out a pitifully thin sheaf of papers, clipped together, read the title of the script almost reverently:

"Unfinished Philosophical Proposition and Related Notes of Juwain."

It would take a mind that knew no groove of logic, a mind unhampered by the pattern of four thousand years of human thought, to carry on the torch the dead hand of the Martian philosopher had momentarily lifted. A torch that lit the way to a new concept of life and purpose, that showed a path that was easier and straighter. A philosophy that would have put mankind ahead a hundred thousand years in two short generations.

Juwain had died and in this very house a man had lived out his haunted years, listening to the voice of his dead friend, shrinking from the censure of a cheated race.

A stealthy scratch came at the door. Startled, Grant stiffened, listened. It came again. Then, a little, silky whine.

Swiftly Grant stuffed the papers back in the portfolio, strode to the door. As he opened it, Nathaniel oozed in, like a sliding black shadow.

"Oscar," he said, "doesn't know I'm here. Oscar would give it to me if he knew I was."

"Who's Oscar?"

"Oscar's the robot that takes care of us."

Grant grinned at the dog. "What do you want, Nathaniel?"

"I want to talk to you," said Nathaniel. "You've talked to

everyone else. To Bruce and Grandpa. But you haven't talked to me and I'm the one that found you."

"O.K.," invited Grant. "Go ahead and talk."

"You're worried," said Nathaniel.

Grant wrinkled his brow. "That's right. Perhaps I am. The human race is always worried. You should know that by now, Nathaniel."

"You're worrying about Juwain. Just like Grandpa is."

"Not worrying," protested Grant. "Just wondering. And hoping."

"What's the matter with Juwain?" demanded Nathaniel. "And who is he and—"

"He's no one, really," declared Grant. "That is, he was someone once, but he died years ago. He's just an idea now. A problem. A challenge. Something to think about."

"I can think," said Nathaniel, triumphantly. "I think a lot, sometimes. But I mustn't think like human beings. Bruce tells me I mustn't. He says I have to think dog thoughts and let human thoughts alone. He says dog thoughts are just as good as human thoughts, maybe a whole lot better."

Grant nodded soberly. "There is something to that, Nathaniel. After all, you must think differently than man. You must—"

"There's lots of things that dogs know that men don't know," bragged Nathaniel. "We can see things and hear things that men can't see nor hear. Sometimes we howl at night, and people cuss us out. But if they could see and hear what we do they'd be scared too stiff to move. Bruce says we're . . . we're—"

"Psychic?" asked Grant.

"That's it," declared Nathaniel. "I can't remember all them words."

Grant picked his pajamas off the table.

"How about spending the night with me, Nathaniel? You can have the foot of the bed."

Nathaniel stared at him round eyed. "Gee, you mean you want me to?"

"Sure I do. If we're going to be partners, dogs and men, we better start out on an even footing now."

"I won't get the bed dirty," said Nathaniel. "Honest I won't. Oscar gave me a bath tonight."

He flipped an ear.

"Except," he said, "I think he missed a flea or two."

Grant stared in perplexity at the atomic gun. A handy thing, it performed a host of services, ranging from cigarette lighter to deadly weapon. Built to last a thousand years, it was foolproof, or so the advertisements said. It never got out of kilter—except now it wouldn't work.

He pointed it at the ground and shook it vigorously and still it didn't work. He tapped it gently on a stone and got no results.

Darkness was dropping on the tumbled hills. Somewhere in the distant river valley an owl laughed irrationally. The first stars, small and quiet, came out in the east and in the west the green-tinged glow that marked the passing of the sun was fading into night.

The pile of twigs was laid before the boulder and other wood lay near at hand to keep the campfire going through the night. But if the gun wouldn't work, there would be no fire.

Grant cursed under his breath, thinking of chilly sleeping and cold rations.

He tapped the gun on the rock again, harder this time. Still no soap.

A twig crunched in the dark and Grant shot bolt upright.

Beside the shadowy trunk of one of the forest giants that towered into the gathering dusk, stood a figure, tall and gangling.

"Hello," said Grant.

"Something wrong, stranger?"

"My gun—" replied Grant, then cut short the words. No use in letting this shadowy figure know he was unarmed.

The man stepped forward, hand outstretched.

"Won't work, eh?"

Grant felt the gun lifted from his grasp.

The visitor squatted on the ground, making chuckling noises. Grant strained his eyes to see what he was doing, but the creeping darkness made the other's hands an inky blur weaving about the bright metal of the gun.

Metal clicked and scraped. The man sucked in his breath and laughed. Metal scraped again and the man arose, holding out the gun.

"All fixed," he said. "Maybe better than it was before."

A twig crunched again.

"Hey, wait!" yelled Grant, but the man was gone, a black ghost moving among the ghostly trunks.

A chill that was not of the night came seeping from the ground and travelled slowly up Grant's body. A chill that set his teeth on edge, that stirred the short hairs at the base of his skull, that made goose flesh spring out upon his arms.

There was no sound except the talk of water whispering in the dark, the tiny stream that ran just below the campsite.

Shivering, he knelt beside the pile of twigs, pressed the trigger. A thin blue flame lapped out and the twigs burst into flame.

Grant found old Dave Baxter perched on the top rail of the fence, smoke pouring from the short-stemmed pipe almost hidden in his whiskers.

"Howdy, stranger," said Dave. "Climb up and squat a while."

Grant climbed up, stared out over the corn-shocked field, gay with the gold of pumpkins.

"Just walkin'?" asked old Dave. "Or snoopin'?"

"Snooping," admitted Grant.

Dave took the pipe out of his mouth, spat, put it back in again. The whiskers draped themselves affectionately, and dangerously, about it.

"Diggin'?" asked old Dave.

"Nope," said Grant.

"Had a feller through here four, five years ago," said Dave, "that was worse'n a rabbit dog for diggin'. Found a place where there had been an old town and just purely tore up the place. Pestered the life out of me to tell him about the town, but I didn't rightly remember much. Heard my grandpappy once mention the name of the town, but danged if I ain't forgot it. This here feller had a slew of old maps that he was all the time wavin' around and studying, tryin' to figure out what was what, but I guess he never did know."

"Hunting for antiques," said Grant.

"Mebbe," old Dave told him. "Kept out of his way the best I could. But he wasn't no worse'n the one that was tryin' to trace some old road that ran through this way once. He had some maps, too. Left figurin' he'd found it and I didn't have the heart to tell him what he'd found was a path the cows had made."

He squinted at Grant cagily.

"You ain't huntin' no old roads, be you?"

"Nope," said Grant. "I'm a census taker."

"You're what?"

"Census taker," explained Grant. "Take down your name and age and where you live."

"What for?"

"Government wants to know," said Grant.

"We don't bother the gov'ment none," declared old Dave. "What call's the gov'ment got botherin' us?"

"Government won't bother you any," Grant told him. "Might even take a notion to pay you something some day. Never can tell."

"In that case," said old Dave, "it's different."

They perched on the fence, staring across the fields. Smoke curled up from a chimney hidden in a sunny hollow, yellow with the flame of birches. A creek meandered placidly across a dun autumn-colored meadow and beyond it climbed the hills, tier on tier of golden maple trees.

Hunched on the rail, Grant felt the heat of the autumn sun soak into his back, smelled the stubbled field.

A good life, he told himself. Good crops, wood to burn, plenty of game to hunt. A happy life.

He glanced at the old man huddled beside him, saw the unworried wrinkles of kindly age that puckered up his face, tried for a moment to envision a life like this—a simple, pastoral life, akin to the historic days of the old American frontier, with all the frontier's compensations, none of its dangers.

Old Dave took the pipe out of his face, waved it at the field.

"Still lots of work to do," he announced, "but it ain't agittin' done. Them kids ain't worth the power to blow 'em up. Huntin' all the time. Fishin' too. Machinery breakin' down. Joe ain't been around for quite a spell. Great hand at machinery, Joe is."

"Joe your son?"

"No. Crazy feller that lives off in the woods somewhere. Walks in and fixes things up, then walks off and leaves. Scarcely ever talks. Don't wait for a man to thank him. Just up and leaves. Been doin' it for years now. Grandpappy told me how he first came when he was a youngster. Still comin' now."

Grant gasped. "Wait a second. It can't be the same man."

"Now," said old Dave, "that's the thing. Won't believe it, stranger, but he ain't a mite older now than when I first saw him. Funny sort of cuss. Lots of wild tales about him. Grandpappy always told about how he fooled around with ants."

"Ants!"

"Sure. Built a house—glass house, you know, over an ant hill and heated it, come winter. That's what grandpappy always said. Claimed he'd seen it. But I don't believe a word of it. Grandpappy was the biggest liar in seven counties. Admitted it hisself."

A brass-tongued bell clanged from the sunny hollow where the chimney smoked.

The old man climbed down from the fence, tapped out his pipe, squinting at the sun.

The bell boomed again across the autumn stillness.

"That's ma," said old Dave. "Dinner's on. Squirrel dumplings, more than likely. Good eatin' as you ever hooked a tooth into. Let's get a hustle on."

A crazy fellow who came and fixed things and didn't wait for thanks. A man who looked the same as he did a hundred years ago. A chap who built a glasshouse over an ant hill and heated it, come winter.

It didn't make sense and yet old Baxter hadn't been lying. It wasn't another one of those tall yarns that had sprung up and still ran their course out here in the backwoods, amounting now to something that was very close to folklore.

All of the folklore had a familiar ring, a certain similarity, a definite pattern of underlying wit that tagged it for what it was. And this wasn't it. There was nothing humorous, even to the backwoods mind, in housing and heating an ant hill. To qualify for humor a tale like that would have to have a snapper, and this tale didn't have one.

Grant stirred uneasily on the cornshuck mattress, pulling the heavy quilt close around his throat.

Funny, he thought, the places that I sleep in. Tonight a cornshuck mattress, last night an open campfire, the night before that a soft mattress and clean sheets in the Webster house.

The wind sucked up the hollow and paused on its way to flap a loose shingle on the house, came back to flap it once again. A mouse skittered somewhere in the darkened place. From the bed across the loft came the sound of regular breathing—two of the Baxter younger fry slept there.

A man who came and fixed things and didn't wait for thanks. That was what had happened with the gun. That was what had been happening for years to the Baxters' haywire farm machinery. A crazy feller by the name of Joe, who didn't age and had a handy bent at tinkering.

A thought came into Grant's head; he shoved it back, repressed it. There was no need of arousing hope. Snoop around some, ask guarded questions, keep your eyes open, Grant. Don't make your questions too pointed or they'll shut up like a clam.

Funny folk, these ridge runners. People who had no part of progress, who wanted no part of it. People who had turned their backs upon civilization, returning to the unhampered life of soil and forest, sun and rain.

Plenty of room for them here on Earth, lots of room for everyone, for Earth's population had dwindled in the last two hundred years, drained by the pioneers who flocked out to settle other planets, to shape the other worlds of the system to the economy of mankind.

Plenty of room and soil and game.

Maybe it was the best way after all. Grant remembered he had often thought that in the months he had tramped these hills. At times like this, with the comfort of the handmade quilt, the rough efficiency of the cornshuck mattress, the whisper of the wind along the shingled roof. Times like when he sat on the top rail of the fence and looked at the groups of golden pumpkins loafing in the sun.

A rustle came to him across the dark, the rustle of the cornshuck mattress where the two boys slept. Then the pad of bare feet coming softly across the boards.

"You asleep, mister?" came the whisper.

"Nope. Want to crawl in with me?"

The youngster ducked under the cover, put cold feet against Grant's stomach.

"Grandpappy tell you about Joe?"

Grant nodded in the dark. "Said he hadn't been around, lately."

"Tell you about the ants?"

"Sure did. What do you know about the ants?"

"Me and Bill found them just a little while ago, keeping it a secret. We ain't told anyone but you. But we gotta tell you, I guess. You're from the gov'ment."

"There really was a glasshouse over the hill?"

"Yes, and . . . and—" the boy's voice gasped with excitement, "and that ain't all. Them ants had carts and there was chimneys coming out of the hill and smoke comin' from the chimneys. And . . . and—"

"Yes, what else?"

"We didn't wait to see anything else. Bill and me got scared. We ran."

The boy snuggled deeper into the cornshucks. "Gee, ever hear of anything like it? Ants pulling carts!"

The ants were pulling carts. And there were chimneys sticking from the hill, chimneys that belched tiny, acrid puffs of smoke that told of smelting ores.

Head throbbing with excitement, Grant squatted beside the nest, staring at the carts that trundled along the roads leading off into the grass-roots land. Empty carts going out, loaded carts coming back—loaded with seeds and here and there dismembered insect bodies. Tiny carts, moving rapidly, bouncing and jouncing behind the harnessed ants!

The glassite shield that once had covered the nest still was there, but it was broken and had fallen into disrepair, almost as if there were no further use of it, as if it had served a purpose that no longer existed.

The glen was wild, broken land that tumbled down toward the river bluffs, studded with boulders, alternating with tiny patches of meadow and clumps of mighty oaks. A hushed place that one could believe had never heard a voice except the talk of wind in treetops and the tiny voices of the wild things that followed secret paths.

A place where ants might live undisturbed by plow or vagrant foot, continuing the millions of years of senseless destiny that dated from a day before there was anything like man—from a day before a single abstract thought had been born on the Earth. A closed and stagnant destiny that had no purpose except that ants might live.

And now someone had uncoiled the angle of that destiny, had set it on another path, had given the ants the secret of the wheel, the secret of working metals—how many other cultural handicaps had been lifted from this ant hill, breaking the bottleneck of progress?

Hunger pressure, perhaps, would be one cultural handicap that would have been lifted for the ants. Providing of abundant food which gave them leisure for other things beyond the continued search for sustenance.

Another race on the road to greatness, developing on the social basis that had been built in that long gone day before the thing called Man had known the stir of greatness.

Where would it lead? What would the ant be like in another million years? Would ant and Man—could ant and Man find any common denominator as dog and Man would find for working out a co-operative destiny?

Grant shook his head. That was something the chances were against. For in dog and Man ran common blood, while ant and Man were things apart, life forms that were never meant to understand the other. They had no common basis such as had been joined in the paleolithic days when dog and Man dozed beside a fire and watched against the eyes that roved out in the night.

Grant sensed rather than heard the rustle of feet in the high grass back of him. Erect, he whirled around and saw the man before him. A gangling man with stooping shoulders and hands that were almost hamlike, but with sensitive fingers that tapered white and smooth.

"You are Joe?" asked Grant.

The man nodded. "And you are a man who has been hunting me."

Grant gasped. "Why perhaps I have, Not you personally, perhaps, but someone like you."

"Someone different," said Joe.

"Why didn't you stay the other night?" asked Grant. "Why did you run off? I wanted to thank you for fixing up the gun."

Joe merely stared at him, unspeaking, but behind the silent lips Grant sensed amusement, a vast and secret amusement.

"How in the world," asked Grant, "did you know the gun was broken? Had you been watching me?"

"I heard you think it was."

"You heard me think?"

"Yes," said Joe. "I hear you thinking now."

Grant laughed, a bit uneasily. It was disconcerting, but it was logical. It was the thing that he should have expected—this and more.

He gestured at the hill. "Those ants are yours?"

Joe nodded and the amusement again was bubbling just behind his lips.

"What are you laughing for?" snapped Grant.

"I am not laughing," Joe told him and somehow Grant felt rebuked, rebuked and small, like a child that has been slapped for something it should have known better than to do.

"You should publish your notes," said Grant. "They might be correlated with the work that Webster's doing."

Joe shrugged his shoulders. "I have no notes," he said.

"No notes!"

The lanky man moved toward the ant hill, stood staring down at it. "Perhaps," he declared, "you've figured out why I did it."

Grant nodded gravely. "I might have wondered that. Experimental curiosity, more than likely. Maybe compassion for a lower form of life. A feeling, perhaps, that just because man himself got the head start doesn't give him a monopoly on advancement."

Joe's eyes glittered in the sunlight. "Curiosity—maybe. I hadn't thought of that."

He hunkered down beside the hill. "Ever wonder why the ant advanced so far and then stood still? Why he built a nearly perfect social organization and let it go at that? What it was that stopped him in his tracks?"

"Hunger pressure, for one thing," Grant said.

"That and hibernation," declared the lanky man. "Hibernation, you see, wiped out the memory pattern from one season to the next. Each spring they started over, began from scratch again. They never were able to benefit from past mistakes, cash in on accumulated knowledge."

"So you fed them—"

"And heated the hill," said Joe, "so they wouldn't have to hibernate. So they wouldn't have to start out fresh with the coming of each spring."

"The carts?"

"I made a couple, left them there. It took ten years, but they finally figured out what they were for."

Grant nodded at the smokestacks.

"They did that themselves," Joe told him.

"Anything else?"

Joe lifted his shoulders wearily. "How should I know?"

"But, man, you watched them. Even if you didn't keep notes, you watched."

Joe shook his head. "I haven't laid eyes on them for almost fifteen years. I only came today because I heard you here. These ants, you see, don't amuse me any more."

Grant's mouth opened, then shut tight again. Finally, he said: "So that's the answer. That's why you did it. Amusement."

There was no shame on Joe's face, no defense, just a pained expression that said he wished they'd forget all about the ants. His mouth said: "Sure. Why else?"

"That gun of mine. I suppose that amused you, too."

"Not the gun," said Joe.

Not the gun, Grant's brain said. Of course, not the gun, you dumbbell, but you yourself. You're the one that amused him. And you're amusing him right now.

Fixing up old Dave Baxter's farm machinery, then walking off without a word, doubtless had been a screaming joke. And probably he'd hugged himself and rocked for days with silent mirth after that time up at the Webster house when he'd pointed out the thing that was wrong with old Thomas Webster's space drive.

Like a smart-Aleck playing tricks on an awkward puppy.

Joe's voice broke his thoughts.

"You're an enumerator, aren't you? Why don't you ask me the questions? Now that you've found me you can't go off and not get it down on paper. My age especially. I'm one hundred sixty-three and I'm scarcely adolescent. Another thousand years at least."

He hugged his knobby knees against his chest and rocked slowly back and forth. "Another thousand years and if I take good care of myself—"

"But that isn't all of it," Grant told him, trying to keep his voice calm. "There is something more. Something that you must do for us."

"For us?"

"For society," said Grant. "For the human race."

"Why?"

Grant stared. "You mean that you don't care."

Joe shook his head and in the gesture there was no bravado, no defiance of convention. It was just blunt statement of the fact.

"Money?" suggested Grant.

Joe waved his hands at the hills about them, at the spreading river valley. "I have this," he said. "I have no need of money."

"Fame, perhaps?"

Joe did not spit, but his face looked like he had.

"The gratitude of the human race?"

"It doesn't last," said Joe and the old mockery was in his words, the vast amusement just behind his lips.

"Look, Joe," said Grant and, hard as he tried to keep it out, there was pleading in his voice, "this thing I have for you to do is important . . . important to generations yet to come, important to the human race, a milestone in our destiny—"

"And why should I," asked Joe, "do something for someone who isn't even born yet? Why should I look beyond the years of my own life? When I die, I die, and all the shouting and the glory, all the banners and the bugles will be nothing to me. I will not know whether I lived a great life or a very poor one."

"The race," said Grant.

Joe laughed, a shout of laughter. "Race preservation, race advancement. That's what you're getting at. Why should you be concerned with that? Or I?"

The laughter lines smoothed out around his mouth and he shook a finger in mock admonishment. "Race preservation is a myth . . . a myth that you all have lived by—a sordid thing that has arisen out of your social structure. The race ends every day. When a man dies the race ends for him—so far as he's concerned there is no longer any race."

"You just don't care," said Grant.

"That," declared Joe, "is what I've been telling you."

He squinted at the pack upon the ground and a flicker of a smile wove about his lips. "Perhaps," he suggested, "if it interested me—"

Grant opened up the pack, brought out the portfolio. Almost reluctantly he pulled out the thin sheaf of papers, glanced at the title:

"Unfinished Philosophical—"

He handed it across, sat watching as Joe read swiftly and even as he watched he felt the sickening wrench of terrible failure closing on his brain.

Back in the Webster house he had thought of a mind that knew no groove of logic, a mind unhampered by four thousand years of moldy human thought. That, he had told himself, might do the trick.

And here it was. But it still was not enough. There was something lacking—something he had never thought of, something the men in Geneva had never thought of, either. Something, a part of the human make-up that everyone, up to this moment, had taken for granted.

A social pressure, the thing that had held the human race together through all millennia—held the human race together as a unit just as hunger pressure had held the ants enslaved to a social pattern.

The need of one human being for the approval of his fellow humans, the need for a certain cult of fellowship—a psychological, almost physiological need for approval of one's thought and action. A force that kept men from going off at unsocial tangents, a force that made for social security and human solidarity, for the working together of the human family.

Men died for that approval, sacrificed for that approval, lived lives they loathed for that approval. For without it a man was on his own, an outcast, an animal that had been driven from the pack.

It had led to terrible things, of course—to mob psychology, to racial persecution, to mass atrocities in the name of patriotism or religion. But likewise it had been the sizing that held the race together, the thing that from the very start had made human society possible.

And Joe didn't have it. Joe didn't give a damn. He didn't care what anyone thought of him. He didn't care whether anyone approved or not.

Grant felt the sun hot upon his back, heard the whisper of the wind that walked in the trees above him. And in some thicket a bird struck up a song.

Was this the trend of mutancy? This sloughing off of the basic instinct that made man a member of the race?

Had this man in front of him, reading the legacy of Juwain, found within himself, through his mutancy, a life so full that he could dispense with the necessity for the approval of his fellows? Had he, finally, after all these years, reached that stage of civilization where a man stood independent, disdaining all the artificiality of society?

Joe looked up.

"Very interesting," he said. "Why didn't he go ahead and finish it?"

"He died," said Grant.

Joe clucked his tongue inside his cheek. "He was wrong in one place." He flipped the pages, jabbed with a finger. "Right here. That's where the error cropped up. That's what bogged him down."

Grant stammered. "But . . . but there shouldn't be an error. He died, that's all. He died before he finished it."

Joe folded the manuscript neatly, tucked it in his pocket.

"Just as well," he said. "He probably would have botched it, anyhow."

"Then you can finish it? You can—"

There was, Grant knew, no use of going on. He read the answer in Joe's eyes.

"You really think," said Joe, and his words were terse and measured, "that I'd turn this over to you squalling humans?"

Grant shrugged in defeat. "I suppose not. I suppose I should have known. A man like you—"

"I," said Joe, "can use this thing myself."

He rose slowly, idly swung his foot, plowing a furrow through the ant hill, toppling the smoking chimneys, burying the toiling carts.

With a cry, Grant leaped to his feet, blind anger gripping him, blind anger driving the hand that snatched out his gun.

"Hold it!" said Joe.

Grant's arm halted with the gun still pointing toward the ground.

"Take it easy, little man," said Joe. "I know you'd like to kill me, but I can't let you do it. For I have plans, you see. And, after all, you wouldn't be killing me for the reason that you think."

"What difference would it make why I killed you?" rasped Grant. "You'd be dead, wouldn't you? You wouldn't be loose with Juwain's philosophy."

"But," Joe told him, almost gently, "that's not why you would kill me. You'd do it because you're sore at me for mussing up the ant hill."

"That might have been the reason first," said Grant. "But not now—"

"Don't try it," said Joe. "Before you ever pressed the trigger you'd be meat yourself."

Grant hesitated.

"If you think I'm bluffing," Joe taunted him, "go ahead and call me."

For a long moment the two stood face to face, the gun still pointing at the ground.

"Why can't you throw in with us?" asked Grant. "We need a man like you. You were the one that showed old Tom Webster how to build a space drive. The work you've done with ants—"

Joe was stepping forward, swiftly, and Grant heaved up the gun. He saw the fist coming at him, a hamlike, powerful fist that fairly whistled with its vicious speed.

A fist that was faster than his finger on the trigger.

Something wet and hot was rasping across Grant's face and he lifted a hand and tried to brush it off.

But it went on, licking across his face.

He opened his eyes and Nathaniel did a jig in front of them.

"You're all right," said Nathaniel. "I was so afraid—"

"Nathaniel!" croaked Grant. "What are you doing here?"

"I ran away," Nathaniel told him. "I want to go with you."

Grant shook his head. "You can't go with me. I have far to go. I have a job to do."

He got to his hands and knees and felt along the ground. When his hand touched cold metal, he picked it up and slid it in the holster.

"I let him get away," he said, "and I can't let him go. I gave him something that belonged to all mankind and I can't let him use it."

"I can track," Nathaniel told him. "I track squirrels like everything."

"You have more important things to do than tracking," Grant told the dog. "You see, I found out something today. Got a glimpse of a certain trend—a trend that all mankind may follow. Not today nor tomorrow, nor even a thousand years from now. Maybe never, but it's a thing we can't overlook. Joe may be just a little farther along the path than the rest of us and we may be following faster than we think. We may all end up like Joe. And if that is what is happening, if that is where it all will end, you dogs have a job ahead of you."

Nathaniel stared up at him, worried wrinkles on his face.

"I don't understand," he pleaded. "You use words I can't make out."

"Look, Nathaniel. Men may not always be the way they are today. They may change. And, if they do, you have to carry on; you have to take the dream and keep it going. You'll have to pretend that you are men."

"Us dogs," Nathaniel pledged, "will do it."

"It won't come for thousands and thousands of years," said Grant. "You will have time to get ready. But you must know. You must pass the word along. You must not forget."

"I know," said Nathaniel. "Us dogs will tell the pups and the pups will tell their pups."

"That's the idea," said Grant.

He stooped and scratched Nathaniel's ear and the dog, tail wagging to a stop, stood and watched him climb the hill.

AUK HOUSE

In the very first paragraph of this story, Clifford Simak uses the names of three towns that were part of his life—but he uses the names only, for the towns he referred to are actually located far from the East Coast.

But that's not important, that's a mere detail. The fact is, this story, although clearly about the abuse of economic power by rich corporations, is really an exploration of the reactions of the victims of that abuse. And the ending to this exploration is one that led me to blink.

"Auk House" was originally written for Judy-Lynn del Rey, editor of Stellar 3, *an original anthology that was published in 1977. Judy-Lynn and her husband, Lester, were longtime friends of Cliff's, in addition to being the editors who handled much of the work he did for Ballantine Books.*

This is a deep and thoughtful story. And it's for adults.

—dww

David Latimer was lost when he found the house. He had set out for Wyalusing, a town he had only heard of but had never visited, and apparently had taken the wrong road. He had passed through two small villages, Excelsior and Navarre, and if the roadside signs were right, in another few miles he would be coming into Montfort. He hoped that someone in Montfort could set him right again.

The road was a county highway, crooked and narrow and bearing little traffic. It twisted through the rugged headlands that ran down to the coast, flanked by birch and evergreens and rarely out of reach of the muted thunder of surf pounding on giant boulders that lay tumbled on the shore.

The car was climbing a long, steep hill when he first saw the house, between the coast and road. It was a sprawling pile of brick and stone, flaunting massive twin chimneys at either end of it, sited in front of a grove of ancient birch and set so high upon the land that it seemed to float against the sky. He slowed the car, pulled over to the roadside, and stopped to have a better look at it.

A semicircular brick-paved driveway curved up to the entrance of the house. A few huge oak trees grew on the well-kept lawn, and in their shade stood graceful stone benches that had the look of never being used.

There was, it seemed to Latimer, a pleasantly haunted look to the place—a sense of privacy, of olden dignity, a withdrawal from the world. On the front lawn, marring it, desecrating it, stood a large planted sign:

FOR RENT OR SALE

See Campbell's Realty—Half Mile Down the Road

And an arrow pointing to show which way down the road.

Latimer made no move to continue down the road. He sat quietly in the car, looking at the house. The sea, he thought, was just beyond; from a second-story window at the back, one could probably see it.

It had been word of a similar retreat that had sent him seeking out Wyalusing—a place where he could spend a quiet few months at painting. A more modest place, perhaps, than this, although the description he had been given of it had been rather sketchy.

Too expensive, he thought, looking at the house; most likely more than he could afford, although with the last couple of sales he had made, he was momentarily flush. However, it might not be as expensive as he thought, he told himself; a place like this would have small attraction for most people. Too big, but for himself that would make no difference; he could camp out in a couple of rooms for the few months he would be there.

Strange, he reflected, the built-in attraction the house had for him, the instinctive, spontaneous attraction, the instant knowing that this was the sort of place he had had in mind. Not knowing until now that it was the sort of place he had in mind. Old, he told himself—a century, two centuries, more than likely. Built by some now forgotten lumber baron. Not lived in, perhaps, for a number of years. There would be bats and mice. He put the car in gear and moved slowly out into the road, glancing back over his shoulder at the house. A half mile down the road, at the edge of what probably was Montfort, although there was no sign to say it was, on the right-hand side, a lopsided, sagging sign on an old, lopsided shack, announced Campbell's Realty. Hardly intending to do it, his mind not made up as yet, he pulled the car off the road and parked in front of the shack.

Inside, a middle-aged man dressed in slacks and turtleneck sat with his feet propped on a littered desk.

"I dropped in," said Latimer, "to inquire about the house down the road. The one with the brick drive."

"Oh, that one," said the man. "Well, I tell you, stranger, I can't show it to you now. I'm waiting for someone who wants to look at the Ferguson place. Tell you what, though. I could give you the key."

"Could you give me some idea of what the rent would be?"

"Why don't you look at it first. See what you think of it. Get the feel of it. See if you'd fit into it. If you like it, we can talk. Hard place to move. Doesn't fit the needs of many people. Too big, for one thing, too old. I could get you a deal on it."

The man took his feet off the desk, plopped them on the floor. Rummaging in a desk drawer, he came up with a key with a tag attached to it and threw it on the desk top.

"Have a look at it and then come back," he said. "This Ferguson business shouldn't take more than an hour or two."

"Thank you," said Latimer, picking up the key.

He parked the car in front of the house and went up the steps. The key worked easily in the lock and the door swung open on well-oiled hinges. He came into a hall that ran from front to back, with a staircase ascending to the second floor and doors opening on either side into ground-floor rooms.

The hall was dim and cool, a place of graciousness. When he moved along the hall, the floorboards did not creak beneath his feet as in a house this old he would have thought they might. There was no shut-up odor, no smell of damp or mildew, no sign of bats or mice.

The door to his right was open, as were all the doors that ran along the hall. He glanced into the room—a large room, with light from the westering sun flooding through the windows that stood on either side of a marble fireplace. Across the hall was a smaller room, with a fireplace in one corner. A library or a study, he thought. The larger room, undoubtedly, had been thought of, when the house was built, as a drawing room. Beyond the larger room, on the right-hand side, he found what might have been a kitchen with a large brick fireplace that had a utilitarian look to it—used, perhaps, in the olden days for cooking, and across from it a much larger room, with another marble fireplace, windows on either side of it and oblong mirrors set into the wall, an ornate chandelier hanging from the ceiling. This, he knew, had to be the dining room, the proper setting for leisurely formal dinners.

He shook his head at what he saw. It was much too grand for him, much larger, much more elegant than he had thought. If someone wanted to live as a place like this should be lived in, it would cost a fortune in furniture alone. He had told himself that during a summer's residence he could camp out in a couple of rooms, but to camp out in a place like this would be sacrilege; the house deserved a better occupant than that.

Yet, it still held its attraction. There was about it a sense of openness, of airiness, of ease. Here a man would not be cramped; he'd have room to move about. It conveyed a feeling of well-being. It was, in essence, not a living place, but a place for living.

The man had said that it had been hard to move, that to most people it had slight appeal—too large, too old—and that he could make an attractive deal on it. But, with a sinking feeling, Latimer knew that what the man had said was true. Despite its attractiveness, it was far too large. It would take too much furniture even for a summer of camping out. And yet, despite all this, the pull—almost a physical pull—toward it still hung on.

He went out the back door of the hall, emerging on a wide veranda that ran the full length of the house. Below him lay the slope of ancient birch, running down a smooth green lawn to the seashore studded by tumbled boulders that flung up white clouds of spume as the racing waves broke against them. Flocks of mewling birds hung above the surging surf like white phantoms, and beyond this, the gray-blue stretch of ocean ran to the far horizon.

This was the place, he knew, that he had hunted for—a place of freedom that would free his brush from the conventions that any painter, at times, felt crowding in upon him. Here lay that remoteness from all other things, a barrier set up against a crowding world. Not objects to paint, but a place in which to put upon his canvases that desperate crying for expression he felt within himself.

He walked down across the long stretch of lawn, among the age-striped birch, and came upon the shore. He found a boulder and sat upon it, feeling the wild exhilaration of wind and water, sky and loneliness.

The sun had set and quiet shadows crept across the land. It was time to go, he told himself, but he kept on sitting, fascinated by the delicate deepening of the dusk, the subtle color changes that came upon the water.

When he finally roused himself and started walking up the lawn, the great birch trees had assumed a ghostliness that glimmered in the twilight. He did not go back into the house, but walked around it to come out on the front.

He reached the brick driveway and started walking, remembering that he'd have to go back into the house to lock the back door off the hall.

It was not until he had almost reached the front entrance that he realized his car was gone. Confused, he stopped dead in his tracks. He had parked it there; he was sure he had. Was it possible he had parked it off the road and walked up the drive, now forgetting that he had?

He turned and started down the driveway, his shoes clicking on the bricks. No, dammit, he told himself, I did drive up the driveway—I remember doing it. He looked back and there wasn't any car, either in front of the house or along the curve of driveway. He broke into a run, racing down the driveway toward the road. Some kids had come along and pushed it to the road—that must be the answer. A juvenile prank, the pranksters hiding somewhere, tittering to themselves as they watched him run to find it. Although that was wrong, he thought—he had left it set on 'Park' and locked. Unless they broke a window, there was no way they could have pushed it.

The brick driveway came to an end and there wasn't any road. The lawn and driveway came down to where they ended, and at that point a forest rose up to block the way. A wild and tangled forest that was very dark and dense, great trees standing up where the road had been. To his nostrils came the damp scent of forest mold, and somewhere in the darkness of the trees, an owl began to hoot.

He swung around, to face back toward the house, and saw the lighted windows. It couldn't be, he told himself quite reasonably.

There was no one in the house, no one to turn on the lights. In all likelihood, the electricity was shut off.

But the lighted windows persisted. There could be no question there were lights. Behind him, he could hear the strange rustlings of the trees and now there were two owls, answering one another.

Reluctantly, unbelievingly, he started up the driveway. There must be some sort of explanation. Perhaps, once he had the explanation, it would all seem quite simple. He might have gotten turned around somehow, as he had somehow gotten turned around earlier in the day, taking the wrong road. He might have suffered a lapse of memory, for some unknown and frightening reason have experienced a blackout. This might not be the house he had gone to look at, although, he insisted to himself, it certainly looked the same.

He came up the brick driveway and mounted the steps that ran up to the door, and while he was still on the steps, the door came open and a man in livery stepped aside to let him in.

"You are a little late, sir," said the man. "We had expected you some time ago. The others waited for you, but just now went in to dinner, thinking you had been unavoidably detained. Your place is waiting for you."

Latimer hesitated.

"It is quite all right, sir," said the man. "Except on special occasions, we do not dress for dinner. You're all right as you are."

The hall was lit by short candles set in sconces on the wall. Paintings also hung there, and small sofas and a few chairs were lined along the wall. From the dining room came the sound of conversation.

The butler closed the door and started down the hall. "If you would follow me, sir."

It was all insane, of course. It could not be happening. It was something he imagined. He was standing out there, on the bricks of the driveway, with the forest and the hooting owls behind him, imagining that he was here, in this dimly lighted hallway with the talk and laughter coming from the dining room.

"Sir," said the butler, "if you please."

"But, I don't understand. This place, an hour ago . . ."

"The others are all waiting for you. They have been looking forward to you. You must not keep them waiting."

"All right, then," said Latimer. "I shall not keep them waiting."

At the entrance to the dining room, the butler stood aside so that he could enter.

The others were seated at a long, elegantly appointed table. The chandelier blazed with burning tapers. Uniformed serving maids stood against one wall. A sideboard gleamed with china and cut glass. There were bouquets of flowers upon the table.

A man dressed in a green sports shirt and a corduroy jacket rose from the table and motioned to him.

"Latimer, over here," he said. "You are Latimer, are you not?"

"Yes, I'm Latimer."

"Your place is over here, between Enid and myself. We'll not bother with introductions now. We can do that later on."

Scarcely feeling his feet making contact with the floor, moving in a mental haze, Latimer went down the table. The man who stood had remained standing, thrusting out a beefy hand. Latimer took it and the other's handshake was warm and solid.

"I'm Underwood," he said. "Here, sit down. Don't stand on formality. We've just started on the soup. If yours is cold, we can have another brought to you."

"Thank you," said Latimer. "I'm sure it's all right."

On the other side of him, Enid said, "We waited for you. We knew that you were coming, but you took so long."

"Some," said Underwood, "take longer than others. It's just the way it goes."

"But I don't understand," said Latimer. "I don't know what's going on."

"You will," said Underwood. "There's really nothing to it."

"Eat your soup," Enid urged. "It is really good. We get such splendid chowder here."

She was small and dark of hair and eyes, a strange intensity in her.

Latimer lifted the spoon and dipped it in the soup. Enid was right; it was a splendid chowder.

The man across the table said, "I'm Charlie. We'll talk later on. We'll answer any questions."

The woman sitting beside Charlie said, "You see, we don't understand it, either. But it's all right. I'm Alice."

The maids were removing some of the soup bowls and bringing on the salads. On the sideboard the china and cut glass sparkled in the candlelight. The flowers on the table were peonies. There were, with himself, eight people seated at the table.

"You see," said Latimer, "I only came to look at the house."

"That's the way," said Underwood, "that it happened to the rest of us. Not just recently. Years apart. Although I don't know how many years. Jonathon, down there at the table's end, that old fellow with a beard, was the first of us. The others straggled in."

"The house," said Enid, "is a trap, very neatly baited. We are mice caught in a trap."

From across the table, Alice said, "She makes it sound so dreadful. It's not that way at all. We are taken care of meticulously. There is a staff that cooks our food and serves it, that makes our beds, that keeps all clean and neat . . ."

"But who would want to trap us?"

"That," said Underwood, "is the question we all try to solve—except for one or two of us, who have become resigned. But, although there are several theories, there is no solution. I sometimes ask myself what difference it makes. Would we feel any better if we knew our trappers?"

A trap neatly baited, Latimer thought, and indeed it had been. There had been that instantaneous, instinctive attraction that the house had held for him—even only driving past it, the attraction had reached out for him.

The salad was excellent, and so were the steak and baked potato. The rice pudding was the best Latimer had ever eaten. In spite of himself, he found that he was enjoying the meal, the bright and witty chatter that flowed all around the table.

In the drawing room, once dinner was done, they sat in front of a fire in the great marble fireplace.

"Even in the summer," said Enid, "when night come on, it gets chilly here. I'm glad it does, because I love a fire. We have a fire almost every night."

"We?" said Latimer. "You speak as if you were a tribe."

"A band," she said. "A gang, perhaps. Fellow conspirators, although there's no conspiracy. We get along together. That's one thing that is so nice about it. We get along so well."

The man with the beard came over to Latimer. "My name is Jonathon," he said. "We were too far apart at dinner to become acquainted."

"I am told," said Latimer, "that you are the one who has been here the longest."

"I am now," said Jonathon. "Up until a couple of years ago, it was Peter. Old Pete, we used to call him."

"Used to?"

"He died," said Enid. "That's how come there was room for you. There is only so much room in this house, you see."

"You mean it took two years to find someone to replace him."

"I have a feeling," said Jonathon, "that we belong to a select company. I would think that you might have to possess rather rigid qualifications before you were considered."

"That's what puzzles me," said Latimer. "There must be some common factor in the group. The kind of work we're in, perhaps."

"I am sure of it," said Jonathon. "You are a painter, are you not?"

Latimer nodded. "Enid is a poet," said Jonathon, "and a very good one. I aspire to philosophy, although I'm not too good at it. Dorothy is a novelist and Alice a musician—a pianist. Not only does she play, but she can compose as well. You haven't met Dorothy or Jane as yet."

"No. I think I know who they are, but I haven't met them."

"You will," said Enid, "before the evening's over. Our group is so small we get to know one another well."

"Could I get a drink for you?" asked Jonathon.

"I would appreciate it. Could it be Scotch, by any chance?"

"It could be," said Jonathon, "anything you want. Ice or water?"

"Ice, if you would. But I feel I am imposing."

"No one imposes here," said Jonathon. "We take care of one another."

"And if you don't mind," said Enid, "one for me as well. You know what I want."

As Jonathon walked away to get the drinks, Latimer said to Enid, "I must say that you've all been kind to me. You took me in, a stranger . . ."

"Oh, not a stranger really. You'll never be a stranger. Don't you understand? You are one of us. There was an empty place and you've filled it. And you'll be here forever. You'll never go away."

"You mean that no one ever leaves?"

"We try. All of us have tried. More than once for some of us. But we've never made it. Where is there to go?"

"Surely there must be someplace else. Some way to get back."

"You don't understand," she said. "There is no place but here. All the rest is wilderness. You could get lost if you weren't careful. There have been times when we've had to go out and hunt down the lost ones."

Underwood came across the room and sat down on the sofa on the other side of Enid.

"How are you two getting on?" he said.

"Very well," said Enid. "I was just telling David there's no way to get away from here."

"That is fine," said Underwood, "but it will make no difference. There'll come a day he'll try."

"I suppose he will," said Enid, "but if he understands beforehand, it will be easier."

"The thing that rankles me," said Latimer, "is why. You said at the dinner table everyone tries for a solution, but no one ever finds one."

"Not exactly that," said Underwood. "I said there are some theories. But the point is that there is no way for us to know which one of them is right. We may have already guessed the reason for it all, but the chances are we'll never know. Enid has the most romantic notion. She thinks we are being held by some super-race from some far point in the galaxy who want to study us. We are specimens, you understand. They cage us in what amounts to a laboratory, but do not intrude upon us. They want to observe us under natural conditions and see what makes us tick. And under these conditions, she thinks we should act as civilized as we can manage."

"I don't know if I really think that," said Enid, "but it's a nice idea. It's no crazier than some of the other explanations. Some of us have theorized that we are being given a chance to do the best work we can. Someone is taking all economic pressure off us, placing us in a pleasant environment, and giving us all the time we need to develop whatever talents we may have. We're being subsidized."

"But what good would that do?" asked Latimer. "I gather we are out of touch with the world we knew. No matter what we did, who is there to know?"

"Not necessarily," said Underwood. "Things disappear. One of Alice's compositions and one of Dorothy's novels and a few of Enid's poems."

"You think someone is reaching in and taking them? Being quite selective?"

"It's just a thought," said Underwood. "Some of the things we create do disappear. We hunt for them and we never find them."

Jonathon came back with the drinks. "We'll have to settle down now," he said, "and quiet all this chatter. Alice is about to play. Chopin, I believe she said."

It was late when Latimer was shown to his room by Underwood, up on the third floor. "We shifted around a bit to give this one to you," said Underwood. "It's the only one that has a skylight. You haven't got a straight ceiling—it's broken by the roofline—but I think you'll find it comfortable."

"You knew that I was coming, then, apparently some time before I arrived."

"Oh, yes, several days ago. Rumors from the staff; the staff seems to know everything. But not until late yesterday did we definitely know when you would arrive."

After Underwood said good night, Latimer stood for a time in the center of the room. There was a skylight, as Underwood had said, positioned to supply a north light.

Standing underneath it was an easel, and stacked against the wall were blank canvases. There would be paint and brushes, he knew, and everything else that he might need. Whoever or whatever had sucked him into this place would do everything up brown; nothing would be overlooked.

It was unthinkable, he told himself, that it could have happened. Standing now, in the center of the room, he still could not believe it. He tried to work out the sequence of events that had led him to this house, the steps by which he had been lured into the trap, if trap it was—and on the face of the evidence, it had to be a trap. There had been the realtor in Boston who had told him of the house in Wyalusing. "It's the kind of place you are looking for," he had said. "No near neighbors, isolated. The little village a couple of miles down the road. If you need a woman to come in a couple of times a week to keep the place in order, just ask in the village. There's bound to be someone you could hire. The place is surrounded by old fields that haven't been farmed in years and are going back to brush and thickets. The coast is only half a mile distant. If you like to do some shooting, come fall there'll be quail and grouse. Fishing, too, if you want to do it."

"I might drive up and have a look at it," he had told the agent, who had then proceeded to give him the wrong directions, putting him on the road that would take him past this place. Or had he? Had it, perhaps, been his own muddleheadedness that had put him on the wrong road? Thinking about it, Latimer could not be absolutely certain. The agent had given him directions, but had they been the wrong directions? In the present situation, he knew that he had the tendency to view all prior circumstances with suspicion. Yet, certainly, there had been some psychological pressure brought, some misdirection employed to bring him to this house. It could not have been simple happenstance that had brought him here, to a house that trapped practitioners of the arts. A poet, a musician, a novelist, and a philosopher—although, come to think of it, a philosopher did not seem to exactly fit the pattern. Maybe the pattern was more apparent, he told himself, than it actually was. He still did not know the professions of Underwood, Charlie, and Jane. Maybe, once he did know, the pattern would be broken.

A bed stood in one corner of the room, a bedside table and a lamp beside it. In another corner three comfortable chairs were grouped, and along a short section of the wall stood shelves that were filled with books. On the wall beside the shelves hung a painting. It was only after staring at it for several minutes that he recognized it. It was one of his own, done several years ago.

He moved across the carpeted floor to confront the painting. It was one of those to which he had taken a special liking—one that, in fact, he had been somewhat reluctant to let go, would not have sold it if he had not stood so much in need of money.

The subject sat on the back stoop of a tumbledown house. Beside him, where he had dropped it, was a newspaper folded to the 'Help Wanted' ads. From the breast pocket of his painfully clean, but worn, work shirt an envelope stuck out, the gray envelope in which welfare checks were issued. The man's work-scarred hands lay listlessly in his lap, the forearms resting on the thighs, which were clad in ragged denims. He had not shaved for several days and the graying whiskers lent a deathly gray cast to his face. His hair, in need of barbering, was a tangled rat's nest, and his eyes, deep-set beneath heavy, scraggly brows, held a sense of helplessness. A scrawny cat sat at one corner of the house, a broken bicycle leaned against the basement wall. The man was looking out over a backyard filled with various kinds of litter, and beyond it the open countryside, a dingy gray and brown, seared by drought and lack of care, while on the horizon was the hint of industrial chimneys, gaunt and stark, with faint wisps of smoke trailing from them.

The painting was framed in heavy gilt—not the best choice, he thought, for such a piece. The bronze title tag was there, but he did not bend to look at it. He knew what it would say:

UNEMPLOYED
David Lloyd Latimer

How long ago? he wondered. Five years, or was it six? A man by the name of Johnny Brown, he remembered, had been the model. Johnny was a good man and he had used him several times. Later on, when he had tried to find him, he had been unable to locate him. He had not been seen for months in his old haunts along the waterfront and no one seemed to know where he had gone.

Five years ago, six years ago—sold to put bread into his belly, although that was silly, for when did he ever paint other than for bread? And here it was. He tried to recall the purchaser, but was unable to.

There was a closet, and when he opened it, he found a row of brand-new clothes, boots and shoes lined up on the floor, hats ranged neatly on the shelf. And all of them would fit—he was sure they would. The setters and the baiters of this trap would have seen to that. In the highboy next to the bed would be underwear, shirts, sock, sweaters—the kind that he would buy.

"We are taken care of," Enid had told him, sitting on the sofa with him before the flaring fire. There could be, he told himself, no doubt of that. No harm was intended them. They, in fact, were coddled.

And the question: Why? Why a few hand-picked people selected from many millions?

He walked to a window and stood looking out of it. The room was in the back of the house so that he looked down across the grove of ghostly birch. The moon had risen and hung like a milk-glass globe above the dark blur of the ocean. High as he stood, he could see the whiteness of the spray breaking on the boulders.

He had to have time to think, he told himself, time to sort it out, to get straight in his mind all the things that had happened in the last few hours. There was no sense in going to bed; tense as he was, he'd never get to sleep. He could not think in this room, nor, perhaps, in the house. He had to go some place that was uncluttered. Perhaps if he went outside and walked for an hour or so, if no more than up and down the driveway, he could get himself straightened out.

The blaze in the fireplace in the drawing room was little more than a glimmer in the coals when he went past the door.

A voice called to him: "David, is that you?"

He spun around and went back to the door. A dark figure was huddled on the sofa in front of the fireplace.

"Jonathon?" Latimer asked.

"Yes, it is. Why don't you keep me company. I'm an old night owl and, in consequence, spend many lonely hours. There's coffee on the table if you want it."

Latimer walked to the sofa and sat down. Cups and a carafe of coffee were on the table. He poured himself a cup.

"You want a refill?" he asked Jonathon.

"If you please." The older man held out his cup and Latimer filled it. "I drink a sinful amount of this stuff." said Jonathon. "There's liquor in the cabinet. A dash of brandy in the coffee, perhaps."

"That sounds fine," said Latimer. He crossed the room and found the brandy, brought it back, pouring a dollop into both cups.

They settled down and looked at one another. A nearly burned log in the fireplace collapsed into a mound of coals. In the flare of its collapse, Latimer saw the face of the other man—beard beginning to turn gray, an angular yet refined face, eyebrows that were sharp exclamation points.

"You're a confused young man," said Jonathon.

"Extremely so," Latimer confessed. "I keep asking all the time why and who."

Jonathon nodded. "Most of us still do, I suppose. It's worst when you first come here, but you never quit. You keep on asking questions. You're frustrated and depressed when there are no answers. As time goes on, you come more and more to accept the situation and do less fretting about it. After all, life is pleasant here. All our needs are supplied, nothing is expected of us. We do much as we please. You, no doubt, have heard of Enid's theory that we are under observation by an alien race that has penned us here in order to study us."

"Enid told me," said Latimer, "that she did not necessarily believe the theory, but regarded it as a nice idea, a neat and dramatic explanation of what is going on."

"It is that, of course," said Jonathon, "but it doesn't stand up. How would aliens be able to employ the staff that takes such good care of us?"

"The staff worries me," said Latimer. "Are its members trapped here along with us?"

"No, they're not trapped," said Jonathon. "I'm certain they are employed, perhaps at very handsome salaries. The staff changes from time to time, one member leaving to be replaced by someone else. How this is accomplished we do not know. We've kept a sharp watch in the hope that we might learn and thus obtain a clue as to how we could get out of here, but it all comes to nothing. We try on occasions, not too obviously, to talk with the staff, but beyond normal civility, they will not talk with us. I have a sneaking suspicion, too, that there are some of us, perhaps including myself, who no longer try too hard. Once one has been here long enough to make peace with himself, the ease of our life grows upon us. It would be something we would be reluctant to part with. I can't imagine, personally, what I would do if I were turned out of here, back into the world that I have virtually forgotten. That is the vicious part of it—that our captivity is so attractive, we are inclined to fall in love with it."

"But certainly in some cases there were people left behind—wives, husbands, children, friends. In my own case, no wife and only a few friends."

"Strangely enough," said Jonathon, "where such ties existed, they were not too strong."

"You mean only people without strong ties were picked?"

"No, I doubt that would have been the case. Perhaps among the kind of people who are here, there is no tendency to develop such strong ties."

"Tell me what kind of people. You told me you are a philosopher and I know some of the others. What about Underwood?"

"A playwright. And a rather successful one before he came here."

"Charlie? Jane?"

"Charlie is a cartoonist, Jane an essayist."

"Essayist?"

"Yes, high social consciousness. She wrote rather telling articles for some of the so-called little magazines, even a few for more prestigious publications. Charlie was big in the Middle West.

Worked for a small daily, hut his cartoons were widely reprinted. He was building a reputation and probably would have been moving on to more important fields."

"Then we're not all from around here. Not all from New England."

"No. Some of us, of course. Myself and you. The others are from other parts of the country."

"All of us from what can be roughly called the arts. And from a wide area. How in the world would they—whoever they may be—have managed to lure all these people to this house? Because I gather we had to come ourselves, that none of us was seized and brought here."

"I think you are right. I can't imagine how it was managed. Psychological management of some sort, I would assume, but I have no idea how it might be done."

"You say you are a philosopher. Does that mean you taught philosophy?"

"I did at one time. But it was not a satisfactory job. Teaching those old dead philosophies to a group of youngsters who paid but slight attention was no bargain, I can tell you. Although, I shouldn't blame them, I suppose. Philosophy today is largely dead. It's primitive, outdated, the most of it. What we need is a new philosophy that will enable us to cope with the present world."

"And you are writing such a philosophy?"

"Writing at it. I find that as time goes on, I get less and less done. I haven't the drive any longer. This life of ease, I suppose. Something's gone out of me. The anger, maybe. Maybe the loss of contact with the world I knew. No longer exposed to that world's conditions, I have lost the feel for it. I don't feel the need of protest, I've lost my sense of outrage, and the need for a new philosophy has become remote."

"This business about the staff. You say that from time to time it changes."

"It may be fairly simple to explain. I told you that we watch, but we can't have a watcher posted all the time. The staff, on the other hand, can keep track of us. Old staff members leave, others come in when we are somewhere else."

"And supplies. They have to bring in supplies. That would not be as simple."

Jonathon chuckled. "You've really got your teeth in this."

"I'm interested, dammit. There are questions about how the operation works and I want to know. How about the basement? Tunnels, maybe. Could they bring in staff and supplies through tunnels in the basement? I know that sounds cloak-and-dagger, but . . ."

"I suppose they could. If they did, we'd never know. The basement is used to store supplies and we're not welcome there. One of the staff, a burly brute who is a deaf-mute, or pretends to be, has charge of the basement. He lives down there, eats and sleeps down there, takes care of supplies."

"It could be possible, then?"

"Yes," said Jonathon. "It could be possible."

The fire had died down; only a few coals still blinked in the ash. In the silence that came upon them, Latimer heard the wind in the trees outside.

"One thing you don't know," said Jonathon. "You will find great auks down on the beach."

"Great auks? That's impossible. They've been . . ."

"Yes, I know. Extinct for more than a hundred years. Also whales. Sometimes you can sight a dozen a day. Occasionally a polar bear."

"Then that must mean . . ."

Jonathon nodded. "We are somewhere in prehistoric North America. I would guess several thousand years into the past. We hear and, occasionally, see moose. There are a number of deer, once in a while woodland caribou. The bird life, especially the wildfowl, are here in incredible numbers. Good shooting if you ever have the urge. We have guns and ammunition."

Dawn was beginning to break when Latimer went back to his room. He was bone-tired and now he could sleep. But before going to bed he stood for a time in front of the window overlooking the birch grove and the shore. A thin fog had moved off the water and everything had a faery, unrealistic cast.

Prehistoric North America, the philosopher had said, and if that was the case, there was little possibility of escape back to the world he knew. Unless one had the secret—or the technology—one did not move in time. Who, he wondered, could have cracked the technique of time transferral? And who, having cracked it, would use it for the ridiculous purpose of caging people in it?

There had been a man at MIT, he recalled, who had spent twenty years or more in an attempt to define time and gain some understanding of it. But that had been some years ago and he had dropped out of sight, or at least out of the news. From time to time there had been news stories (written for the most part with tongue firmly in cheek) about the study. Although, Latimer told himself, it need not have been the MIT man; there might have been other people engaged in similar studies who had escaped, quite happily, the attention of the press.

Thinking of it, he felt an excitement rising in him at the prospect of being in primitive North America, of being able to see the land as it had existed before white explorers had come—before the Norsemen or the Cabots or Cartier or any the others. Although there must be Indians about—it was funny that Jonathon had not mentioned Indians.

Without realizing that he had been doing so, he found that he had been staring at a certain birch clump. Two of the birch trees grew opposite off another, slightly behind but on opposite sides of a large boulder that he estimated at standing five feet high or so. And beyond the boulder, positioned slightly down the slope, but between the other two birch trees, was a third. It was not an unusual situation, he knew; birch trees often grew in clumps of three. There must have been some feature of the clump that had riveted his attention on it, but if that had been the case, he no longer was aware of it and it was not apparent now. Nevertheless, he remained staring at it, puzzled at what he had seen, if he had seen anything at all.

As he watched, a bird flew down from somewhere to light on the boulder. A songbird, but too far away for identification. Idly he watched the bird until it flew off the rock and disappeared.

Without bothering to undress, simply kicking off his shoes, he crossed the room to the bed and fell upon it, asleep almost before he came to rest upon it.

It was almost noon before he woke. He washed his face and combed his hair, not bothering to shave, and went stumbling down the stairs, still groggy from the befuddlement of having slept so soundly. No one else was in the house, but in the dining room a place was set and covered dishes remained upon the sideboard. He chose kidneys and scrambled eggs, poured a cup of coffee, and went back to the table. The smell of food triggered hunger, and after gobbling the plate of food, he went back for seconds and another cup of coffee.

When he went out through the rear door, there was no one in sight. The slope of birch stretched toward the coast. Off to his left, he heard two reports that sounded like shotguns. Perhaps someone out shooting duck or quail. Jonathon had said there was good hunting here.

He had to wend his way carefully through a confused tangle of boulders to reach the shore, with pebbles grating underneath his feet. A hundred yards away the inrolling breakers shattered themselves upon randomly scattered rocks, and even where he stood he felt the thin mist of spray upon his face.

Among the pebbles he saw a faint gleam and bent to see what it was. Closer to it, he saw that it was an agate—tennis-ball size, its fractured edge, wet with spray, giving off a waxy, translucent glint. He picked it up and polished it, rubbing off the clinging bits of sand, remembering how as a boy he had hunted agates in abandoned gravel pits. Just beyond the one he had picked up lay another one, and a bit to one side of it, a third. Crouched, he hunched forward and picked up both of them. One was bigger than the first, the second slightly smaller. Crouched there, he looked at them, admiring the texture of them, feeling once again, after many years, the thrill he had felt as a boy at finding agates. When he had left home to go to college, he remembered there had been a bag full of them still cached away in one corner of the garage. He wondered what might have become of them.

A few yards down the beach, something waddled out from behind a cluster of boulders, heading for the water. A bird, it stood some thirty inches tall and had a fleeting resemblance to a penguin. The upper plumage was black, white below, a large white spot encircled its eye. Its small wings shifted as it waddled. The bill was sharp and heavy, a vicious striking weapon.

He was looking at, he knew, a great auk, a bird that up in his world had been extinct but which, a few centuries before, had been common from Cape Cod to far north in Canada. Cartier's seamen, ravenous for fresh meat as a relief from sea rations, had clubbed hundreds to death, eating some of them at once, putting what remained down in kegs with salt.

Behind the first great auk came another and then two more. Paying no attention to him, they waddled down across the pebbles to the water, into which they dived, swimming away.

Latimer remained in his crouch, staring at the birds in fascination. Jonathon had said he would find them on the beach, but knowing he would find them and actually seeing them, were two different things. Now he was convinced, as he had not been before, of exactly where he was.

Off to his left, the guns banged occasionally, but otherwise there were no signs of the others in the house. Far out across the water, a string of ducks went scuddling close above the waves. The pebbled beach held a sense of peace—the kind of peace, he thought, that men might have known long years ago when the earth was still largely empty of humankind, when there was still room for such peace to settle in and stay.

Squatting there upon the beach, he remembered the clump of birch and now, suddenly and without thinking of it, he knew what had attracted his attention to it—an aberration of perspective that his painter's eye had caught. Knitting his brow, he tried to remember exactly what it was that had made the perspective wrong, but whatever it had been quite escaped him now.

He glimpsed another agate and went to pick it up, and a little farther down the beach he found yet another one. This, he told himself, was an unworked, unpicked rock-hunters paradise. He put the agates in his pocket and continued down the beach. Spotting other agates, he did not pick them up. Later, at some other time, if need be, he could find hours of amusement hunting them.

When he climbed the beach and started up the slope, he saw that Jonathon was sitting in a chair on the veranda that ran across the back of the house. He climbed up to where he sat and settled down in another chair.

"Did you see an auk?" asked Jonathon.

"I saw four of them," said Latimer.

"There are times," said Jonathon, "that the beach is crowded with them. Other times, you won't see one for days. Underwood and Charlie are off hunting woodcock. I suppose you heard them shooting. If they get back in time, we'll have woodcock for dinner. Have you ever eaten woodcock?"

"Only once. Some years ago. A friend and I went up to Nova Scotia to catch the early flight."

"I guess that is right. Nova Scotia and a few other places now. Here I imagine you can find hunting of them wherever you can find alder swamps."

"Where was everyone?" asked Latimer. "When I got out of the sack and had something to eat, there was no one around."

"The girls went out blackberrying," said Jonathon. "They do that often. Gives them something to do. It's getting a little late for blackberries, but there are some around. They got back in time to have blackberry pie tonight." He smacked his lips. "Woodcock and blackberry pie. I hope you are hungry."

"Don't you ever think of anything but eating?"

"Lots of other things," said Jonathon. "Thing is, here you grab onto anything you can think about. It keeps you occupied. And I might ask you, are you feeling easier than you were last night? Got all the immediate questions answered?"

"One thing still bothers me," said Latimer. "I left my car parked outside the house. Someone is going to find it parked there and will wonder what has happened."

"I think that's something you don't need to worry over," said Jonathon. "Whoever is engineering this business would have seen to it. I don't know, mind you, but I would guess that before morning your car was out of there and will be found, abandoned, some other place, perhaps a hundred miles away. The people we are dealing with would automatically take care of such small details. It wouldn't do to have too many incidents clustered about this house or in any other place. Your car will be found and you'll be missing and a hunt will be made for you. When you aren't found, you'll become just another one of the dozens of people who turn up missing every year."

"Which leaves me to wonder," said Latimer, "how many of these missing people wind up in places such as this. It is probable this is not the only place where some of them are being trapped."

"There is no way to know," said Jonathon. "People drop out for very many reasons."

They sat silent for a time, looking out across the sweep of lawn. A squirrel went scampering down the slope. Far off, birds were calling. The distant surf was a hollow booming.

Finally, Latimer spoke. "Last night, you told me we needed a new philosophy, that the old ones were no longer valid."

"That I did," said Jonathon. "We are faced today with a managed society. We live by restrictive rules, we have been reduced to numbers—our Social Security numbers, our Internal Revenue Service numbers, the numbers on our credit cards, on our checking and savings accounts, on any number of other things. We are being dehumanized and, in most cases, willingly, because this numbers game may seem to make life easier, but most often because no one wants to bother to make a fuss about it. We have come to believe that a man who makes a fuss is antisocial. We are a flock of senseless chickens, fluttering and scurrying, cackling and squawking, but being shooed along in the way that others want us to go. The advertising agencies tell us what to buy, the public relations people tell us what to think, and even knowing this, we do not resent it. We sometimes damn the government when we work up the courage to damn anyone at all. But I am certain it is not the government we should be damning, but, rather, the world's business managers. We have seen the rise of multinational complexes that owe no loyalty to any government, that think and plan in global terms, that view the human populations as a joint labor corps and consumer group, some of which also may have investment potential. This is a threat, as I see it, against human free will and human dignity, and we need a philosophical approach that will enable us to deal with it."

"And if you should write this philosophy," said Latimer, "it would pose a potential threat against the managers."

"Not at first," said Jonathon. "Perhaps never. But it might have some influence over the years. It might start a trend of thinking. To break the grip the managers now hold would require something like a social revolution . . ."

"These men, these managers you are talking about—they would be cautious men, would they not, farseeing men? They would take no chances. They'd have too much at stake to take any chances at all."

"You aren't saying . . ."

"Yes, I think I am. It is, at least, a thought."

Jonathon said, "I have thought of it myself but rejected it because I couldn't trust myself. It follows my bias too closely. And it doesn't make sense. If there were people they wanted to get out of the way, there'd be other ways to do it."

"Not as safely," said Latimer. "Here there is no way we could be found. Dead, we would be found . . ."

"I wasn't thinking of killing."

"Oh, well," said Latimer, "it was only a thought. Another guess."

"There's one theory no one has told you, or I don't think they have. An experiment in sociology. Putting various groups of people together in unusual situations and measuring their reactions. Isolating them so there is no present-world influence to modify the impact of the situation."

Latimer shook his head. "It sounds like a lot of trouble and expense. More than the experiment would be worth."

"I think so, too," said Jonathon.

He rose from his chair. "I wonder if you'd excuse me. I have the habit of stretching out for an hour or so before dinner. Sometimes I doze, other times I sleep, often I just lie there. But it is relaxing."

"Go ahead," said Latimer. "We'll have plenty of time later to talk."

For half an hour or more after Jonathon had left, he remained sitting in the chair, staring down across the lawn, but scarcely seeing it.

That idea about the managers being responsible for the situation, he told himself, made a ragged sort of sense. Managers, he thought with a smile—how easy it is to pick up someone else's lingo.

For one thing, the idea, if it worked, would be foolproof. Pick up the people you wanted out of the way and pop them into time, and after you popped them into time still keep track of them to be sure there were no slipups. And, at the same time, do them no real injustice, harm them as little as possible, keep a light load on your conscience, still be civilized.

There were two flaws, he told himself. The staff changed from time to time. That meant they must be rotated from here back to present time and they could be a threat. Some way would have had to be worked out to be sure they never talked, and given human nature, that would be a problem. The second flaw lay in the people who were here. The philosopher, if he had remained in present time, could have been a threat. But the rest of them? What threat could a poet pose? A cartoonist, maybe, perhaps a novelist, but a musician-composer—what threat could lie in music?

On the surface of it, however, it was not as insane as it sounded if you happened not to be on the receiving end of it. The world could have been spared a lot of grief in the last few hundred years if such a plan had been operative, spotting potential troublemakers well ahead of the time they became a threat and isolating them. The hard part of such a plan—from where he sat, an apparently impossible part of it—would lie in accurately spotting the potential troublemakers before they began making trouble. Although that, he supposed, might be possible. Given the state of the art in psychology, it might be possible.

With a start, he realized that during all this time, without consciously being aware of it, he had been staring at the birch clump. And now he remembered another thing. Just before he had stumbled off to bed, he had seen a bird light on the boulder, sit there for a time, then lift itself into the air and disappear—not fly away, but disappear. He must have known this when he saw it, but been so fogged by need of sleep that the significance of it had not made an impression. Thinking back on it, he felt sure he was not mistaken. The bird had disappeared.

He reared out of the chair and strode down the slope until he stood opposite the boulder with the two trees flanking it and the other growing close behind it. He took one of the agates out of his pocket and tossed it carefully over the boulder, aimed so that it would strike the tree behind the rock. It did not strike the tree; he could not hear it fall to the ground. One by one, he tossed all the other agates as he had tossed the first. None of them hit the tree, none fell to the ground. To make sure, he went around the tree to the right and, crouching down, crawled behind the boulder. He carefully went over the ground. There were no agates there.

Shaken, his mind a seething turmoil of mingled doubt and wonder, he went back up the hill and sat in the chair again. Thinking the situation over as calmly as he could, there seemed to be no doubt that he had found a rift of some sort in—what would you call it?—the time continuum, perhaps. And if you wriggled through the rift or threw yourself through the rift, you'd not be here. He had thrown the agates and they were no longer here; they had gone elsewhere. But where would you go? Into some other time, most likely, and the best guess would seem to be back into the time from which he had been snatched. He had come from there to here, and if there were a rift in the time continuum, it would seem to be reasonable to believe the rift would lead back into present time again. There was a chance it wouldn't, but the chance seemed small, for only two times had been involved in the interchange.

And if he did go back, what could he do? Maybe not a lot, but he damn well could try. His first move would be to disappear, to get away from the locality and lose himself. Whoever was involved in this trapping scheme would try to find him, but he would make it his business to be extremely hard to find. Then, once he had done that, he would start digging, to ferret out the managers Jonathon had mentioned, or if not them, then whoever might be behind all this.

He could not tell the others here what he suspected. Inadvertently, one of them might tip off a staff member, or worse, might try to prevent him from doing what he meant to do, having no wish to change the even tenor of the life they enjoyed here.

When Underwood and Charlie came up the hill with their guns, their hunting coats bulging with the woodcock they had bagged, he went inside with them, where the others had gathered in the drawing room for a round of before-dinner drinks.

At dinner, there was, as Jonathon had said there would be, broiled woodcock and blackberry pie, both of which were exceptionally tasty, although the pie was very full of seeds.

After dinner, they collected once again before the fire and talked of inconsequential things. Later on Alice played and again it was Chopin.

In his room, he pulled a chair over to the window and sat there, looking out at the birch clump. He waited until he could hear no one stirring about, and then two more hours after that, to make sure all were safely in their beds, if not asleep. Then he went softly down the stairs and out the back door. A half-moon lighted the lawn so that he had little trouble locating the birch clump. Now that he was there, he was assailed by doubt. It was ridiculous to think, he told himself, what he had been thinking. He would climb up on the boulder and throw himself out toward the third tree that stood behind the boulder and he would tumble to the ground between the tree and boulder and nothing would have happened. He would trudge sheepishly up the slope again and go to bed, and after a time he would manage to forget what he had done and it would be as if he had never done it. And yet, he remembered, he had thrown the agates, and when he had looked, there had not been any agates.

He scrambled up the face of the boulder and perched cautiously on its rounded top. He put out his hands to grasp the third birch and save himself from falling. Then he launched himself toward the tree.

He fell only a short distance, but landed hard upon the ground. There had not been any birch to catch to break his fall.

A hot sun blazed down upon him. The ground beneath him was not a greasy lawn, but a sandy loam with no grass at all. There were some trees, but not any birches.

He scrambled to his feet and turned to look at the house. The hilltop stood bare; there was no house. Behind him, he could hear the booming of the surf as it battered itself to spray against the rocky coastline.

Thirty feet away, to his left, stood a massive poplar, its leaves whispering in the wind that blew off the sea. Beyond it grew a scraggly pine tree and just down the slope, a cluster of trees that he thought were willows. The ground was covered—not too thickly covered, for rain-runneled soil showed through—by a growth of small ferns and other low-growing plants he could not identify.

He felt the perspiration starting from his body, running in rivulets from his armpits down his ribs—but whether from fear or sun, he did not know. For he was afraid, stiff and aching with the fear.

In addition to the poplar and the pine, low-growing shrubs were rooted in the ground among the ferns and other ground cover. Birds flew low, from one clump of shrubbery to another, chirping as they flew. From below him, their cries muted by the pounding of the surf, other birds were squalling. Gulls, he thought, or birds like gulls.

Slowly the first impact of the fear drained from him and he was able to move. He took a cautious step and then another and then was running toward the hilltop where the house should be, but wasn't.

Ahead of him, something moved and he skidded to a halt, poised to go around whatever had moved in the patch of shrubbery. A head poked out of the patch and stared at him with unblinking eyes. The nose was blunt and scaly and farther back the scales gave way to plates of armor. The thing mumbled at him disapprovingly and lurched forward a step or two, then halted.

It stood there, staring at him with its unblinking eyes. Its back was covered by overlapping plates. Its front legs were bowed. It stood four feet at the shoulder. It did not seem to be threatening; rather, it was curious.

His breath caught in his throat. Once, long ago, he had seen a drawing, an artist's conception, of this thing—not exactly like it, but very much the same. An anky, he thought—what was it?—an ankylosaurus, that was what it was, he realized, amazed that he should remember, an ankylosaurus. A creature that should have been dead for millions of years. But the caption had said six feet at the shoulder and fifteen feet long, and this one was nowhere near that big. A small one, he thought, maybe a young one, maybe a different species, perhaps a baby ankywhatever-the-hell-it-was.

Cautiously, almost on tiptoe, he walked around it, while it kept turning its head to watch him. It made no move toward him. He kept looking over his shoulder to be sure it hadn't moved. Herbivorous, he assured himself, an eater of plants—posing no danger to anything at all, equipped with armor plate to discourage the meat eaters that might slaver for its flesh. He tried hard to remember whether the caption had said it was herbivorous, but his mind, on that particular point, was blank.

Although, if it were here, there would he carnivores as well—and, for the love of God, what had he fallen into? Why hadn't he given more thought to the possibility that something like this might happen, that he would not, necessarily, automatically go back to present time, but might be shunted off into another time? And why, just as a matter of precaution, hadn't he armed himself before he left? There were high-caliber guns in the library and he could have taken one of them and a few boxes of ammunition if he had just thought about it.

He had failed to recognize the possibility of being dumped into a place like this, he admitted, because he had been thinking about what he wanted to happen, to the exclusion of all else, using shaky logic to convince himself that he was right. His wishful thinking, he now knew, had landed him in a place no sane man would choose.

He was back in the age of dinosaurs and there wasn't any house. He probably was the only human on the planet, and if his luck held out, he might last a day or two, but probably not much more than that. He knew he was going off the deep end again, thinking as illogically as he had been when he launched himself into the time rift. There might not be that many carnivores about, and if a man was observant and cautious and gave himself a chance to learn, he might be able to survive. Although the chances were that he was stuck here. There could be little hope that he could find another rift in time, and even if he did, there would be no assurance that it would take him to anything better than this. Perhaps, if he could find the point where he had emerged into this world, he might have a chance to locate the rift again, although there was no guarantee that the rift was a two-way rift. He stopped and looked around, but there was no way to know where he had first come upon this place. The landscape all looked very much the same.

The ankylosaurus, he saw, had come a little out of the shrub thicket and was nibbling quite contentedly at the ground cover. Turning his back upon it, he went trudging up the hill.

Before he reached the crest, he turned around again to have a look. The ankylosaurus was no longer around, or perhaps he did not know where to look for it. Down in the swale that had been the alder swamp where Underwood and Charlie had bagged the woodcock, a herd of small reptiles were feeding, browsing off low-growing shrubs and ground cover.

Along the skyline of the hill beyond which the herd was feeding, a larger creature lurched along on its hind legs, its body slanted upright at an angle, the shriveled forearms dangling at its side, its massive, brutal head jerking as it walked. The herd in the swale stopped their feeding, heads swiveling to look at the lurching horror. Then they ran, racing jerkily on skinny hind legs, like a flock of outsize, featherless chickens racing for their lives.

Latimer turned again and walked toward the top of the hill. The last slope was steep, steeper than he remembered it had been on that other, safer world. He was panting when he reached the crest, and he stopped a moment to regain his breath. Then, when he was breathing more easily, he turned to look toward the south.

Half-turned, he halted, amazed at what he saw—the last thing in the world that he had expected to see. Sited in the valley that lay between the hill on which he stood and the next headland to the south, was a building. Not a house, but a building. It stood at least thirty stories high and looked like an office building, its windows gleaming in the sun.

He sobbed in surprise and thankfulness, but even so, he did not begin to run toward it, but stood for a moment looking at it, as if he must look at it for a time to believe that it was there. Around it lay a park of grass and tastefully planted trees. Around the park ran a high wire fence and in the fence at the foot of the hill closest to him was a gate, beside which was a sentry box. Outside the sentry box stood two men who carried guns.

Then he was running, racing recklessly down the hill, running with great leaps, ducking thickets of shrubs. He stubbed his toe and fell, pinwheeling down the slope. He brought up against a tree and, the breath half-knocked out of him, got to his feet, gasping and wheezing. The men at the gate had not moved, but he knew that they had seen him; they were gazing up the hill toward him.

Moving at a careful, slower pace, he went on down the hill. The slope leveled off and he found a faint path that he followed toward the gate.

He came up to the two guards and stopped.

"You damn fool," one of them said to him. "What do you think you're doing, going out without a gun? Trying to get yourself killed?"

"There's been an old Tyranno messing around here for the last several days," said the other guard. "He was seen by several people. An old bastard like that could go on the prod at the sight of you and you wouldn't have a chance."

The first guard jerked his rifle toward the gate. "Get in there," he said. "Be thankful you're alive. If I ever catch you going out again without a gun, I'll turn you in, so help me."

"Thank you, sir," said Latimer.

He walked through the gate, following a path of crushed shells toward the front entrance of the office building. But now that he was there, safe behind the fence, the reaction began setting in. His knees were wobbly and he staggered when he walked. He sat down on a bench beneath a tree. He found that his hands were shaking and he held them hard against his thighs to stop the trembling.

How lucky could one get? he asked himself. And what did it mean? A house in the more recent past, an office building in this place that must be millions of years into the past. There had not been dinosaurs upon the earth for at least sixty million years. And the rift? How had the rift come about? Was it something that could occur naturally, or had it come about because someone was manipulating time? Would such rifts come when someone, working deliberately, using techniques of which there was no public knowledge, was putting stress upon the web of time? Was it right to call time a web? He decided that it made no difference, that the terminology was not of great importance.

An office building, he thought. What did an office building mean? Was it possible that he had stumbled on the headquarters of the project/conspiracy/program that was engaged in the trapping of selected people in the past? Thinking of it, the guess made sense. A cautious group of men could not take the chance of operating such an enterprise in present time, where it might be nosed out by an eager-beaver newsman or a governmental investigation or by some other means. Here, buried in millions of years of time, there would be little chance of someone unmasking it.

Footsteps crunched on the path and Latimer looked up. A man in sports shirt and flannels stood in front of him.

"Good morning, sir," said Latimer.

The man asked, "Could you be David Latimer, by any chance?"

"I could be," said Latimer.

"I thought so. I don't remember seeing you before. And I was sure I knew everyone. And the guards reported . . ."

"I arrived only an hour or so ago."

"Mr. Gale wanted to see you as soon as you arrived."

"You mean you were expecting me?"

"Well, we couldn't be absolutely sure," said the other. "We are glad you made it."

Latimer got off the bench and the two of them walked together to the front entrance, climbed the steps, and went through the door. They walked through a deserted lounge, then into a hallway flanked by numbered doors with no names upon them. Halfway down the hall, the man with Latimer knocked at one of the doors.

"Come in," a voice said.

The man opened the door and stuck his head in. "Mr. Latimer is here," he said. "He made it."

"That is fine," said the voice. "I am glad he did. Please show him in."

The man stepped aside to allow Latimer to enter, then stepped back into the hall and closed the door. Latimer stood alone, facing the man across the room.

"I'm Donovan Gale," said the man, rising from his desk and coming across the room. He held out his hand and Latimer took it. Gale's grasp was a friendly corporate handshake.

"Let's sit over here," he said, indicating a davenport. "It seems to me we may have a lot to talk about."

"I'm interested in hearing what you have to say," said Latimer.

"I guess both of us are," said Gale. "Interested in what the other has to say, I mean."

They sat down on opposite ends of the davenport, turning to face one another.

"So you are David Latimer," said Gale. "The famous painter."

"Not famous," said Latimer. "Not yet. And it appears now that I may never be. But what I don't understand is how you were expecting me."

"We knew you'd left Auk House."

"So that is what you call it. Auk House."

"And we suspected you would show up here. We didn't know exactly where, although we hoped that it would be nearby. Otherwise you never would have made it. There are monsters in those hills. Although, of course, we could not be really sure that you would wind up here. Would you mind telling us how you did it?"

Latimer shook his head. "I don't believe I will. Not right now, at least. Maybe later on when I know more about your operation. And now a question for you. Why me? Why an inoffensive painter who was doing no more than trying to make a living and a reputation that might enable him to make a better living?"

"I see," said Gale, "that you have it figured out."

"Not all of it," said Latimer. "And, perhaps, not all of it correctly. But I resent being treated as a bad guy, as a potential threat of some sort. I haven't got the guts or the motive to be a bad guy. And Enid, for Christ's sake. Enid is a poet. And Alice. All Alice does is play a good piano."

"You're talking to the wrong man," Gale told him. "Breen could tell you that, if you can get him to tell you. I'm only personnel."

"Who is Breen?"

"He's head of the evaluation team."

"Those are the ones who figure out who is going to be picked up and tossed into time."

"Yes, that is the idea, crudely. There's a lot more to it than that. There is a lot of work done here. Thousands of newspapers and other periodicals to be read to spot potential subjects. Preliminary psychological determinations. Then it's necessary to do further study back on prime world. Further investigation of potential subjects. But no one back there really knows what is going on. They're just hired to do jobs now and then. The real work goes on here."

"Prime world is present time? Your old world and mine?"

"Yes. If you think, however, of prime world as present time, that's wrong. That's not the way it is. We're not dealing with time, but with alternate worlds. The one you just came from is a world where everything else took place exactly as it did in prime world, with one exception—man never evolved. There are no men there and never will be. Here, where we are now, something more drastic occurred. Here the reptiles did not become extinct. The Cretaceous never came to an end, the Cenozoic never got started. The reptiles are still the dominant species and the mammals still are secondary."

"You're taking a chance, aren't you, in telling me all this."

"I don't think so," said Gale. "You're not going anywhere. There are none of us going anywhere. Once we sign up for this post, we know there's not any going back. We're stuck here. Unless you have a system . . ."

"No system. I was just lucky."

"You're something of an embarrassment to us," said Gale. "In the years since the program has been in operation, nothing like this has happened at any of the stations. We don't know what to make of it and we don't quite know what to do with you. For the moment, you'll stay on as a guest. Later on, if it is your wish, we could find a place for you. You could become a member of the team."

"Right at the moment," said Latimer, "that holds no great attraction for me."

"That's because you aren't aware of the facts, nor of the dangers. Under the economic and social systems that have been developed in prime world, the great mass of mankind has never had it so good. There are ideological differences, of course, but there is some hope that they eventually can be ironed out. There are underprivileged areas; this cannot be denied. But one must also concede that their only hope lies in their development by free-world business interests. So-called big-business interests are the world's one hope. With the present economic structure gone, the entire world would go down into another Dark Age, from which it would require a thousand years or more to recover, if recovery, in fact, were possible at all."

"So to protect your precious economic structure, you place a painter, a poet, a musician into limbo."

Gale made a despairing gesture with his hands. "I have told you I can't supply the rationale on that. You'll have to see Breen if he has the time to see you. He's a very busy man."

"I would imagine that he might be."

"He might even dig out the files and tell you," said Gale. "As I say, you're not going anywhere. You can pose no problem now. You are stuck with us and we with you. I suppose that we could send you back to Auk House, but that would be undesirable, I think. It would only upset the people who are there. As it is, they'll probably figure that you simply wandered off and got killed by a bear or bitten by a rattlesnake, or drowned in a swamp. They'll look for you and when they don't find you, that will be it. You only got lost; they'll never consider for a moment that you escaped. I think we had better leave it at that. Since you are here and, given time, would nose out the greater part of our operation, we have no choice but to be frank with you. Understandably, however, we'd prefer that no one outside this headquarters knew."

"Back at Auk House, there was a painting of mine hanging in my room."

"We thought it was a nice touch," said Gale. "A sort of friendly thing to do. We could bring it here."

"That wasn't why I asked," said Latimer. "I was wondering—did the painting's subject have something to do with what you did to me? Were you afraid that I would go on painting pictures pointing up the failures of your precious economic structure?"

Gale was uncomfortable. "I couldn't say," he said.

"I was about to say that if such is the case, you stand on very flimsy ground and carry a deep guilt complex."

"Such things are beyond me," said Gale. "I can't even make a comment."

"And this is all you want of me? To stand in place? To simply be a guest of all these big-hearted corporations?"

"Unless you want to tell us how you got here."

"I have told you that I won't do that. Not now. I suppose if you put me to the torture . . ."

"We wouldn't torture you," said Gale. "We are civilized. We regret some of the things that we must do, but we do not flinch from duty. And not the duty to what you call big-hearted corporations, but to all humankind. Man has a good thing going; we can't allow it to be undermined. We're not taking any chances. And now, perhaps I should call someone to show you to your room. I take it you got little sleep last night."

Latimer's room was on one of the topmost floors and was larger and somewhat more tastefully furnished than the room at Auk House. From a window, he saw that the conformation of the coastline was much the same as it had been at Auk House. The dirty gray of the ocean stretched off to the east and the surf still came rolling in to break upon the boulders. Some distance off shore, a school of long-necked creatures were cavorting in the water. Watching them more closely, Latimer made out that they were catching fish. Scattered reptilian monstrosities moved about in the hills that ran back from the sea, some of them in small herds, some of them alone. Dwarfed by distance, none of them seemed unusually large. The trees, he saw, were not a great deal different from the ones he had known. The one thing that was wrong was the lack of grass.

He had been a victim of simplistic thinking in believing, he told himself, that when he threw himself into the rift he would be carried to present time or prime world or whatever one might call it. In the back of his mind, as well, although he had not really dared to think it, had been the idea that if he could get back to the real world, he could track down the people who were involved and put a stop to it.

There was no chance of that now, he knew, and there never had been. Back on prime world, there would be no evidence that would stand up, only highly paid lackeys who performed necessary chores. Private investigators, shady operators like the Boston realtor and the Campbell who had listed Auk House for sale or rent. Undoubtedly, the sign announcing the house was available was posted only when a potential so-called customer would be driving past. Campbell would have been paid well, perhaps in funds that could not be traced, for the part he played, offering the house and then, perhaps, driving off the car left behind by the customer. He took some risks, certainly, but they were minimal. Even should he have been apprehended, there would be no way in which he could be tied into the project. He, himself, would have had no inkling of the project. A few men in prime world would have to know, of course, for some sort of communications had to be maintained between this operations center and prime world. But the prime-world men, undoubtedly, would be solid citizens, not too well known, all beyond suspicion or reproach. They would be very careful against the least suspicion, and the communications between them and this place must be of a kind that could not be traced and would have no record.

Those few upright men, perhaps a number of hired hands who had no idea of what was being done, would be the only ones in prime world who would play any part in the project. The heart of the operation was in this building. Here the operations were safe. There was no way to get at them. Gale had not even bothered to deny what was being done, had merely referred him to Breen for any further explanation. And Breen, should he talk with him, probably would make no denial, either.

And here he stood, David Latimer, artist, the one man outside the organization who, while perhaps not realizing the full scope of the project, still knew what was happening. Knew and could do nothing about it. He ran the facts he had so far acquired back and forth across his mind, seeking some chink of weakness, and there seemed to be none.

Silly, he thought, one man pitting himself against a group that held the resources of the earth within its grasp, a group at once ruthless and fanatical, that commanded as its managers the best brains of the planet, arrogant in its belief that what was good for the group was good for everyone, brooking no interference, alert to even the slightest threat, even to imagined threat.

Silly, perhaps absurdly quixotic—and, yet, what could he do? To save his own self-respect, to pay even lip service to the dignity of humanity, he must make at least a token effort, even knowing that the possibility of his accomplishing anything was very close to zero.

Say this much for them, he thought, they were not cruel men. In many ways, they were compassionate. Their imagined enemies were neither killed nor confined in noisome prisons, as had been the case with historic tyrants. They were held under the best of circumstances, all their needs were supplied, they were not humiliated. Everything was done to keep them comfortable and happy. The one thing that had been taken from them was their freedom of choice.

But man, he thought, had fought for bitter centuries for that very freedom. It was not something that should be lightly held or easily relinquished.

All this, at the moment, he thought, was pointless. If he should be able to do anything at all, it might not be until after months of observation and learning. He could remain in the room for hours, wallowing in his doubt and incompetency, and gain not a thing by it. It was time to begin to get acquainted with his new surroundings.

The parklike grounds surrounding the buildings were ringed by the fence, twelve feet high or more, with a four-foot fence inside it. There were trees and shrubs and beds of flowers and grass—the only grass he had seen since coming here, a well-tended greensward.

Paths of crushed shell ran among the trees and underneath them was a coolness and a quiet. A few gardeners worked in flower beds and guards stood at the distant gate, but otherwise there were few people about. Probably it was still office hours; later on, there might be many people.

He came upon the man sitting on the bench when the walk curved sharply around a group of head-high shrubbery. Latimer stopped, and for a moment they regarded one another as if each was surprised at the appearance of the other.

Then the man on the bench said, with a twinkle in his eye, "It seems that the two of us are the only ones who have no tasks on this beautiful afternoon. Could you be, possibly, the refugee from Auk House?"

"As a matter of fact, I am," said Latimer. "My name is David Latimer, as if you didn't know."

"Upon my word," said the other, "I didn't know your name. I had only heard that someone had escaped from Auk House and had ended up with us. News travels swiftly here. The place is a rumor mill. There is so little of consequence that happens that once some notable event does occur, it is chewed to tiny shreds.

"My name, by the way, is Horace Sutton and I'm a paleontologist. Can you imagine a better place for a paleontologist to be?"

"No, I can't," said Latimer.

"Please share this bench with me," invited Sutton. "I take it there is nothing of immediate urgency that requires your attention."

"Not a thing," said Latimer. "Nothing whatsoever."

"Well, that is fine," said Sutton. "We can sit and talk a while or stroll around for a bit, however you may wish. Then, as soon as the sun gets over the yardarm, if by that time you're not totally disenchanted with me, we can indulge ourselves in some fancy drinking."

Sutton's hair was graying and his face was lined, but there was something youthful about him that offset the graying hair and lines.

Latimer sat down and Sutton said to him, "What do you think of this layout? A charming place, indeed. The tall fence, as you may have guessed, is electrified, and the lower fence keeps stupid people such as you and I from blundering into it. Although, there have been times I have been glad the fence is there. Comes a time when a carnivore or two scents the meat in here and is intent upon a feast, you are rather glad it's there."

"Do they gather often? The carnivores, I mean."

"Not as much as they did at one time. After a while, the knowledge of what to keep away from sinks into even a reptilian brain."

"As a paleontologist you study the wildlife here."

"For the last ten years," said Sutton. "I guess a bit less time than that. It was strange at first; it still seems a little strange. A paleontologist, you understand, ordinarily works with bones and fossil footprints and other infuriating evidence that almost tells you what you want to know, but always falls short.

"Here there is another problem. From the viewpoint of prime world, many of the reptiles, including the dinosaurs, died out sixty-three million years ago. Here they did not die out. As a result, we are looking at them not as they were millions of years ago, but as they are after millions of additional years of evolutionary development. Some of the old species have disappeared, others have evolved into something else in which you can see the traces of their lineage, and some entirely new forms have arisen."

"You sound as if your study of them is very dedicated," said Latimer. "Under other circumstances, you would probably be writing a book . . ."

"But I am writing a book," said Sutton. "I am hard at work on it. There is a man here who is very clever at drawing and he is making diagrams for me and there will be photographs . . ."

"But what's the point?" asked Latimer. "Who will publish it? When will it be published? Gale told me that no one ever leaves here, that there is no going back to prime world."

"That is right," said Sutton. "We are exiled from prime world. I often think of us as a Roman garrison stationed, say, on Britain's northern border or in the wilds of Dacia, with the understanding that we'll not be going back to Rome."

"But that means your book won't be published. I suppose it could be transmitted back to prime world and be printed there, but the publishing of it would destroy the secrecy of the project."

"Exactly how much do you know about the project?" Sutton asked.

"Not much, perhaps. Simply the purpose of it—the trapping of people in time—no, not time, I guess. Alternate worlds, rather."

"Then you don't know the whole of it?"

"Perhaps I don't," said Latimer.

"The matter of removing potentially dangerous personnel from prime world," said Sutton, "is only part of it. Surely if you have thought of it at all, you could see other possibilities."

"I haven't had time to think too deeply on it," said Latimer. "No time at all, in fact. You don't mean the exploitation of these other worlds?"

"It's exactly what I mean," said Sutton. "It is so obvious, so logical. Prime world is running out of resources. In these worlds, they lie untouched. The exploitation of the alternate worlds not only would open new resources, but would provide employment, new lands for colonization, new space for expansion. It is definitely a better idea than this silly talk you hear about going off into outer space to find new worlds that could be colonized."

"Then why all the mummery of using it to get rid of potential enemies?"

"You sound as if you do not approve of this part of the project."

"I'm not sure I approve of any of it and certainly not of picking up people and stashing them away. You seem to ignore the fact that I was one of those who was picked up and stashed away. The whole thing smells of paranoia. For the love of God, the big business interests of prime world have so solid a grip on the institutions of the Earth and, in large part, on the people of the Earth, that there is no reason for the belief that there is any threat against them."

"But they do take into account," said Sutton, "the possibility of such threats rising in the years to come, probably based upon events that could be happening right now. They have corps of psychologists who are pursuing studies aimed against such possibilities, corps of economists and political scientists who are looking at possible future trends that might give rise to antibusiness reactions. And, as you know, they are pinpointing certain specific areas and peoples who could contribute, perhaps unwittingly, either now or in the future, to undesirable reactions. But, as I understand it, they are hopeful that if they can forestall the trends that would bring about such reactions for a few centuries, then the political, the economic, and the social climates will be so solidly committed in their favor, that they can go ahead with the exploitation of some of the alternate worlds. They want to be sure before they embark on it, however, that they won't have to keep looking over their shoulders."

"But hundreds of years! All the people who are engaged in this project will have been long dead by then."

"You forget that a corporation can live for many centuries. The corporations are the driving force here. And, in the meantime, those who work in the project gain many advantages. It is worth their while."

"But they can't go back to Earth—back to prime world, that is."

"You are hung up on prime world," said Sutton. "By working in the project, you are showered with advantages that prime world could never give you. Work in the project for twenty years, for example, and at the age of fifty—in some cases, even earlier—you can have a wide choice of retirements—an estate somewhere on Auk world, a villa on a paradise world, a hunting lodge in another world where there is a variety of game that is unbelievable. With your family, if you have one, with servants, with your every wish fulfilled. Tell me, Mr. Latimer, could you do as well if you stayed on prime world? I've listed only a few possibilities; there are many others."

"Gale told me it would be possible to send me back to Auk House. So people can move around these alternate worlds, but not back to prime world?"

"That is right. Supplies for all the worlds are transported to this world and from here sent out to other stations."

"But how? How is this done?"

"I have no idea. There is an entire new technology involved. Once I had thought it would be matter transmitters, but I understand it's not. Certain doors exist. Doors with quote marks around them. I suppose there is a corps of elite engineers who know, but would suspect that no one else does."

"You spoke of families."

"There are families here."

"But I didn't see . . ."

"The kids are in school. There aren't many people about right now. They'll be showing up at the cocktail hour. A sort of country-club routine here. That's why I like to get up early. Not many are about. I have this park to myself."

"Sutton, you sound as if you like this setup."

"I don't mind it," Sutton said. "It's far preferable to what I had in prime world. There my reputation had been ruined by a silly dispute I fell into with several of my colleagues. My wife died. My university let me stay on in sufferance. So when I was offered a decent job..."

"Not telling you what kind of job?"

"Well, no, not really. But the conditions of employment sounded good and I would be in sole charge of the investigation that was in prospect. To be frank with you, I jumped at it."

"You must have been surprised."

"In fact, I was. It took a while to reconcile myself to the situation."

"But why would they want a paleontologist?"

"You mean, why would money-grabbing, cynical corporations want a paleontologist?"

"I guess that's what I mean."

"Look, Latimer—the men who make up the corporations are not monsters. They saw here the need for a study of a truly unique world—a continuation of the Cretaceous, which has been, for years, an intriguing part of the planet's history. They saw it as a contribution to human knowledge. My book, when it is published, will show this world at a time before the impact of human exploitation fell upon it."

"When your book is published?"

"When it is safe to make the announcement that alternate worlds have been discovered and are being opened for colonization. I'll never see the book, of course, but nevertheless, I take some pride in it. Here I have found confirmation for my stand that brought about condemnation by my colleagues. Fuzzy thinking, they said, but they were the fuzzy thinkers. This book will vindicate me."

"And that's important? Even after you are dead?"

"Of course it is important. Even after I am dead."

Sutton looked at his watch. "I think," he said, "it may be time now. It just occurred to me. Have you had anything to eat?"

"No," said Latimer. "I hadn't thought of it before. But I am hungry."

"There'll be snacks in the bar," said Sutton. "Enough to hold you until dinner."

"One more question before we leave," said Latimer. "You said the reptiles showed some evolutionary trends. In what direction? How have they changed?"

"In many ways," said Sutton. "Bodily changes, of course. Perhaps ecological changes as well—behavioral changes, although I can't be sure of that. I can't know what their behavior was before. Some of the bigger carnivores haven't changed at all. Perhaps a bit more ability in a number of cases. Their prey may have become faster, more alert, and the carnivores had to develop a greater agility or starve. But the most astonishing change is in intelligence. There is one species, a brand-new species so far as I know, that seems to have developed a pronounced intelligence. If it is intelligence, it is taking a strange direction. It's hard to judge correctly. You must remember that of all the stupid things that ever walked the earth, some of the dinosaurs ranked second to none. They didn't have a lick of sense."

"You said intelligence in a strange direction."

"Let me try to tell you. I've watched these jokers for hours on end. I'm almost positive that they handle herds of herbivores—herbivorous reptiles, that is. They don't run around them like sheepdogs manage sheep, but I am sure they do control them. There are always a few of them watching the herds, and while they're watching them, the herds do no straying—they stay together like a flock of sheep tended by dogs. They move off in orderly fashion when there is need to move to a new pasture. And every once in a while, a few members of the herd will detach themselves and go ambling off to a place where others of the so-called intelligent dinosaurs are hanging out, and there they are killed. They walk in to be slaughtered. I can't get over the feeling that the herbivores are meat herds, the livestock of the intelligent species. And another thing. When carnivores roam in, these intelligent jokers shag them out of there. Not by chasing them or threatening them. Just by moving out where they can be seen. Then they sit down, and after the carnivores have looked them over, the carnivores seem to get a little jittery, and after a short time they move off."

"Hypnotism? Some sort of mental power?"

"Possibly."

"That wouldn't have to be intelligence. It could be no more than an acquired survival trait."

"Somehow I don't think so. Other than watching herds and warning off carnivores—if that is what they're doing—they sit around a lot among themselves. Like a bunch of people talking. That's the impression I get, that they are talking. None of the social mannerisms that are seen among primates—no grooming, horseplay, things like that. There seems to be little personal contact—no touching, no patting, no stroking. As if none of this were needed. But they dance. Ritualistic dancing of some sort. Without music. Nothing to make music with. They have no artifacts. They haven't got the hands that could fashion artifacts. Maybe they don't need tools or weapons or musical instruments. Apparently they have certain sacred spots. Places where they go, either singly or in small groups, to meditate or worship. I know of one such place; there may be others. No idols, nothing physical to worship. A secluded spot. Seemingly a special place. They have been using it for years. They have worn a path to it, a path trod out through the centuries. They seem to have no form of worship, no rituals that must be observed. They simply go and sit there. At no special time. There are no Sundays in this world. I suspect they go only when they feel the need of going."

"It is a chilling thought," said Latimer.

"Yes, I suppose it is."

He looked at his watch again. "I am beginning to feel the need of that drink," he said. "How about you?"

"Yes" said Latimer, "I could do with one."

And now, he told himself, he had a few more of the answers. He knew how the staff at Auk House was changed, where the supplies came from. Everything and everyone, apparently, was channeled and routed from this operations center. Prime world, from time to time, furnished supplies and personnel and then the rest was handled here.

He found himself puzzled by Sutton's attitude. The man seemed quite content, bore no resentment over being exiled here. They are not monsters, he had said, implying that the men in this operation were reasonable and devoted men working in the public interest. He was convinced that someday his book would be published, according him posthumous vindication. There had been, as well, Latimer remembered, Enid's poems and Dorothy's novel. Had the poems and the novel been published back in prime world, perhaps under pseudonyms, works so excellent that it had been deemed important that they not be lost?

And what about the men who had done the research that had resulted in the discovery of the alternate worlds and had worked out the technique of reaching and occupying them? Not still on prime world, certainly; they would pose too great a danger there. Retired, perhaps, to estates on some of the alternate worlds.

They walked around one of the clumps of trees with which the park was dotted, and from a distance Latimer heard the sound of children happy at their play.

"School is out," said Sutton. "Now it's the children's hour."

"One more thing," said Latimer, "if you don't mind. One more question. On all these other alternate worlds you mention, are there any humans native to those worlds? Is it possible there are other races of men?"

"So far as I know," said Sutton, "man rose only once, on prime world. What I have told you is not the entire story, I imagine. There may be much more to it. I've been too busy to attempt to find out more. All I told you are the things I have picked up in casual conversation. I do not know how many other alternate worlds have been discovered, nor on how many of them stations have been established. I do know that on Auk world there are several stations other than Auk House."

"By stations, you mean the places where they put the undesirables."

"You put it very crudely, Mr. Latimer, but yes, you are quite right. On the matter of humans arising elsewhere, I think it's quite unlikely. It seems to me that it was only by a combination of a number of lucky circumstances that man evolved at all. When you take a close look at the situation, you have to conclude that man had no right to expect to evolve. He is a sort of evolutionary accident."

"And intelligence? Intelligence rose on prime world, and you seem to have evidence that it has risen here as well. Is intelligence something that evolution may be aiming at and will finally achieve, in whatever form on whatever world? How can you be sure it has not risen on Auk world? At Auk House, only a few square miles have been explored. Perhaps not a great deal more around the other stations."

"You ask impossible questions," said Sutton shortly. "There is no way I can answer them."

They had reached a place from which a full view of the headquarters building was possible and now there were many people—men and women walking about or sunning themselves, stretched out on the grass, people sitting on terraces in conversational groups, while children ran gaily, playing a childish game.

Sutton, who had been walking ahead of Latimer, stopped so quickly that Latimer, with difficulty, averted bumping into him.

Sutton pointed. "There they are," he said.

Looking in the direction of the pointing finger, Latimer could see nothing unusual. "What? Where?" he asked.

"On top of the hill, just beyond the northern gate."

After a moment Latimer saw them, a dozen squatting creatures on top of the hill down which, a few hours ago, he had run for the gate and safety. They were too distant to be seen clearly, but they had a faintly reptilian look and they seemed to be coal-black, but whether naturally black or black because of their silhouetted position, he could not determine.

"The ones I told you about," said Sutton. "It's nothing unusual. They often sit and watch us. I suspect they are as curious about us as we are about them."

"The intelligences?" asked Latimer.

"Yes, that is right," said Sutton.

Someone, some distance off, cried in a loud voice—no words that Latimer could make out, but a cry of apprehension, a bellow of terror. Then there were other cries, different people taking up the cry.

A man was running across the park, heading for its northeast corner, running desperately, arms pumping back and forth, legs a blur of scissoring speed. He was so far off that he looked like a toy runner, heading for the four-foot fence that stood inside the higher fence. Behind him were other runners, racing in an attempt to head him off and pull him down.

"My God, it's Breen," gasped Sutton. His face had turned to gray. He started forward, in a stumbling run. He opened his mouth to shout, but all he did was gasp.

The running man came to the inner fence and cleared it with a leap. The nearest of his pursuers was many feet behind him.

Breen lifted his arms into the air, above his head. He slammed into the electrified fence. A flash blotted him out. Flickering tongues of flame ran along the fence—bright and sparkling, like the flaring of fireworks. Then the brightness faded and on the fence hung a black blot that smoked greasily and had a fuzzy, manlike shape.

A hush, like an indrawn breath, came upon the crowd. Those who had been running stopped running and, for a moment, held their places. Then some of them, after that moment, ran again, although some of them did not, and the voice took up again, although now there was less shouting.

When he looked, Latimer saw that the hilltop was empty; the dinosaurs that had been there were gone. There was no sign of Sutton.

So it was Breen, thought Latimer, who hung there on the fence. Breen, head of the evaluation team, the one man, Gale had said, who could tell him why he had been lured to Auk House. Breen, the man who pored over psychological evaluations, who was acquainted with the profile of each suspected personage, comparing those profiles against economic charts, social diagnostic indices, and God knows what else, to enable him to make the decision that would allow one man to remain in prime world as he was, another to be canceled out.

And now, thought Latimer, it was Breen who had been canceled out, more effectively than he had canceled any of the others.

Latimer had remained standing where he had been when Sutton and he had first sighted the running Breen, had stood because he could not make up his mind what he should do, uncertain of the relationship that he held or was expected to assume with those other persons who were still milling about, many of them perhaps as uncertain as he of what they should do next.

He began to feel conspicuous because of just standing there, although at the same time he was certain no one noticed him, or if they did notice him, almost immediately dismissed him from their thoughts.

He and Sutton had been on their way to get a drink when it had all happened, and thinking of that, Latimer realized he could use a drink. With this in mind, he headed for the building. Few noticed him, some even brushing against him without notice; others spoke noncommittal greetings, some nodded briefly as one nods to someone of whose identity he is not certain.

The lounge was almost empty. Three men sat at a table in one corner, their drinks before them; a woman and a man were huddled in low-voiced conversation on a corner of a davenport; another man was at the self-service bar, pouring himself a drink.

Latimer made his way to the bar and picked up a glass.

The man who was there said to him, "You must be new here; I don't remember seeing you about."

"Just today," said Latimer. "Only a few hours ago."

He found the Scotch and his brand was not among the bottles. He selected his second choice and poured a generous serving over ice. There were several trays of sandwiches and other snack items. He found a plate, put two sandwiches on it.

"What do you make of Breen?" asked the other man.

"I don't know," said Latimer. "I never met the man. Gale mentioned him to me."

"Three," said the other man. "Three in the last four months. There is something wrong."

"All on the fence?"

"No, not on the fence. This is the first on the fence. One jumped, thirteen stories. Christ, what a mess! The other hanged himself."

The man walked off and joined another man who had just come into the lounge. Latimer stood alone, plate and glass in hand. The lounge still was almost empty. No one was paying the slightest attention to him. Suddenly he felt a stranger, unwanted. He had been feeling this all the time, he knew, but in the emptiness of the lounge, the feeling of unwantedness struck with unusual force. He could sit down at a table or in one of a group of chairs or on the end of an unoccupied sofa, wait for someone to join him. He recoiled from the thought. He didn't want to meet these people, talk with them. For the moment, he wanted none of them.

Shrugging, he put another sandwich on the plate, picked up the bottle, and filled his glass to the top. Then he walked out into the hallway and took the elevator to his floor.

In his room, he selected the most comfortable chair and sat down in it, putting the plate of sandwiches on a table. He took a long drink and put down the glass.

"They can all go to hell," he told himself.

He sensed his fragmented self pulling back together, all the scattered fragments falling back into him again, making him whole again, his entire self again. With no effort at all, he wiped out Breen and Sutton, the events of the last hours, until he was simply a man seated comfortably in his room.

So great a power, he thought, so great and secret. Holding one world in thrall, planning to hold others. The planning, the foresight, the audacity. Making certain that when they moved into the other worlds, there would be no silly conservationists yapping at their heels, no environmentalist demanding environmental impact statements, no deluded visionaries crying out in protest against monopolies. Holding steadily in view the easy business ethic that had held sway in that day when arrogant lumber barons had built mansions such as Auk House.

Latimer picked up the glass and had another drink. The glass, he saw, was less than half full. He should have carried off the bottle, he thought; no one would have noticed. He reached for a sandwich and munched it down, picked up a second one. How long had it been since he had eaten? He glanced at his watch and knew, even as he did, that the time it told might not be right for this Cretaceous world. He puzzled over that, trying to figure out if there might be some time variance between one world and another. Perhaps there wasn't—logically there shouldn't be—but there might be factors . . . he peered closely at the watch face, but the figures wavered and the hands would not stay in line. He had another drink.

He woke to darkness, stiff and cramped, wondering where he was. After a moment of confusion, he remembered where he was, all the details of the last two days tumbling in upon him, at first in scattered pieces, then subtly arranging themselves and interlocking into a pattern of reality.

He had fallen asleep in the chair. The moonlight pouring through the window showed the empty glass, the plate with half a sandwich still upon it, standing on the table at his elbow. The place was quiet; there was no noise at all. It must be the middle of the night, he thought, and everyone asleep. Or might it be that there was no one else around, that in some strange way, for some strange reason, the entire headquarters had been evacuated, emptied of all life? Although that, he knew, was unreasonable.

He rose stiffly from the chair and walked to the window. Below him, the landscape was pure silver, blotched by deep shadows. Somewhere just beyond the fence, he caught a sense of movement, but was unable to make out what it was. Some small animal, perhaps, prowling about. There would he mammals here, he was sure, the little skitterers, frightened creatures that were hard-pressed to keep out of the way, never having had the chance to evolve as they had back in prime world when something had happened millions of years before to sweep the world clean of its reptilian overlords, creating a vacuum into which they could expand.

The silver world that lay outside had a feel of magic—the magic of a brand-new world as yet unsullied by the hand and tools of men, a clean place that had no litter in it. If he went out and walked in it, he wondered, would the presence of himself, a human who had no right to be there, subtract something from the magic?

Out in the hall, he took the elevator to the ground floor. Just off the corridor lay the lounge and the outer door opened from the lounge. Walking softly, although he could not explain why he went so softly, for in this sleeping place there was no one to disturb, he went into the lounge.

As he reached the door, he heard voices and, halting in the shadow, glanced rapidly over the room to locate the speakers. There were three of them sitting at a table in the far end of the lounge. Bottles and glasses stood upon the table, but they did not seem to be drinking; they were hunched forward, heads close together, engaged in earnest conversation.

As he watched, one of them reared back in his chair, speaking in anger, his voice rising. "I warned you," he shouted. "I warned Breen and I warned you, Gale. And you laughed at me."

It was Sutton who was speaking. The man was too distant and the light too dim for Latimer to recognize his features, but the voice he was sure of.

"I did not laugh at you," protested Gale.

"Perhaps not you, but Breen did."

"I don't know about Breen or laughter," said the third man, "but there's been too much going wrong. Not just the three suicides. Other things as well. Miscalculations, erroneous data processing, bad judgments. Things all screwed up. Take the generator failure the other day. Three hours that we were without power, the fence without power. You know what that could mean if several big carnivores . . ."

"Yes, we know," said Gale, "but that was a mere technical malfunction. Those things happen. The one that worries me is this fellow, Latimer. That was a pure and simple foul-up. There was no reason to put him into Auk House. It cost a hell of a lot of money to do so; a very tricky operation. And when he got there, what happens? He escapes. I tell you, gentlemen, there are too many foul-ups. More than can be accounted for in the normal course of operation."

"There is no use trying to cover it up, to make a mystery out of it," said Sutton. "You know and I know what is happening, and the sooner we admit we know and start trying to figure out what to do about it, the better it will be. If there is anything we can do about it. We're up against an intelligence that may be as intelligent as we are, but in a different way. In a way that we can't fight. Mental power against technical power, and in a case like that, I'd bet on mental power. I warned you months ago. Treat these jokers with kid gloves, I told you. Do nothing to upset them. Handle them with deference. Think kindly toward them, because maybe they can tell what you're thinking. I believe they can. And then what happens? A bunch of lunkheads go out for an afternoon of shooting and when they find no other game, use these friends of ours for casual target practice . . ."

"But that was months ago," said the third man.

"They're testing," said Sutton. "Finding out what they can do. How far they can go. They can stop a generator. They can mess up evaluations. They can force men to kill themselves. God knows what else they can do. Give them a few more weeks. And, by the way, what particular brand of idiocy persuaded prime world to site the base of operations in a world like this?"

"There were many considerations," said Gale. "For one thing, it seemed a safe place. If some opposition should try to move in on us . . ."

"You're insane,' shouted Sutton. "There isn't any opposition. How could there be opposition?"

Moving swiftly, Latimer crossed the corner of the lounge, eased his way out of the door. Looking back over his shoulder, he saw the three still sitting at the table. Sutton was shouting, banging his fist on the table-top.

Gale was shrilling at him, his voice rising over Sutton's shouting: "How the hell could we suspect there was intelligence here? A world of stupid lizards . . ."

Latimer stumbled across the stone-paved terrace and went down the short flight of stone stairs that took him to the lawn. The world still was silver magic, a full moon riding in a cloudless sky. There was a softness in the air, a cleanness in the air.

But he scarcely noticed the magic and the cleanness. One thing thundered in his brain. A mistake! He should not have been sent to Auk House. There had been a miscalculation. Because of the mental machination of a reptilian intelligence on this world where the Cretaceous had not ended, he had been snatched from prime world. Although the fault, he realized, did not lie in this world, but in prime world itself—in the scheme that had been hatched to make prime world and the alternate worlds safe, safe beyond all question, for prime world's business interests.

He walked out across the sward and looked up at the northern hilltop. A row of huddled figures sat there, a long row of dumpy reptilian figures solemnly staring down at the invaders who had dared to desecrate their world.

He had wondered, Latimer remembered, how one man alone might manage to put an end to the prime-world project, knowing well enough that no one man could do it, perhaps that no conceivable combination of men could do it.

But now he need wonder no longer. In time to come, sooner or later, an end would come to it. Maybe by that time, most of the personnel here would have been transferred to Auk House or to other stations, fleeing this doomed place. It might be that in years to come, another operations center would be set up on some safer world and the project would go on. But at least some time would be bought for the human race; perhaps the project might be dropped. It already had cost untold billions. How much more would the prime-world managers be willing to put into it? That was the crux of it, he knew, the crux of everything on prime world: was it worth the cost?

He turned about to face the hilltop squarely and those who squatted there. Solemnly, David Latimer, standing in the magic moonlight, raised an arm in salutation to them.

He knew even as he did it that it was a useless gesture, a gesture for himself rather than for those dumpy figures sitting on the hilltop, who would neither see nor know. But even so, it was important that he do it, important that he, an intelligent human, pay a measure of sincere respect to an intelligence of another species in recognition of his belief that a common code of ethics might be shared.

The figures on the hilltop did not stir. Which, he told himself, was no more than he had expected of them. How should they know, why should they care what he instinctively had tried to communicate to them, not really expecting to communicate, but at least to make some sign, if to no other than himself, of the sense of fellowship that he, in that moment, felt for them?

As he was thinking this, he felt a warmness come upon him, encompassing him, enfolding him, as when he had been a child, in dim memory, he remembered his mother tucking him snugly into bed. Then he was moving, being lifted and impelled, with the high guard fence below him and the face of the great hill sliding underneath him. He felt no fright, for he seemed to be in a dreamlike state inducing a belief, deep-seated, that what was happening was not happening and that, in consequence, no harm could come to him.

He faced the dark and huddled figures, all sitting in a row, and although he still was dream-confused, he could see them clearly. They were nothing much to look at. They were as dumpy and misshapen as they had seemed when he had seen them from a distance. Their bodies were graceless lumps, the details vague even in the bright moonlight, but the faces he never would forget. They had the sharp triangle of the reptilian skull, the cruelty of the sharpness softened by the liquid compassion of the eyes.

Looking at them, he wondered if he was really there, if he was facing them, as he seemed to be, or if he still might be standing on the greensward of the compound, staring up the hill at the huddled shapes, which now seemed to be only a few feet distant from him. He tried to feel the ground beneath his feet, to press his feet against the ground, a conscious effort to orient himself, and, try as he might, he could feel no ground beneath his feet.

They were not awesome creatures and there was nothing horrible about them—just a faint distastefulness. They squatted in their lumpy row and stared at him out of the soft liquid of their eyes. And he felt—in some strange way that he could not recognize, he felt the presence of them. Not as if they were reaching out physically to touch him—fearing that if they did touch him, he would recoil from them—but in another kind of reaching, as if they were pouring into him, as one might pour water in a bottle, an essence of themselves.

Then they spoke to him, not with voice, not with words, with nothing at all that he could recognize—perhaps, he thought wildly, they spoke with that essence of themselves they were pouring into him.

"Now that we have met," they said, "we'll send you back again."

And he was back.

He stood at the end of the brick-paved driveway that led up to the house, and behind him he heard the damp and windy rustle of a primeval forest, with two owls chuckling throatily in the trees behind him. A few windows in the house were lighted. Great oaks grew upon the spreading lawn, and beneath the trees stood graceful stone benches that had the look of never being used.

Auk House, he told himself. They had sent him back to Auk House, not back to the grassy compound that lay inside the fence in that other world where the Cretaceous had not ended.

Inside himself he felt the yeasty churning of the essence that the squatting row of monstrosities had poured into him, and out of it he gained a knowledge and a comfort.

Policemen, he wondered, or referees, perhaps? Creatures that would monitor the efforts of those entrepreneurs who sought a monopoly of all the alternate worlds that had been opened for humans, and perhaps for many other races. They would monitor and correct, making certain that the worlds would not fall prey to the multinational financial concepts of the race that had opened them, but would become the heritage and birth-right of those few intelligent peoples that had risen on this great multiplicity of worlds, seeing to it that the worlds would be used in a wiser context than prime world had been used by humans.

Never doubting for a moment that it would or could be done, knowing for a certainty that it would come about, that in the years to come men and other intelligences would live on the paradise worlds that Sutton had told him of—and all the other worlds that lay waiting to be used with an understanding the human race had missed. Always with those strange, dumpy ethical wardens who would sit on many hilltops to keep their vigil.

Could they be trusted? he wondered, and was ashamed of thinking it. They had looked into his eyes and had poured their essence into him and had returned him here, not back to the Cretaceous compound. They had known where it was best for him to go and they would know all the rest of it.

He started up the driveway, his heels clicking on the bricks. As he came up to the stoop the door came open and the man in livery stood there.

"You're a little late," said the butler. "The others waited for you, but just now sat down to dinner. I'm sure the soup's still warm."

"I'm sorry," said Latimer. "I was unavoidably detained."

"Some of the others thought they should go out looking for you, but Mr. Jonathon dissuaded them. He said you'd be all right. He said you had your wits about you. He said you would be back."

The butler closed the door behind him. "They'll all be very happy to find you're back," he said.

"Thank you," said Latimer.

He walked, trying not to hurry, fighting down the happiness he felt welling up inside himself, toward the doorway from which came the sound of bright laughter and sprightly conversation.

CLIFFORD D. SIMAK, during his fifty-five-year career, produced some of the most iconic science fiction stories ever written. Born in 1904 on a farm in southwestern Wisconsin, Simak got a job at a small-town newspaper in 1929 and eventually became news editor of the *Minneapolis Star-Tribune*, writing fiction in his spare time.

Simak was best known for the book *City*, a reaction to the horrors of World War II, and for his novel *Way Station*. In 1953 *City* was awarded the International Fantasy Award, and in following years, Simak won three Hugo Awards and a Nebula Award. In 1977 he became the third Grand Master of the Science Fiction and Fantasy Writers of America, and before his death in 1988, he was named one of three inaugural winners of the Horror Writers Association's Bram Stoker Award for Lifetime Achievement.

DAVID W. WIXON was a close friend of Clifford D. Simak's. As Simak's health declined, Wixon, already familiar with science fiction publishing, began more and more to handle such things as his friend's business correspondence and contract matters. Named literary executor of the estate after Simak's death, Wixon began a long-term project to secure the rights to all of Simak's stories and find a way to make them available to readers who, given the fifty-five-year span of Simak's writing career, might never have gotten the chance to enjoy all of his short fiction. Along the way, Wixon also read the author's surviving journals and rejected manuscripts, which made him uniquely able to provide Simak's readers with interesting and thought-provoking commentary that sheds new light on the work and thought of a great writer.

THE COMPLETE SHORT FICTION OF CLIFFORD D. SIMAK

FROM OPEN ROAD MEDIA

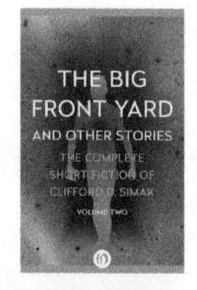

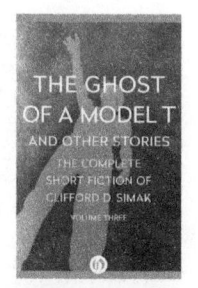

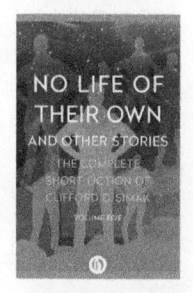

OPEN ROAD
INTEGRATED MEDIA

OPEN ROAD
INTEGRATED MEDIA

Find a full list of our authors and
titles at www.openroadmedia.com

FOLLOW US
@OpenRoadMedia